W9-BZX-195

Great reviews for SHE DRIVES ME CRAZY

"Good ole boy attitudes and laid back charm make this splendid tale a local delicacy. Author Leslie Kelly brings wit, humor and exuberance to this story of one woman's reluctant attempt to go home again."
—*Romantic Times*

"I know this is only a March release but I think I've already found my favorite book of the year in Leslie Kelly's *She Drives Me Crazy*. This is such an outstanding book on so many levels that it's hard to mention them without giving away one of the many surprises found between the pages. A Recommended Read."
—*Fallen Angel Reviews*

"Spend an evening of pleasure and fun, and treat yourself to an intensely emotional, funny, spine-tingling, and well-written book. A Perfect 10!"
—*Romance Reviews Today*

"Sexy, funny and a little outrageous, Leslie Kelly is a must read!"
—*New York Times* bestselling author Carly Phillips

"Leslie Kelly's books are the perfect blend of sass and class. Her cheeky style makes her one of the strongest voices in romance today."
—*New York Times* bestselling author Vicki Lewis Thompson

"Leslie Kelly is a future star of romance."
—*New York Times* bestselling author Debbie Macomber to *Publishers Weekly*

More rave reviews for the books of Leslie Kelly!

"Ms. Kelly never fails to deliver a captivating story."
—*Romance Reviews Today*

"Top Pick! Leslie Kelly introduces characters you'll
love spending time with; explores soulmates
you'll dream about; and a hero to die for."
—*Romantic Times* on *Naturally Naughty*

"Entertaining is just too tame a word.
This is pure reading pleasure."
—*The Romance Reader* on *Night Whispers*

"Leslie Kelly writes with a matchless combination
of sexiness and sassiness that makes
every story a keeper."
—*Fallen Angel Reviews*

"Kelly tells a high-energy story and
delivers a satisfying read."
—*All About Romance* on *Killing Time*

"Leslie Kelly writes hot, steamy stories with lots
of humor and tons of romance thrown in."
—*Romance and Friends*

Leslie Kelly

she's got the look

HQN™

ISBN 0-373-77058-8

SHE'S GOT THE LOOK

www.HQNBooks.com

Printed in U.S.A.

To my cousin, Louis Smith, and all his pals from the 1st Marine Expeditionary Force...you're all heroes.

To my girlfriends, past and present, who've always been there for the laughing, griping, celebrating, crying, plotting, whining and wine. Most especially Jill, Brenda, Julie, Karen, Janelle, Camille and Roxanne. Life wouldn't be the same without you.

And to my hubby, Bruce...you'll always be number one on my list. Just above Hugh Jackman.

she's got the
LOOK

PROLOGUE

Six Years Ago

"EVERY WOMAN NEEDS a list of men she'll have sex with, no questions asked, if she ever gets the chance."

Amazingly, despite her friend's outrageous comment, Melody Tanner managed to avoid spewing the mouthful of margarita she'd just sipped. She stared at Tanya Williams, one of her bridesmaids, who cocked an unrepentant brow. The two additional women at the table—her other closest friends—snorted and laughed.

Since they were sitting in a crowded Mexican restaurant, and since Tanya was such an attention getter, anyway, with her beautiful ebony skin, striking features and imposing height, she didn't figure there was much chance the comment had gone unheard by those around them. But she cast a quick glance anyway.

Nope. Definitely not unheard. The pudgy guy at the next table looked like he'd swallowed a lemon. The owner of the place, who *always* watched them, was keeping an extra close eye, as well.

Oblivious to the attention, Tanya added, "Married, single, in a relationship or not, a woman's gotta have a go-for-it list." She narrowed her eyes. "Especially if she's stupid enough to get married at twenty-one."

"Lovely idea," said Rosemary, her maid of honor. "A get-out-of-adultery-free card." Rosemary's lyrical Southern accent could make anything sound elegant. Even a sex list.

"You're both high," Melody muttered before taking another sip of her drink, not taking offense at Tanya's comment about her age. Her friend had made her opinion very clear on that matter. As had everyone else.

"Come on," Tanya said. "You're not married *yet*. Be honest, there have got to be at least five guys you'd leap on if you had the chance."

Paige, her final bridesmaid, interrupted. "She probably doesn't need a sex list." Paige made up for her lack of height by speaking about three decibels louder than anyone else, so they were almost *certainly* being overheard now. "Face it, Mel's probably *on* the lists of half the men in this country."

Melody wrinkled her nose. "The blond twit in the swimsuit edition might be. But I'm *not* her anymore, remember?"

No, she wasn't. She'd gotten as far away from her former career as she could in the two years since she'd shocked everyone—especially her mother—and quit modeling. She'd stopped coloring her reddish-brown hair blond, stopped starving herself to keep slim, stopped constantly traveling with no friends close by, no family.

No family…well, you couldn't really miss what you'd never had, could you? Her mother had been family in only the most technical sense and she had no idea who her father was. So, to her, family was a fairly loosely defined word.

The three other women sitting around this table with her had been her real family—her *chosen* family—for a very long time. Rosemary, Tanya and Paige were the sisters she'd never had, the ones who'd supported her when she'd walked away from the job her mother had thrust on her as a baby.

Her mother, on the other hand, had stuck around just long

enough to make sure Melody wouldn't change her mind. Once she'd accepted that—and realized the money that had supported them was going to stop rolling in—she'd married a foreign designer and moved to England.

She'd sent a Crock-Pot for Mel's upcoming wedding. It had a European plug. That pretty much summed up Mother.

But it was okay. Melody had been dealing with her mother's less-than-maternal instincts for years. Melody had her friends. She had a normal life. She was finally going to pursue the passion she'd never gotten to explore since she'd always been in front of a camera: she planned to work *behind* one.

And tomorrow, to make things perfect, she'd have another new member of her chosen family. A husband. Her marriage to a nice, smart, nonglamorous dentist would be the dot on the exclamation point as she renounced the first two decades of her life.

"Well, if you're making a Men Most Wanted list, I want to make one, too," said Paige. She bent under the table to dig into her purse, until all Mel could see of her were the puffy, light brown curls on the top of her head. When she came back up, she was holding a pen and a small notebook. "Now, Mel goes first since she's the one getting married. Tonight's her last night to do this…since it'd be tacky to make a list of men you want to have sex with *after* you're married, right?" She glanced at her friends, looking for confirmation.

At the table next to them, the pudgy old man began choking on a tortilla chip. Or his tongue.

"Turn the volume down, girl," Tanya said. "And let me do it, your writing's awful." Grabbing the notebook, Tanya looked at Mel. "Okay, let's do your sex list. Tell us everything. After all, who can you share your deepest fantasies with if not us?"

Melody glanced around the room. "Uh, half of Savannah?"

Tanya leaned in. "We won't tell. We're your best friends."

"Yes, you are," she murmured, silently thanking them for their support. For being here when they all thought she was making a mistake. For loving her as much as she loved them.

The four of them were an unlikely group—Rosemary, an elegant blonde and a member of one of Savannah's wealthiest families. Paige, the loud, giggly one who discarded jobs like some people discarded tissues. Tanya, the nearly six-feet-tall African-American who was such a perfect foil to Rosemary's spoiled Southern belle act.

Then there was Melody, whose face had been plastered on baby-food jars as an infant, whose famous diaper commercials had become a pop-culture reference. The one who'd hammed it up on a bunch of kiddie TV shows, and whose teenage butt had filled out the curves of designer jeans. The one who smiled to show sparkling teeth and cried to sell booboo medicine and who'd landed a spot in a swimsuit issue at seventeen.

Most importantly, Mel realized, she was the one who'd kept her most valued friendships alive by winning one battle against her mother: she'd insisted they have a real home in Savannah. Which was why Paige, Tanya and Rosemary had been there for every major event in her life. Like the one tomorrow. Her wedding. To nice, handsome, considerate Dr. Bill Todd of Atlanta.

The only man she'd ever have sex with again.

Grabbing for her margarita, she drained the glass. Then she reached for the pitcher, suddenly wondering if twenty-one really *was* too young to give up sex with every man in the world but one. Almost without thinking about it, she mumbled, "Brad Pitt."

Tanya snorted. "Oh, please, be a *little* original. If that man had sex with every woman who wanted him, he'd have to be on an intravenous Viagra drip with Spanish fly on the side."

"I thought this was *my* fantasy list."

Paige agreed with Tanya. "Fantasy, but with a shot of reality. Still, I suppose if a man knew you were the Luscious Lingerie Peacock Feather Girl you could get—"

"Ugh, don't remind me!" Mel snapped. "People *still* ask me about that stupid one-of-a-kind bra-and-panty set. I would burn it, but I have a feeling it could fund my retirement."

She'd only done one photo shoot for Luscious Lingerie, yet it seemed that's how most of *male* America was going to remember her. As the Peacock Feather Girl. Funny, that particular job—which she hadn't wanted to do in the first place—was what had made her decide to quit her former profession. Her mother-manager had insisted the exposure would be wonderful. In Melody's opinion, the exposure had been nearly X-rated. Only if she wanted to be a porn star would the Luscious Lingerie shoot have been a wise move. Tanya had compared it to Shirley Temple posing for *Penthouse* after she'd gotten off the Good Ship Lollipop.

After the catalog had come out, she'd been stalked by so many men she'd had to hide out in her apartment for months. But hearing a fan say how proud he was that he'd walked in on his twelve-year-old son having his first yank-and-pull session while holding the photo of Mel in the peacock ensemble had been the last straw. Being a pinup girl for prepubescent boys to get off on was gross to the nth degree.

That'd been the moment she'd decided to quit. And finally—thankfully—she'd begun feeling she could go out without people whispering about her. The hair-color change had been a big help. So had her co-ed wardrobe and normal-person lifestyle.

"I think I'd rather be remembered for almost anything

else," she said, shaking her head. Maybe as the three-year-old running to the bathroom with her hands frantically clutching her training pants. Or, gads, as the scrub-faced teen who sang the praises of a certain brand of tampons. Like at age fifteen, she'd wanted the whole world thinking about her being on her period!

Still, they'd be better than the Peacock Feather Girl.

"I know," Paige said. "But what I meant was, the lingerie model might have had a shot. Movie stars, however, are not in the future of Mrs. Bill the Dentist from Atlanta."

Melody sipped again, trying to laugh at Paige's words. Deep inside, however, she wasn't laughing. She was wincing.

She loved Bill. She felt sure she did. He was the first man who hadn't treated her like an object, who'd supported her decision to change her life. Marriage to him would be perfect.

So will the sex.

That was when she figured out what was *really* bothering her about this list thing. It was bizarre to think about having sex with a stranger—even jokingly—when she hadn't had it with her fiancé. Bill was old-fashioned and wanted to wait.

Oh, God, what if we just don't click in bed?

Forcing the traitorous thought away, she said, "So it's my fantasy list, but I don't get to say who's on it?"

"There just have to be some ground rules," Tanya announced.

"Why, Tanya, honey, I thought you never paid any attention to rules," Rosemary said, sounding amused.

"First of all," Tanya said, ignoring Rosemary, "we each need to write down copies of all four lists and hold on to them so we can keep an eye out for each other's men."

Paige nodded. "Good idea. And the men should be improbable—not impossible. What fun is having a fantasy if there's not a teeny chance of it happening? It's like buying a lottery ticket when you know you have better odds of getting hit by a low-flying seven forty-seven than winning. But you do it anyway because *somebody's* gotta win."

Melody wasn't convinced. "This is only a joke, right? So who cares if I put Brad Pitt on there?"

Tanya blew out an impatient breath. "Of course it's just for fun. We know you're not a hootchie mama who'd hook up with a dude because he's on some list. But don't you sometimes like to wonder 'what if?' What fun is wondering 'what if' if there's never a chance in a million years that it'll happen?"

"Hootchie mama?" Rosemary rolled her eyes. "Really, Tanya, you're so…descriptive."

"Up yours," Tanya said sweetly. She lifted the pen. "Now, Mel, your list?"

Nibbling on her lip for a second, Mel thought about it. Thankfully, the margaritas were finally kicking in. Besides, these were her best friends and, like Tanya had said, it was just silly fun. No way would any of them *really* jump into bed with a man at first sight. Well…maybe Rosemary, who, to be honest, had a more-than-active libido. But probably not.

Tapping her index finger on her cheek, she came up with what she thought they'd find an acceptable choice. "Jonathan Rhodes."

"Ooh, our hunky new congressman?" Paige said.

"What can I say? I had to admire his guts with the sexy way he said his slogan." She lowered her voice and did a bad Austin Powers impression. "*I will take you* with me to Washington, baby."

He hadn't done the baby part, but it was implied. Every time she'd heard it, Mel had given reluctant credit to the guy for appealing to female voters, who were obviously supposed to ignore the second half of that sentence and vote for him on innuendo.

The others nodded their approval, so Melody added another name—of a local guy who'd been making a name for himself on the PGA tour. His preferences meant he wasn't much of a possibility, but he did have a cute smile. And a decent backswing.

"You know, honey, that sweet-looking man is probably *not* out of the realm of possibility," Rosemary pointed out. "I bet he'd let you handle his *putter* any old time you asked him."

"I hear he's gay."

"Ahh." Rosemary nodded, not doubting Melody's infamous sources, who'd kept them all in-the-know in the old days.

"Isn't that cheating if he's gay?" Paige asked indignantly.

"You said improbable. Not impossible. Besides, this is for fun, right? I don't have to be *too* realistic. Even if he *is* gay, he's still more likely than Brad Pitt." Then, thinking of someone else, she added the name of a local TV reporter. "Drake Manning."

Paige wrinkled her nose. "Slimy."

That was surprising coming from Paige, who was, to be honest, the nicest one of their group. "You think?"

She nodded. "His hair never moves. I think you could hit it with a sledgehammer and it'd bounce right back into place."

Tanya harrumphed. "It's Mel's list. You can put nothing but fluffy-haired heterosexuals on yours but it's *not your turn.*"

"Sorry," Paige said, looking sheepish. "Go on, Mel."

Melody continued to think, but it was tough. Eliminating movie stars cut out about eighty percent of the men she'd ever fantasized about. Frankly, she'd never had much time for men. Her few sexual experiences before her chaste fiancé had been on-the-run affairs with an ambitious photographer who wanted to take her picture more than he'd wanted to take *her*. And then there'd been a male model who made friends with every mirror he met. That was it.

She sighed. "Lately my only fantasies have been about the chocolate volcano cake at Chez Jacques. I'm dying for some, but one bite'll make my butt bulge out of my wedding gown."

Tanya grunted, probably because she was thin as a rail and ate like a linebacker. Unlike Melody, who had been taking note of every morsel she consumed since her ninth birthday when her mother had given her an electronic calorie counter instead of the Hello Kitty play set she'd asked for.

"My father knows the chef at Chez Jacques," Rosemary said. "His name's not Jacques, it's Charlie."

"Okay, Charlie the chef," Mel said. "He's fourth. A man who makes art out of chocolate must be good with his hands."

Then there was one slot left. One more fantasy guy. One more traitorous thought of another man before she ended the naughty game and focused on her fiancé. Her *reality*.

Draining the rest of her margarita, she contemplated naming whoever had invented fat-free cheese curls, if only to balance things out with the chocolate guy. The words were on her lips when suddenly the big-screen TV over the bar caught her eye. Or, rather, the news segment playing on it did.

She couldn't hear well, but she didn't have to. She knew the story. Everyone was talking about the Georgia hero who'd rescued some orphans in a third-world country. A photographer had captured the amazing moment, right in the heat of battle, and the picture had graced the cover of *Time* magazine last week.

It was the magazine cover that filled the screen right now as the Savannah station picked up on the Georgia-boy-done-good angle. Melody stared, unable to tear her eyes away from the haunting image. The thick-armed marine—strikingly handsome even while covered with grime and streaked with soot—was heroism personified. In one arm, he cradled a baby while, with the other, he braced an older child against his side. A tiny pair of hands and a little tear-streaked face peering above his shoulder said there was a third youngster clinging to his back.

The soldier's dusty face was grim with resolve, his body reportedly wounded yet still so strong. The taut cords in his neck spoke of adrenaline, anger and battle—all so stark against the tenderness with which he held the children. Behind him was the outline of a burning building, orange flames merging with streaks of light that could only have been mortar fire.

But it was the eyes that got to her. The dark brown eyes, full of determination, emotion. Anger and mourning. Eyes that said he had seen too much and been cut too deeply for someone as young as he appeared to be.

His image burned itself into her brain, remaining there long after the news segment had ended and the picture had disappeared.

"Mel? You okay?" Paige asked.

She nodded slowly. Then, without having to give it another thought, she whispered, "Move everyone on the list down one."

Melody didn't even know the guy's name or where he lived. Or even if he'd make it back from his next mission in whatever war-ravaged country he was in now.

She wanted him. Passionately. Unequivocally. Undeniably.

"Marine hero on *Time* magazine. He's in first place," she murmured, still visualizing his face.

There was no doubt in her mind that if she ever met the

man with the haunting brown eyes—which had seemed to
stare directly at her from the cover of the magazine—he'd be
absolutely impossible to resist. He was larger than life, a
once-in-a-lifetime fantasy man. A hero.

And now, the number-one guy on her Men Most Wanted
list.

CHAPTER ONE

Present Day

THE REDHEAD WITH the camera was spying on him again.

Nick Walker glanced into his rearview mirror and saw the woman skulking around the corner of the church across the square. Every once in a while, she lifted the big camera that hung from one shoulder, swinging it in front of her face to snap off a shot of the trees. The birds. The sky. The church.

All of which was to hide her real photographic subject. *Him.*

He sighed deeply, shaking his head, wondering how long he could wait—and how far he could let her go—before his cover was blown. Not too much longer, that was for sure.

He hadn't figured on going unnoticed when he'd started this undercover assignment a couple of days ago. Nobody dressed in his ratty clothes, with the shaggy beard, and two-days-past-needing-a-shower hair *wouldn't* be looked at in old Savannah. Not to mention the car. It was a standard, city-issued, undercover P.O.S—Piece Of Shit—the color showing through the rust falling somewhere between puce and putrid.

But the cover was still a good one, considering the eclectic nature of the population in this area. There were just as likely to be panhandlers as millionaires moseying around some of the city's famous squares. This getup was noticeable, but quickly forgotten by the busy residents who really didn't want to think too much about how the "other half" lived.

So yeah, he'd been prepared for *some* attention. What he hadn't expected was a frigging Nancy Drew out with her camera, snapping clandestine shots of a suspected bad guy and his license plate. She was about as clandestine as a tank.

"Lady, go home," he pleaded softly, willing the woman to retreat into the building where she'd recently moved. The building where he was *supposed* to be conducting this stakeout.

That'd been the plan, anyway, which made the woman's nosiness even more aggravating. His partner, Dex Delaney, was involved with the daughter of the building's owner. Dex had felt sure his girlfriend, Rosemary, could arrange to let them use the building. It would have been perfect—discreet, vacant. An ideal place to stake out the first-floor apartment in the building across the street where a suspected drug trafficker resided.

Then, after Nick had grown in a beard and scavenged clothes from Goodwill, the ax had fallen. Rosemary's father had refused, saying he'd rented the building to a family friend in need. Considering Rosemary's social circles, the woman probably needed a place to stay so her mansion could be painted.

One thing *he* hadn't needed was to have his stakeout made ten times tougher because of a rich woman's whim. "Why the hell couldn't she have moved in next month?" he muttered, still frustrated by the change in plans that had him sitting here on a sweltering ninety-five-degree day in a car that smelled like the last ninety-five men who'd been in it.

Sometimes he really didn't like his job.

"But not often," he admitted to himself.

Most times, he *loved* his job. Being a cop gave him more satisfaction than he'd ever dreamed of having in his civilian life. Funny, coming out of the marines four years ago, he hadn't been sure what he'd do. Going back to his hometown had been impossible. College? A fantasy. He'd gotten used to being in action, to fighting and surviving. To nailing bad guys. On a big scale or on a small one, taking criminals out of commission was what he did best…he'd figured that out back when he wasn't sure he'd ever give a damn about anything again.

Nick liked to think of it as weeding out the bullies. Pushers or terrorists, they were all the same. Narrow-minded. Violent. Caring nothing for anyone else. Just like any other loud, abusive, small-town bully trying to impose his will on everyone around him.

The one he'd grown up with, for instance.

So yeah, being a cop was a perfect fit. He'd never regretted his choice of careers. Except maybe a *tiny* bit on days like today. "Come on, Rupert, you punk, come visit Mr. Miller here so I can go home, shave and take a shower," he said under his breath. Rupert was a low-level dealer. Miller was the big fish who brought in the shit that poisoned kids, ruined lives and sparked crime by addicts desperate to get one more high.

Nailing Miller would help a lot of people…which meant a lot to Nick. Because he'd discovered something else when he'd been fighting half a world away in a war-torn area foreign to anything he'd ever known: he was good at helping people who couldn't help themselves. That was his talent, his calling.

He'd picked up that burden in Kosovo. And he'd never been able to put it back down.

"Hey, partner, you still awake?"

He slid down, trying not to let his head come in contact with the headrest. His personal ick-limit wouldn't stand for it.

"I'm here," he said softly into the small, handheld radio, keeping it concealed by his fingers. "Nancy Drew's back on the beat, keeping the area safe from miscreants and jaywalkers."

Dex laughed. He *could*. He was covering the back of the building. In the shade. In a newer car. With air-conditioning.

Nick was the rookie detective. So he got the P.O.S.

"You ever find out from Rosemary why this friend simply *had* to move in *now?*" he asked, his voice still low, his eyes constantly scanning the street.

"She's an old friend of Rosie's who's starting a new photography business," Dex said.

Hence the camera.

"Apparently she just came out of a really ugly divorce."

"Wait…there's a truck pulling up." Nick lowered the radio, watching in his side mirror as a sizable U-Haul truck maneuvered up the street. It almost clipped a BMW and came damn close to taking out a street sign. As the truck passed, he casually glanced over and saw a small woman with curly light brown hair clutching the wheel as if she was a lion tamer holding a chair.

"*No,*" he bit out when the truck stopped. "Keep going."

The radio crackled. "What is it?"

"Trouble. A big truck just pulled up in front of Rosemary's father's building and double-parked. It's completely blocking my visual on the perp's apartment. Not to mention traffic."

"Want me to get a uniform out there to tell them to move?"

"Absolutely," he said when he realized the driver was getting out of the truck. The woman called to someone. Somehow, Nick couldn't muster up much surprise when he saw she was waving at the nosy photographer, who came jogging over.

That female was destined to be the bane of his existence this week.

He waited, tapping his fingers on the dash, watching the two women from behind his dark sunglasses. They stood beside the truck and talked for a while, looking upset. Finally the short, curly-haired driver pulled a cell phone out of her purse. Crossing the street to the shady square, she sat on a bench and started an animated phone conversation.

"No, you are *not* doing this," he muttered, shaking his head as he observed the other one—the tall photographer—open the back of the truck and climb inside.

But she *was* doing it. As he watched in disbelief, she came staggering down the truck ramp carrying a double mattress. All he could see of her behind the mattress was two sandal-clad feet at the bottom, and two hands clutched on either side. Her oblivious friend was turned the other way, not even watching.

"Dammit."

He looked at his watch. Tried again to peer around the truck. Wondered just how long it was going to take a beat cop to get his ass here and get the truck off the street. But most of all, he wondered what the heck the woman thought she was doing schlepping furniture all by herself on a hot summer day.

"Watch it, lady, you're gonna fall," he whispered when she reached the curb, which he thought she might not see.

Nope. She didn't see it. Realizing what was going to happen, he called, "No!" and leaped out of his car. But it was too late. She tripped and fell forward. It was her extreme good fortune, however, that she landed right on her own mattress.

Before he could think better of it, Nick jogged the few yards over to her. "You okay?"

The woman was still lying there, facedown on the mattress in the middle of the sidewalk. She mumbled something but since her face was buried, he couldn't make out what.

While waiting for her to move, he noted the richness of her thick hair, which, on closer inspection, was more auburn than true red. It was a warm shade, the color of vibrant earth after a rain. And he definitely noted her tall, curvy form, clad in tight jeans and a sleeveless white tank top.

If he'd thought she was really hurt, he might not have taken a second to appreciate the way she filled out those jeans. But she'd landed on something soft, and the view was definitely worth appreciating. *Definitely.* Hell, a saint would have looked, and no Walker had ever been accused of being a saint. A devil straight from hell was a more frequent expression.

Breathing deeply, he swallowed his libido back into his gut. "Ma'am? Do you need help getting up?" He cast a quick look to the side, noting that Miller's blinds were closed tight. Hopefully he wasn't sitting there in the darkness of his apartment, watching the world through his warped little drug-pushing eyes.

"I'm fine," he heard as the woman pushed herself up to her knees, until she was on all fours right below him.

Lord have mercy.

Nick closed his eyes briefly, thrusting every low-down wicked Walker thought out of his head by sheer force of will. Trying to find the good manners his mama had tried so hard to teach him, he got hold of himself. When he opened his eyes again, the woman had risen to her feet. Thank God.

It took him less than a second to realize she was afraid of him. Though she jutted her chin out and kept her head up, she did step back. She obviously recognized him as the suspected pervert from the rust bucket parked at the curb around the corner.

He put his hands up, palms out. "I just wanted to make sure you were okay."

The tension in her body eased a bit, which gave Nick a chance to study her from behind his tinted sunglasses.

She was tall, and as nicely curved in the front as she was in the back. Though dark circles hinted of stress and her cheeks were a little pale—maybe even gaunt—her face didn't suffer for it. In fact, she had a *great* face—wide mouth that would probably be beautiful when she smiled. Big old eyes that he figured were blue, but couldn't tell for sure because of his glasses. Long lashes, creamy complexion, high cheekbones. Yes, indeed, his Nancy Drew was a pretty woman. Even if she was a busybody.

"If you'll excuse me, I have to get this done," she said, her voice sounding shaky. As if she hadn't completely accepted that he was merely a nice bystander wanting to help out. Considering how he looked, he couldn't blame her.

Then she turned her back on him and bent over again—heaven help him for being a *bad* man—and tried picking up the mattress.

"You're gonna hurt yourself," he said, his throat tight.

"I'm stronger than I look." Still bent over, she stared doubtfully at the building and added under her breath, "Though the stairs up to the third floor may be…difficult."

"*Third* floor?" he snapped in disbelief.

"It'll be fine," she insisted, straightening up—without the mattress. "I'm just bringing a few things up there. Not much."

He followed the airy hand she waved and looked into the truck. No, not much. Just a frigging box spring, dresser, small table, two chairs and a love seat. "You're nuts. For God's sake, wait for the movers." Then, remembering he had a job to get back to, he added, "And you *have* to move this truck."

She stiffened. "I don't have any movers. Paige's—my friend's husband was supposed to be here, but he's not." Her voice rose a little and she stepped closer, as if she didn't even realize it. "I have to empty that truck and return it before four o'clock or I'm going to owe Paige for another day's rental." Another step. Another flash of spirit. Another decibel and she was almost shouting. "And dammit, that truck is not going anywhere until I get *this* furniture into *that* building."

Feisty. He liked that. He almost smiled, but figured she wouldn't appreciate it.

Despite a little quiver in her bottom lip, and her initial fear of him, the woman was standing her ground. But that quiver, and a hint of moisture in her big eyes, made him suspect she was hanging on to her bravado by a thin thread. Remembering what Dex had started to say a few minutes ago, he realized this woman was probably moving out on her own for the first time after her…how had his partner described it? *Ugly* divorce. With nothing but a bed, a table and a few chairs.

His heart twisted, even while a voice in his head whispered, *No, this is not your problem.*

Damn. The last thing he needed was to worry about her, but he couldn't help it. Despite being a better-than-average-height female, she had such a look of vulnerability. Particularly in that unsmiling mouth and those darkly circled eyes. Empty eyes. Frightened eyes, he'd say, if he didn't already know she had guts, because of the way she'd been standing up to him.

Before he could decide what to do, a marked car pulled up behind the truck and a young beat cop Nick recognized from the station got out. Their eyes met for one second and the kid's mouth quirked in a smile as he took in Nick's getup.

"Someone's going to have to move this truck," he said as he approached them. "It's blocking traffic."

Nancy Drew's friend finally realized what was going on and came running from across the street. "Wait, please, we'll be so quick unloading it you won't even know we were here."

"I'm sorry, you have to get it out of here," the cop said.

The pretty, sad-looking woman at the center of all of this blinked, looking back and forth between them. Then she wrapped her arms around herself, as if needing strength. Needing support.

Needing.

Nick mentally kicked himself. But even as his internal voice told him he was an idiot, he opened his mouth and surprised them all. "Officer," he said, looking at the younger man, "between the two of us, we could empty this thing and have these ladies on their way within ten minutes. Don't you think?"

The kid flinched, not expecting the response. With a slight shake of his head, Nick stopped any questions and got his point across. They *were* going to do this. If Miller looked out his window, he'd see a cop and a guy helping a lady move in. Not anything unusual in a Southern town known for its hospitality.

Dex might not agree, but Nick's decision was made. He couldn't explain it, couldn't understand it himself, really. But something inside him wouldn't let this haunted-looking woman load her mattress back on that truck and drive away.

She needed help. And he was going to give it to her.

VANDALIZING A BILLBOARD to announce to the world that your husband was a cheating scumbag might not be the best way to save a marriage, but it was one hell of a way to end one.

Melody Tanner-Todd—now just Tanner again, thankfully—had discovered that when she'd sought retaliation against her bastard of an ex, who'd slept his way across Atlanta during their marriage. It had been hugely public, hugely satisfying and it had hugely entertained the city's commuting population. It had also cost her nearly everything she owned.

"You mean he gets practically all your money just because you painted some graffiti on a billboard?" said Paige Winston—now Suffolk—sounding shocked and dismayed.

Rosemary and Tanya wore similar looks of disbelief, which probably matched the one that had been on Mel's own face for the past two months—since the day a judge had given her ex most of what she had earned during nineteen years as a model and actress.

"This is unbelievable! The house? The boat? That cheating sack of shit gets it *all?* Gawd, I'm *never* getting married. Vibrators are just as good and they don't come with six-foot-tall walking dicks attached." Six years might have turned Tanya into a softer-looking, mature woman, but they hadn't done anything to smooth out that ballsy attitude.

Melody had a flash of déjà vu. It'd been almost exactly six years ago that the four of them had been sitting in this same restaurant, with the same watchful owner, at this same table, drinking margaritas out of possibly these same glasses, on the night before her wedding. Her blissful, lovely, elegant wedding that was supposed to be the start of her perfect life.

The perfection had lasted about ten months. Until Melody had started hearing rumors that her devoted husband was devoted to anything with two parted legs. It had taken another three years for her to grasp the scope of Bill's betrayals. But eventually she'd realized that her dentist husband was willing to drill absolutely any woman who opened wide.

"The judge agreed with his lawyer that I'd damaged his

professional reputation," Melody murmured, knowing the others were waiting to hear the rest of the story.

They'd heard bits and pieces, of course. Though they lived several hours away, her friends had been a great source of support—even with only their telephone calls—during the ugly, rancorous split-up. They'd wanted to come to see her, but Melody had put them off, not wanting them to know how bad it was.

Only Tanya, who was a flight attendant and visited Atlanta a lot anyway—and who would never take no for an answer—had ignored her request. She'd shown up at Mel's door one day last May with a bottle of tequila and a big cheesecake. So she knew something about Melody's disgrace. Just like Rosemary knew the most about her unhappiness. And Paige knew the most about her dreams for the future. But none of them knew the *whole* story.

"I know you've all been wanting to hear everything, but I needed a couple of weeks to pull myself together," Melody said. "I only want to tell the story once. This is the first time all four of us have been together since I got back, so I guess tonight it's time to let it all come out."

Paige reached across the table and took her hand. Rosemary listened quietly, and Tanya gave her a nod of encouragement.

"So to start, yes, he got almost everything." She squeezed Paige's fingers. "You know, letting me borrow that furniture to camp out while Rosemary's father had renovations done on the building was a godsend. I *finally* got the stuff the judge said I could take from the house, but up until a week ago, I wasn't sure Bill would let me have even *that* without another battle."

"I asked you to stay with me," Rosemary said.

Rosemary's frown emphasized some unusual dark smudges beneath her eyes, and Melody realized just how tired and pale her friend looked. She had to wonder what was up with Rosemary, who was usually very precise about her appearance.

"Or me," Tanya added.

Yes, they'd all offered. But starting a new life on her own had meant just that. *On her own.* "I know, and thank you. But it was fine. Paige's stuff was all I needed. Thanks again."

Paige grinned. "You're welcome. It was worth it—that cop looked cute carrying stuff up the stairs in his tight pants."

Frankly, Melody had been too shaken by the scruffy, bearded stranger in the dingy jeans to pay much attention to the boyish policeman who'd helped them move furniture a couple of weeks ago. She still wondered about the man, who, she had to admit, had come to her aid at a time when she'd nearly been at the end of her rope. Odd, since she'd started out being afraid of him—wondering if Bill had hired someone to stalk her when she saw his car parked around the corner two days in a row.

When she'd actually spoken to him—after she'd so stupidly fallen on the mattress—she'd been taken aback by his smooth, sexy voice. There'd also been something nice about his lean jaw, even though it had been almost hidden by his scraggly beard.

Then there'd been his eyes. During one moment when he was helping carry a table up the stairs, his glasses had slid down briefly, allowing her a glimpse of his brown eyes. Nice. Very nice. She liked brown-eyed men. Maybe because Bill's were green.

Melody had wondered once or twice what had happened to the dangerous-looking stranger who'd been so helpful. He must have accomplished whatever he'd been doing on her street, because she hadn't seen him since that day.

Mel shrugged off her curiosity. "Anyway, like I said, Bill got almost everything."

Sipping her sweet tea, Rosemary murmured, "I can't believe this, sugar. These things don't happen here in Georgia. All of my friends have lived like queens off their divorce settlements."

"Atlanta's not Savannah," Melody replied. "Here, it'd be perfectly understandable for a wife to take retribution against a cheating husband by having that voodoo queen, Lula Mae Dupré, curse him. Or by breading his Southern-fried steak with rat droppings. But Atlanta's different. More…"

"Northern," Rosemary said with audible disdain.

"They said that, because I painted a billboard advertising Bill's *business,* I hurt him professionally and damaged his ability to practice dentistry. Meaning, I owe him a living for the rest of his rotten life. And oh, how he loves to rub that in. Can you believe he had the balls to come visit me *here?* Just to throw it in my face one more time that he *won.*"

That was the hardest part to swallow. The man could live off her money for a long time. Meanwhile, Melody could be out of funds in as little as two months if she didn't start working fast. Or if she didn't sell her famous peacock-feather lingerie on eBay, which she'd seriously considered.

It'd serve Bill right, the bastard, since he'd tried to get *that* in the divorce settlement, too.

It shouldn't get that bad. Thankfully, she had her photography *hobby*—as Bill had called it—to fall back on. She'd tried to pursue it after the wedding, always having a talent for instinctively knowing how to photograph something—or someone—to make a statement. But Bill had been less than supportive, almost petulant, saying she was wasting her time. Eventually it just hadn't seemed worth the fight and she'd let it go.

Now, though, she had the chance to try again, to prove she was every bit as good behind the camera as she'd been in front of it. She'd already set up her new studio, right downstairs from the small apartment Rosemary's family had rented to her in one of their historic district townhomes. The Chiltons had been wonderfully supportive; Rosemary's brother even arranging for some renovations so she'd have a darkroom. She was all set to begin her new life in Savannah as a photographer.

And a single woman.

That was the silver lining in this whole thing. She was free. Free of everyone for the first time in her life. Free to choose what she wanted—not what her mother or her husband wanted for her. Melody intended to enjoy the hell out of her new life. Not as a kid model with the world watching her every move and a controlling mother on her back. Not the immature, desperate-to-be-wanted-for-herself young woman she'd been before she'd married Bill. Not the wife of an up-and-coming society dentist.

Just Melody. Free, independent and ready to *live,* back here in the only place she'd ever considered home, with the only people she'd ever considered family.

"So," Paige said, "you never were clear on this. What *exactly* did you do, and how did Bill know *you'd* done it? People vandalize signs all the time. You should have denied it." A few people looked over. Six years and a husband hadn't done much to quiet Paige's big voice. Or tame her big curls.

Nibbling her lip, Melody shook her head. A thick lock of reddish-brown hair fell across her eye, and she brushed it back, loving the way her new, shorter hairdo felt. She'd chopped half of it off to frame her face in chunky layers that barely touched her shoulders. Returning to her natural auburn color had been an extra perk—another up-yours to her ex. Bill had adored her long hair, which he'd talked her into dyeing blond again after the wedding.

So much for saying he wanted her for who she was, not the model the world knew. Within a month of their marriage, she'd looked just like the twit who'd gushed to *Teen Magazine* that what she most wanted was world peace.

World peace would be great. But right now, she'd settle for a five-figure balance in her money-market account.

"Mel?" Paige prompted. "Why did you admit you did it?"

"I couldn't deny it when I was plastered all over the eleven-o'clock news standing up on the billboard platform with the paint can in my hand," she said. "Not to mention that the fresh paint was the same Cherry Cordial I'd used to redo the guest room."

"Cherry Cordial? Gosh, the room must have been so dark," Paige said, immediately distracted.

"Hush up, I want to hear the rest," Rosemary said as she tapped a long, pink-tinted nail on the table. "Now, honey, what was it you said that was so damaging to your lesser half?"

Rubbing her eyes wearily, Melody didn't even look at her friends as she explained, "The billboard was directly over his building, by an exit ramp, so it was pretty high profile."

High profile, indeed. God, she still couldn't believe she'd been so damned furious at Bill that she'd climbed up a rickety scaffold ladder with a paint can in one hand and a thick paintbrush clasped tightly in her teeth.

Being honest with herself, she acknowledged that it hadn't been just his cheating that had driven her to seek revenge. She'd gotten used to the infidelity. Her feelings for Bill had been dead for a long time—she'd just been biding her time, waiting for the opportune moment to hit him with divorce papers. Her lawyer had been looking into ways to separate their money first since she'd been too young and too stupid to demand a prenup.

In that instance, she *should* have listened to her mother.

She'd waited patiently, trusting her lawyer. But finding out *who* Bill had had that last fling with had sent her right out of her mind. Shaking her head, she murmured, "The billboard had this big giant picture of Bill, smiling his phony 'you can count on me' smile, with the caption 'Trust Dr. Bill to Drill.'"

Tanya snickered at the cheesiness of it, as Melody had a few years ago when her husband had informed her of the slogan he planned to use in a new ad campaign.

"I wouldn't trust him to clean my litter box," Paige said. Then she smiled. "Did I tell you about my new cat? He's so—"

"Shh!" Tanya hissed, silencing Paige. Never an easy feat.

"I had planned to wait him out—let him ruin himself," Melody said. "But that day, I learned from one of our closest friends that Bill had seduced her eighteen-year-old daughter…a kid we'd bought Girl Scout cookies from a few years back. I sort of lost it. So I got what I needed and drove to his office."

Around them, the cacophony of noise seemed to diminish, as if everyone were waiting for her to continue. A look confirmed a few eavesdroppers. But considering everyone in Atlanta had seen her swinging like a deranged monkey from a billboard, she'd pretty well used up her lifetime supply of embarrassment.

In a low, shaky voice, Paige asked, "What'd you do, Mel?"

Reaching for her glass, she admitted, "I added a few words to his slogan until it read, 'You can Trust Dr. Bill to Drill… your wives, your daughters and certain barnyard animals.'"

A snort from the two women at the next table and the grin on the face of the owner—who'd been hovering over Melody since the minute she'd arrived—confirmed her wider audience. At her own table, her three friends made no effort to hide their laughter. "Oh, my goodness, I would have paid to see that," Paige said, her face growing red as she giggled helplessly.

With a droll lift of her brow, Melody replied, "You could have, if you lived in Atlanta and happened to be watching the eleven-o'clock news that night. The Channel Six helicopter was flying to the scene of an accident and spotted me. They lit me up like a prisoner going over the wall and broadcast the image all over the airwaves for the entire city to see."

Rosemary shook her head. "Ouch."

"It gets better," Tanya mumbled as she dipped a chip.

Yeah. It got better, in a sick, oh-God-can-you-believe-she-actually-did-that way. "I panicked," Mel said flatly. "Dropped the evidence. Dashed for the ladder. Slipped in the spilled paint—which got all over me—and fell off the end of the platform. The Cherry Cordial should've been called Blood Red, because I looked like a monster out of a horror movie dangling up there. King Kong's mutant baby or something."

Beside her, Tanya tried to look sympathetic while also trying to hide a grin. Maybe someday Melody would laugh about it, too. Maybe when she was ninety and had managed to forget how stupid she must have looked on TV, hanging from the platform waiting for the firemen who'd rescued her with a ladder truck.

She had thought that was the most humiliating moment of her life, of all the humiliating moments she'd endured during her marriage to the prick with the drill. It'd been close. But it still couldn't beat the day her divorce decree had come down.

"Oh, sugar, haven't you heard?" Rosemary said, her lips curved in a smile. "Like Scarlett O'Hara used to say, 'Revenge is a dish best served cold.'"

Paige frowned. "I thought Hannibal Lechter said that."

Melody reached for a handful of tortilla chips, not caring how many calories were in each one. Without Bill frowning at her, she didn't give a damn what she ate or how much weight she gained.

"I think," Tanya interjected with a disgusted grunt, "it's Klingon. Though *I* would have taken the Lechter approach."

"I didn't mind billboard vandalism, but I hadn't reached the point where I wanted to kill my husband and eat his liver with some fava beans." Melody ate a chip, then added, "So that's the story. My life of crime and my fifteen minutes of fame."

"You had a couple of decades of fame," Paige reminded her.

Right. But no more. She was completely finished with all of that and intended to live life out of the spotlight from now on. Quiet, low-key, no scandals, no adventures.

"Do you have a copy of that news program?" Tanya asked, still looking amused. "You oughta keep it as a warning for any man you consider marrying in the future."

"Ha-ha, I know, it's all funny until a male judge who probably cheats on his wife, too, decided Bill's reputation had been damaged for life and I owed him everything but my internal organs. Which will probably be awarded to him if I appeal."

"But you *are* going to appeal, right?" Tanya suddenly sounded serious. They'd had this conversation before, and Melody knew her friend, the fighter, believed this situation could be fixed.

Mel wasn't so sure. Not that she wouldn't like her money back, or to at least make sure Bill didn't get it. But she didn't want to go back to her old life when she'd been the duped wife, the vengeful ex. Not to mention the target of Bill's incessant anger and malicious threats.

He hadn't liked being humiliated and her money apparently hadn't eased the sting. *He's gone,* she reminded herself, refusing to think of his visit to Savannah. Not to mention the heavy-breathing calls she'd received her first weeks in town…until she'd had her number changed. *Long gone.* And she was done with the past. It was time to find herself again. To stop looking back, to move on, focusing on the future.

Paige suddenly changed the subject. "Do you remember the last time we all came here? The night before Mel's wedding?"

So much for not looking back. That'd lasted ten seconds.

"We were practically kids," Tanya replied.

"Well, I happened to stumble across a souvenir from that night," Paige said with a secretive smile. She reached into the duffel bag she'd been carrying when she'd arrived, and dug out a pad of paper. "Remember *everything* we talked about?"

It took Melody a moment to recall the entire evening, which seemed like the last truly happy one she'd had. Any happy ones she'd shared with Bill had been zapped out of her memory around year three of their marriage. But when Paige flipped open the notebook and turned it around to show the rest of them, she remembered. "Oh, our infamous Adultery Free Zone lists."

"Right. We were going to go for it, no questions asked, no guilt, if we ever had the chance with one of these guys."

"Well," Rosemary said, "my go-for-it list is on my fridge. I've crossed off number five…that Atlanta Braves player? Met him at a New Year's Eve party and we had sex in a coat closet as the ball was dropping." Almost purring, she added, "Fortunately, he spent a lot more time going down than the ball did."

Melody couldn't help wondering if Rosemary would ever find *one* man who satisfied her as much as so *many* men did. "Uh, I thought the lists were a joke."

"They were…until I met that Braves player." Rosemary's

smile was definitely catlike. "Speaking of our lists, I've kept my copies of all of them. I even dug yours out, Mel, once I knew you were divorcing the dick with the drill and coming home."

Grunting, Melody said, "Well, someone talking about me having sex is about as close to a sex life as I've had in a long time, so I guess I can't gripe about it."

The middle-aged owner with thinning dark hair walked by just in time for that comment; his speculative look made her grab for her margarita.

Tanya shuddered. "Quick, Paige, find Mel's list. If there's anybody who needs to get laid in this town, it's *her*."

Wrinkling her nose, Melody ignored her friend. But Paige had already started flipping through the notebook. "Oh, my," she said. "Jonathan Rhodes…there's a blast from the past."

Glancing over her friend's shoulder, Melody scooted her chair around to get a closer look. "Yikes. I forgot about him. He sure didn't last long in Washington."

"Probably only a bit longer than he lasted in the hooker's bed," Tanya said. "He didn't even run for reelection after he got caught in that police raid at a sleazy hotel. He came back here to Savannah and returned to his law practice."

Rosemary nodded, a speculative look in her eye. "Hmm…so he's still around. A definite possibility, Mel."

Melody shook her head. "Not happening. Even if the list was serious—which it's *not*—I'm not interested in sex. I'm not feeling very charitable toward men right now."

"Which is why you need to think like a man," Rosemary said. "Go out and live a little, take what you can get. You might not have meant it the night we wrote these down, but you can mean it now." Leaning forward, Rosemary continued almost fiercely, "*Live,* Mel. Get back to being the happy, confident girl you were that night and don't let the bastard you married cause you one more minute of pain or self-doubt."

Rosemary was the languid one, not the passionate one, so Melody was somewhat taken by surprise. It said a lot about how worried her friends were, which touched her. Deeply.

Knowing, however, that Rosemary was involved in a somewhat serious on-again, off-again romance, which she was keeping pretty close to her vest, Melody didn't believe her friend was living by her own advice. But she had once. And it didn't appear to have hurt her. So maybe...

No. She needed sex like a nun needed edible underwear.

Before Rosemary could keep arguing, Paige yelped, "Oh, yikes, this guy—number five—didn't fare so well. Chef Charlie of Chez Jacques died about a month ago, in his own restaurant."

"I heard he got drunk and choked on a meatball," Tanya said. "Sounds like that man swallowed some dumb-ass pills first."

"Creepy," Paige said. Then she made the sign of the cross.

Tanya rolled her eyes. "You're not Catholic."

"It seemed appropriate." In typical Paige fashion, she allowed herself to be completely distracted by a random thought. "Why do you think he was making meatballs? Isn't Chez Jacques a French place? Do they serve meatballs? Is Charlie a French name?"

Tanya gave Paige an impatient glare. Then she pointed at the notebook. "Who else did Mel list?"

Yeah, who else? Melody had been so focused on her rocky marriage and horrible divorce for such a long time, she hadn't thought about the list in ages. She didn't even know where her originals were and had to read over Paige's shoulder to remind herself who she'd once wanted so badly.

When her gaze fell on the name of a golfer who'd had a

chance in the PGA some years ago, but had quickly fizzled out, she gasped.

"What?" Rosemary asked.

"You're not going to believe this, but Kenny Traynor, that golfer who was supposedly gay? He was all over the news in Atlanta last month. He was killed in a weird accident in the locker room of the country club where he was a golf pro."

They all fell silent as the reality sunk in. Two of the men Melody had joked about sleeping with had died since that night. Young men, healthy men. Paige was right…it *was* creepy.

Suddenly looking relieved, Paige smiled. "But number four—Drake Manning, the reporter—is still around. He's an anchor on Channel Nine. And his hair hasn't moved since you left."

"He's a pig," Tanya said, her mouth tight.

Paige continued before Melody could question Tanya's comment. "Now we come to number one, which was why I brought our lists. I saw this on eBay and had to get it for you."

Reaching into her bag, Paige retrieved a plastic-wrapped magazine. Melody recognized it—and the picture on the cover—immediately. It was her marine, the one who'd saved the children. Her number-one fantasy man.

"You sure were drooling into your burrito when his picture came on the TV screen that night. Wasn't she?" Paige said.

Tanya nodded. "Uh-*huh!* That boy was *fine.*"

Rosemary, for some reason, remained silent, just staring at the picture, a half smile on her lips. Melody couldn't blame her. She was enraptured by the photo on the magazine, too. "Oh, my God, I hope I didn't jinx this guy."

"It would have made the news," Paige said. "He was a Georgia hero. We would have heard if he hadn't made it back."

She prayed Paige was right. Because she'd hate to think of this particular man meeting some strange fate like the others.

The picture was every bit as dramatic—as compelling—as it had been that night six years ago. More so, really, since she was a woman now, not an immature girl, as she'd been when she got married. The only thing that hadn't changed was the *hunger.*

The sudden flash of want surprised her. But it was there…strong, insistent. She was attracted to this stranger like she hadn't been attracted to anyone in a long time.

"He looks familiar for some reason," she murmured.

"Well, duh, of course he looks familiar," Paige said. "You only lusted after him more than any guy you'd ever seen."

"I know that. But there's something else. I just can't quite put my finger on it." The little flash of intuition, recognition or memory disappeared as quickly as it had popped into her brain. "I wonder what happened to him after…"

"You have to go to the police."

Shocked by Rosemary's words, Melody just gaped. "Huh?"

"I mean it. Two out of five men on your list have died, both very recently. Both right here in Georgia, and under strange circumstances. We're calling the police."

Melody was shaking her head throughout Rosemary's spiel. "That's utterly ridiculous. This has nothing to do with me."

Ignoring her, Rosemary reached for her cell phone. "I know someone on the Savannah PD."

Though outwardly scoffing, a hint of concern did go through Melody's mind. Still, she insisted, "I can't do it. I'm not going to tell some cop that men I once wanted to have sex with are dropping like flies throughout the state of Georgia."

"You sure won't get a date that way," Paige offered.

"Hush up, Paige," Rosemary said. "Mel, I am not kidding. You just came through a divorce with a husband out for revenge." Her eyes widened. "Bill *knew* about this list! I remember it came up during one of my visits to Atlanta a few years ago. He was joking about it, while you seemed to have forgotten the whole thing."

She *had* almost forgotten about the list, which had at first been just a joke to her. Later, when it had become clear that her marriage had been an enormous mistake, the silly game had provided some fodder for late-night fantasies and dreams, but eventually, she'd stopped even dreaming. Fantasies, dreams and thoughts of her list had faded away…as had her marriage.

"Yeah, he knew," she finally said. "He found all four of our lists in my purse during our honeymoon. We laughed about them and he even wrote out his own top five."

Of course, Bill probably *hadn't* been joking. She wouldn't be surprised if the son of a bitch had crossed every name off his list before their fourth anniversary.

Don't go there. She took a deep breath, forcing herself to focus on the bright, wide-open future with people who loved her. Not the gut-wrenching, humiliating past with people who'd been pitying her. Like all of her Atlanta friends, who had to have known about Bill's affairs long before she did.

"That does it," Rosemary said. "You've got to tell someone."

By now, even skeptical Tanya was looking convinced, and Paige's eyes were wide as she whispered, "Maybe she's right."

"I can't tell a stranger that I sat down the night before my wedding and made a list of men I wanted to have sex with."

Rosemary was already pushing buttons on her cell phone

with the pointed tip of her nail. "You don't have to go into that much detail, sugar. Just call it a little bridesmaid game. Men you're attracted to—you don't have to mention the adultery-free-zone part of it." Then, before pushing the send button, she added, "This detective's nice and discreet." She glanced away, not meeting Mel's eye. "He's older. Kindly. Fatherly."

Never having known for sure who—or where—her father was, Melody couldn't take much comfort in that. "Rosemary…"

But before she could finish her sentence, she realized Rosemary was already talking in hushed tones to someone, her hand curved around the phone for privacy. *A little late for that.*

Outnumbered, confused and a teeny bit apprehensive, Melody realized she had no choice. Which was why, a minute later, she agreed to meet with Rosemary's detective friend. Adamant about not barging into the police station, she at least got Rosemary to agree to set up an informal meeting in a public place.

It was ridiculous, of course. But she'd do it. At ten o'clock the next morning, at a diner on Abercorn Street not far from her own apartment, she'd meet with this detective, carefully tell him what she knew, hear him laugh, then forget about it.

Grabbing a pen, she jotted down the man's name, writing it on the list Paige had torn out of the notebook. For *evidence.*

Yeesh. Her sexual-fantasy list possible evidence. How utterly embarrassing. She could only hope this Detective Walker was as nice and fatherly as Rosemary said he was.

And that he was *very* understanding.

CHAPTER TWO

"WAIT A MINUTE," Nick Walker said, eyeing his partner on the Savannah-Chatham Metropolitan PD. "You're telling me some woman thinks a chef who choked on a meatball while drunk was actually *murdered?* And that his death might have something to do with the death of a golf pro in Atlanta?"

Nick made no effort to keep the skepticism out of his voice as he stared across his desk at his partner. Dex didn't flinch away from the pointed look and Nick sat back in his chair, sighing heavily. Because apparently his friend *was* serious.

The two of them sat in the bustling station on Habersham Street, getting ready to start another day filled with the promise of lots of crime. First up was investigating a robbery-homicide at a nearby antique store that had been filling the local media. The case had brought pressure on the whole precinct—they'd just come from a bitch-out meeting during which their lieutenant had threatened bodily injury if it wasn't solved soon.

It was a typical weekday morning—already over eighty degrees and sweltering, with air that smelled like used motor oil and felt about as thick. The window air conditioner chugged lazily, managing to circulate a breeze that could only be described as cool by a recent refugee from hell.

At every other desk sat another member of the squad,

making calls, writing reports, delaying the inevitable moment when they'd have to leave the building and venture out into the wicked September morning. Because, damn, it hurt to breathe out there. The heat wave gripping the city had lasted nine weeks now. Might be another month before it dropped below eighty.

He hated the heat and not only because his skin hadn't felt dry since Memorial Day. The hotter it got—the *stickier* it got—the more people heated up and committed crimes. Quick to anger, slow to reason, the city had been on a low rolling boil all summer and September hadn't seemed to evaporate any of the steam.

"I know it's probably a long shot, but it's worth a conversation, isn't it?" Dex asked, his tone even, his voice reasonable. As usual. The guy was nearly impossible to rile, unlike Nick who, truth be told, hadn't been too sure he'd ever make detective given his tendency to erupt every now and again. He thought he'd done a pretty good job escaping his badass teenage years, when he'd literally fought his way out of his family's Walkers-are-all-no-good-drunks reputation with his fists. But that old Walker temper did kick up once in a while.

"You're really serious about this?" Nick asked.

"I am. It's a long shot, but maybe there is some kind of connection between these two cases."

"The Chez Jacques death isn't a case—it was ruled an accident. The investigation's been closed for a month."

"So this tip probably won't go anywhere. But since you caught the original call, isn't it worth a conversation?"

If the request had come from Draco, Jones or one of the others, he would have immediately suspected some kind of setup. A practical joke at the very least. A blind date at the worst.

As the youngest on the squad, the newest detective *and* one of the only two unmarried men on this floor—the other being his partner—he was the target of a lot of jokes. Not to mention a lot of schemes to get him as tied-around-the-balls as every other poor married sucker he worked with.

But this was Dex. Mr. Serious. The most straightforward, honest, no-nonsense guy in the building. And his partner.

Dex was *also* the only one in the building who knew that Nick had once been married. Briefly. *Badly.* To a woman who'd then sabotaged Nick's relationship with his entire family, separating them for a decade with her lies. So Dex wouldn't play some kind of setup game with him.

"I know how it sounds, but Rosemary swears it's true."

Nick grunted but said nothing against Rosemary. He still hadn't quite forgiven her for the stakeout snafu a few weeks ago, when he'd nearly blown his cover trying to help some woman move her furniture.

Some woman. Yeah, she had been that.

For some reason, he hadn't been able to put her completely out of his mind since. Occasionally he'd even considered cruising by her place, seeing how she was doing. Seeing if she had any more chairs she needed moved.

He hadn't done it. Not only because he just wasn't in the market to meet a woman right now, but also because she'd seemed so damned vulnerable. So hurt. So desolate.

The last thing she needed was a visit from a workaholic cop who'd deceived her about who he was on the day they'd met.

"Rosemary swears, huh?" he finally said, knowing Dex was waiting for an answer.

"Yeah. And you know how she is."

Oh, yes, he knew. Frankly, Nick didn't know how his friend had hooked up with the woman, who was the spoiled, pampered daughter of one of the former mayors of Savannah. Yeah, she was hot, and she managed to keep Dex a lot more on edge than any woman he'd ever dated—which seemed a good thing for someone as quiet and uninvolved as his partner. The differences in their financial situations were glaringly obvious, and Dex had made more than one comment about trying to keep up with Rosemary.

Besides being rich, she was flighty. Not to mention oversexed, bored and pretentious.

Dex was about as down-to-earth and unpretentious as they came, which was one reason he and Nick got along so well. Nick hated pretension. He had no patience for the old guard who hadn't yet realized the Civil War was over and the grand and glorious days of plantation owners were mere textbook footnotes.

Coming from a white trash Georgia family in a small town in the northwest corner of the state, he'd never realized the elitist culture still existed elsewhere. Sure, Joyful had been full of the haves and the have-nots, like every other town— the Walkers definitely being on the have-not list. But until he'd started working to solve some of the crimes targeting the upper crust of this old, proud city, he hadn't realized how far in the past some people seemed to live.

That was how Dex had met Rosemary. Somebody had robbed a pricey house she had listed with her real-estate agency.

"I told Rosemary you'd meet the woman today at ten." After naming the location, Dex added, "You'll know her by her red hat."

Nick didn't respond right away, merely studying his friend, watching for a shift of the eyes or a tiny grin that would say he was being had. He saw neither. Just stalwart, calm Dex. The nice, stoic, friendly side of their good-cop, bad-cop routine.

"Why, exactly, did Rosemary decide I was the person who had to meet with this mystery woman? Why not you?"

"She apparently doesn't like Northerners."

The explanation wouldn't make a whole lot of sense in a lot of other places. But this was Savannah. Dex, who hailed from Pennsylvania, had never lost the clipped tone or flat accent that pegged him as someone from above the Mason-Dixon line. This wouldn't be the first time he'd been eyed with suspicion by some spoiled wannabe Southern belle.

Nick disliked the woman already.

He gave it one more shot. "Last I checked, Rosemary didn't exactly admire my tact with women."

A half smile appeared on Dex's face. "Only because you told that reporter doing a story on Rosie's real-estate business that you'd rather go to bed with a cross-dressing, three-armed circus freak than ever go out with her again."

He remembered.

"I think Rosemary's changed her mind," Dex said. "She never liked Angie Jacobs anyway and didn't much care that Angie dropped the story once she found out you were a friend of ours."

Just as well, because Angie was a piranha.

"Rosemary now thinks you might just have great instincts."

"Until the next time she decides I'm a cretin because you have a beer with me instead of meeting her at some party where they serve bait on crackers and call it gourmet cookin'."

"Careful, your moonshiner background is showing."

Rolling his eyes, Nick rose to his feet and tossed a file at Dex. "Make yourself useful while I'm chasing your girlfriend's boogeymen. See if you can find anything on this plate. Could be connected to the break-in on Wright Square."

He hadn't really expected Dex to complain, and he didn't. Instead, he gave Nick a relieved smile. "Thanks. I owe you one."

"You owe me many, especially for having to drive the P.O.S. during the Miller stakeout. But who's counting?"

"Hey, we got him, didn't we?"

That they had. They'd gotten him and the scumbag wouldn't be putting his filth onto the streets of Savannah anytime soon.

Muttering under his breath about spoiled society brats with conspiracy complexes, Nick left the precinct and drove the short distance to the café. He could have walked the few blocks, but it was too hot and he was too irritated.

Dex had to have named the location for the meeting, which was the one good thing about this whole mess. Because this place sure knew how to serve biscuits and gravy.

"Red hat," he reminded himself, shaking his head as he walked in the front door. "Just what I need, a red-hat lady."

Once inside, he remembered another good thing about this restaurant. The air-conditioning worked a darn sight better than it did at the precinct. Or in his city-issued car.

Standing in the doorway and taking in a resigned breath, he looked around the place, which was decades old but still popular with locals and tourists. He kept his eye out for a red hat and blue hair. Because, really, if the woman was one of those red-hat ladies, she had to be at least one hundred and four.

No red hat. No big red feathers, or jewels or lace, like he'd seen on the more flamboyant headgear sold at the boutiques around here, which catered to the rich and to the tourists. Definitely not his shopping grounds. He felt much more at home at the Wal-Mart near his west Chatham apartment.

A few late-morning customers chatted at a couple of the tables in the front room, occasionally beckoning to a harried-looking waitress who carried a steaming pot of coffee. Two men sat at the counter, and another was paying at the cash register.

Skirting the edge of the place, he walked into the second room, where a dozen more tables took up nearly all the available floor space. Several of the tables were occupied, but only one had a person sitting completely alone. And that person, he realized, was wearing a baseball cap. A *red* baseball cap.

So maybe she's only ninety.

Unfortunately, the woman sat below a stained-glass window depicting the most overutilized image in all of Savannah—the Bird Girl statue that'd been on the cover of The Book...*Midnight In The Garden of Good And Evil.* Nick could happily live the rest of his life without seeing another book, window, magnet, bookmark, T-shirt, mug, poster or postcard with that particular picture. But it'd never happen, not unless he moved away from Savannah. It was as intrinsic to this city as the Gordon Low house, where giddy, giggling Girl Scouts flocked by the thousands to worship their founder.

Pulling his attention off the window, he peered around the few customers and waitresses, staring at the woman in the cap. He noted a pair of tanned shoulders, exposed by the sleeveless blue tank top the woman wore. And, of course, the cap, with a short, dark-colored ponytail sticking out the opening in the back, looking too damn bouncy and jaunty in this wilting heat.

Reminding himself that Dex would never send him on a wild-goose chase when they were working a case, he made his way down the narrow aisle, nodding to the waitress. The busy woman paused to stare back and give him a once-over. Nick didn't necessarily like the attention he got from women—particularly because of the bullshit he caught about it from the other guys in the squad. But, on occasion, it came in handy. Like now. Because with one quick smile and a hand gesture, he had the woman promising to be right over with a fresh pot. If history was any indication, he'd have a cup of coffee within twenty seconds of sitting down.

Moving toward the woman he was to meet, he continued to study her without her knowledge. Each step that brought him closer to his target seemed slower than the one before. Because the more he saw, the more suspicious he became.

Her shoulders weren't merely tanned and soft looking against the pale blue shirt. They were also toned. Curved. Leading to long, slim arms. Definitely young looking.

She moved one of those arms, reaching to adjust her ball cap. Her movements were graceful. Fluid. They drew his eyes to the thick dark hair, a rich, reddish-brown. A *familiar* reddish-brown. "My, oh my," he whispered.

It was her. He knew it as sure as he knew the way the sun winked orange and purple as it went down over the horizon. Sitting in front of him was the woman he'd helped a few weeks ago. The one who'd fallen on the mattress the day he'd nailed Manny Miller, the drug trafficker.

Nick's heartbeat kicked up a notch as a nearly unfamiliar sensation crawled through his veins. *Interest.* It was as unexpected as it was exciting, and for some reason the quiet, stale morning suddenly seemed ripe with expectation.

He'd been thinking about her for weeks. And fate, or Rosemary Chilton, had given him another chance to meet her.

Suddenly the woman looked to the side, her attention drawn by a passing busboy. The movement gave him a glimpse of her profile. Long enough to confirm her identity by the full lips, the stubborn curve of her chin, the sweep of her long lashes. More importantly, it was long enough to see the absence of those shadows beneath her eyes. And to notice that her face had filled out, looking less gaunt, less distressed. More beautiful.

The cop in him analyzed her features and noted the changes.

The man in him took a much more *carnal* inventory.

Setup or not…he wanted her with a rush of attraction so completely overwhelming it turned his feet into lead weights until he couldn't take another step. He just stood there, a foot behind her, staring down at the top of her head.

Then she turned around again, as if aware of his presence. Slowly tilting her head back, she peered up from beneath the rim of her baseball cap, looking at him with those big baby blues.

He paused, studying her head-on. The glimpses he'd had of her as he'd made his way through the diner had only provided tantalizing clues. Now, under the full-frontal assault of that face, those wide eyes, that sexy mouth—now parted in surprise as she returned his stare—he realized he was already in deep.

He'd been attracted to her weeks ago. But now that the sadness seemed to be gone from her eyes, his attraction took a big leap forward. He *wanted* her. Sex with this woman instantly became number two on his list of personal goals for the year. Right after saving enough money to put a down payment on a house, but before getting his mutt Fredo to stop chewing his shoes.

"I think I'm supposed to be meeting you," he murmured. He stepped closer until his thigh touched the edge of her table, coming very close to her hands, which were flat on the surface. "I'm Detective Walker." He gave her a little smile, just to put her at ease since she still had that deer-in-the-headlights look on her face. Then, with an exaggerated shrug, he added, "You're the only person here wearing a red hat."

Still nothing. Nada. Not one word, not one gesture. Not a smile. Certainly not a phone number and an invitation, which were, to be honest, the words he'd really like to hear coming out of her incredible mouth. But she merely sat there, frozen.

"Ma'am? Are you okay?"

And finally...*finally*...she blinked. Her mouth snapped shut. Her jaw visibly tensed. On the table, her hands curled into fists, as if she were suddenly feeling violent.

When she spoke, he realized she *was* feeling violent. Because in a low, shaking voice, she said, "You'd better arrest me, because I swear to God, the minute I find Rosemary Chilton, I'm going to *murder* her."

UNLESS ROSEMARY HAD gone into the witness-protection program last night after she'd set up this outrageous meeting, she was dead meat. Because Melody was going to track her down and kill her for this. *After* she tortured her by throwing her entire collection of Manolo Blahniks into the Savannah River.

She'd been set up. Completely, totally, shockingly blind-sided...by one of her best friends. She hadn't felt this taken for a ride since her divorce hearing.

It was humiliating enough to tell a cop that people might be getting killed because of a sex list she'd made as a joke six years ago. That was when she'd figured she'd be talking to some cuddly Father Bear of a cop.

This guy was no Father Bear. And cuddling was the *last* thing a woman would want to do if she got him into bed. Because Detective Walker was *him*. Her ultimate fantasy. Her marine from *Time* magazine. And oh, God, was he to die for.

"Why do I get the feeling we've been set up?" he asked, lifting one corner of his wide, drool-worthy mouth in a smile.

Melody had to swallow, not yet able to answer. Her throat

was tight, her voice having dried up when she'd made the mistake of glancing at his jean-clad hips, mere inches from her arm.

Soft, slouchy, threadbare jeans were made for bodies like these. Made to ride low on lean hips, to bulge in the most interesting places, and to hug long, hard legs.

She jerked her attention up, trying to focus on his face. That move was just as bad…and every bit as dangerous. Because his face—those eyes, that intensity—had been what had drawn her to him the first time she'd seen him six years ago. And they hadn't changed a bit. She wondered if he was the real reason she'd always had a thing for dark-eyed men, up to this very day.

"You *do* think we've been set up, right?" he asked, obviously trying to pry her out of her silence.

"Yeah. Definitely a setup," she finally muttered, already wondering if he'd chase her down and arrest her if she got up and ran for the door. They always arrested people who took off from the police on the TV cop shows. But only after patting them down.

Oh, Lord, she was better off sitting here with her face turning twenty shades of red and her butt feeling as if it were superglued to the chair than being patted down by this man. Being touched by him at all would be like throwing a lit match on a box of Fourth of July firecrackers. She'd start sparking and popping and two seconds later she'd be on the man like an actor on an Oscar statue.

"Can I sit down anyway?" he asked.

He didn't wait for permission. He simply moved to the other side of the table and slid into the seat, facing her.

Facing. Goodness gracious, his face. The handsomeness she'd imagined behind the blood and grime in the magazine photo hadn't come close to the reality. His face was lean, his cheeks closely shaven, emphasizing the strength of his jaw. His lose-yourself-in-them eyes were the color of rich chocolate. He had a strong nose, and a mouth she wanted to suck on like a lollipop.

The body simply defied description. From the broad shoulders clad in a tight black T-shirt, to the thick arms bulging with muscle, the man personified strength. His chest was impossibly broad and she'd already gotten a load of what he could do for a pair of aged jeans. Delightful things. Sinful things.

Somehow, it seemed impossible that he should look exactly the same. Just as big. Just as masculine. Just as intense and brooding, but God, so incredibly *sexy*.

He somehow seemed to have been plucked out of the field of battle and dropped right here into civilized Savannah, but hadn't quite caught up with his change of venue. Because he looked dangerous. From the thick, dark head of hair to the glitter in his eyes, to the coiled strength of his body, held so tight and aware, he screamed danger.

"My first name's Nick," he said, breaking the silence.

Nick Walker. A good name. A strong name. Definitely *not* a cuddly, fatherly name. *Rosemary, you demon.*

"And you are?"

"Call me Mel," she mumbled.

So, there was the introduction. What happened next depended on how single he was and whether Melody decided her list was more than just a joke, like Rosemary had.

Of course, she didn't even know if he'd *want* to have wild, passionate, completely unexpected sex with her. She didn't know if *she'd* want to.

Liar.

"So, what story did Rosemary use to get you here?" His voice was low, gravelly almost, but in a few drawn-out syllables there was an unmistakable Southern softness. A bit of twang that she liked a lot. And, she had to acknowledge, she didn't like only the soft lilt in his voice, she also liked the way his mouth moved with every word he spoke. "I figure she made up some excuse for you to come down here and meet with a complete stranger."

Before Melody could reply, the waitress appeared beside their table with a mug and a steaming pot of coffee. She quickly served the newcomer, giving him a warm look. Mel waved her fingers toward her own nearly empty, rapidly cooling cup, but was totally ignored by the woman.

For some reason, the smile on Nick Walker's face after the waitress breezed away without a single glance at Melody really annoyed her. *Cocky.* He was cocky. She hadn't seen that in his picture, though she shouldn't be surprised. A man as handsome and as obviously brave would have a lot to be cocky about, right?

But she didn't like it…she'd never liked arrogant men. Which was good. Because she *needed* to find things she didn't like about this man, and fast. She could start by amending the rules of the list, by adding a cocky out-clause. Otherwise, she could end up making a fool of herself by oh, say, asking him if he wanted to retreat to the nearest hotel.

He stirred his coffee. "Judging by the look in your eye, I'd say Rosemary told you who I really am."

Melody closed her eyes and counted to three, clenching her fingers together in her lap. The man knew she knew he was the *Time* magazine hero. Meaning Rosemary had to have told him. But please, oh, please, God, she couldn't have told him about the list. She wouldn't have, right? Rosemary was her best friend. She *wouldn't* have.

If she had, Mel was going to die. Collapse right across the

table and land face-first in his nice, hot, steaming cup of coffee and die.

"I guess we didn't get off to the best start, huh?"

"I've always thought it was the finish that mattered," she mumbled before she thought better of it.

"Don't tell me you're leaving already." With a boyish smile that suited the way a thick, dark lock of his hair fell over his brow, he added, "Can I confess I'm surprised you came anyway, despite my, uh, disreputable appearance the first time around?"

"Disreputable?" Shock made her eyes widen. "No, you weren't disreputable looking at all." Heroic, admirable, determined and courageous were more like it. How could he possibly think a little dirt and some blood would make him look disreputable when he'd been holding three children whose lives he'd just saved?

"Not at all," she repeated, not wanting him to think he had reason to be embarrassed. Lord, there went the whole cocky out-clause, because the man obviously had no idea how amazing that picture had really been. Or how it had affected her.

"You *do* know who I am, right?"

She swallowed hard. "Yes. Sure. I mean…who doesn't?"

His brow shot up in surprise and his head tilted to one side. "Really? You think I'm that easily recognizable?"

The man had been the hunk of the known universe six years ago on the cover of one of the most widely circulated magazines in the world. Of course he was recognizable! "Hate to break it to you, but yes, you are."

Her answer didn't seem to make him feel any better. He rubbed a hand across his smooth jaw and muttered, "I must be losing my touch."

Goodness, he really was feeling bad about that. As if he wasn't happy being recognized as a national hero.

And suddenly, she thought she understood. Hadn't she hated being recognized for one photograph that didn't represent the real person she was inside? The journalist who'd taken this man's picture and circulated it around the world had caught only one moment, one selfless act. There was a lot more man here to be seen. A *lot* more man.

Like there was a lot more woman to Melody than was revealed in that horrid peacock-feather ensemble. Not *physically,* since almost all of her body had been revealed. But emotionally.

"I think I understand," she said, wanting to comfort him, to let him know he really wasn't alone in what he was feeling. "We all project an image for the world to see. It can be a little disconcerting when someone sees the person behind the mask."

"Or the person beneath the dirty clothes," he said with a rueful laugh. "For the record, I do bathe regularly."

Huh? He was embarrassed because he hadn't been able to bathe in the middle of a war-ravaged battlefield? Good Lord, her first instincts had been *way* off base. Far from being cocky, this man had hardly any self-confidence at all!

"You really don't have to make any excuses to me, Nick." Almost unable to help it, she reached across the table and touched the back of his hand. She'd meant to be consoling, comforting. That would have seemed strange if she were reaching out to the big, strong, larger-than-life man who'd been on the cover of the magazine. But she was reaching out to the nice, low-confidence guy she'd been speaking with.

Somehow, though, she realized that the big, sexy stranger was the one she was touching the moment their hands connected. Because as soon as her fingers brushed against his skin, something snapped and sparked a reaction, surprising her. She suddenly got all hot and flustered, though the room was cool enough.

He was so warm, that was it. The electric warmth of his skin had just taken her by surprise. But his next move nearly made her come right out of her seat. He turned his hand a bit, so he could scrape the tip of one finger on the fleshy pad of her palm, and the touch was so unexpected, so…personal, somehow, that she could barely remember to breathe.

She finally pulled her hand away, reaching for her water glass in a stall for time. After swallowing, she admitted, "You should never make excuses for doing something heroic. Something wonderful. You stepped in and helped when others wouldn't."

Looking at him, she noticed the confused expression on his face. As if he couldn't quite figure her out. Shrugging his shoulders, he said, "It wasn't that big a deal."

"Yes it *was* a big deal." Hadn't the whole world thought so?

"I mean, it wasn't like it was that heavy a load."

Three small children might not have weighed a lot in terms of pounds, but the responsibility for them must have been an enormous weight. "I don't agree with you there."

He sipped his coffee. "I've lifted more at the gym."

"Well, of course you have," she said, "but nothing that was so important. So *critical*."

He frowned and his jaw tightened. Suddenly he looked more the dangerous marine and less the guy-next-door. "It really was that critical? Was it all you had?"

She didn't follow.

"I mean, I don't know the whole story, but did you really end up with nothing but a couple of mattresses and some chairs?"

Now she was completely lost. "What?"

He put his hands up, palms out. "Sorry. I shouldn't have asked that. It's none of my business."

The hands-off gesture seemed familiar. It tugged something in her memory, but she was too focused on his odd words. Was he talking about furniture, when she was talking about orphans?

Suddenly he laughed. "I guess it's a good thing you started out with the mattress. I don't think that box spring would have been as comfortable to land on face-first."

"The mattress…"

The word dying on her lips, Melody froze. In a second everything clicked into place. Somehow managing to keep her mouth from falling open in utter shock, she stared at him, finally seeing what she *should* have seen the minute he'd sat down.

Add a rough beard and some dark glasses, mess up his hair and throw him in filthy clothes, and he became the stranger from the street. The one who'd kept the cop from towing her truck. Who'd hauled her furniture up several flights of stairs. Who'd stepped in when she'd been ready to collapse in exhaustion and fear that Bill was never going to let her get on with her life, since he'd come to harass her in Savannah that very morning.

"Um, will you excuse me for a minute?" she mumbled, already rising to her feet. Without waiting for his answer, she beelined straight to the ladies' room, went inside and locked the door behind her. Leaning her forehead against the doorjamb, she sucked in a few deep breaths and took it all in.

The guy she'd wanted so desperately at first sight all those years ago wasn't simply a gorgeous fighting man, not just a war hero. No, he was also her *personal* one. At least, the closest thing to a hero she'd had in her life lately.

Then something else dawned on her. "He doesn't know," she whispered. He thought she recognized him from the day he'd helped her move in. Not from his brief bout of celebrity six years ago. He had no idea she'd recognized him from his famous photo. Which meant, if God was kind, he had no idea about the list.

So maybe Rosemary was going to survive the week after all.

"ROSEMARY, WHAT DID YOU get me mixed up in?"

Rosemary Chilton smiled at the sound of Dex's voice, her body going warm and soft. She always had that reaction when it came to this man who'd come out of nowhere and changed her world a year ago. "Well, hello to you, too, Detective Delaney."

"Nick just called."

"Really?" Rosemary murmured. "And how is his day going? As fine as mine? What about yours…you feelin' okay after your, um, hard workout on Sunday?"

He cleared his throat. "This isn't a social call."

Rosemary leaned back in her chair, swiveling it around to look out her blinds into the back garden behind her house. A beautiful, sunny day from this angle. If only it were about twenty degrees cooler, she'd love to be rolling around in that thick green grass with Dex the way she'd been rolling around in her bed with him for much of the previous weekend.

"Rosemary, tell me what you did this morning."

"Well," she murmured, her tone sultry, "I got up and took a long shower. I rubbed a soft sponge all over my body. It was real soapy, with that lilac-scented soap you like to smell on my skin. And I noticed these red marks on the inside of my thighs… I think they've been there since Sunday, when you, um, decided to put maple syrup on more than your pancakes."

Those were lies. Actually, she'd slept late and had woken up feeling like the inside of a dog's mouth. She just wasn't used to late nights with girlfriends anymore. Either that or she was getting old. Because she was having a really hard time getting motivated to do much of anything today.

She practically heard his face pull into a frown. "You're not going to distract me."

"I'd like to," she purred, knowing that in spite of his stiff tone, Dex liked it when she played sexy games with him.

"Stop it. Did you send Nick on a wild-goose chase?"

"Wild-goose chase?" She laughed softly. "Oh, no, honey, I sent him on a fantasy quest."

Dex was silent for a moment, that heavy, disapproving silence he could use to leave her squirming like a naughty girl.

Hmm…sounded like *that* could be fun some night.

Knowing she couldn't tease her way out of this one, she admitted, "I sent him to meet my friend Melody."

"I know. He called me and told me she's disappeared into the ladies' room, obviously pretty upset."

Rosemary frowned, though she wasn't really surprised. Melody had run out on her fantasy guy, obviously unable to get past her shock to grab the chance she was being offered. Hopefully her friend wasn't too mad. Though she knew Melody would probably be a bit embarrassed, Rosemary had figured the excitement of coming face-to-face with her hunky hero would make her forget all that.

Oh, honey, give yourself a chance.

God, she hated the way Melody had come out of her six-year stint in hell. If she could get her hands around Bill Todd's throat, she'd cheerfully strangle the man for crushing her best friend's spirit, leaving her unsure of herself and so unhappy.

"How did Nick sound when he called?" she had to ask.

"I dunno…anxious? A little confused."

"Interested?"

Dex sighed, knowing better than to try to keep it from her. "Yeah. I'd say he was interested."

Excellent. She'd known he would be.

Hopefully Mel would get over her cold feet, because Nick was exactly the man to warm them up. If Rosemary hadn't met and fallen for Dex first, she might have considered giving Mel a serious run for her money for the *Time* magazine hero. But she had met Dex first. And wow had she fallen…for the first time in her life.

Besides, deep down, she knew she wouldn't have stabbed Melody in the back by stealing her number-one guy. Not that she'd even realized he *was* her number-one guy at first. When she'd first met Dex's partner, Rosemary hadn't recognized him right away. It wasn't until Dex mentioned that his new partner had been a fifteen-minutes-of-fame war hero that she'd begun getting the whole picture. That had been right around the time Melody had been talking about coming back to Savannah after her divorce.

It had seemed like an omen.

But it wasn't going to go anywhere if Mel didn't have the guts to go after what she'd always wanted. Self-confidence was among the things her bastard of an ex had stolen from her, along with her money. When she closed her eyes, Rosemary could still hear the raw pain that had been in her best friend's voice over the past year, when Melody had let her rotten marriage undermine her belief in herself as a woman. She needed that confidence back. And a hot man was a good place to start getting it.

As for whether Nick would go for it? Well, he was…unpredictable. She had the feeling, however, that he was going to like Melody Tanner just fine. That the two of them were somehow meant to come together. Figuratively *and* literally.

Rosemary was a superstitious woman—most people born and raised in Savannah were. So she fully believed in fate. And it seemed like fate had fixed this up. That Melody had seen Nick's face that night and fantasized about him for a long time for a *reason*. That a house Rosemary had been brokering had been robbed, requiring her to call the police—which was how she'd met Dex—for a *reason*. And that Nick had become Dex's new partner for a *reason*. That her sweet friend was gullible enough to believe in the plausibility of a cockamamie murder idea for a *reason*.

Fate. Who was she to argue with it? And if she had to nudge it along a little by concocting murder plots? Well, so be it.

"Don't be mad, sugar," she told Dex. "Nick's not gonna be."

He quickly figured out what she'd done. "Your friend Melody, is she one of the ones who did those silly lists with you? The one you wave at me when you don't get your way?"

She chuckled because there was no real anger in his voice. The man did react so nicely when she teased him to try to make him jealous. Telling him about her sexual-fantasy list last winter had inspired a delightfully powerful reaction. That night had been one of the sexiest she'd ever experienced. "Uh-huh."

"And Nick's name is on hers?"

"Right again."

Dex tsked into the phone. "When are you going to learn to stop meddling? She's not going to thank you for embarrassing her."

Not now, maybe. But someday she would. Rosemary was absolutely sure of it.

CHAPTER THREE

WHEN MELODY FELT she'd pulled herself together as much as she was able, she emerged from the ladies' room and returned to the table in the café. Nick was watching her closely, his expression serious. "Are you all right?" he asked when she sat down.

Oh, great. She'd been in the ladies' room having a meltdown, and he'd been sitting here thinking she was throwing up. Lovely.

"I'm fine."

As for whether or not she was really okay? No, she wasn't. She was losing it. She'd been spinning whimsical fantasies in her mind about this poor, wonderful, wounded soldier she'd met this morning, when, in reality, he'd been dressed like a criminal, hanging around doing heaven-knows-what in her neighborhood.

The possibilities had filled her mind during her time-out in the bathroom. She'd gotten past his hero qualities enough to wonder what the heck he'd been doing that day. Who he really was…a real cop? Or had that been another one of Rosemary's embellishments. "Why were you parked by my building that week?" Keeping her anger—and her concern—in check, she leaned in. "Did my ex-husband hire you to spy on me? Is *that* why you were in a disguise? Are you one of *those* detectives…guys who get a badge off the Internet then go out and spy on people?"

It was his turn to look shocked, even a little indignant. "No, of course not. It had nothing to do with you."

"So what did it have to do with?"

He leaned in over the table, as well, until their faces were only a few inches apart, right above their cups. His coffee was hot, steamy and fragrant, recently freshened up. Her cup was still empty. She could have hit him just for that.

"I'm with the Savannah-Chatham PD's Crime Investigation Unit. Didn't Rosemary tell you why I was undercover? Didn't you hear about your neighbor, the drug importer?"

A *real* undercover cop. And she had heard something about an arrest near her home. The relief flooding through her couldn't be denied. "I'm sorry." She tugged her ball cap off her head and tossed it onto the table, suddenly feeling a headache coming on. "I didn't know for sure who you were."

"So who did you *think* I was when we were talking a few minutes ago?"

She sighed, wondering what to say. About him, the list, his fifteen minutes of fame. Before she had to decide, he spoke again.

"It's okay, I think I get it. Rosemary spun some kind of story to get you here, right?" He shook his head. "That woman sure loves to pull people's strings, doesn't she?"

Melody seized on the explanation. "Rosemary. Yes, of course." Forcing a laugh, she added, "She is rather outrageous."

"How do you know her?" he asked. Waiting for her to respond, he leaned back in his chair, kicking his legs out in front of him and crossing one foot over the other.

Those long legs. Those big feet. Which instantly had her trying to remember what they said about big feet.

Then he crossed his arms in front of his chest.

Those thick arms. Those big hands. Which also got her wondering about the whole big-hands, long-fingers thing.

God, she had to get out of here. Because now he was even more dangerous to her peace of mind than he'd been before, when she'd thought he was *just* the guy from her list.

Now he was the guy who'd helped her move into her new place. The one who'd risked his own undercover assignment, somehow seeing the desperation Melody had thought she'd been doing a pretty good job of hiding, and helped her when she was most in need.

He was gorgeous. He was sexy. He was a hero. And *she* was in way over her head.

Because even if she did something unthinkable, like go for it with a man she'd once named on a list, *he* wouldn't be one she could do it with. Nick wasn't the kind of man a woman could have and then forget. He was completely unforgettable; she knew that already after their two brief interactions. Which kind of defeated the purpose of the list, didn't it? Joke or no joke.

"You still breathing over there?" he asked, a teasing look in his twinkling brown eyes.

Before she could respond, the waitress came over to their table. "He took the dregs, and said to get you a nice fresh pot," the woman said, giving Melody an impersonal smile.

Oh, no. He'd done something kind again. Something thoughtful. She really needed him to stop doing that if she was going to be able to maintain any willpower at all around the man.

Once the waitress had filled her cup and left, Mel answered Nick's question. "Rosemary and I met as kids. She and Paige, the woman who was helping me move in that day, were my best friends from fourth grade on." She smiled, remembering how it had felt to have a normal kid life for the first time. "Then Tanya burst into our lives. A strong-willed, feisty black girl who had no idea the kind of crap that could go on in the genteel South. The three of us rallied around her because some of the stuck-up white kids in our private school were so rotten to her."

"Rosemary wasn't one of them?" He sounded skeptical.

"Rosemary's spoiled and is from a rich Southern family, but she's definitely *not* a racist." Chuckling, she added, "The two of them love to harass each other. They're a riot when the one-liners start flying—the pampered Southern belle and the tough, proud, African-American woman. They are a perfect foil to each other. I guess, when you think about it, all of us complemented one another pretty well, which is why we got along from day one."

His jaw tightened almost imperceptibly. "So are you like Rosemary? A real-live Southern belle?"

"I was born in Florida. My mother and I moved here when I was ten and we rented a place in this area."

She didn't elaborate. He didn't need to know that they'd moved to Savannah precisely so her mother could play Southern belle. Or that the place they'd rented had been a gorgeous estate a few blocks from the river. Or that the money Melody had been making as the most popular kid on just about every TV commercial on the air and almost every kiddie show on PBS had paid for it.

That was all on a need-to-know basis. And this man didn't need to know anything more than the three spots on Melody's body that could give her an almost-instant orgasm.

In five-and-a-half years of marriage, Bill had found *one* of them. Sort of. But she'd bet this guy could zone in on all three in under five minutes if they ever got naked.

It's not happening. The list was a joke!

"You're not a native," he said. "Me neither."

"You're not from Georgia?" she asked, surprised since that's about all she'd ever known about her *Time* magazine hero.

"Yeah, but not here. I moved here after high school. I'm from the northwest part of the state, a place called Joyful."

Joyful, Georgia. "Sounds quaint and sweet, like a picture-postcard small town."

"It's hell with white picket fences," he replied matter-of-factly, indicating that subject was closed. "Now, come on, tell me. How'd Rosemary get you here?" he asked. "And *why?*"

Uh-uh. No way was she going into detail on either of those questions. "Doesn't matter. She was obviously playing a joke on both of us, so I think I'll get my check and go."

His eyes narrowed. "Not so fast. I think it does matter. She got me here with some story about you knowing of a link between a murder in Atlanta and the death of a local restaurant owner."

Though her heart skipped a beat, Melody managed to keep her expression serene. "Really? How strange."

He stared for a moment, then slowly asked, "So you're saying you don't know anything about the death of Charles Pulowski in the kitchen of his own restaurant?"

She gaped. "Pulowski? His last name was Pulowski? And he owned a restaurant named Chez Jacques?"

"So you *do* know him."

Shaking her head, she said, "No, but I've heard of him. I lived on his chocolate volcano cake during finals in college."

He didn't react at all. Some men would have made a comment about the cake not hurting her figure. Some women might have been fishing for such a comment. But he wasn't such a man. And she wasn't even going to *think* about whether she was such a woman.

"You didn't answer my question," Detective Walker murmured, his voice steady, that soft drawl low and warm but strictly business…as if he wasn't the least bit distracted by any thoughts of her appearance.

This man was so different from most of the men she met. So completely the opposite of her ex-husband, whose smooth delivery back when they were dating had made his incessant compliments and comments about her looks seem almost charming, instead of piggish. Now she knew better.

Detective Walker seemed to have flipped a switch. From self-deprecating charmer when he'd arrived, to no-nonsense cop now.

His current disinterest was…unsettling. Not that she was drop-dead gorgeous or anything. She'd always been more of a fresh-faced, wholesome, big-smile model rather than a classically beautiful one…which was why the Luscious Lingerie thing had been such a fluke. And an embarrassment.

She'd put on a few pounds after she'd quit modeling. And she'd *eaten* her way through her divorce, needing to sample every form of chocolate ever invented. So she was nowhere near her size-four model days. Several sizes from it, in fact.

But she still turned heads on occasion when she made the effort. Then again, she hadn't made much of an effort this morning, doing nothing more than yanking her hair into a ponytail and scraping some lipstick across her lips. So maybe that explained it. *Mental note: start making an effort. You never know when you're going to run across somebody from your sex list.*

Realizing he was still waiting for an answer, Mel finally said, "I can say with perfect honesty that I have never met this Charles Pulowski, and unless he disguised himself as a waiter and delivered my chocolate volcano cake, I have never even laid eyes on him." Perfectly truthful. And as much as he needed to know.

"I don't think he'd have gone incognito as a waiter without you noticing him." He sipped his coffee, then added, "He was seventy years old and weighed almost four-hundred pounds."

Gulping, Melody sent up a quick thanks that she hadn't met the man and that the list had been a joke. Besides, even if Rosemary thought it hadn't been, the list was still only a guideline…she was *allowed* to hop into bed with any of the men on it. That didn't mean she was required to. At least, that's how she interpreted it.

She wasn't so sure Rosemary would say the same. Especially after today. Then again, Rosemary might still be dead by the end of the week, depending on how much she groveled over this ambush, so who cared what she thought?

"Well, then I definitely never met him," she replied.

He didn't appear entirely convinced, but didn't press. "So it was a scam. Why is Rosemary trying to set you up?"

Again, no flattery. No smarmy comment like Bill might have made when trying to pick up a woman he'd just met about how ludicrous it was to think she'd *need* someone to set her up.

A part of her wondered briefly if he wasn't flirting simply because he wasn't interested in her. But she quickly put that thought under a sharp stiletto heel in her brain and ground it out of existence. Considering she'd wanted him with every molecule in her body at first sight, she'd have to get violent if she thought he felt absolutely *nothing* in return.

She doubted that. He might not be flirting or sizing her up, now, but he had earlier. Besides, there was an intensity about the way he watched her that made her think he was every bit as aware of her as she was of him.

"She have some idea that you need to hop back on the horse because you fell off the marriage wagon?" he asked.

"Something like that, I guess," she admitted. "She's determined to throw me kicking and screaming into—" *your bed* "—the dating pool. But one thing I do not need is a date."

No, she merely needed an orgasm. Or a hundred.

"So why does Rosemary think you do? Or is it just her being her spoiled puppeteer self, deciding to pull your strings the way she tries to pull everyone else's?"

Ooh. He didn't like Rosemary. There was a point against the man. If he said he hated cats, she'd have to scratch him off her list altogether. That'd been her first real indication that Bill was a jerk—he'd hated her cat. Which was why she'd gotten another one a couple of years ago.

Since this guy was destined to be delisted, anyway, given her way-too-unmanageable-and-dangerous response to him, she considered mentioning her two felines, Oscar and C.C. Instead, she answered his question with a pointed stare. "Rosemary is my best friend. She was my maid of honor."

"How long were you married?"

"Almost six years. The divorce was final a few months ago."

"That's tough. I went through it several years ago."

"Is that why Rosemary's trying to set *you* up?"

Nick—she was mentally calling him Nick now, instead of Detective Walker, which probably wasn't too smart but she couldn't help it—rolled his eyes. "No, she's doing that because she's a pain in the ass."

Sharing his rueful grin, because it was *true* and because his voice held a hint of amusement rather than dislike, she murmured, "She can be."

"And," he continued, "I suspect she thinks if I get distracted by someone, I won't have as much time to corrupt Dex."

"Dex?"

"My partner."

Melody nearly fell out of her chair. In fact, it actually did wobble a bit because she instinctively reared straight up on the rickety old seat. It almost went over backward, and probably would have if not for the grace of God and the luck of fools.

"Partner?" she whispered.

He nodded. Confirming he had a *partner.* Holy shit on a shallot, this guy—her fantasy guy—was *gay?*

Reality immediately set back in. *Not gay, dummy.* A cop…all cops had partners, right? He had to be talking about his partner on the police force. *Had* to be. Because a man as masculine, rugged and sexy as this one being gay would be a crime against humanity. Well, *half* of humanity. The half that didn't pee standing up.

It wasn't just the idea of the man sitting *across* from her being gay that bothered her. It was the idea that the man she'd once had such long, torrid fantasies about—in the early days of her less-than-satisfactory marriage—could be.

She'd allowed her *Time* magazine marine to slip out of her mind sometime over the past few years, when she'd been so focused on pain, failure and betrayal. So she'd forgotten the many long, sleepless nights she'd lain in her bed and wondered about the stranger, picturing his dark brown eyes and the grim, intense expression on his face. She remembered now, though. And she feared it wasn't going to be so easy to forget him again.

There was one way to make sure of his leanings. "Uh, I take it you mean your partner on the police force. Not your partner…in life?"

Lowering his coffee cup, he stared at her. Hard. "Yeah. My partner on the police force. Were you thinking…"

Her face grew hot. And probably twenty shades of red. But there was only one way out of this and that was to brazen through it. "Well, only for a second."

He chuckled. "That's some friend you have there, if you think she'd set you up with somebody who didn't even like women."

She wouldn't put it past Rosemary, who probably wouldn't see anything wrong in having a one-night stand with someone who was a little, um…*open*…in his preferences. Maybe that was because Rosemary hadn't had a close brush with a venereal disease. Unlike Melody. Who'd learned from her enraged ex-husband that the reason he hadn't had sex with her during their engagement was because he'd been afraid he'd give her an STD and she'd never marry him.

Uh, yeah, that'd been a pretty good bet.

Thank God the prick with the drill had been so scared of getting busted that he'd always used condoms—using the too-soon-for-kids excuse. Then, typical of men who collect things, he'd quickly tired of her and had moved on to other conquests. Mel had been tested a number of times and, like most of her money, a sexually transmitted disease was *not* among the things she'd taken with her when she'd left her marriage.

"It was just a brief thought," she said with a smile.

"An incorrect one."

"Okay. I'm convinced."

"You sure you don't need proof?"

Heat rose in her face as she imagined the kind of proof he could offer. As if he could read her mind, Nick started to laugh.

She blushed some more, she could feel it. In comparison with some of the other ways she'd humiliated herself in the past few years, this really wasn't so bad. So she'd kind of accused a big, gorgeous, hunky former-marine-turned-cop of liking men. Not a huge deal in the scheme of things, right? She really shouldn't be feeling so utterly mortified.

But she did. She really wanted to sink under the table and crawl out of here on all fours. That was another reason to forget about the man, along with the fact that he disliked her best friend. He could mortify her. That was a very bad combination and one Melody wasn't about to allow.

"Dex, my partner in the Criminal Investigation Unit, has been dating Rosemary on and off for over a year," he explained, still looking amused. "Hasn't she told you about him?"

She hadn't. Not in any detail. She certainly hadn't mentioned that she was dating a Savannah cop. That was very unexpected for Rosemary, who, to be honest, was expected to marry into some old, rich, Southern family like her sister had done. *If* she ever settled down at all.

"I've been sort of distracted with my divorce," Mel finally said, figuring that was the reason Rosemary hadn't been any more forthcoming about her romance. She wondered if Paige and Tanya knew Rosemary was involved with the marine hero's partner, but figured not. Paige couldn't keep a secret longer than six-and-a-half minutes. And Tanya would never have let Rosemary get away with this morning's setup. "I knew she was seeing someone but never knew who. I'm sure she figured I had enough to think about."

"Ahh."

Then, curious, she said, "You're not freaking out that I thought you were gay."

"No, I'm not." He sipped his coffee, not quite successful in an attempt to hide a chuckle. "Unlike you."

"I was embarrassed," she mumbled.

That cocky look returned as he smoothly seized the chance to take the upper hand. "You were upset at the idea, Melanie, admit it. Upset and disappointed."

"My name's *Melody.*" Somehow, down deep inside, she

grabbed hold of a bit of strength. Giving him a look of disdain that had reduced international designers to stammering little boys, she added, "You're very amusing, but I absolutely was not upset, *or* disappointed. Now, I do have to go."

Oh, that had sounded good. Perfect. Just the right tone and the right expression and now she could exit stage left and forget this disconcerting conversation had ever taken place.

Only, something funny happened. Funny strange, not funny ha-ha. Because instead of looking deflated or resigned, Nick Walker was smiling. A big, huge, good-ol'-boy smile that lit up his amazing eyes and brought out two enormous dimples in his cheeks.

God, what a smile.

What a smile? The question should be *why* a smile! She'd insulted him.

"*Melody,* huh? A very unusual name. And you're Rosemary's best friend?" he said, laughter in his voice. "I should have known."

Her heart rate kicking up a notch, Mel whispered, "Why?"

"Well," he replied with that boyish grin still glued to his face, "because I've heard about you. Rosemary does like to throw her parties, and yes, indeed, I do believe your name has come up a time or two when I've been at her place."

Dead? Did she say Rosemary was dead? That wasn't good enough. Eviscerated…that might do. For a start.

She didn't want to know, even though the curiosity was gnawing at her stomach with painful intensity. Slowly rising, she gave him a noncommittal smile. "Really? How funny. Well, it was nice meeting you, and I'm sorry for the inconvenience."

The man didn't rise. He just sat there, looking up at her. Then he slowly shook his head and tsked. Actually *tsked!*

"What?" she snapped.

"Seems to me," he said, "you're going about this all the wrong way. Getting up and running isn't exactly going to get you what you want."

She closed her eyes briefly, willing him not to mean what she suspected he meant.

"Because, honey, if you're supposed to be working on me, you really ought to stick around."

Her jaw clenched. "*Working* on you?"

Slowly—as if intentionally drawing out her torment—he rose from his chair, unfolding himself with unconscious grace and simmering sexiness. He stepped closer, around the table, until they stood toe-to-toe. Nearly hip to hip. Almost chest to chest and definitely breath to breath—if, of course, she ever remembered to start breathing again.

Then he laughed—a low, sultry sound that slid across all her nerve endings—and said, "Well, yeah, we haven't even named the place yet."

Dread filling her mind as much as his sultry, masculine scent was filling her head, she bit out, "The place?"

He nodded, stepping even closer until their chests did meet and her nipples tightened in a sudden, instinctive response. "You know," he said softly, for her ears alone. "For us to get workin' on that list of yours."

Oh, God.

"After all," he continued, "if I'm the number-one man on your sexual-fantasy list, I think we'd better go someplace a little more private."

NICK COULDN'T REMEMBER the last time he'd been so amused, aroused and intrigued by a woman all at the same time. Melody…this friend of Rosemary's with her sassy ponytail and her pouty, kissable lips and those deep blue eyes…she amused him for sure. And she aroused him nearly out of his mind.

As for intriguing him? Well, she'd been doing that for ages, since long before he'd ever set eyes on her. Now that he knew who she was, he had the feeling there wasn't going to be any way to shake off this hunger except by giving them both what she'd once claimed to most desire.

"You're deranged," she whispered hoarsely.

"Uh-uh. I've seen your list." That was entirely true. He had seen her list—he just hadn't realized it was *hers* until a moment ago when she'd revealed her actual name.

Melody…not Melanie. Not a name he'd soon forget. After all, it wasn't every day you learned a woman had named you her number-one fantasy man. That'd been the intriguing part.

"You've *seen* it?" Her jaw dropped. He reached up and touched her chin with his finger, stroking the soft skin there the tiniest bit as he tipped her mouth closed. Her face was incredibly soft, perfectly smooth. Sensual to the touch.

Melody's eyes widened even more as she stared directly into his, not having to tilt her head back too far to do so. Reminding him that she was tall. *Perfect.* They were so very close. He could lean a few inches and catch that mouth in the kind of kiss that would make them both weak in the knees.

If only they weren't entirely surrounded. But they were, and that knowledge gave him the strength to step away.

"Rosemary wouldn't have…"

"I don't think she meant to. She was digging for hers to annoy Dex and yours kinda fell out. It was sort of an accident, and I only caught a little glimpse."

"An accident? How can someone *accidentally* show the world her best friend's sexual-fantasy list?"

Ahh. He had her. "So you admit it?"

Her jaw tightened. "I'm not admitting a thing."

"You said you were mad at Rosemary for talking about your sexual-fantasy list."

"That was a 'just supposing' type of thing. As in, just supposing I did have such a list—which I *don't*—there's no way my best friend would share it with anybody, much less you."

He shrugged. "But she did."

She looked ready to growl, but before she could say anything, a loud throat clearing interrupted. That's when he realized they'd stopped talking in whispers.

"*You* are a jerk," she muttered.

"And *you* are a liar."

Her jaw clenched. "Well, then it's a good thing we'll never be seeing each other again."

Shaking his head, he shrugged. "I wouldn't say that." Finally, unable to keep teasing her, he laughed. "Come on, ease up, I'm giving you a hard time. I know the list is a joke."

Some of the tension eased out of her body. "You do?"

"You really think I believe women sit down on the night before they're getting married and give themselves *permission* to cheat?" Then, thinking of his own ex-wife, he qualified that. "I mean, *normal* women?"

"It was a stupid game," she mumbled.

"I know."

"Never intended to be taken seriously."

"More's the pity."

That got her attention. She lifted one brow.

"I said I *know* it was a joke," he said with an unrepentant shrug. "Not that I'm *glad* it was."

Her shoulders stiffened again, and Nick almost chuckled at how easy she was to rile. So unlike the sad-looking, life-weary woman he'd met a few weeks ago, struggling to be strong but unable to hide the truth of her desperation.

He much preferred this Melody, the one whose eyes were sparkling, not tearing up.

"Are you the type of guy who'd do something like that?"

"You don't have to sound all judgmental," he said, not denying it, even though her accusation wasn't true. "You were the one who wrote the list in the first place. What'd you call it? Your Men Most Wanted? I gotta say, I'd really like to hear more about how I was lucky enough to win first place."

This time, he thought he heard her spine snap as she straightened up. *Good.* Definitely no more quivering lip, no more lowered eyes, shaking hands or sad expression. Now her mouth was moving a little, as if she were telling him off under her breath. Her whole body was so stiff and indignant, as if she were ready to pound him…or jump on him. Yessir, he was definitely enjoying seeing another glimpse of this redhead's temper. "So how about we sit back down and talk about this list of yours?"

"How about you take your breakfast and shove it up your—"

"Ahem!"

This time the throat clearing came from a frazzled-looking mama with a toddler in a high chair and a wide-eyed preschooler beside her. Tsking, he murmured, "Not very ladylike."

Melody didn't reply. Instead, giving a quick, apologetic look to the woman with the little ones, she swung around, her purse smacking him in the arm on the way by. She didn't say another word as she stalked through the restaurant.

"Nice meeting you, Melody," he called after her, unable to keep the laughter out of his voice.

Her response made him laugh even more. Without turning around—without a word—she lifted her hand up and shot him the finger over her shoulder as she blew out the door.

Apparently the mama with the little ones didn't mind nonverbal insults, because she was grinning, too, once Melody was gone. "I don't think that went well," she said.

"I think that went just fine," he replied, still chuckling.

Yeah. It'd gone *very* well. He'd say their relationship was off to a rousing start. They'd talked and flirted, taunted and argued. Most of all, they'd pushed each other's buttons.

She had awakened something in him—something he hadn't felt in a good long time, if ever. It wasn't merely lust. The sex-list thing had been a joke, he knew that. He'd simply liked teasing her with it to see the way her eyes snapped with fire, her chin jutted out and her sexy mouth turned mulish.

No, it wasn't because of any list that he couldn't wait to seek out Miss Tanner again. It was because for the first time in a number of years, he'd met a woman who'd gotten in the last word and left him practically begging for more. That, and because he was genuinely *interested* in getting to know her.

"Don't you think you should go after her?" the waitress said as she came by with his check.

He shook his head. "Too soon."

"Suit yourself," the woman said as she walked away.

The young mother apparently agreed with the waitress. "No, it's not too soon." She kept on talking even while doing that nasty spit-on-a-napkin-to-wipe-the-kid's-face thing all mothers did. "You need to strike while the iron is hot."

Nick caught the kid's resigned look and winked. "Oh?"

"She's all flustered now. Once she gets home and thinks about it, she's going to forget how charming you were and only remember how you yanked her chain about that list of hers."

Nick winced. The woman had heard every word they'd said.

"Listen, when you have babies you develop ears like a hawk. And your conversation was a mite bit more interesting than ours."

He laughed, dropping his hand to the preschooler's head to rustle his soft hair. "You got a smart mama, you know that?"

The little boy nodded. Then, lifting his hand, he said, "What does this mean?"

Nick knew the middle finger was gonna pop up about two seconds before it actually did. "Yikes, sorry," he muttered.

The mother sighed heavily and waved a hand, shooing him off while she dealt with the child.

Nick didn't plan to act on the young woman's advice. He had a feeling Melody wouldn't take kindly to being followed down the streets of Savannah. Besides, he didn't *need* to follow her. He knew where she lived.

Glancing at the table they'd shared, he spied Mel's half-empty cup. It was smeared with a bit of her lipstick, the rosy color shining brightly against the white mug. Strange, he could still almost see her slim hand curled around it and the way her lips pursed as she blew on it to take off some of the steam.

Crazy. He'd never been so focused, so aware of a woman before. Of her every movement, the way she lifted her hand to brush back an errant strand of hair. The hitchy little sound she made in the back of her throat when she was upset. That brilliant, full-lipped smile.

Still looking at the mug, he started to chuckle as he realized something. Even though she'd blown him off with a resounding silent hand gesture, he'd obviously gotten under her skin. Melody had been so flustered she'd forgotten to even pay for her coffee, leaving him stuck with the bill. His *and* hers.

He didn't mind, he'd have wanted to pay anyway. But he'd bet anything she wouldn't have wanted him to.

When he actually looked at the check, his chuckle turned

into a full laugh. Because Melody hadn't *only* walked out without paying for a cup of coffee. "Biscuits and gravy," he read aloud.

Mel had left him with the bill for her breakfast, and she'd had his favorite. Somehow that made him like her even more.

And reaffirmed just how much he couldn't wait to see her again.

AFTER HER SILENT parting shot, Melody hadn't been able to get out of the restaurant fast enough. She'd almost tripped over a couple of people as she'd made her escape, but she didn't think she'd have been able to stop if someone who'd eaten one too many cholesterol-laden scrambled eggs keeled over of a heart attack right in front of her.

"Too much," she muttered as she stood outside in the hot Savannah morning a few moments later. She'd had to pause to make her heart stop pounding and to regain her calm.

Nick Walker *was* too much. She just couldn't take him today. Or tomorrow. Or next year. Maybe when she was fifty she could handle a man like Nick, but until then, uh-uh.

Why, oh why had Rosemary done this to her? Setting her up, telling him about that stupid list? She'd thrown Melody to the wolves...at least one Big Bad Wolf...when Rosemary, better than anyone, knew how deeply Bill's betrayals had hurt her.

A product of a home broken by infidelity herself when she was very young, Rosemary had been the one Mel had confided in during the last miserable months of her marriage. Before she'd gone to the billboard, before she'd made a laughingstock of herself, Melody had poured her heart out to Rosemary.

And this was how her friend had repaid her.

"Maybe that's why she did it," she admitted under her

breath. Because on one or two occasions when the self-doubt had been overwhelming, she'd told her best friend about her deepest fear—that Bill's description of her as a pretty, lifeless, sexless doll was true. Rosemary had been a quiet, comforting voice of support. But she'd also wanted to go find a voodoo priestess and have some juju put on Bill so he could never get it up again.

Hmm…if the bastard didn't stay out of her life from now on, Melody might just think about it.

Rosemary believed in action, not words. So Melody could almost hear her justifying today's actions. Her friend had undoubtedly figured that the minute Melody recognized her *Time* magazine hero, she'd forget the list had been a joke, let her libido take over for her brain, and end up wiling away the rest of the day in this guy's bed.

Finally realizing she'd better go before Nick came outside and assume she'd been waiting for him, she started walking back toward her place. "He'd probably think I was out here planning to pounce on him because of that stupid list," she muttered.

It wasn't that she hadn't been tempted—the man was temptation on two legs. But she wasn't ready for it. Sex with anybody required a level of trust she wasn't sure she was capable of giving anymore.

And sex with somebody who could crush her with one bored look, or a lack of interest in a second round? No way. Her ego couldn't stand it. She'd be better off going to bed with the unsexiest, most boring, unattractive guy she could find. That way, if she wasn't inspiring enough to command a repeat performance, at least she wouldn't give a damn.

With Nick, she'd give a damn.

She really didn't deserve this, not now when she finally felt that things were coming together. Because Nick Walker made her feel anything but together. He confused her. Angered her. Amused her. Oh, Lord, definitely aroused her. But she didn't have time in her life for *any* of that right now. Not confusion or anger, not distraction or embarrassment.

Not sex. Not him.

"Not sex *with* him."

"Excuse me?"

She realized she'd spoken aloud when she glanced up and saw a man standing directly in front of her on the sidewalk. She'd almost barreled into him, paying attention only to what was going on in her head and not what was happening in front of her face. For a second she thought she'd just made an idiot of herself for about the tenth time in an hour in front of a complete stranger. But this wasn't a stranger.

She wasn't sure whether that made it better or worse.

"Uh, hi," she said, clearing her throat. "I almost didn't recognize you without salsa music or the smell of enchiladas."

The Hispanic owner of the Mexican restaurant where Melody had hung out with her friends for years gave her a warm smile. "Believe it or not, this is my *second* favorite place to eat." He pointed to the café she'd just left, which was only a few yards behind her. "I come here for grits and biscuits."

The restaurant owner, who kept his few strands of overly shiny black hair brushed across his bald head in a blatant attempt to defy late middle-age, didn't look like the grits-and-biscuits type. Though judging by the pendulous belly straining the buttons of his short-sleeved white dress shirt, Mel supposed he hadn't been living on tortillas alone.

"You're not with your friends this morning?" he asked, looking around as if expecting to see Paige, Rosemary or Tanya hiding behind a car parked at the curb. "I didn't think you girls ever did anything without each other."

She really hated the way some men called grown women "girls." That was on her pet-peeve list. Along with men who called their cars their "ride" and their wives "baby." Like her ex had.

"Not today. I'm all by myself," she said.

He shook his head. "That is not good, *señora*. You shouldn't be alone at this time. You should be with people…people who appreciate you and make you smile in that beautiful way." His eyes glittered as he repeated, "Such a *beautiful* smile."

His words were friendly, but something about the way he was looking at her made her uncomfortable. It was almost personal. Flirtatious. If he weren't twenty years her senior and hadn't been serving her and her friends chicken burritos since they were in middle school, she'd suspect the guy was coming on to her.

"I would give *anything* to see that smile every day."

Okay, he *was* coming on to her. *Eww.*

Suddenly the idea of hooking up with an unsexy, unappealing guy for the sake of her ego became less palatable. Particularly when she, uh, pictured the possibilities with this one.

Nope. She couldn't do it. Couldn't have sex with someone who didn't attract her, not even for the sake of her banged-up pride. Not for fun, not because of a list, not to get back in the saddle, not for *anything*. So, really, the only solution was to have no sex at all. Not for a long, long time. Years. Decades.

Then she pictured Nick's face…his big hands, his hard body, his soft, sexy voice.

And wondered if she'd last the week.

CHAPTER FOUR

THE NEXT MORNING, as Nick headed from the station over to the D.A.'s office to pick up some paperwork, he realized he was still thinking about the woman he'd met for breakfast the day before. He hadn't been able to get Melody off his mind since she'd walked out of the diner, leaving him there with a big smile on his face and a strong sense of anticipation in his mind.

It'd been a good long time since any woman had occupied his thoughts as she had over the past twenty-four hours. The past couple of weeks, really, since he'd been a little fascinated by her ever since he'd seen her spying on him with her camera.

A good long time? Hell, he couldn't remember *ever* being so instantly attracted to someone. He'd had a hard time throwing off the image of her smile while he and Dex talked to their informant yesterday, and it'd been even harder to get to sleep last night with the sound of her laughter bouncing around in his head. He'd been so distracted, he hadn't even noticed that Fredo was in his closet turning shoe leather into beef jerky for a good bit of the evening.

He was still wondering why that particular woman wouldn't leave his thoughts as he got into his car in the parking lot outside the station. Before he could even turn the key in the ignition, however, his cell phone rang. Checking the caller ID and recognizing the number, he answered, "Walker."

"That's my line."

He shook his head, still not used to answering the phone and hearing Johnny's voice on the other end. Damn, it'd been a long ten years without his one-year-older brother in his life. "Hey, Mr. Hotshot D.A. Does the town council know you're making personal calls from the office?"

"Does the chief of police know you had breakfast with a strange woman yesterday?" his brother replied.

"Now, if we were both in Joyful, I wouldn't even have to ask how you knew that."

"Dex told me. I called you at your desk two minutes ago."

Shaking his head as he buckled his seat belt, Nick said, "Knowing my partner is not a gossipy old woman, I gotta wonder what exactly you said to get that information out of his mouth."

Johnny chuckled. "I asked him if you had any kind of social life whatsoever, since I suspect you haven't been laid since making detective. You work too hard, little brother."

Nick wasn't going to argue that one. Because damned if Johnny wasn't right.

Johnny had the courtesy not to rub it in. "So who was the woman?"

"I don't know yet," he admitted, knowing it was true. He didn't know for sure *who* Melody was. "She's a puzzle."

Johnny understood. "Have fun figuring it out."

No doubt about it. He was going to enjoy every minute of figuring what made her tick. "So what's going on?"

"I promised Emma Jean I'd call and remind you about getting measured for your tux."

Emma Jean was Johnny's fiancée, the infamous woman who'd landed the former most eligible bachelor of Joyful.

One more reason he'd never move back home...he sure didn't want to inherit *that* title. "I *have* to wear an undertaker suit?"

"Undertakers don't wear cummerbunds."

"What the hell is a cummerbund?"

"Don't worry. Your job is to show up, wear what you're told to wear and not lose the ring."

"I don't suppose you'd consider eloping to Vegas?"

"I suggested it, but she didn't bite," Johnny said with a sigh. "And as best man, you have to suffer with me."

Best man. It still boggled the mind. Even though his brother had thought the worst of him, along with everyone else in Joyful, Johnny had been among the first to listen—and to *hear*—the truth when Nick had finally gone home a few months ago to set things right...with his brother, with their mother. With his ex-wife, Daneen. Even with Daneen's ten-year-old son, Jack.

The boy Nick had once prayed would be his.

"Emma wants an old-fashioned wedding, so we're both stuck with the penguin suits." Johnny didn't really sound upset, which wasn't surprising. His brother was totally gone on his fiancée.

Funny, thinking of Emma Jean as his brother's bride... considering Nick had once asked her to marry *him*. Of course, that was years ago, before he'd walked out on her on prom night so he could run away and marry Daneen, who'd named him as the father of her unborn baby. One lie among many.

Things sure had worked out, because Johnny had always been the one Em had wanted. Nick had figured that out long ago. "Jack sounds pretty excited to be an usher."

His brother was silent for a moment. "I didn't realize you've been talking to Jack."

"He e-mailed me in July. Seems he has no problem with me not being his father, but he still wants me to be his friend. We've talked a few times," Nick said, still surprised himself.

"I told you that kid was something special." Johnny had doted on Jack for years, so he'd been the one who'd taken Nick to meet the boy for the first time in June. Somehow, Johnny had known—as no one else did—that Nick was still raw when it came to Daneen's son…the child who should have been his.

They could never have predicted how Jack would react. He'd been incredibly mature, admitting he'd known since age six that his mother had lied about his paternity. He'd overheard the truth but had kept silent, not wanting to *embarrass* Daneen or upset his Grandma. He'd also thanked Nick for helping them out financially over the years…something *no one* else knew about.

Some kid, that one. Made Nick wonder how things might have turned out if he'd reacted differently. If instead of lashing out in anger at Daneen and joining the marines, he'd stuck around to be some kind of father to the boy.

Too late. Much too late.

"You are coming back for the engagement party, right?"

"Will that get me out of wearing the cumbersome thing?"

"Cummerbund," Johnny said with a chuckle. "And no."

Nick gave an exaggerated sigh. "I suppose I'll come anyway."

"Good. Gotta go," Johnny said. "I have an hour with the courthouse secretary before she has to go on dog-tag duty."

Ahh, Joyful. Some things never changed.

Disconnecting, and starting the car, Nick couldn't help thinking about how different his life was from three months ago. He had a family again…a connection to Joyful, of all places. Things he'd never expected. So maybe the idea of finding a special woman wasn't so ridiculous. Hell…maybe he already had.

Emma Jean would crow about that. His future sister-in-law had been urging him to believe he could meet someone, have something better in his future than he'd had in his past. Frankly, though he'd never admit something so sappy, having a relationship with his family again had given him a better future. And the other relationships from his old life seemed to be resolved now, too. Like the one with his ex-wife.

No, he was never going to forget that Daneen had lied to him—giving him the expectation of being a father, then yanking it away a month after their marriage. Or that she'd gone back home after their divorce and made him out as a villain who'd abandoned her and *their* child.

But he'd somehow been able to finally let go of his anger and come to an understanding with Daneen. She'd been as much a kid as him—just a couple of teenagers trying to escape from their shitty lives. And God knows she'd gone through hell lately. He pitied her, really, because at some point, he'd forgiven her.

A year ago, forgiveness hadn't even been in his vocabulary. Now he had a more than passing acquaintance with the word.

So, yeah, maybe Em was right. Maybe things could be different. Nick had certainly changed, in more ways than one.

What had happened yesterday was a prime example. Because he sure couldn't remember ever being as fascinated by a woman as he was with the sassy, ponytailed redhead who'd flipped him off.

The woman who, he realized as he cruised down Habersham Street, was almost directly in front of him. He'd recognize that bouncy reddish ponytail anywhere, not to mention the camera stuck in front of her face as she photographed a carriage driver and his horse. Then she waved at the guy and started walking down the street.

Though Nick had planned to wait a couple of days to seek her out, fate seemed to think sooner was better than later. As he pulled up beside her, he slowed the car to a crawl, expecting her to look over. He planned to offer her a lift. He didn't figure she'd appreciate it if he offered her a *ride*.

She never looked.

Pulling the car over, he parked and quickly got out. "Good morning, Miss Tanner."

She immediately looked across and saw him. Nick was close enough to note the expressions passing over her face. Starting with interest, flipping to embarrassment, and ending with stiff resolve.

The woman had her guard up. Unfortunately.

"Fine day," he said as he joined her on the sidewalk.

"It *was*," she said with a frown. Without so much as a goodbye—much less a hello—she turned on her heel to walk away.

"Melody, wait a second," he called. "I'm sorry, I didn't mean to offend you yesterday. I was kinda tickled by... things."

She slowly turned around. "You're apologizing?" she said, her tone skeptical.

He walked to her side. "Uh-huh."

"For assuming I had some wild, completely inappropriate sexual interest in you?"

"Uh-uh. For laughing. Because you having a wild, completely inappropriate sexual interest in me is no laughing matter."

Eyes narrowing, she crossed her arms in front of her chest, which only drew his attention there. To her chest, clad in a tight tank top that scooped low on some very feminine cleavage. The strap of her camera resting between her breasts only served to emphasize her curves and he imagined any carriage driver in Savannah would be happy to pose for the woman.

The rest of her was just as feminine—the shapely waist, the curvy hips and slim legs clad in a cute, brightly colored pair of cropped pants. Yeah. He imagined she could fill a whole portfolio with pictures of every single man in this town, all of whom would stop in a heartbeat for a chance to meet her.

"You are very arrogant, aren't you?" she asked.

"Only when I know I've made a pretty good first impression."

"You made a pretty *lousy* first impression."

"Then why'd you put me on your list?"

Uncrossing her arms, she stuck her index finger out at him. "You were not on my list. *If* there was such a list."

"There is. Exactly like Rosemary's, which she hangs up on her refrigerator whenever she wants to piss off Dex."

"Bet it hangs there all the time, then," she muttered under her breath. "She's an expert at pissing people off."

He grinned. Obviously the woman *was* a good friend of Rosemary's. "She tapes it there when they're fighting. Whenever he sees it, he scratches out the names, changing all of them to his. He calls it her Dex list instead of her sex list."

A rueful smile tugged at those pretty lips of hers, softening her face and almost easing the tension from her body. He liked teasing her. Liked the way her eyes went from sapphire to sky-blue in the bright sunshine. Liked seeing her happy.

How very, very strange, considering he'd gotten such a kick out of seeing her mad and spittin' fire yesterday morning.

"Sounds like he might be good for Rosemary," she said. "As long as he doesn't mind that she's already checked one man off."

That surprised him. He seriously doubted Dex knew that. But it also made him wonder how serious these women had been about their lists. Until now it had seemed like nothing more than a joke. A silly game played by some bridesmaids.

But if Rosemary had actually started checking people off hers…maybe this list thing was more serious than he'd expected. And maybe Melody was looking to do the same thing.

That made him pause. To reassess things. And it disturbed him. Because it just didn't match up with the woman he'd been getting to know. The one he'd been getting to *like*.

"Though," she continued, "I honestly doubt she told him."

"Probably not," he replied, shaking off the concern. "They might be able to make it work—if he doesn't kill her."

"Or if *I* don't."

Chuckling, he asked, "So you going to let me make it up to you for laughing at you?"

She held his stare for one long instant. When her little pink tongue darted out to moisten her lips, Nick almost groaned.

"I don't think so," she murmured. Then she walked away.

Frowning, he jogged behind her, knowing how to get her to stop. "Isn't that against the rules of the list?"

"You're *not* on my list," she growled, still walking.

"Sure I am, I'm number one. The marine from *Time* magazine."

Melody did stop at that, her expression rife with curiosity, as if she couldn't figure him out. "Did you really rescue those kids from the bombed orphanage in Bosnia like the articles said?"

Nick stiffened, unable to help it. His career in the marines wasn't something he was ashamed of. God knows, it'd straightened him out when he'd been a stupid kid—fresh out of high school, recently married and even more recently divorced.

He sometimes had a hard time reconciling the relatively normal life he lived now with the erratic one he'd lived then.

He'd been eighteen and pumped full of anger, bitterness and indignation after his brief marriage. Estranged from his family, a pariah in his hometown, he'd been crushed to realize he truly *had* wanted Daneen's unborn child to be his. He'd wanted something of his own, a fresh start, a new life. Away from Joyful, where his family name was mud and his own father lived up to every evil, vile rumor attributed to him.

When that fantasy had been snatched from him, Nick had done what a lot of messed-up guys did: he'd joined the military, figuring he could work out his anger by kicking some enemy ass. His life had seemed over and he hadn't cared whether he got hurt or not. Maybe that was why he'd thrived on the dangerous missions. Why he'd volunteered for the riskiest assignments.

Or maybe he'd just been a dumb, reckless punk.

Whatever the case, he seldom thought about it and didn't like talking about his time in the marines. He especially didn't like talking about the media coverage he'd gotten because of that photograph. Any other guy in his unit would have done exactly what he did, and some of them *had*. He'd just been the one the photographer had focused in on.

"Well?" she prompted. "Were you?"

"It wasn't Bosnia, it was Kosovo. And I was only doing my job," was all he said. "Now, back to your list. Are you denying that number one was the marine on the cover of *Time* magazine?"

Thankfully, she let him get away with his evasion. "That doesn't mean it was you. You're not the only hero to ever be on the cover of a magazine, you know. Maybe I meant someone else."

Grinning, he shook his head. "Sorry. The list was dated. Plus Rosemary flat-out told me her best pal Melody had the hots for me once she found out who I was. Of course, you shouldn't blame her…as I recall, it was after one of her parties, and Rosemary'd been hitting the champagne pretty hard."

"I'd like to hit her with champagne. A whole magnum of it."

He gave her his sternest cop look. "Assault with a deadly."

"Are champagne bottles deadly?"

"If they're swung upside somebody's head, I'd say yeah." Then he grinned ruefully. "Or if it's the cheap stuff like I drank at my high-school homecoming dance."

She wasn't charmed. "I don't really want to kill her…though if she doesn't stop avoiding my calls, I might change my mind." Nibbling her lip, she said, "But I can't believe she set me up like that. I mean, set *us* up. It's really ridiculous."

"The setup?"

"The list."

He stepped closer, until his pants brushed against her bare calf. "Sex is a lot of things, but ridiculous isn't one of them."

She frowned. "Stop flirting with me."

"Not flirting, ma'am. Just stating a fact." Crossing his arms, he added, "And the fact is, you wanted me."

Eyes narrowing, she snapped, "I wanted a fantasy guy." She raked a look over him, an assessing one. But she couldn't quite manage disdain when she added, "Not *you*."

He could only grin, liking how she sassed him, how she didn't give any ground. "You really want to go about it this way?"

"What way?"

"With these denials? We can play it that way if you want, but frankly, I like your list idea better."

Her jaw dropped. "You really think we should go ahead and sleep together right now?"

No, he *really* didn't. He wasn't a big fan of one-night—
or one-morning—stands. He'd been down the easy-sex road
a time or two and figured *nothing* was without strings, not
even no-strings sex.

But this woman sure made it seem tempting. She also
made him want to see how far she'd go, to try to get an idea
of what kind of a person she was. Reckless, daring and oversexed like her friend, Rosemary? Or something else. "It was
your idea."

"A bad one."

"I don't know, some folks'd say it's pretty smart. Avoids
a lot of questions and wondering that go along with the dating process."

One of her brows arched up. "Are you asking me on a date?"

Shaking his head, he replied, "I don't date."

"Ever?"

"Not anytime recently," he muttered. "Let's just say most
of the women I meet aren't as up-front about what they want
as you are, and I haven't had enough time or interest to figure it out."

Until now.

He'd meant to maintain the teasing tone, to keep things
light and playful. But even he couldn't deny the hint of intensity in his voice. Not many people knew about his once-
burned, twice-shy attitude toward relationships and he
preferred to keep it that way.

"You know," he said, suddenly remembering something,
"if you think about it, I suppose we already had a date. Considering I bought you breakfast and all."

She lifted a hand to her mouth and whispered softly, "Oh."

"Yeah. You ran off without paying. You're lucky you didn't
spend your afternoon washing dishes." Crossing his arms, he
added, "Or that nobody called the cops."

Casting a quick look over his clothing, she muttered, "You sure weren't dressed like a cop yesterday."

He supposed today's khaki-colored pants and golf shirt were a bit of an improvement in her eyes. Not exactly the dress code, but the lieutenant had been relaxing that a little bit. Because nobody wanted to wear a damn dress shirt and tie on a ninety-degree day. "Yesterday I was going to talk to an informant in a part of town where I want to blend in, not stand out."

She opened her purse. "I'll pay you back for breakfast."

"No, you won't. But tell me one thing. What happens next?"

"You're serious about this?"

He nodded, very serious about this. He wanted to know what she thought, what she wanted. Whether she'd *really* go through with it. And how he'd feel about it. Because there was no doubt he was feeling something for this woman he'd just met.

Damn, he should be running in the other direction. Not stepping even closer to the danger she represented. For some strange reason, though, he couldn't walk away. Probably because of that danger-loving side of him he'd never fully subdued. She was *definitely* the dangerous kind. The unforgettable kind.

"So let me get this straight," she said, tapping the tip of her finger against her cheek. "You don't date, you don't want to get to know me, you just want to go somewhere, get a room and have wild, hot, monkey sex all afternoon?"

He couldn't contain a grin. "Uh, wild, hot, monkey sex?"

Her cheeks pinkened.

"I'm working this morning," he said before she had a chance to recant. Then he stepped closer, until one of his feet was almost between her sandal-clad ones.

Lifting a hand to her cheek, he brushed back a strand of hair that had loosened from her ponytail, unable to resist fingering its silkiness. He heard the hoarseness in his own voice as he said, "Besides, wild, hot, incredible sex is better late at night when the air smells ripe and fragrant and wraps you in its coolness after a steamy summer day. When it's so quiet you can hear every sigh or deep breath and the moon is bright enough to create shadows and pools of light on the bed. And whoever's on it." He breathed in deeply then added, "No distractions. No interference. Nothing but long hours of indulgence."

Even as he said the words, he wondered who had taken over his vocal cords. Even if he'd thought such things, Nick had never said anything like them to a woman before. And certainly not one he barely knew.

She said nothing for a moment while she thought it over. He knew she was reacting, though…he could see the way her lips parted a little, and she licked at them. Plus a sudden flush of color rose from her collarbone all the way up her face.

Her voice husky, she said, "You sound like you know what you're talking about."

He did. Not because of his own experiences—there hadn't been a lot of those lately. He hadn't been kidding her about the no-dating thing, since he'd been working crazy hours lately. Plus, the last woman he'd even considered taking up with—the reporter who'd been doing a story on Rosemary—had been a psycho bitch just this side of needing to be Baker Acted. So there hadn't been anything resembling romance *or* sex in his life for a good six months now.

But he had fantasies. Had long sleepless nights wondering why he felt so…*hungry.* "Maybe I do."

She tugged her bottom lip into her mouth and her eyes

widened the tiniest bit, as if she were thinking things over. Wondering if she should really go for it.

Part of him—the part below his belt that was already impatient and restless—was dying for her to say she would.

Another part—his brain, which was much more cynical when it came to women and their desires—was hoping she wouldn't. Because hopping into bed with him now would mean he was just a body. A quick means to an end, a name to scratch off. Damned if he wanted to be that. For her or anybody.

But Lord Almighty, this woman did tempt him.

Whatever happened next would be determined by who Melody Tanner really was. A lonely female who'd take a joke sex list and turn it into a one-night stand with a practical stranger? Or a funny, vulnerable woman who might actually make him want to change his opinion on dating. "What are you thinking?" he asked.

After what seemed like forever, she cleared her throat. "About what to say," she said. "And now I know."

He waited.

"You, Nick Walker," she added, leaning forward until their noses were inches apart, "are definitely *off* my list."

Without another word, the woman who'd once named him as her number-one sexual fantasy spun on her heel and walked away. Leaving him standing there on the sidewalk, ready to throw his head back, look up at the blue sky and shout hallelujah.

No, his crotch wasn't doing a happy dance. But the rest of him was. She didn't want only a *body*. Which meant maybe she wanted a *man*.

She hadn't seen the last of him, that was for sure. And no way was he going to let her scratch him off her list forever…though, just for now was okay.

As long as it was *just* for now.

"WHAT DO YOU MEAN you're not coming to my party? You *have* to come, you're the guest of honor!"

Melody pulled the phone away from her ear as Rosemary screeched. She'd expected the reaction. But…tough. Not going to Rosemary's party was minor punishment, considering Melody had spent much of yesterday and today thinking of ways to kill her best friend.

Mel still hadn't forgiven Rosemary for the farce at the diner the previous morning. In fact, as time had passed and Rosemary had ignored all of her calls, Melody had gotten more and more angry. By the time she'd locked up her studio downstairs—which had been woefully empty again today except for a visit from the UPS guy—she'd been dying for a big glass of Pinot Grigio and a hot bubble bath. And revenge.

She'd started on her second glass of wine and her third hour of whine—and had been buried up to her neck in steamy water and bubbles—when she'd figured out the perfect way to get Rosemary to answer her damn phone. Hopping out of the lovely old claw-foot tub, she'd dripped her way across the aged oak floor all the way to her bedroom. Grabbing the cordless phone off her bed, she'd brought it back with her to the bathroom and stepped back into the tub. This latest time when the answering machine had picked up, she'd said, "You might as well cancel Saturday night's party. I'm not coming."

That'd gotten a response. Rosemary had picked up before Mel had finished speaking. "No more nonsense, now. You know how much you've been looking forward to it. Tanya rearranged her flight schedule to be there, and Paige is bringing the corpse."

Rosemary wasn't overly fond of Paige's engineer husband. "So you *are* coming," she continued.

When Rosemary finally took a breath, Mel said, "Oh, so you *are* there? You *have* been avoiding my calls?"

"I was out," Rosemary said, the lie so smooth that if Mel didn't know her better, she'd have believed it.

"Since yesterday morning?" Melody asked, her tone dry. Without waiting for an answer, she asked, "How could you do it to me? How could you set me up like that?"

Her friend didn't apologize. "How could *you* not obey the rules of the list and go for it when you had the chance?"

Immediately on the defensive, Melody cleared her throat. "The list was a joke, Rosemary, remember? Besides, it didn't say I *had* to do the nasty with one of the men if I ever met him, it just said I could—without feeling guilty about it."

"Same difference."

Maybe for Rosemary. Not for Melody.

Taking a sip of her wine and sinking deeper into the bubbles, Mel sighed. "So why did you do it? I was absolutely humiliated." Then, remembering the depth of Rosemary's betrayal, she shot right back up, sloshing water onto the floor. "And furthermore, what business do you have telling people about my sex list?"

"Are you telling me that now, having met him, you don't think Nick Walker is just as sexy and hot as you did six years ago?"

"Answer the question."

Rosemary sighed heavily. "Oh, all right. I tricked you into meeting him because I didn't think you'd go if I told you the truth. In spite of how badly you need some cock, I know you think you're not ready to have sex with somebody else."

That startled a laugh out of her, then another sigh. Because the second part of Rosemary's accusation was probably true. Mel was nowhere near ready to have any relationship—even an uncomplicated one-night stand—with a man. The thought of getting naked in front of someone made her fear she'd break out in hives.

Aside from Bill, the only man who'd seen her naked in the past six years was a creepy workman who'd spied on her through a skylight at their old house in Atlanta. Typical of her inconsiderate ex, he'd arranged for some roof repairs and hadn't told her. She'd put on quite a show for the roofer while taking a bath. Thankfully, there had been lots of bubbles blocking most of his view—at least, *after* she'd gotten into the water.

The creep had been leering—one hand down his pants—when she'd spied him through the skylight and screamed. Whether he'd been jerking off or not, he'd *definitely* jerked when he'd gotten caught. Jerked so hard he fell off the roof. God, it had galled her to call an ambulance for him, especially since he got a free vacation courtesy of her home-owner's insurance.

Apparently perverts weren't excluded from filing claims.

"As for why I told him about the list?" Rosemary continued, distracting Melody from her trip down bad-memory lane. "Well…"

"I know. Nick told me you'd had a bit too much champagne."

Rosemary didn't reply at first. "That's partly true."

"What do you mean?"

"Well…I wasn't tipsy. I kind of did it on purpose."

Her head pounding now, Melody pulled the receiver away from her head so she could call her friend a bunch of foul names without actually *calling* her them.

Rosemary heard, anyway. When Mel was done, her friend said, "You finished, sugar?"

"Why did you show him my list?"

"Fate." Rosemary said the word softly, and that got Melody's attention like nothing else could have.

"What do you mean?"

"I mean, have you wondered why this whole thing happened? Why you picked him that night? Why he ended up here—where *you* are? Why I happened to meet him? It all seemed like…fate."

Melody rolled her eyes. "If it was fated to happen, you didn't need to tell him about my list, our grocery carts would have bumped into each other at the Piggly Wiggly or something."

"Sometimes fate needs a swift kick in the ass."

That was a Rosemary-ism for sure. "So you interfered."

"I interfered. Now, tell me, having met him, do you really expect me to believe you don't want him like mad?"

Nibbling her lip, Melody admitted, "I'm not saying that."

"And," Rosemary added, having the courtesy to not sound triumphant, "that any woman would love to end up in his bed?"

"Not denying that, either."

"Then what's the problem?"

"The problem is, I'm not *any* woman. I'm your best friend and I deserve better than to be ambushed by someone I trust."

That shut Rosemary up. A lengthy silence followed. Mel didn't say anything, knowing from experience that Rosemary never intended for her schemes or her interference to hurt anyone. But once she realized they had, she was usually very remorseful.

"I'm not sorry."

So much for that theory.

"Don't try to tell me that you're fine and capable of making decisions about your romantic life, because I know you're not. And if I had to help you for your own good, well, I'm not going to apologize for it."

Melody didn't even try to argue the point.

Rosemary's tone softened. "Honey, I've known you for seventeen years. I know when you're hurting and I know that if it's left up to you, you will hide in your apartment, bury yourself in your photography and watch life through a lens instead of living it. The longer it goes on, the more you'll let yourself dry up because of what that bastard did to you. I know you weren't having sex with that pig you married for a couple of years, so how long has it been since you've had a man?"

"A *man?* More than six years. Bill's a pig, remember?"

As Rosemary chuckled, Melody fell silent. Was her friend right? Sure, for much of the past year she'd been dealing with her divorce. But she'd been a free woman for a few months now and she'd had opportunities both in Atlanta, and here in Savannah, to reenter the world of the living. The world that included *men.*

She hadn't. She'd clung to her old friends, to all that was familiar to her. She'd frozen off any man she met, hadn't explored anything or anyone outside of her comfort zone. And today, she'd fled from a guy she'd been dying to have for *years.*

So maybe…just maybe…Rosemary had a point.

"You know," she said, not ready to forgive Rosemary yet, "it takes two to do the deed. I can't climb aboard a man and start going at it if he's not interested. Aside from the physical limitations, it wouldn't be very polite."

Rosemary chuckled. "Oh, he was interested, all right."

For some reason, that made her sit right up in the tub again. "He was? How do you know?"

"Well, he asked Dex to get your number."

Part of her got excited at the thought. Another part was horrified. "Tell me you didn't give it to Dex."

A pause. "I didn't."

Liar.

As if hearing the accusation, Rosemary sighed. "Okay, I did. But I also told Dex you *aren't* the type of woman to be pushed. That if you're interested, you'll make the next move."

Ha. Make the next move? Melody wasn't sure she even remembered how. Or that she wanted to!

Okay, now *she* was the liar.

"So say you'll come Saturday night," Rosemary urged. "Don't let the dick with the drill rule your life across the state."

Rosemary obviously knew her well enough to push the right buttons, because the idea that she was making decisions based on her past with her ex was entirely repugnant.

Melody still had to know one thing. "Rosemary, did you invite Nick Walker to this party?"

"No."

Mel didn't say a word.

"Oh, all right, *yes*. But that doesn't mean for sure that he'll come. He almost never comes over when I invite him. I think he thinks I'm a bad influence on Dex."

She probably was. Rosemary sure wasn't great in the whole truth-telling department.

"So please say you'll be here. *If* he shows up, you can ignore him if you want. But if you do want another chance, he'll be right here for you to work your magic on."

Magic? Melody felt closer to a carny con man than to Houdini on the magic scale. Any magic she'd once had with men seemed to have dried up over the past six years.

"You'll come, won't you?"

She could use Nick as an excuse not to go. But there really wasn't any reason to, was there? After all… "He's off my list."

It was Rosemary's turn to drop the phone. When she came back on again, she was sputtering. "You mean you did it? You put me through all this torture and you already *did* him?"

"No," she said with a helpless laugh. "I mean, I removed him from my list. Scratched him off…not *checked* him off."

"I think that's cheating," Rosemary said matter-of-factly.

"I don't think I care what you think."

"Tell me why you did it and I'll tell you if it's allowed."

Tell her why? Well, that was the question of the hour, wasn't it? Because Melody wasn't entirely sure she could explain why she'd decided Nick Walker was unsuitable for a wild, reckless, go-for-it fling. Not to Rosemary. Not even to herself.

But she had her suspicions and she could come up with several little reasons. She'd frozen him out for more than his teasing, more than his dislike of her best friend, which, to be honest, was pretty warranted today. More than the way he made her feel like a stammering twit instead of a grown woman.

When she really thought about it, she knew it came down to one thing. She'd taken him off her list because, somehow, even only knowing him a little while, she'd already realized that one time would not be enough. Not with a man like that. She couldn't have an amazing, reckless, one-night stand and then walk away. With a man like Nick, there would be regrets. Longing. Hunger.

Repercussions.

None of which she could afford right now. Especially because if she went and did the unthinkable—if she actually *fell* for a man like him—she'd be setting herself up for another miserable failure of a relationship.

God Almighty, if she couldn't hold the interest of bland, boring Dr. Bill Todd, what on earth could she possibly have to offer someone as sexy and powerful as Detective Nick Walker?

"Mel?" Rosemary prodded.

"Don't ask me any more questions," she said with a sigh,

wondering how she'd become such an emotional mess. And how long it might take before she began feeling anything like herself again. The strong Mel. The secure Mel. The confident Mel.

"Okay, no more questions. Say you'll come." Rosemary quickly added, "That wasn't a question, it was an order."

Unable to help it, Melody laughed. Rosemary was a pain in the ass…but oh, how she'd missed her. "Be good and don't try any more tricks and maybe, just *maybe*…I'll show up Saturday night."

CHAPTER FIVE

"SHE'S NOT GOING TO show up," Nick mumbled to Dex as they stood in Rosemary's lush walled garden Saturday night. He'd arrived an hour ago, on edge, his pulse already revved up as he anticipated another verbal game of one-on-one with Melody. A good prelude to the physical game of one-on-one they'd be playing sooner or later, if he had his way.

But she wasn't here.

He cast another thorough look around the yard, trying to spot her familiar auburn hair. A wasted effort—no woman at the party was quite as tall as Melody. And not one woman here made his heart pound a little harder in his chest.

He couldn't believe he'd been thinking about her almost nonstop for days. It had been a long time—maybe forever—since he'd been as instantly attracted, as immediately intrigued. as he was by Melody Tanner. Thankfully, he'd managed to control his interest well enough to keep doing his job. He and Dex had even come up with a good lead on the tourist murder case, which had kept him busy and focused at work during the day.

His nights? Well, they were a different story. Because all he'd been able to think about for the past few nights when he'd gone to bed were the images he'd put in both of their heads the other morning. Images of sweaty, late-night love-making. Of the heady fragrance of the air and her skin, wrapping together to fill his head. The way her lips would taste and the way she'd look wearing nothing but moonlight as she lay in his bed.

It had been damned frustrating. And incredibly arousing.

"Rosemary swears she'll be here, because Melody is the guest of honor." Dex's eyes were twinkling. He was unsuccessful at hiding a smile as he lifted his glass, adding, "And I'm sure she wouldn't miss seeing you again, getting to sample that famous Walker charm."

"'F' you," Nick said before sipping his beer. He hadn't gone out of his way to charm Melody. In fact, he'd done nearly everything he could to tease and taunt her. She just brought out the devil in him…a devil he thought he'd long since shaken off.

Maybe back during his teenage years he'd been more of a charming, flirting kind of guy. He wasn't that guy anymore…in fact, most people thought of him as pretty serious these days. *Intense.* That was the word most often associated with him.

So how on earth had one sassy female managed to make him unsure whether to laugh or groan; to tease his way past her defenses or just grab her and kiss the taste out of her mouth?

"Your girlfriend sure goes all out, doesn't she?" Nick muttered, needing to change the subject.

"That she does." Dex glanced around, a frown furrowing his brow. Nick knew the look. Dex was troubled. With reason. It couldn't be easy to be in love with a woman like Rosemary.

"I don't particularly like this crowd, but I have to say there's something special about this place," Nick said.

"Special…and expensive."

There was that note of tension again, which Nick had heard more and more frequently in his friend's voice lately.

Dex fell silent, keeping his quiet counsel, as always. But his eyes were constantly shifting over the party. As, of course, were Nick's. Cop instinct. It was ingrained.

The broad expanse of lawn between the mansion, where Rosemary lived, and the carriage-house-turned garage, was filled with people. Small groups stood chatting on stone patios, in shadowy corners, beside gurgling fountains or beds profuse with flowers. Lanterns provided soft atmospheric lighting throughout the yard. Huge oaks shaded much of the lawn from the starry night sky and long loops of Spanish moss provided effective curtains from any curious passersby who might try to peer through the side gate. If not for the modern-day clothes, this could have been a garden party from a previous century.

Everyone was having a wonderful time eating the catered food, drinking from the open bar—where a uniformed bartender served nearly any drink ordered. Always precise to the last detail, Rosemary had even hired a three-piece band to provide light classical music in the background.

A typical Rosemary party. Elegant, rich, and leaving Nick wondering what the hell *Dex* was doing here…much less *him!*

But he knew the answer to his own question. He was here for *her.* Here to see if Melody would show up tonight when she had to have figured Rosemary would invite him.

"So she's really something, this friend of Rosemary's?"

Sensing that Dex was simply curious and not setting him up, Nick nodded. "Yeah." *I'm just not sure what.*

Was she the witty, open, easygoing woman he'd chatted with the other morning? The one who'd had no problem flipping him off, but who'd probably also had a most adorable blush on her face while doing it? Or was she a horny woman on the prowl, ready to dive into bed the moment she met the right man?

He took another swallow of beer.

"I guess she has to be beautiful, given her background."

That got him curious. "Background?"

"Didn't she tell you? She used to be a child model."

Nick absorbed that bit of information, surprised, though he shouldn't have been, given her height and her looks. He thought about it, trying to place her name—or her face. But he couldn't.

"She apparently did TV shows, commercials and photo ads when she was a kid, and as a teenager," Dex explained. "I haven't actually seen it, but Rosemary swears there's a shot of her in a famous swimsuit edition from about ten years back."

A swimsuit model? Lord knows the woman had the figure for it, but it didn't seem to fit the Melody he'd begun to know.

"And," Dex added, pausing for a moment to make sure he had Nick's attention, "she was the Peacock Feather Girl."

Nick's jaw dropped open in shock and his slippery beer bottle nearly fell out of his hand. "You are shitting me."

"Nope. Rosemary swears it's true."

"The Peacock Feather Girl," he mumbled, having a really hard time wrapping his mind around that. Melody was *the* Peacock Feather Girl? The lingerie model whose picture had nearly set records for how fast it had spread across the Internet, before such things became almost hourly occurrences? Hell, Nick had been overseas in the service and he'd *still* seen that picture.

The model had been blond, but when he thought about it, he realized she indeed could have been Melody before a hair-color change. Frankly, her face and hair hadn't been what he and most of the guys in his unit had been looking at.

A brilliant sapphire-blue, the bra and panties set being

modeled had been skimpy to the point of nothingness. The bra, he recalled, had pretended to cover the essentials and had actually been pretty, as well as incredibly sexy. Its vivid, satiny fabric had been accented by soft-looking blue-green feathers, which had curled up from beneath each breast to curve into two carefully placed peacock "eyes." Dead center.

They were supposed to cover the wearer's breasts. But the brownish, provocative swirls had instead made the bra look wickedly salacious, as if the model had been wearing one with the front cut out to expose her nipples.

As for the panties? Well, hell, they might as well not have existed at all. A tiny ropy string of sapphire material and a long, slim feather had curved over each of the model's hips before dipping down in the front. *Way* down. And again there were those pretty, feathery swirls—the peacock eyes—all running together and overlapping. They formed a small triangle, right below the vulnerable hollow beneath the model's pelvis.

There'd been no denying what that gorgeous, feathery little beige triangle had looked like at first glance, either.

"Damn, it's hot out here," he said, tugging at his collar.

"Very," someone murmured.

Not just someone. *Her.* The woman had sneaked up on him and caught him unawares, distracted, turned-on and shifting in his pants. How *had* she managed to get the better of him already?

Pasting on a lazy smile, Nick slowly turned around to face her. Then the smile faded. Because she looked incredible.

No simple ponytail for Melody Tanner this night. Her dark auburn hair was swept back off her face, with a few soft curls dropping onto her shoulders. That amazing face, which didn't seem to even need makeup the other day, had been shadowed and powdered until she almost glittered with sophistication.

He'd known she was lovely when they'd met in the diner. Tonight, however…well, she was stunning. She sure didn't look like his red-baseball-cap-wearing informant anymore.

He probably should have kept his attention on her face. Then, perhaps, he would have been able to smile pleasantly and not let her see how sucker punched he felt by her looks. Most likely he could have held it together, murmured something normal, like "Hello," but instead he made the colossal mistake of looking down. Raking a slow, thorough look down her entire body to the tips of her toes, he tensed before slowly looking up.

Good God Almighty.

Nick's breathing slowed, the thick night air almost sticking in his chest, the heavy fragrance of flowers nearly cloying as he struggled to regain control of himself. Because it was blue. That was the color of her glittery little dress. Peacock-blue.

Why did it have to be that *particular* shade of blue? Why did it have to be so tight, so perfectly fitted to her body? Why did the thing have no sleeves, and of what use were the silly, beaded straps? Why did the front drape so low into a V to draw attention to some positively mouthwatering cleavage?

Nick's pulse started to pound in his temple as he grew more and more irritated.

Why did the damn fabric hug her like skin and why did it emphasize her slim waist and her just-right hips? And why did he have to now notice that most of her height came from incredibly long legs that would wrap just perfectly around him when he had her? As he was now even more determined to do.

Finally he pulled his desire-zapped brain back together enough to say, "Hello, Ms. Tanner. Isn't this a surprise?"

"It's my party," she said evenly.

"You're late."

"Maybe I like to make an entrance."

"Maybe you had to work up your nerve."

She cocked a brow. "I can't imagine what you mean."

"Sure you can. I'm quite sure, if you think about it real hard, you'll realize why I had the feeling you wouldn't show."

She was breathing harder now, getting riled like she had the other morning. Letting him push her buttons. But he had to hand it to her, she pulled herself together, pasting that serene smile back on her lips. "Now why on earth would you think that?"

With a nonchalant shrug, he said, "Well, I don't know, maybe it was watching you practically run away the other day. I guess I was wondering if you'd ever work up the nerve to face me again."

Her laugh sounded forced. "Really, Detective, you give yourself too much credit. If I stayed away from places simply to avoid men who annoy me, well, I'd never get to go anywhere."

Beside him, Nick heard Dex snort. Even Nick had to give a rueful grin because, damn, the girl could sound lofty and ladylike as hell, even when throwing insults in someone's face.

"Nice to see you again, too," he replied, meaning it. It *was* nice to see her—if only she hadn't walked up on him when he'd been picturing her in the sexiest lingerie ever made. "You been practicing that line since Wednesday?"

Her chin went up a notch. "That would imply I've thought about you at least once since Wednesday."

"You saying you haven't?"

"Not once."

Shaking his head, he tsked. "Good thing you're not wearing pants."

She glanced down at her dress, obviously not following his meaning.

"'Cause there'd be flames around your ankles by now."

Scrunching her eyes shut, she groaned at his liar-liar-pants-on-fire reference. "That was really lame."

He chuckled, unable to hold on to any grouchiness about how damned beautiful she looked in that blue dress. Not when she was making him remember how cute she was when she got all huffy and annoyed. "What can I say? You bring out the dork in me."

"I somehow doubt you were ever dork material, Detective," she said with a wry smile. "I picture you being more the motorcycle-riding bad boy than the Steve Urkel of your high school."

"Oh, he was definitely Steve Urkel," Dex said, interjecting himself into their conversation. "I've seen the pictures. Jeans too short, thick glasses, class valedictorian. Can't you tell?"

Tapping the tip of her finger on her cheek, she gave Nick a visual once-over. But her saucy, playful smile quickly faded.

Nick didn't particularly care for the kind of clothes required for this type of evening. But when he saw her pretty lips part and her chest move as she pulled in deeper breaths, he couldn't help thinking it wasn't such a bad thing to put on a well-cut suit once in a while. Because she obviously liked it. Judging by the way she swallowed so hard her throat bobbed, he'd say she liked it a lot.

Finally, though, she squared her shoulders. "I think you're right. I can definitely see the class nerd in him."

Dex snickered.

"Hate to disappoint you two," Nick said, "but I was the white-trash country boy driving the ancient pickup truck that was held together by duct tape and what was left of its paint."

"Let me guess," she said. "You kept a sleeping bag in the back of it for all the girls you took stargazing."

He gave her a lazy smile, because she wasn't far from the truth.

"Ugh. I think I liked you better as Steve Urkel."

He looked up at the night sky. "There's Cassiopeia," he murmured softly, his voice as smooth as the warm night air. His best seduction voice. "You know, upside down, she looks almost like an *M*. For Melody." He stared deeply into her eyes. "Your name is written in the stars."

"Gag me."

Shrugging, he said, "It worked *really* well on sixteen-year-old girls."

"So save it for them."

Dex cleared his throat. "Uh, please don't. I'd hate to arrest you now that I've finally started breaking you in."

"Ha. Nobody else would put up with you," Nick said. "Now, as much as I enjoy being the butt of your jokes, I suppose I ought to introduce you two, though I might live to regret it. Dex, meet Melody Tanner. Melody, this is my partner Dex Delaney, more recently known as Rosemary Chilton's arm candy."

Snorting, Dex stuck out his hand and Melody shook it. "Thank you for not killing Rosemary. I was checking the odds on that right up until it was time to come here tonight," he said.

"*I* was checking the odds on whether she'd *be* here tonight," Nick added.

"Back to that again?" Melody said. Glancing at Dex, she said, "I haven't killed her *yet*." Then she turned to Nick. "And I haven't said I'm staying."

A smile making his green eyes sparkle, Dex said, "I'd really prefer to keep Rosemary alive for a little longer. At least long enough for me to teach that woman how to make a bagel without burning it."

Melody sighed and shook her head. "I'm afraid if you want Rosemary, you're going to have to get used to room service and crêpes suzette for breakfast."

"Spoiled brat," Dex said. "I need to take her up into the mountains to do some camping and fishing."

"I think she'd prefer that I kill her," Melody said.

Dex laughed aloud. "She can be a handful, can't she?"

"But you seem to be doing okay," Melody replied. Her tone grew a little more serious as she admitted, "She seems happy."

Dex didn't respond to that. Instead he offered to go get Melody a drink. Leave it to his partner to know without asking that Nick wanted a minute alone with her.

"Actually, I don't want anything. Why don't you tell me how you and Rosemary met? Have you met the rest of her family? I think they're coming tonight." Her words were hurried, and she actually put her hand on Dex's arm to prevent him from leaving.

Coward. In spite of being surrounded by people, she was afraid to be alone with Nick. Which really amused him.

Melody might claim to have crossed him off her list on paper. But he didn't think she'd done so in her head.

"I've met Deidre and Brian," Dex said. Turning to Nick, he explained, "Rosemary's sister and her stepbrother." Then he lifted his nearly empty glass to his mouth and drained it before stiffly adding, "But not her parents. I don't think they're exactly thrilled that the princess is dating…"

"A cop?" Nick asked, stiffening on his partner's behalf.

"A *Northern* cop."

Melody nodded in commiseration. Since she'd known Rosemary and her family for years, maybe she could grasp the whole rich-parents-disapproving thing. But as far as Nick was concerned, Rosemary's parents were morons. Because their daughter would never in her lifetime find a better guy than Dex Delaney.

"They're actually not so bad," Melody murmured. "Her whole family has helped me out a lot since I've been back." She glanced around the crowded party. "Speaking of which, I should probably track down Brian. He's in charge of Rosemary's father's rental properties. And I've got some leaky pipes."

"Nick is pretty handy," Dex said, looking so innocent that even Nick almost believed he was being nothing but helpful. But he knew better. Dex might be honest and forthright, but he did occasionally like to amuse himself by yanking other people's chains. Maybe that was why he and Rosemary got along so well.

Melody stammered something—probably excuses about why she'd want anyone *except* Nick near her *pipes*—when someone interrupted.

"Mel, honey! Welcome home!" An older version of Rosemary descended on them, the resemblance so strong that Nick immediately pegged her as the sister. Beside her was a man about her age but not resembling the flamboyant woman in any way. His shoulders were slightly hunched and he kept his head tilted down so that his pale hair fell over his eyes, as if he were terribly shy.

Unlike the blonde. "I'm *so* sorry to hear about the nonsense you went through up in Atlanta, but you're home now." The woman air-kissed both of Melody's cheeks, then put her hands on her shoulders and looked her over. "You've gained weight."

Nick bristled on Melody's behalf, but before he could say anything, the woman continued, "Which is wonderful. Darling, you were skin and bones in the old days. Now you look like a *woman*."

"Nice to see you, too, Deidre," Melody said. Then she turned toward the man. "Brian, we were *just* talking about you."

The guy's eyes widened in surprise, as if he'd never expect a beautiful woman to talk about him for any reason. No self-confidence, that was for sure. He was surprised the man was related to Rosemary and her sister at all, even if only through marriage, because judging by this brief glimpse of Deidre, she was every bit the outspoken spoiled princess her sister was.

"Hi, Melody. How is the darkroom w-working out? Is there anything you n-need?" Brian said, his voice soft and tentative.

She squeezed his shoulder. "It's great, thank you so much for your hard work. But I did want to ask you about something."

Before she could ask Brian to check out her pipes—which would probably have sent the man right over the edge and destroyed his speaking ability completely—they were startled by a woman's shriek. Nick and Dex reacted in nearly synchronized timing, spinning toward the noise, instantly going into cop mode.

Thankfully, he didn't see any crime being committed. No woman was being manhandled, nor had anybody stumbled into the fountain or had a drink tossed in her face. Instead, there was simply the same attractive, petite woman with curly, light brown hair and freckles who'd been driving the moving truck the first time he'd met Melody. She was staring wide-eyed and openmouthed.

At *him*.

"Oh, my God," she sputtered.

Staring? No. This had quickly progressed to gawking. The woman's mouth was hanging open and her eyes were almost protruding out of their sockets.

Others at the party had apparently heard her squeal, because a dozen or more people stared over in curiosity. The buzz of conversation throughout the lawn diminished a bit.

"Ma'am?" he said, wondering if she'd had too much to drink, though it was pretty early in the evening. "Are you all right?"

"She's fine," a voice snapped from behind him. *Melody.* She stepped between him and Dex, shooting the woman a quelling glance. "That's Paige and she's just fine. *Aren't* you, Paige?"

"But…but, Mel…"

"It's so *nice* to see you. I'm glad you could come. Now let's go find Rosemary," Melody ordered, taking a few long strides toward the other woman, whom she grabbed by the arm and tried to turn toward the house.

The woman—Paige—didn't move. "But, Mel…"

"*Now,* Paige. Let's go."

The woman's feet still didn't move. Then, finally, she lifted her hand and pointed a shaky finger. Directly at Nick.

"It's *him!*" she exclaimed in a whisper so loud it could likely be heard at the River Walk. "It's the *Time* magazine hero."

Nick suddenly understood and controlled a sudden urge to smile. Obviously this was one of the other bridesmaids. One who knew a little too much. Which was why Melody was struggling so hard to drag her away before she could say anything embarrassing.

Too late.

"Don't you recognize him, Mel?" the woman exclaimed, her voice growing even louder in her excitement. "It's the number-one man on your gotta-have-sex-with-him list!"

MAYBE SHE'D LIKE PRISON. True, orange had never really been her color, and with her reddish hair, it'd probably clash horribly. And Melody couldn't stand stripes. But maybe she'd be lucky and the prison jumpsuit would have vertical stripes…which were slimming, unlike those hideously rounding horizontal ones.

So yes, she might do okay. Which was a good thing, because she was plotting her second murder in three days. If this kept up, she'd be in Rikers by the end of September for sure.

"Paige!" someone snapped, finally interrupting the deafening silence that had followed her friend's outrageous announcement. "You have the biggest mouth in the known universe. Melody's sexual-fantasy list isn't up for public discussion."

Tanya. Imposing Tanya, who was nearly yelling with indignation. Gee, what a help. At this rate, she was going to have to kill all *three* of her best friends, and then what fun would it have been to come back to Savannah?

"Uh, friends of yours?" Nick murmured. He lifted a brow, watching her, his dark eyes glittering under the light from the torches lining the lawn. "You sure know how to pick 'em."

If he smiled, she was going to take a swing. Fist or knee. One or the other would be flying if he so much as grinned. And God help the man if he laughed. "You are *so* off my list," she whispered under her breath, though she knew he heard.

This just *couldn't* be happening. She'd come so close to pulling it off. So very close to sticking to her plan to come to the party and prove to Nick Walker that he hadn't gotten under her skin like a wicked itch she couldn't reach.

It hadn't been easy—her first sight of the man had nearly sent her fleeing into the night. But she'd somehow managed to keep from swallowing her tongue at how utterly perfect

Nick Walker looked in a dark, well-cut suit, with his jaw cleanly shaved and his dark hair smoothed back.

He'd been funny and flirtatious, sexy and charming, but she'd held it together. During a few unforgettable moments when she'd caught him staring at her with glittering eyes that spoke of hunger, want and sweet desire, she'd succeeded in remaining clothed and upright when her impulse had said to strip and drop.

Maintaining the right level of cordial but cool, accessible but aloof, she'd been certain that by the end of the evening he'd have accepted the fact that the list—and his possible presence on it—was a joke. A complete joke.

Fate, it seemed, had other plans. Good old fate, Rosemary's excuse for everything. Right now she'd like to take fate and shove it down her best friend's throat.

"What's going on out here?"

Speak of the devil.

Rosemary came barreling down the back steps from the veranda, her heels click-clicking on the stone terrace like teeny little gunshots. Lucky thing for her—and for Paige—that there were no guns within grabbing distance.

"Mel, honey, you're here," Rosemary said, her tone bright. "I'm so glad you could make it. Did you sneak in the back way? Come in and say hello to everyone." Then, beneath her breath, she added, "I heard from the patio. We'll brazen it out."

Rosemary probably figured she was the cavalry. Melody instead pictured her as a moving target.

All around she heard whispers, subdued laughs. Some of these people she recognized as friends from the old days, some were even nice enough to *not* be laughing their asses off at what had happened. But a lot of them were strangers— Rosemary's set—whom she'd apparently invited to broaden Melody's social circle.

Hmm…she'd have to ask Rosemary just how *that* had worked out.

"If you'll all excuse me," she murmured, amazed at how steady she sounded when inside she was tied in knots, "I think I'll go drown myself in the koi pond."

"I bet it's not deep enough," said a low, masculine voice. Nick. Of course, who else would it be?

"Well, maybe you could stand on me to hold me down," she responded from between clenched teeth. She kept her chin up and forced herself to ignore the laughs, the winks and the mumbling.

"Jeez, Mel, I'm sorry," Paige said, apparently realizing what she'd done. Looking sheepish, Paige nibbled her lip as she moved closer. Lowering her voice to a real whisper— *about frigging time*—she added, "Would it help if I told everyone we *all* had sex lists? Eddie's around here somewhere, and he doesn't know about it, but if it'll make you feel better, I'll do it."

Eddie, Paige's reserved, quiet, engineer husband would probably fall over dead if he found out *half* the intimate details Paige had shared with her friends over the past couple of years.

Melody was tempted for about a second. "Forget it." Swallowing down a heaping helping of humiliation, she blinked to ensure no stupid tears made it past her lashes. "Hopefully most of these people have had enough to drink that they won't even remember," she said, hearing the doubt in her voice.

"I wish, darlin'. But I don't think you're that lucky," Nick said. He sounded amused, though he still didn't dare smile.

"I think my luck ran out Tuesday morning," she snapped.

"Well, now you've wounded me. Come on, let's go for a walk so you can apologize." He stepped closer, taking her arm in his, almost imperceptibly bracing her against his tall, hard body. Lending her his quiet support, his strength to lean in-to. And suddenly she saw the veiled concern in his expression.

He was worried about her. Embarrassed for her. Maybe even feeling a little guilty. She didn't have time to evaluate the absurd fluttering in her stomach caused by his tenderness. It was just so unexpected, so unlike the tough cop she knew him to be. But very much like the guy who'd carried her furniture.

In any case, he wasn't laughing at her, unlike most of the other people here. Which was the *only* reason she let him lead her away without a word to anyone. The last thing she noted was the concern—and a hint of speculation—in Rosemary's eyes.

Strolling down the garden path, he steered her toward the carriage house. From behind, it probably looked as if they were merely admiring the night-blooming jasmine instead of escaping.

He didn't say a word for the first several steps, and he didn't remove his arm, either. He simply walked with her, kept her close and held her tight enough that she couldn't compound the humiliation of this awful night by bolting for the street.

Behind them, she finally heard the sound of activity resuming. The musicians began to play. Rosemary's voice rose above the din as she entertained her guests with some bit of historical lore. At last Melody could breathe again.

"You okay?" he asked softly.

"Is everyone still staring?" she whispered.

He slowly turned his head, casting a casual glance behind them. "Nope. Nary a one."

Good. That meant she could step away. Gain some distance. Take back possession of her arm.

But she didn't.

"Those are some friends you've got," he said with a disbelieving shake of his head. "Remind me to go look up that Paige woman whenever I'm on a case and need to hear everything that's goin' on in this city."

"She doesn't mean any harm. She's got a good heart."

"And a big mouth."

Finally relaxing, she even managed a smile. "I suppose."

Curiosity furrowed his brow. "So who was on *her* list?"

"Say the word *list* one more time and I'm shoving you in the koi pond ahead of me."

He chuckled, low and deep, and she wondered why the sound washed over her the way it did. All warm and soft. Like something physical, tangible. She swallowed hard, trying to dispel the feeling but unable to completely manage it.

"I hope you're kidding about there being some koi pond back here, because if this heat wave doesn't let up, your friend Rosemary's going to be serving up boiled fish at her parties."

"Eww."

"Though, I suppose it's better than the raw fish they're serving back there."

Scrunching up her nose, she couldn't help agreeing. "I've never developed a taste for sushi, either."

"Fish eggs are bad enough."

"Ah, caviar, now *that's* another story."

"You like that stuff?"

She licked her lips. "Mmm."

Nick finally slid his arm out from around hers and moved away. Stepping off the stone path onto the lawn—out of the last bit of lantern night—he crossed his arms and leaned against the trunk of a huge oak tree, watching her with hooded eyes.

Melody stepped closer, brushing aside some long tangles

of Spanish moss, until she, too, was close enough to lean against the tree. Not that she *would*—the glitter from her dress wouldn't last ten seconds against the bark. And it wouldn't do to get that close to the man watching her so intently in the shadowy night.

Turning a little, she glanced across the lawn, toward the party going on twenty yards away. Yet they seemed almost separated from it. Hidden by the trees, as if curtained in some private wooded glade.

That was when her senses really kicked up a notch and she caught the danger of the situation. Escaping had seemed like a good idea. Escaping with *him* into a dark, shadowy corner full of sweet night smells and tangible expectation? Well... that had been about as wise as the Trojans bringing a big wooden horse into the middle of their city.

"So tell me about your caviar days," he said.

"Hmm?"

"Well, from what I hear tell, I'm not the only one who ended up in a magazine. You were famous." A grin tugged at his lips. *God, those lips.* "A *Sports Illustrated* swimsuit model? Am I a creep for saying I would have liked to see that?"

Rosemary's ruthless campaign of complete exposure of all Melody's secrets had obviously swung right back into full force. If she'd told Nick—or *anyone*—about the billboard incident in Atlanta, Mel was going to go all over town blabbing about the Braves player and the New Year's Eve party. "It wasn't *Sports Illustrated,*" she mumbled. "It was a little knockoff magazine that was probably only purchased by the mothers of the minor-league players interviewed in it. And I was wearing a one-piece."

"I'd bet the dads bought at least *one* issue every year."

Her eyes narrowed.

He backtracked. "So you don't model anymore, I take it?"

"No. I quit several years ago, before I got married."

That distracted him. "How old are you, anyway?"

Well, how polite. "Why?"

"I'm just wondering. Judging by when you had to have made your list, I figure you got married around six years ago. What were you, all of eighteen?"

"I was twenty-one," she replied primly. "Not a kid."

"Not far from it."

Remembering something he'd said once, she asked her own questions. "What about you? You said you went through something similar some years back. Were you eighteen when you got married?"

His answer stunned her. "Yeah. I was."

"Really?"

His jaw tightened. "I had what you might call a shotgun wedding. And a quickie divorce." He didn't sound teasing and flirtatious anymore. Now he seemed tense. As if he regretted starting the conversation.

Well, so did she. She was nowhere near ready to talk about her marriage, to him, or to anyone new in her life. So she couldn't blame him for not wanting to share the details of his. "Maybe we should get back to the party."

"Chicken?"

"Hardly."

"You sure?" Straightening, he dropped his arms to his sides and stepped closer. The moonlight cast shadows of light and dark on his face. Shadows shaped like the leaves of the tree and the tangled gray moss. He looked mysterious, his eyes glittering. His big body seemed almost dangerous, though she wasn't afraid he'd do her any harm. Not physically, anyway.

He lifted a hand and traced the tip of one finger along her shoulder strap. Because the strap was thin, his warm touch brushed her skin as well as the fabric. She hissed out a slow breath. Because *that* was the danger. Her reaction to him.

"You're not nervous being out here in the dark with me?"

"N-no. Of course not." Melody crossed her fingers behind her back at that lie. Because she was definitely nervous. The longer she spent here in the shadows with this man, the more in trouble she could be. When he touched her, whispered to her, she began to think about those late-night fantasies she'd once had about him. And the harder it was to remember all the reasons she'd told herself she couldn't act on her attraction…or her list.

He leaned in. "Your pulse is racing, Melody."

Oh, she liked how he said her name. That low, husky whisper scraped over all her nerve endings. He was close enough that she felt the warmth of his breath on her cheek. Close enough that she could breathe deeply and inhale his clean-scented cologne.

What were those reasons again?

"I think I'm going to kiss you before the night is out," he whispered, his voice floating over her like the evening breeze.

"You can try," she replied, going for a flip dare. But there was no doubt in her mind, or probably in his, that her words had sounded like a plea instead.

Meeting her gaze, he stared at her for one long second, gauging her mood. Judging her seriousness. Then, with a helpless, throaty groan, he leaned in and touched his mouth to hers.

He tasted like the night. Warm and moist. Heady and erotic. His lips slid across hers, slowly, as if he savored the feel of skin on skin. Then he licked delicately at the seam of her lips until, with a sigh, she opened for him and met his tongue for a slow, deliberate exploration.

Heat uncoiled inside her and rolled through her blood,

making her hotter than the Savannah summer ever could. His mouth was heavenly on hers and the way he delicately stroked her tongue with his own made her sure she'd melt into a puddle of want.

She moved closer, resting her hand on his impossibly broad chest, feeling the pounding of his heart beneath her fingers. Their bodies brushed against each other, lightly, effortlessly, almost swaying to the music from the party, which somehow seemed very far away. As did the rest of the world.

The kiss continued with lazy eroticism. No frenzy, no frantic thrusts, just a lethargic exploration that hinted of long, sultry nights filled with sensuous pleasures.

Melody sighed when Nick lifted his hand to cup her face, his touch incredibly tender but also evocative. Possessive. The feel of his other hand on the small of her back made her arch closer against him in helpless response. Instead of that suggestive scrape of dress on jacket, they were now pressed close together. Melody's breasts grew tight and heavy and her legs went weak at the feeling of his hard form—so *very* hard—pressed against hers.

She hungered. Truly, *wanted,* for the first time in a very long time. Physically *and* mentally.

Finally he ended the kiss, lifting his head to look down at her with dark eyes that caught and reflected the sheen of moonlight above them. They stood there, face-to-face for a long moment. Melody heard her harsh breaths, felt her heart pounding and slowly let thought return and sensation slide away.

Of course, as thought returned, she began to wonder what she'd just allowed to happen.

Not the kiss. Yes, it had been divine—the first time she'd kissed a man other than Bill in more than seven years. But the kiss had only been part of it.

She'd acted on her attraction. Encouraged it. Thrown gasoline on the fire she'd already sensed she could feel for the man. The fire she knew could rage out of control if she didn't get a grip on herself. "Oh, my," she whispered.

"Yeah," he murmured softly. "You think I've earned back my number-one spot?"

Her instinctive reaction was to nod, but she kept herself from doing it. Because every concern, every fear she'd had about going for it with Nick—her number-one fantasy—had been justified by that one kiss.

He could shatter her. He could leave her quivering and shaking with desire, desperate to have him, growing addicted to whatever he offered.

Once wouldn't be enough, but once was all she could allow herself with any man. No more than that, not until she pulled herself back together emotionally from her miserable marriage.

She knew she needed to begin living her new life, but she didn't want to open up her heart and let somebody start shooting holes through it again. One night of sex with no emotions shouldn't be too dangerous. So until she felt good enough about herself to think she might be able to bring something to the table in terms of a real relationship, she needed to steer clear of anything more than a single, forgettable encounter.

Nick Walker would be utterly unforgettable. His kiss had proved that beyond a shadow of a doubt.

This was definitely a case of the wrong man, wrong place, wrong time. Or maybe he was the right one. But it didn't matter. It was still the wrong place and wrong time.

Perhaps Rosemary would have been strong and determined enough to take what she wanted and forget about it. But Melody already knew she was never going to forget this man. He could never be meaningless. Now, having been in his arms, she was absolutely certain of it.

So, stepping away, she slowly shook her head. Wondering

if he could hear the heavy regret in her voice, she said, "No, I don't think so. I'm sorry…so sorry. But you *definitely* can't be on my list anymore."

Stiffening her shoulders—and her resolve—she silently turned and walked back to the party before he could say a word.

CHAPTER SIX

THOUGH ROSEMARY WAS BUSY entertaining her guests and trying hard to come up with something her father might have in common with Dex that they could talk about—instead of just avoiding each other like they had since she'd introduced them—she kept one eye out toward the rear of the gardens. Just in case.

Melody could be out there going for it—healing her broken heart and salving her wounded spirit with a man hot enough to tempt a saint into sinning.

Okay, hopefully they weren't going for it right in her backyard. Particularly since her gardener had fertilized very recently. But still, Melody might be indulging in a few stolen kisses and planning for a future assignation.

She had to sigh at the romanticism of it.

"What was that heartfelt sound for?"

Dropping the lace curtains draped across the dining-room window, she spun on her heel and greeted Dex with a smile. Oh, he did look *fine* in his dark suit, so nicely fitted against his big, hard body, and such a good shade with his light brown hair. He was a very handsome man, capable of taking her breath away.

"Just thinking about Melody," she finally replied.

He crossed his arms and gave her a scolding look. "When are you going to learn to mind your own business?"

She waved an airy hand. "I do mind my own business."

"Rosemary…"

"*Most* of the time. But when someone I care about is hurting, well, I can't help it if I want to do something."

"She might not forgive you for it, you know," he murmured, relaxing his rigid stance. "Even if you did it for her own good."

"If it gets that bastard she married off her mind and gives her something to smile about for a few nights, I think she will."

"A few nights?"

"Well, yes, if she has a fling with her fantasy man, it'll be the perfect way to start her life over."

"And that's all she's after? A fling? A couple of nights?" He looked tense again. Dex's pale green eyes narrowed.

"What?"

"Rosemary, I don't know that Nick's the kind of guy who'll take that very well—being used for a couple of nights by a woman who needs to make herself feel better."

She hadn't thought that far ahead, frankly. "What red-blooded American man doesn't dream about being used as a sex object by a gorgeous former lingerie model?"

He shook his head and frowned deeply. "One who's a loner. Who's been burned by women one too many times and doesn't have much faith in them as it is."

She refused to look at it that way. What difference did it make if Nick had faith in women or not? It wasn't as if he and Mel were going to fall madly in love. They just needed to fall passionately between the sheets.

Determined not to worry about it anymore, she walked over to Dex and slipped her arms around his neck. "Have I told you how handsome you look tonight?"

His lips quirked up a tiny bit. "Yeah."

She waited for a reciprocal remark and when she didn't get it, she yanked his hair.

Laughing, he pulled her close. "You're beautiful." His laughter faded as he stared intently into her face. "I sometimes look at you across the room and wonder how this ever happened."

"How what happened?"

"You and me," he replied, stroking a lazy circle on the small of her back that soon had her ready to melt. Like his touch always did. "How we're making it work." His smile faded. "How long we're going to be able to keep making it work."

Rosemary didn't even want to think that way. What mattered was that they *were* making it work. And they'd continue to do so, if it was the last thing she ever did.

Before she could say so, Dex lifted his hand to her face. Gently rubbing his thumb on her cheek, he murmured, "You look tired. Have you eaten anything?"

"You know I can never eat at my own parties," she said. "I get butterflies trying to make sure everything is just right."

"It is tonight. You've outdone yourself. Now sit down and eat a plateful of food."

Ugh. Her stomach rebelled at the very thought, obviously still knotted up with worry over what was happening with Melody and Nick out in the backyard.

But before she could say that, her sister entered the room, Brian close behind her. "Good, you're alone. I can finally get the scoop." Deidre gave Dex a quick smile. "No offense—I meant the *rest* of the party's outside."

"Glad to know I'm considered part of the inner circle," Dex said, his good humor quickly returning. He got along well with Rosemary's siblings, who seemed to see the same streak of honor and integrity that had so drawn Rosemary to him. As her father would—if he ever gave him a chance.

"Don't be too glad," Brian murmured. "You n-never know what these two are going to talk about." Staring at Deidre, he added, "If you start talking about w-women's stuff, I'm leaving."

Rosemary smiled, noting her stepbrother's reddened cheeks. God love poor Brian. He had never known what had hit him when his mother had married their father twenty years ago. He'd suddenly been thrust between two high-strung sisters and had never been quite quick enough to keep up with them.

"I want the dish on Melody. And...*him*. That gorgeous man."

"*He's* my partner, and *I'm* leaving," Dex said, turning on his heel. "Sounds like female stuff, Brian."

Her brother ducked his head and smiled. "I can handle names. Just not body parts."

"Suit yourself." But as Dex strode toward the door, he glanced over his shoulder and gave Rosemary a look with which she'd become very familiar. A warning one. "You've set the wheels in motion, Rosie. Now let it be. Whatever happens, happens."

"Rosie?" Brian said with wide eyes once Dex had left.

Shooting her brother a glare, Rosemary said, "If you ever tell anyone he calls me that, I'll...I'll tell Paige you had a mad crush on her back in high school."

Brian paled, his mouth opening then closing. Rosemary immediately regretted teasing him, because he was so ill-equipped to deal with it. "I'm kidding. Your dark secret is safe with me."

"Now, tell me about this man. And the list! What *is* this list?" Deidre asked, gesturing widely with her arms.

Rosemary didn't keep secrets from her sister, but the story of the lists they'd made the night before Mel's wedding was one she hadn't shared. "It's that silly list I have on my refrigerator. We *all* made one the night before Mel's wedding."

"The list with Dex's name all the way down?" Deidre asked, looking confused.

Dex. He'd changed her list again. Oh, goodness, she did have a good time with that man's possessive streak.

She explained the whole story as quickly as possible, keeping her tone light. But no matter the tone, Brian began to flush, then his eyes grew wide and his earlobes red. "Maybe I should go," he mumbled, edging toward the arched doorway.

Ignoring him, Deidre clapped her hands together. "That's wonderful. I want to make a list."

Rosemary lifted a droll brow. "I don't think Carl would approve. You know, Carl? Your husband."

Brian mumbled something else, then turned to leave the room, as if he couldn't stand hearing any more sex talk from his sisters. But before he could do so, Paige and Tanya burst in. Paige was out of breath, her face bright red. And even tough, implacable Tanya looked upset.

"What is it?" Rosemary asked, more curious than concerned.

"You have to hide," Paige said between choppy breaths. "Because she's going to kill you."

"What?"

"Though, I guess I should thank you for getting me out of the hot seat for opening my big mouth," she continued, still gasping a little as she tripped over her words.

"What are you talking about?" Rosemary asked, instantly stiffening. "Who's going to kill me?"

Tanya answered before Paige could, a feat in and of itself. "Breathe, Paige." Then she stepped closer, her dark brown eyes snapping in righteous anger. "How could you do it? First I hear you sent her out to breakfast with the *Time* magazine guy who showed up here tonight?"

"I need a drink," Paige muttered. She elbowed past Tanya and grabbed a glass of champagne from a tray on the dining-room table. It was half-empty, obviously someone else's, but Paige hardly seemed to notice as she lifted it to her mouth and drained it. Even Brian paused, cringing as he watched, as did Deidre.

"You're toast, Rosemary," Paige said with a mournful shake of her head when she could speak again. "Deader than a doornail."

"You got that right," Tanya said, for once agreeing with Paige when she usually rolled her eyes at their friend's antics.

Rosemary almost stamped her foot out of frustration with these two. She had a feeling that half glass of champagne hadn't been the first drink Paige had had all evening. "Say it!"

"They're here," Paige said, shaking her head mournfully. "I just saw them. That stiff hair of his is hard to miss."

Oh, God. Rosemary's heart tripped as she grasped what they meant. She'd almost forgotten. They hadn't responded to the invitations and she'd figured that was for the best. But now...

Paige continued to shake her head. "Yep, you really did it this time." She glanced frantically around for another drink and finally stared at the watery remnants of a cocktail in a small, nearly empty tumbler. Deidre deftly grabbed it and moved it out of the way, tsking in disapproval.

Groaning, Paige dropped into one of the dining-room chairs and put her chin on her fisted hands. "Oh, I hope she doesn't think we had anything to do with this."

"Me, too," Tanya replied, lowering herself to another chair. "I wouldn't have come if I'd known you'd invited…them."

"Invited who?" Deidre snapped, looking unable to contain herself. "Who's here?" Her sister did stomp her foot, which made Rosemary glad she hadn't, because it was terribly silly to watch.

"Jonathan Rhodes and Drake Manning," Tanya said in disgust.

"Yeah," Paige added, her voice rising in a near wail. "And Mel is going to absolutely go through the roof when she finds out Rosemary arranged for *all three* of the men on her sexual-fantasy list to be here tonight."

AFTER MELODY STUNNED HIM by walking away after their surprising, erotic kiss, Nick remained in the garden for a while. Thinking. Wondering. Reliving.

Yeah. He definitely relived every moment of their conversation, the way the glitter on her dress had reflected in the moonlight. The reddish sheen of her hair under the flickering glow of the lanterns. The sound of her laughter. Their kiss.

God, that kiss. That incredible kiss. He'd kissed a lot of women in his life, going way back to seventh grade when Cherry Hilliard had dragged him into the locker room at Joyful Middle School, and showed him that a tongue was good for a lot more than licking ice-cream cones.

But he'd never shared a kiss that had seemed so…intimate. He'd had sexual encounters that had seemed less erotic.

One kiss. That's all it had been. But he had a feeling he was going to remember it for the rest of his life.

"So why did you walk away?" he wondered aloud as he stood beneath the oak tree for the longest time, watching Melody move through the party. She was so easy to spot in her peacock-blue outfit, which stood out among all the women in their little black cocktail dresses. She mingled and chatted, was air-kissed by a bunch of women and ogled by a bunch of guys.

That made Nick tense up, which was crazy since he had absolutely no claim on the woman. Except that she'd once wanted him above all men. And despite her claims, he wasn't ready to let her stop wanting him.

Finally, about a half hour after she had left him standing alone in the far corner of the yard, Melody worked up the nerve to look at him. She cast a quick glance in his direction, as if making sure he was no longer there. Their eyes met, their stares locking. She went very still, as did he, while they shared a long, revealing moment.

He knew she'd been pretending not to notice him.

She knew he hadn't taken his eyes off her.

Then someone spoke to her. With a quick shake of her head, she looked away, but not before revealing a flash of something in her face. A hint of regret? A promise that they weren't done yet? Maybe even a plea to be left alone?

Well, that was impossible.

She couldn't pretend their kiss hadn't affected her, because they both knew it had. And her protestations about her stupid list meant nothing. The list be damned—they'd met, there was attraction, something was going to happen. The predetermined plan she'd laughingly made up with her girlfriends had *nothing* to do with them from here on out.

The list hadn't made her look at him with those dreamy eyes, hadn't made her whimper and sigh when their lips had touched. Hadn't made her tilt her head and open her mouth wider, meeting every thrust of his tongue with a languorous one of her own.

Now this was just about them, Nick and Melody, who'd kissed in the moonlight.

Realizing he was going to start looking like some kind of voyeur if he kept standing here watching from the shadows, he returned to the party. Melody had disappeared, as had Dex, which was probably for the best. He probably should get out of here. Common sense told him to wait a day or two for Melody Tanner to get her head together—to stop pretending she could control what her body wanted by saying so with her mouth.

Then they could start over. Hell, maybe he'd even risk swimming in the dating waters again. Because spending an evening with her over a leisurely dinner sounded *really* good to him.

Looking for Dex and Rosemary so he could say goodbye, he went inside. Rosemary's home was amazing—the kind of place often used as a B and B or a tourist attraction. He didn't know how her father had made his money, but he knew he had enough to give this house to his younger daughter. Rosemary lived here alone, since Deidre was married and Brian lived in an apartment building he managed for his stepfather.

The place was enormous, yet he doubted there was room for Dex here. Dex didn't fit. Sooner or later, he was going to realize that. Or Rosemary would. Nick didn't want to think about what was going to happen to his friend on that day.

Hearing voices in the dining room, he headed there. He'd reached the arched doorway when he heard Melody's blabbermouth, curly-haired friend say something that made him shake. The blood began to roar in his head and he stalked into the room. "You're telling me there are other men from that goddamned list here tonight? And that you ambushed her?"

Rosemary's mouth opened, but she couldn't say a word. Neither could any of the other people in the room—not even Paige, who he'd figured was never lost for words.

"How the hell could you do that to her? *Again?*"

Rosemary tilted her head up. "I want her to be happy. She needs to take her life back."

"What she needs," he said harshly, "are friends she can *trust*."

With that, he turned on his heel and stalked out of the room, needing to find Melody before she came face-to-face with one of the men Paige had mentioned. He looked for the slimy guy from Channel 9 who'd been involved in a domestic dispute with his outraged and violent wife last year. And for the lawyer, Jonathan Rhodes, who Nick personally loathed after a few run-ins in court.

He didn't allow himself to think about Melody having once desired the two men. His brain couldn't even fathom being put in the same category as them, considering they were both scumbags, as far as he was concerned.

Figuring Mel would be upset, and thankful her bright dress would make her easy to find, he walked out to the veranda searching for a crying redhead in peacock-blue. And there he spotted her. Smiling. Laughing. Looking comfortable and relaxed with a small group of people by the railing.

She obviously hadn't bumped into one of her list guys. Yet.

As he approached her, Nick looked for signs of stress—a gleam of moisture in her eyes that would tell him she was putting on a front. But he saw nothing, not even a stiffness in her beautiful shoulders that said she was uncomfortable.

It wasn't until he got to within three feet of her that Nick realized *who* she was talking to. The two men had been indistinguishable in their dark suits, as was the other woman, who had her back to him. But when he heard the woman in the black dress laugh, he stiffened. There was no mistaking that laugh, or the hardened voice that went with it.

It was Angie Jacobs, the reporter he'd come close to hooking up with six months ago. He groaned inwardly, wondering why the hell the woman was at the party when she'd annoyed Rosemary by dropping the news piece. Then again, knowing Angie, not having an invitation wouldn't stop her from going somewhere she wanted to go. Even if she had to use deceit to get there.

That's how she'd gotten his super to let her into his apartment last spring, where she'd promptly searched for anything she could find on a high-profile case Nick had been working. Then she'd planted herself in his bed, apparently planning to seduce the information out of him. Which had led to their last confrontation and the circus-freak remark.

So, no, he wasn't particularly thrilled at the prospect of coming face-to-face with her again.

But he couldn't think too much about it. Because he suddenly recognized the two men standing with Angie and Melody. One of them was Angie's co-worker, looking just as fake and arrogant as he did on TV. The second guy wasn't hard to recognize either, with his pricey Italian suit and his slimy defense-lawyer smile.

They were Drake Manning and Jonathan Rhodes.

And Melody was standing right between them.

Nick *almost* turned around. Almost judged by the smile on her face and her relaxed posture that Melody was fine and dandy chatting up the two men to see if she was going to hop into the sack with one of them. Almost walked away thinking maybe she was exactly the kind of woman he'd once feared she was…a taker, someone who wanted a meaningless lay to get her confidence back.

Then Manning touched her. And Melody flinched.

She was definitely *not* all right.

"Here you are," he said, striding into the group. "I promised Rosemary I'd bring you in for a toast."

A quick, nearly imperceptible look of relief flashed across

her face. Then her back straightened. "I was getting to know some more of Rosemary's *guests*. Such interesting people in her circle," Melody murmured, her voice tight.

"Well, well, if it isn't Detective Walker," Angie said, her cordial tone countering the malice in her eyes. "You do clean up, don't you? You *almost* look like you belong here."

Melody's sharply inhaled breath told him she hadn't been prepared for Angie. But Nick was used to her. Raking a bored glance over the woman, he said, "Amazing how clothes can make a person look *almost* human, isn't it?"

Drake Manning stiffened and Angie's eyes blazed. Melody, however, sucked her lips into her mouth, as if she were trying not to laugh. Without another word for any of them, Nick reached out and took hold of Mel's arm, tugging her with him. "Let's go."

He felt her stiff resistance at first, but she did finally move her feet and follow him. Once they were out of earshot of the others, she yanked her arm away. "You can't…"

"I just did, Melody," he muttered, not in the mood to hear any excuses. Damned if he was going to leave her there with those three—the scummy TV anchor, the scummier defense lawyer and the bitch queen of Savannah.

Reaching the other end of the veranda, he tried a pair of French doors and found them open. Pushing her inside, he followed her, hoping no one had seen them disappear but not caring too much if they had.

In the silence, he heard her harsh breaths and wondered if she was about to go apeshit on him for manhandling her out of her own party. Not that he cared. Whether she'd realized it or not, she'd needed rescuing. Maybe even from herself…though he hated to think she'd even *consider* letting her dumb-ass list allow her to make a colossal mistake with one of those pricks.

Giving her a chance to cool down, he turned and glanced around the room. They were in Rosemary's office, where she worked at home doing her real-estate stuff. It was empty, nearly dark, lit only by a small lamp in the corner. Dominated by a large antique desk standing right in the middle of the floor, the room was otherwise relatively sparse. A shelving unit stood along one wall, and two overstuffed leather chairs were opposite the desk.

He pushed her toward one of the chairs.

"Would you keep your hands off me?" she snapped.

"I don't see you flinching when I touch you the way you did with that Manning guy. What number was *he* on your list?"

Her eyes widened. "Oh, my God, Rosemary told you the whole thing?" Looking stunned, she dropped into the chair.

"Rosemary didn't tell me. Your friend Paige—"

"*Paige* told you that?" She looked truly stunned. "What, is everybody at this party talking about my sex life?"

"No. She was reaming out Rosemary for inviting the other two and I overheard." Unable to help it, he frowned. "You sure didn't have the best taste in men, did you?"

"Obviously not, since I chose *you*."

She'd just admitted again that she *had* chosen him—but he didn't call her on it. "I've got to say, you looked pretty calm talking to those two."

"I was fine."

"Not ready to murder Rosemary this time?"

She crossed her legs—those endlessly long legs—and leaned back in her chair. "I was…surprised. But not completely shocked. I'd wondered if she'd do it."

He'd expected more indignation. More anger. More *something*. "So, what, you wandered right up to them and engaged them in conversation?" he asked, leaning back until he was half sitting on Rosemary's big desk.

"Something like that," she admitted. "I think the two of them are friends." Her voice was steady, but the way she shifted her eyes away made him wonder if she was being entirely honest.

"And there was no embarrassment, like the other morning at the diner." He raised a disbelieving eyebrow. "No concern, nothing?"

"Nope. They were both friendly, cordial and attractive."

He stiffened, wondering why she'd gotten so damned chummy with the other two men so fast.

"Now, if we've finished the inquisition, Mr. Big Bad Policeman, can I get back to my party?"

Rising, he stepped closer. "Anxious to get back to scoping out the two other guys on your list, huh?"

"Maybe," she retorted, her cheeks reddening. "If I am, it's certainly none of your business."

She was definitely holding back. There was something she did not want him to see. It amazed him, really, how quickly he'd become familiar with her moods. The rapid pulse in her temple told him she was being evasive and the way she shifted her startling blue eyes away reinforced that certainty.

Keeping his voice deceptively quiet, he asked, "So which one's in the lead so far? I mean, for the list thing."

"Would you shut the hell up about my list?" She rose to her feet.

Hot button. "Touchy, touchy." He stepped closer, and so did she. "You are mighty sensitive about it, aren't you? Thought you were relaxed and calm about meeting those two."

"I *am*. They're nice, attractive and not cavemen."

He caught the insult. "I don't know that *nice* is a word I'd use to describe either one of them. That Manning guy has chased so many women in this town, he ended up giving himself a heart attack."

Her chin went higher. "Oh, how nice, making fun of some-one's health."

"Not making fun, darlin', it's true. Happened last year."

"Whatever," she muttered. "But I'm still glad that Rose-mary arranged for them to be here tonight so I could meet them both."

He *nearly* let her words get to him, nearly left the party, like he should have an hour ago. But something made him wait. To think. To figure out what he was missing. So he remained still, staring at her from a few short inches away.

For all her flip words and her confidence, Melody was barely holding on to her control. Her hands were clenched in front of her, her fingers clasped so tightly together they'd turned white. Her breathing was ragged, color brightening her cheeks. The woman was in no way calm, cool and comfortable. In fact, she was totally and completely on edge. On the verge of exploding. Or running.

And suddenly, without another word, he understood. Everything came together in his mind and he got the whole picture. Melody hadn't been uncomfortable with the other two men, because she'd felt absolutely *nothing* for them.

Unlike with him.

Watching her, it was so easy to see the truth. She was upset, shaking, confused and dying to get away now for one simple reason: because she wanted *him*. And only him.

Now he just had to make her admit it.

The realization that she was trying to bluff her way out of here with false bravado, and that she really wasn't interested in anyone else, made a low, grateful laugh escape Nick's lips. The laughter held both amusement at the way she'd been fighting her own reactions, and pure, one-hundred-percent relief that he wasn't the only one feeling the intense, tangible attraction that had erupted between them from the moment they'd met.

"What is so funny?" She looked indignant.

"You," he admitted. "You're trying so damn hard to keep me from figuring out why you're fine and dandy with those two when you can hardly hold it together with me."

Her mouth opened in shock. "You're delusional."

"Uh-uh. I'm not. I just got it. You could talk them up easy because there was *nothing* there. No spark. No interest. Nothing." Knowing he was right and feeling so relieved he wanted to cheer, he moved even closer, until his suit jacket brushed against the front of her sparkly blue dress. "Admit it," he said throatily, "I'm the only man on your so-called list who makes you feel *anything*."

She froze, not pulling away, keeping their bodies close enough that he could practically feel the physical spark of energy and desire snapping between them. "Admit it, Melody."

Breathing even more deeply, she stared searchingly at his face, not responding. She didn't have to. He knew he was right—her silence confirmed it. It only remained to see whether she'd have the guts to say so.

The sound of a voice from outside startled her, shaking her out of her reverie. Her face flushing red, she stepped back. "You're *off* my list. How many times do I have to say it?"

He shrugged. "Until you can convince yourself it's true."

Closing her eyes, she threw her head back and groaned. "Why would I want you? You're arrogant and you don't like my best friend and you don't like cats and you're not a nice guy!"

One of her accusations deeply offended him. "Who told you I don't like cats?"

She opened one eye and peered at him. "So that's the only thing you're denying?"

He answered with a shrug. "Rosemary's okay. Sometimes."

She groaned again and spun away, stalking toward the French doors. As she passed the desk, she reached out angrily and slammed the palm of her hand flat on its surface. "I'll put anyone else in first place on my list instead of you. The UPS guy…hell, my landlord! You are *off* my list and *off* my radar. You make me crazy. And I don't *want* anyone who makes me crazy."

He followed, determined not to let her leave. She'd nearly reached the door but before she could escape outside, she got tangled up in the lacy curtains blowing in on the warm night breeze.

"Honey, stop," he said, putting a hand on her shoulder.

She didn't walk out. Instead, she stayed very still.

Stepping close behind her, he lifted his other hand to her bare arm, stroking up and down. Their bodies were so close he could feel her warmth, could smell the sweetness of her hair and her perfume and her skin. And *her.* "You need someone who makes you crazy," he said, his voice downright hungry. "Someone who makes you wild and insane."

She said nothing. But the tenseness in her arm and shoulder began to disappear. She leaned back, slightly, almost imperceptibly. Just close enough that her back touched his chest and her hair slid across his cheek. Her sweetly curved ass brushed ever so lightly against his groin.

He hissed. And she whimpered. He pushed closer. And she pushed back. Then all restraints were gone. Simply…gone.

"Nick," she moaned. It sounded like a plea.

"Shh." He lowered his hands, twining his fingers with her hand and sliding his other arm around her waist. Pressing his palm flat against her belly, he tugged her closer, tighter, savoring the softness of her body against his. Unable to wait any longer, he bent and sampled the fragrant skin on the side of her neck. Breathing deeply of her scent, he scraped his tongue up to her pulse point, then nibbled on her earlobe.

"If it's any consolation, you drive me crazy, too," he admitted as she arched back, offering him more.

He continued kissing her, bending farther to taste her throat. Letting his hand slide down her front, he brushed tantalizingly close to where he *so* wanted to touch her, and tugged her even tighter against him.

"Oh, God," she whimpered, obviously feeling the way his body was reacting to their embrace.

"See?" he growled. "Crazy. Insane."

"Yes, I see." Melody reached up and behind her to loop one arm around his neck. Her hips thrust back gently, almost reflexively, as if seeking the touch he hinted at.

And oh, how he wanted to give it to her.

As if sensing they were nearing a much more intimate encounter—and *wanting* it—Melody reached out and pushed the French door shut with a click, then adjusted the drapes to ensure it was covered. That left them secluded, with complete privacy.

Almost desperate to taste her mouth, he took her actions as enough of a sign. Turning her around in his arms, he caught her lips in a carnal, openmouthed kiss. They gasped together, plunging and taking and exploring, all hunger and desperation—not the sweet, languorous desire with which they'd kissed earlier in the garden.

This was sexual. Frenzied.

Their mouths clinging together like they needed to share the air, she thrust his jacket off his shoulders, then grabbed at his tie. Tugging it open, she reached to undo the top buttons of his shirt so she could touch him. The feel of her cool fingers on his chest made him even more frantic, more desperate, and he pushed her toward the desk. When the back of her thighs reached it, she slid up onto it, parting her legs for him to step between them.

Perfect. Because, at this minute, between her legs was exactly where he'd give just about anything to be. His future. His life. His soul.

"Please, please," she whimpered, arching harder against him as she wrapped one leg around the back of his. Only his pants and whatever she had on under her dress separated them, and he was desperate to be rid of both.

She seemed to feel the same desperation, because she ground against him. Sliding up and down against his bulging erection, she made them both a little crazier, a little hungrier, until they were each groaning in anticipation. She was greedy, using his hard cock to take the kind of touch she most needed, right where she needed it. Her fast, choppy breaths, coming between parted lips, told him she was getting off on just that.

So was he. It was an incredible turn-on. Even through his trousers, he could feel her heat. The need to sink into her, into that tight, sweet wetness, was nearly overwhelming.

But first he wanted to see her come. "Need some help, darlin', or are you doing okay on your own?"

Ignoring him, she panted, arched again, cried out some more and rode him as if he were her favorite vibrating sex toy.

Of all the reasons to be used by a beautiful woman, he had to say this was one of the few good ones.

He definitely, however, wanted to be more involved. Still giving her the pressure she wanted, he began to kiss his way across her cheek and her jaw. "You taste spicy. Like cinnamon. Vanilla. I want to devour you."

"Oh, my," she whimpered, scraping her cheek against his face, tilting her head to give him access to her soft neck.

He kissed her there, delicately licking his way down her throat until he could taste that vulnerable hollow. Continuing to inhale deeply, to breathe in her fragrance and her sweetness and her taste, he nibbled his way across her nape, then her shoulder, until he reached the tiny strap of her dress. He carefully nudged it aside, until it fell across her shoulder. One more push and the blue fabric fell away, revealing one perfect, plump breast.

His mouth went dry with want. "Beautiful," he muttered through a throat that felt too tight to breathe.

Catching her mouth in another deep, wet kiss—where their tongues mated and danced, gave and took—he lifted a hand to her bare breast. She gasped against his lips and arched in response as he cupped her. When he caught her hard, tight nipple between his fingers and rubbed ever so lightly, she began to whimper, to sigh, to beg. "Nick, please…"

Needing to taste her—now—he moved his hand away, replacing it with his mouth. Giving her absolutely no warning, he covered her nipple and sucked quick, hard and deep.

She finally cried out, jerking against him. Grabbing his hair to hold him close, she shuddered, thrust and got what she'd been seeking. As she slid up and down against his erection, shaking with a powerful orgasm that literally rocked her whole body, he thought for a second that he was going to lose it and follow her over that peak. Fortunately, he was no inexperienced kid who couldn't keep himself under control.

"Yes, yes, yes," she whimpered, still shaking, her breaths choppy and her skin flushed.

She might have reached one milestone, but the race was a long way from over. Having tasted her, he couldn't wait to sample more. To feel more. To touch her as intimately as it was possible to touch a woman. "You taste so good," he whispered, still licking her, sampling her sweet, tender skin. He sucked and nibbled, knowing by her little coos and whimpers how hard to take it and when to back off. And the pressure began to build again—he sensed it by her cries and the desperate look in her eyes.

Needing more—and knowing she needed it, too—Nick reached for her knee and began stroking upward. Higher. Her legs parted, one lifting to invite further exploration. He slid his hand up that endless, smooth thigh as he continued to roll his tongue over her distended nipple, knowing he could have her coming against his hand within a few more inches.

Nick nearly shook in anticipation of letting his fingers glide to the very top of her leg. Touching her there. And *there*. Exploring all that smooth skin and finally sinking into the hot, wet place where he wanted to completely lose himself, knowing she'd get lost again, too.

Then Melody arched too far back and knocked the phone off the desk. It crashed to the floor, striking the hardwood with a crunch and a tiny ring. The sound was so surprising, so unexpected, that they both froze.

And, at almost the same moment, both realized what had almost happened in their hostess's office.

"Oh, this…you…here?" was all Melody could manage to say as she stared at him, wide-eyed, flushed, with her legs still limp and parted and one gorgeous breast exposed.

"Not here," he muttered, trying to breathe again. Trying to think. Wondering how far the sound of the phone might have carried down the hall and who might have heard it. "Let's go."

As if just realizing how revealed she was, Melody yanked at her dress, tugging it over herself. She slid off the desk, shimmying the rest of the blue fabric in place, covering those glorious thighs that he could almost feel wrapped around him.

"Go?"

"You live a lot closer than I do," he said gruffly. "Let's go. Now. While I think I can keep myself from ripping that dress off you and finishing what we started."

"We did start something, didn't we?" She sounded dazed.

"Yeah, I'd say we did." Reaching up, he rebuttoned his shirt and fixed his tie. "I don't want to be a name on a list to you, but damned if I want to wait, either. Not after…this."

He'd meant the words as a joke. Well, sort of. They'd been entirely true, but he'd meant to bring back that sense of wicked expectation that had gripped them a few moments before, hoping it would give them both the strength to get out of here and go straight to the nearest private place. Like her bedroom.

He should have known better. She deflated at his words, judging by the quiver in her lips and the shakiness of her hands. "How could we have been so stupid," she whispered.

"Nothing this good can be stupid." He reached for her, but she ducked away. "Melody, no regrets. You wanted this."

She nodded, admitting that much. "I did. I wanted it."

He pressed her. "And you want to finish it."

"I do."

He tried hard not to let her see his relief. Finishing with his tie, he tucked his shirt back in, wondering where in the hell his jacket had ended up. Spotting it on the floor, he bent to retrieve it, almost not catching what she said next.

"But I'm not going to finish it, Nick."

He quickly straightened. "What?"

She swallowed hard. "I can't. If anything, what happened just now proved everything I suspected. It's too much. Sex with you would be *too* good, not the quick, forgettable experience I need to help me get back in the saddle."

His jaw tightened, but he let her go on.

She laughed bitterly. "Believe me, I know I deserve good sex after three years without it, and part of me says I deserve *you*. But I'm a coward and I'm too screwed up right now to take you."

"You were doin' fine from where I was looking," he said, giving her a teasing smile. This had to be cold feet. Had to be. No woman could say no to something she so obviously wanted. So very badly. "I have to say, I kind of liked watching you *take* what you needed."

Color rose in her face.

"I *cannot* let this happen."

Before he could say a word—before he could think of a word to say—she spun around and dashed out of the room, taking off down the interior hallway as if she were being chased by a knife-wielding maniac.

Nick stood there, stunned, staring at the door, listening to the click of her heels on the hardwood floors of the house. They got softer as she got farther and farther away. And then they were gone completely.

CHAPTER SEVEN

MELODY HAD erotic dreams for the next couple of nights. Intimate, wicked dreams that woke her from her sleep, leaving her restless and needy. Shaking with desire. Hungry to finish what she and Nick Walker had started at the party.

She needed sex. Needed it badly. Needed it now.

The little gadgets she'd become accustomed to using during the last few passionless years of her marriage wouldn't do a thing for her. Not after the amazing things Nick had made her feel Saturday night in Rosemary's office. Having come so close to getting the real thing—a *lot* of the real thing, judging by the bulge she'd felt behind his zipper—she simply couldn't make do with any substitutes.

It was him or nobody. The real thing, or nothing at all.

She still grew hot and flustered just thinking about what had happened. Melody had always liked sex, but she'd never been a greedy little monster about it. Yet Saturday night, she'd rubbed up against the man like a stripper on a pole. Using him for her own fulfillment, she hadn't much cared whether he was getting off on watching her pleasure herself. Though…he *definitely* appeared to be.

How on earth could she ever face him again?

No faces necessary with certain positions…

"Knock it off, stupid," she muttered aloud. Thinking about naughty sexual positions with Nick Walker was not going to do anything to get the man out of her head, or relieve the pressure between her legs.

Judging by her bedside clock, it was nearly one in the morning Tuesday, so thinking about him wasn't helping her get to sleep, either.

C.C. and Oscar both heard her mumbling and came slowly walking up from the foot of the bed, where they'd grown accustomed to sleeping since the move to Savannah. She liked having them there, particularly since Bill had been a closet cat-hater who'd shut them out of their room every night. At least, back when they'd shared a room. That had finished *long* before their breakup.

"He does like cats," she admitted, scratching C.C.'s head and letting Oscar curl up under her neck. "But letting things get that far was still the dumbest thing I've ever done."

The cats just mewed, probably wondering why she'd woken them up at this time of night. "Make that the *second* dumbest thing I've ever done. Marrying Bill, that was number one. But starting things with Nick...*not* finishing things with Nick...oh, hell, I don't know which is worse!"

Nick didn't seem to be much happier about the way they'd left things. He'd called three times over the past few days. She'd ignored the calls and let her machine pick up. The first time he'd sounded almost...well, she'd say *hurt* if she'd been talking about anyone but a big, hunky cop. He'd wanted to know why she'd walked out, and what she planned to do now.

His second call had been flirtatious. Tempting. When he'd told her answering machine that he could still lick his lips and taste her nipple there, she almost came out of her chair and dove for the phone.

The third call, at around ten o'clock Monday night—a few hours ago—had been challenging. He'd nearly ordered her to admit how she felt. To stop hiding behind things like her divorce and a stupid joke sex list and be true to what she really wanted.

She'd been weakening after call two, but call three had strengthened her resolve. Taking what she wanted would be a very dangerous thing. Hadn't Saturday night proved that? Lord have mercy, she'd barely been able to breathe for ten minutes after she'd left Nick standing in Rosemary's office, all rumpled, disheveled, aroused and sexier than any man had the right to be.

That had been after some wildly unexpected foreplay. What if they ever actually made love? Well, she had the feeling the memories would interfere with more than a few nights' sleep. They could interfere with her whole life.

No. As desperate as she was for some mind-blowing sex, she couldn't have it. Not with Nick Walker, anyway. Not when having him would mean throwing her tangled emotions, already so raw and vulnerable, into an even wilder frenzy.

All that made perfect sense. It was the right thing to do and she meant every word. In her conscious hours, with her wits about her, when she was dressed in regular clothes, not a silky short nightie that scraped ever so delicately across the tops of her thighs like a lover's fingers, she would have been strong enough to resist.

But it was late. And it was hot. And her skin ached. And her body was so damn empty.

So when the phone rang—not surprising her, despite the late hour—she couldn't find the strength to ignore it. Somehow, her erotic mood made talking to Nick on the phone not merely acceptable…it made it wickedly desirable.

She almost didn't even realize she was reaching out when she closed her eyes and picked up the receiver. "You just don't give up, do you?" she answered, her voice thick and throaty, slow and sleepy.

He didn't say anything, probably surprised she'd picked up the phone, since she'd avoided his calls for two days.

"You're ruining my sleep, you know. I can't stop thinking about…everything."

Still nothing. Silence. Thick and mysterious. Sultry.

She laughed softly. "Okay, you can talk to my machine, but you can't talk to me? I thought I was going to be the one who'd be embarrassed. You do know how to confuse me, don't you?"

The silence continued. Only now it was interrupted by a rhythmic sound…an airy sound. Breathing. In. Out. Again. Pause.

A frisson of concern crawled up her spine. "Say something."

The sound continued, growing deeper, steadier. What had just a moment ago somehow sounded erotic suddenly scraped across her nerves, heightening her instincts and making her tense up. "Okay, I'm not kidding. Say something, please."

Still nothing. And now her uncertainty turned into fear. "This isn't funny. I want to know who this is. Right now."

The breathing now mingled with a funny sound, which she quickly identified as a little moan.

That was enough for Melody. Her heart racing, she shot up in the bed and slammed the receiver back into its cradle. C.C. and Oscar looked up at her curiously, but she couldn't console them. She wasn't sure she could console herself. Her breathing became ragged and her heart tapped a crazy, staccato beat.

Snapping her bedside light on, she quickly scanned the caller ID on her phone. The last call, from a few minutes ago, had been from an unidentified number. Remembering when each of Nick's calls had come in, she checked the listing and saw they'd all been from the same cellular phone.

So maybe this last time he called from home.

She hoped so. God, she hoped so. Because the thought that Bill was once again going to get his kicks by tormenting her with late-night phone calls or, even worse, unexpected visits was almost more than she could stand.

The thought of waiting for the phone to ring again drove her crazy. So almost without thinking about it, she dialed the cell number—*Nick's* cell number.

"Walker," he mumbled after the fourth ring, sounding as if he'd just woken from a deep sleep.

Damn. He apparently *wasn't* the heavy breather.

"Hello?" he said.

"I'm sorry," she whispered.

"Melody?" His voice was suddenly more alert. "Is that you?"

"It's me." She cleared her throat. "I'm so sorry I woke you. I just had a...a call. I thought it might be you, but you were obviously asleep. Weren't you? It *wasn't* you, was it?" Knowing he probably heard the hopeful note in her voice, she held her breath, waiting for his answer.

"No, it wasn't me. I called earlier, but I've been asleep for...what time is it, anyway?"

She couldn't keep the disappointment from her voice. "It's a little after one. I'm sorry I woke you."

"Don't worry about it. What did the caller say?"

"Nothing," she said, unable to keep the bitterness from her voice. "Just heavy breathing, like before."

"Before?" He instantly sounded more alert. "You've had problems with pervert callers before?"

God, this was embarrassing. "My ex was harassing me for a while after I moved here."

She could almost hear Nick go from sleepy, sexy man into cop mode. "How do you know it was him? Did you investigate? Notify the phone company?"

None of the above. "No. I just figured…"

"How long has it been going on?"

"I got regular calls the first month, but nothing for a couple of weeks now, since I changed my number."

"What if you figured wrong and it wasn't him?"

Mel was already shaking her head, not even willing to think that way. "I didn't. Look, I'm sorry I woke you. I know it's a work night. Go back to sleep."

"Is your door locked?"

"Yes," she said, feeling funny—a little tingly—about the protective tone in his voice. It was unfamiliar, that was all. She wasn't the type of woman who'd ever thought she'd want a big, strong man to protect her. But for a fleeting second, it was kind of nice.

"Does your building have an alarm system?"

"Absolutely. Rosemary's brother took care of it because I have a lot of photography equipment downstairs. I'm safe and snug."

He exhaled, but Nick's breathing comforted her, made her feel he was nearby. Close enough to touch…without the heartrending danger of actually touching the man.

Or the heart-pounding pleasure.

"Why haven't you been taking my calls?" he asked, sounding sleepy and relaxed again.

Turning the lamp back off, she settled down into her bed. "Because you confuse me," she admitted, being completely honest.

"I'm an open book."

"Hardly." The man was part hero, part grump, part cocky flirt and part edgy cop. And every part of him attracted her as she'd never been attracted to anyone before in her life.

"I don't accept confusion as an adequate reason to give up on someone," he said.

She wondered if he realized how serious he sounded. And how some women might take that seriousness.

Oh, God, a year from now, maybe she'd have the courage to do this. But not now. Not this month. Not this night.

If only she could make him understand. It was unlikely, but she still gave it a shot. "Can you imagine what it would be like to find an absolutely perfect bathing suit buried in the back of a clearance rack when you're shopping for a winter coat?"

"Huh?"

She supposed the clothes analogy was a bad way to start with a man. A woman would instantly have known where she was going. "I mean," she explained, "that there's such a thing as really, *really* bad timing. Like finding the adorable pink-and-white bikini for half price when what you need is a nicely tailored, slimming, black leather trench coat."

"So why can't you buy the bathing suit *now* and have it around for next summer when you need it?"

A typical man response.

"Because it might be out of style by next summer. You might have moved to Antarctica and have no need for a bathing suit," she explained, wanting him to understand. "You might have had a crappy winter and eaten your way through a cold February and a rainy April and there's just no way you're going to fit into a bikini by June. Don't you see? The timing is all wrong."

His voice was low and scratchy when he finally replied. "You can eat your way through February and April and I'd still fit you as well as I would right now."

Oh, God. The man fought dirty. Because now all she could imagine was how well they'd fit. How he looked right now, lying in his bed, shirtless, sleepy, aroused. So utterly sexy.

"I can't do this. Not now," she whispered. "I'm sorry I bothered you."

"It wasn't a bother," he said, not accusing her of being a coward, even though that's exactly what she was. "Make sure your doors are locked."

Still worried. That was nice. "I will."

Not giving him a chance to say anything else that might weaken her already paper-thin resolve, Melody hung up the phone. And prepared for a long, sleepless night.

AFTER HANGING UP from Melody's surprising late-night call, Nick got out of bed and pulled on a pair of jeans and a T-shirt. Fredo, his purebred mutt, watched lazily, hardly lifting his head from the end of Nick's king-size bed. "Dog, I'm gonna start shutting the door if you're going to keep sneaking up onto my bed. What's wrong with that nice big doggie pillow I bought you?"

Fredo didn't even spare a glance for the oversize pillow, which he'd once deigned to pee on, just to make sure no other dog got what he, himself, didn't even want. Still sprawled at the foot of the bed, the mutt watched Nick with soulful eyes.

"Man's best friend," Nick muttered. *His* best friend might as well have been flipping Nick the finger as he lazily chewed on something clasped between his furry front paws. Something that looked suspiciously like…

"And stop chewing my shoes!" Nick grabbed his sneaker from the dog's paws, wiped a line of drool off on his jeans. He pulled the shoe on, muttering about bad dogs and heavy-breathing ex-husbands the whole time. "I *do* like cats, you know, no matter what *she* thinks," he said, glaring at the dog as he grabbed his keys, his gun and his cell phone and strode out the bedroom door.

That got a reaction. Fredo gave a mournful little yelp. Glancing over his shoulder, Nick saw the dog hop down and hang his head as he trudged over to his dog pillow.

"You think I'm stupid? I know you're gonna be on the bed before I'm out the front door."

Looking deeply wounded, the dog threw himself down. But by the time Nick unlocked the front door of his apartment, he heard a telltale squeak from his headboard that said Fredo had again commandeered his favorite spot.

Nick muttered about his bad luck with dogs and women throughout his drive to the historic district of Savannah. He was still muttering a half hour later as he parked outside Melody's building, holding a foam cup filled with crappy but hot coffee from a local twenty-four-hour market. It was late, about two in the morning, and the street was quiet. Empty. Most of the residents parked behind their own buildings at night, so there were only a few cars on the block.

Good. That'd make it easier to spot anyone suspicious.

Sipping his coffee, he put his window down, welcoming in the late-night air, which taunted him with a whisper of coolness that would be long gone by eight o'clock. He leaned back in the driver's seat, settling in for the night. It'd be a long one, but what the hell. He wouldn't have been able to sleep, anyway. Not when he'd be worrying about Melody until morning.

He hadn't liked hearing the fear in her voice. Hadn't liked it one bit. "Damn him," he muttered, staring up at the second floor of her building.

He would love to get his hands on her ex-husband, the man who'd left that beautiful, vivacious woman nervous and jumpy, unsure of herself and unhappy. Like the one he'd first met a few weeks ago…the one he'd thought had disappeared for good.

Almost wishing he'd brought Fredo with him for company, he sipped his coffee again, settling farther into the seat. Never taking his eyes off the upstairs window, he immediately noticed when the curtain shifted. Then a silhouette appeared there.

A female silhouette.

Melody stood in the window. She looked down at him, her hair loose around her shoulders. He could barely make out some light-colored fabric floating around her body, a filmy nightgown, most likely.

Sleep was definitely out of the question now.

But hopefully not for her. Nick nodded once, silently urging her to go back to bed. Telling her she was okay, that she could rest easy, because he wasn't going anywhere.

She understood. A small, faint smile widened her lips. And from down on the street, he made out the words she mouthed.

Thank you.

Nodding, Nick continued to sip his coffee and watch the night shadows lengthen over the next couple of hours, until it was nearly dawn. Staying up all night on a stakeout was usually easy because he had Dex either in the car or within radio reach of his position. This was different. Being alone on the silent street left him vulnerable to his own imagination. To the image of Melody standing in her window, wearing that filmy bit of nothingness disguised as sleepwear.

To the way she'd look now, lying in her bed, her hair spilling over her pillow.

To the way she'd feel when he was inside her.

"Damn," he muttered, trying to refocus his thoughts as the night wore on.

Unfortunately, his solitude also gave him a chance to worry. The thought of Melody's ex deciding to follow up his sick phone call with a visit made his entire body tense. "You'd better hope you covered your tracks, you cowardly son of a bitch," he muttered, picturing her ex-husband.

By six o'clock, with no suspicious activity at all, Nick began to relax, confident that Melody was okay. The whole block had been dead silent for hours and she'd hopefully gotten some sleep.

Since the first streaks of orange and gold were appearing on the horizon, he figured it was time to go. Time to get out of here before Melody woke up and felt obligated to come downstairs. With his luck, she'd still be wearing her nightgown and Nick didn't think he was a strong enough man to see *that* close up. Not unless it was for the three seconds it would take him to tear it off her.

Adjusting his seat, he was about to reach for the ignition key when he realized the passenger door had opened.

"Morning," she said. "I brought coffee."

He shifted his gaze and saw Melody sliding into his car to sit beside him. "You didn't have to do that." Then, his throat tight, he added, "You're not even dressed."

And she wasn't. A silky robe dotted with little pink strawberries covered her from her shoulders to the tops of her thighs, but her incredible, mile-long legs were completely bare. As were her feet, so he could see the hot-pink polish on her toenails. His mind filled with the image of the flimsy nightgown she most likely had on underneath the robe. *Lord have mercy.*

"I'm decent."

She might be, but his thoughts definitely weren't.

"And I won't be long. I'm going right back inside." She handed him a small, foil-wrapped paper plate, then a mug of steaming coffee. "I couldn't remember if you took cream, but I figured after an all-nighter you'd probably want some sugar. And I also made you an unburned bagel."

He chuckled. "No crêpes suzette?"

"You're lucky you got the bagel. I'm not much better in

the kitchen than Rosemary." Nibbling her lip, she reached for the door handle, then softly added, "Thank you, Nick. You didn't have to do this. In the light of day, I'm embarrassed that you did, especially because I'm sure you have to go to work today." Looking at him with blatant honesty in her blue eyes, she continued, "But last night, looking out the window and seeing you here, well…I felt very safe. I appreciated it."

Nick wasn't comfortable with the hero role. He never had been. And gratitude was the last thing he wanted from *this* woman, in particular. So he shrugged off her thanks with a frown. "Forget it. Anybody would have done it. Don't make more of it than it was. I am a cop, remember?"

"Don't tell me *anybody* would have gotten up in the middle of the night and sat outside my building so I could get some peace of mind. It was very nice of you."

Nice. He hadn't been called nice in…hell, longer than he could remember. Maybe never.

A loner, a loser, a lost cause—those were the words he most remembered people using about him…about *all* the Walkers, really. So hearing this woman call him nice made him just a mite uncomfortable. Because the last couple of times a woman had mistaken him for nice, he'd been hurt, lied to or royally screwed over. By his high-school girlfriend, who'd really been in love with his brother. By the woman he'd married, who'd been pregnant with somebody else's kid. Most recently by Angie, who'd tried to worm her way into his case files by way of his bed.

"I'm not a nice guy," he muttered, reminding them both of that fact. "You said so yourself."

"I didn't mean that," she countered, obviously remembering her comment. "You've been very nice to me on a couple of occasions."

"Don't get used to it."

She chuckled. "Well, back to Mr. Grouchy. I've met him on a couple of occasions, too. Now I feel better."

He couldn't resist her infectious good mood. Offering her a small smile, he sipped the coffee. *Awful.* But he managed not to grimace. "Hey, with last week, this is our second breakfast date, isn't it?"

"Thought you didn't date."

"You keep tricking me into it," he said, shaking his head mournfully. "You're a wily one, Melody Tanner. I'm going to have to keep my guard up around you. Next thing you know, you'll be calling about your leaky pipes and seducing me with a juicy pot roast and a home-made apple pie."

She giggled, all hint of fear, of sadness gone from her face. Which made the cramp in his leg and the stiffness in his back from sitting in the car for the past four hours completely worthwhile.

"I told you I can't cook. So if I were going to do such a thing, it'd have to be with Kentucky Fried Chicken and Krispy Kreme doughnuts."

"That's almost as dangerous."

"I know. But I promise, I won't trick you into any more dates against your will. Your reputation is safe with me." She made a cross-your-heart thing and lifted two of her fingers.

Nick had lived in this town long enough to know what *that* meant. "Scout's honor?"

"I wasn't a Girl Scout."

His eyes widened. "I thought that was illegal in Savannah. All small females living within a hundred miles of this place have to be Girl Scouts."

"I traveled too much as a kid."

She traveled too much to be a Girl Scout. It made him wonder what else she'd missed out on. Not just because of her lousy marriage—but because of her crazy childhood. "I'd like to hear about it sometime." Shoving an inner voice of caution down deep into his subconscious, he added, "Maybe while I check your pipes and try to resist the smell of fried chicken and twenty crispy, creamy cholesterol points pretending to be breakfast food."

Her smile faded and she began to shake her head. "I can't." Her voice grew softer. "I meant what I said…"

"Don't talk to me about that damn list again," he growled.

"Not that," she whispered. "It's not about any stupid list. It's about…"

"The bathing suit and the leather coat?"

She thought about it, then slowly nodded.

"So you're just a coward, huh?" He'd meant to spark a reaction. Not have her agree with him.

"Yes, I am."

He nearly kicked himself for using the word. "You're not a coward. It took a lot of guts for you to get through that party Saturday night when your *friends* kept surprising you."

"Surprising? Yeah, I guess that's one way to put it. Though humiliating is probably a better one."

"You going to forgive them for that?"

"I did. They called as much as *you* did the past few days."

She fell silent, not opening the door but not looking as if she was ready to share his coffee and nibble his bagel, either.

"Mel…"

"Nick…"

"Sorry," he said with a laugh. Needing to know for sure, he added, "You really are a coward about *some* things, huh?"

"'Fraid so. And you're at the top of the list." Wincing, she added, "My things-to-be-careful-of list. Not the…*other* one."

"Fuck the other one," he couldn't help muttering.

Her rueful laugh told him she wasn't offended. "Uh, I don't think so."

Well, hell, didn't this blow? For the first time in forever, he'd started to let his guard down around a woman who seemed to want him every bit as much as he wanted her. But the timing was wrong.

Timing. What a stupid word.

Still, he could almost hear the thoughts going through her mind. Hadn't those same thoughts gone through his own whenever he'd even considered getting involved with a woman? The doubts and anger and hurt from the past whispered the loudest when the future looked the most uncertain.

"Okay," he finally muttered. "But just so you know, I'm not going to let you get away with that for too long."

"Meaning?"

"Meaning," he explained, reaching over to brush a strand of her hair behind her ear, "that I suspect there's not a cowardly bone in your body. I'm buying it this time, but pretty soon, honey, you won't even be able to sell that line to yourself."

ATTORNEY JONATHAN RHODES HAD two deep, unwavering loves in his life. One had given him his greatest success, and the other had, in effect, taken it away.

His political ambition had been driving him for as long as he could remember. It had made him excel in law school and, when he'd graduated, had helped him in his quest to become a hotshot in the Savannah legal community. He'd then used his young Turk reputation, letting it parlay him into a congressional seat soon after his thirtieth birthday, achieving the first step of his political dream.

Yes…that political dream had been about to begin, with his first campaign just a small step on the journey. He'd had it in the palm of his hand, seeing his brilliant future laid out in front of him like a red carpet unfurling into eternity.

Then it had happened. His *other* favorite thing had cost him the seat in congress. It was lucky for him that the cops who'd caught him with that hooker up in Washington had been bribable, so the full story had never come out. Bad enough to have to leave D.C. without ever going any further than the house of representatives. But the whole truth could've done a lot worse, including preventing him from returning to his legal profession in Savannah.

So now his political dreams were shelved for the time being, but he was making the best of it. Savannah was home, *his* home of loyalty and suspicion, old values and new ambitions. Of secrets and of sex. He was making waves as the somewhat infamous former congressman turned defense attorney. And he still had time to fully explore his other obsession.

So it wasn't entirely a bad thing to be home, he reminded himself Thursday as he stood in his office looking out toward the Savannah River. Especially when he imagined what he might have missed out on if he'd been up in Washington.

He might not have met *her,* Melody Tanner. The Peacock Feather Girl.

He'd recognized her right away. Considering he still had a poster-size print of her hanging among his collection in a secret room in his apartment, it wasn't too surprising. Her hair was different and she'd aged a bit. She was also a little more filled out than she'd been in her Luscious Lingerie days.

But there was no mistaking those blue eyes that had so perfectly matched the bra and panties she'd been modeling. Not to mention that perfect, creamy skin that had complemented the underclothes so very well.

When they'd been introduced, he'd heard her name and had known for sure. It was her…the model from the lingerie catalog he'd lusted over and dreamed about for years.

It was fate, really. Fate or karma or mere good fortune had brought her into his life, just when he'd given up on ever getting what he had desired for a very long time.

Jonathan had tried to track her down once, a couple of years ago. He'd hired a private investigator to find the former officers of Luscious Lingerie. Due to some embezzlement at the highest corporate levels, the company had gone bankrupt shortly after that infamous catalog had been released; the famous peacock-feather set that might have saved them had reportedly never even gone into production.

A former VP accused of the embezzlement had put him on the track of Melody Tanner in exchange for some free legal work, and he'd gone looking for the model. He'd found her agent, but by that time, she'd retired and had taken herself out of the public eye. No one would tell him where she'd gone. He'd given up, eventually forgetting about her. Until Saturday night, when he'd met her right here in Savannah.

Yeah. Fate. What he most desired was right here in his home city. And judging by the surprise—shock, almost—on her face when they'd been introduced, he'd definitely intrigued her. All that remained was to act on that interest, and await his opportunity. He'd put it off for a few days, not wanting to appear too eager. But now, well, he simply couldn't wait any longer to seek her out.

"Melody," he murmured as he looked at the business card she'd given him at the party the other night.

She was a photographer, looking to drum up business. He was a lawyer looking to spruce up his professional portfolio.

Sounded to him like a match made in heaven. Which was why he picked up the phone and dialed her number.

CHAPTER EIGHT

MELODY DIDN'T KNOW where she got the nerve to agree to meet Jonathan Rhodes for lunch on Friday. She'd been very surprised to hear his voice on the phone Thursday afternoon. He'd had to repeat his name a couple of times for it to sink in that another of the men she'd fantasized about all those years ago was calling her.

She almost turned down his invitation because, no matter what she'd thought of the man six years ago, she knew now that there was absolutely no spark of attraction between them. When they'd shaken hands at Rosemary's party, she'd felt absolutely nothing. No tingle. No curiosity. No flash of danger or naughtiness at having once thought about having sex with him.

Her mind, her libido, her waking thoughts and her dreams, every bit of her—except her actual body—was thoroughly involved with Nick Walker. There was no room for anyone else.

In the end, though, that lack of spark was the reason she agreed to meet with Jonathan. Because having no interest in him—unlike what had happened the moment she'd met Nick—might be significant. Maybe feeling no serious connection meant she could go for something with him and feel absolutely no regrets when she walked away the next day.

Yeah. He'd be safe. Unthreatening. Someone she could

have a one-night stand with to get her confidence back without a single regret or repercussion afterward.

If only she had *any* interest in having sex with the man.

"But I don't," she reminded herself as she pulled her car into the parking lot of her favorite Mexican restaurant Friday at noon. She'd suggested the place for their meeting, wanting to be in safe and familiar surroundings. And half wondering if returning to the scene of the crime—the place where she'd made the list—might make Jonathan Rhodes a little more interesting.

It was worth a shot, anyway, just to see if something developed. No, she didn't have any illusions that Jonathan could make her stop fantasizing about Nick Walker, but it could be enlightening to see if she could muster even a slight interest in anyone else.

Besides, even if it didn't, it was worth meeting the man because he *could* end up being a client. He'd mentioned wanting new professional photographs for his entire practice.

If her Men Most Wanted list wasn't worth meeting Jonathan Rhodes for, a job most certainly was.

"Well, hello there, Miss Tanner, all alone today?" she heard as she entered the building, savoring the cool air-conditioning.

Recognizing the restaurant owner, who'd made her feel so uncomfortable last week outside the café, she almost wished she'd chosen another location for today's lunch. If she'd been thinking straight, she would have. The man's smile was already too intimate, knowing. As if he suspected she'd come here today because she couldn't stand not to see him. "I'm meeting someone."

"The dark Amazon, the little curly-haired one or the blonde?" he asked with a suggestive wag of his eyebrows.

"Oh, not one of my girlfriends," she admitted. "I'm meeting a man, Jonathan Rhodes. Do you know if he's here yet?"

His smile faded the tiniest bit. "No. No lone gentlemen here yet." Retrieving two menus, he led her toward a small table just inside the door and pulled out her chair.

Sitting down, Melody accepted the menu and thanked him.

"A margarita on the rocks?"

She shook her head. No alcohol today. She needed all her wits about her for this lunch date…er, meeting. She wanted to be sharp and alert to all her senses so she could determine once and for all if there was any sizzle whatsoever between her and the number-two man on her list. "Sweet tea, please," she said.

"And a chicken burrito? I know it's your favorite."

Surprised, she cocked her head to the side. "You really pay attention to your customers, don't you, uh…"

"Call me Ricky." He leaned down and looked from side to side, as if making sure he wasn't being overheard. "And I only pay such attention to the *very* special ones."

Not sure whether he was trying to flirt, or just being a good host, Mel stammered, "Well, uh, thanks. But I think I'll wait to see what my companion's going to have before I order."

He immediately straightened and gave her a stiff nod.

The front door opened again, a stream of harsh sunlight flooding across the reddish tile floor, blinding her for a second. Then a man appeared in the doorway. Jonathan Rhodes.

He was still handsome, with thick blond hair, green eyes that probably twinkled when he smiled. Good body. It was no wonder the man had gotten elected to congress. No wonder also that he'd attracted enough women to ruin himself in D.C.

"Melody," he said as he strode over to her table. He bent down as if to kiss her, and she quickly stuck out her hand.

"Nice to see you, Mr. Rhodes."

"Please, if we're going to be working together, I insist that you call me Jonathan."

Working together. That sounded promising.

During the next hour, Melody found herself quite enjoying the witty attorney. He was a Savannah native, so he had lots of stories to share. The broad hints he gave about defending some Mafia types who lived for danger made her wonder if Jonathan, himself, didn't have a thrill-seeking streak.

Well-spoken, attentive, charming…he was everything she'd imagined him to be six years ago when she'd put him on her fantasy list. Only…she didn't want to have sex with him.

There was definitely no spark. While it might be easy to walk away from him the morning after, with no regrets and no looking back, there couldn't *be* a morning after with a man who did absolutely nothing to light her fire the night before.

Damn. Only Nick Walker did that. And he wouldn't be easy to walk away from. He'd be the kind she'd be chasing after.

"So," he said after they'd finished eating and he'd called for the check, "you really think you can handle the individual shots as well as a group portrait for our entire office? As much as I loathe legal advertising, it does seem to be the name of the game these days, and we need some high-quality portraiture."

"Absolutely. My studio is large, and I have state-of-the-art equipment." Thank God the judge had left her with the equipment she'd already had, and enough money to fund the rest and still eat for a couple of months.

He lifted his half-empty glass, dripping with condensation. "Is your studio convenient for you? Close to home?"

She laughed. "Very convenient. I live right upstairs."

His eyes widened and he immediately lowered his glass. "Really? That's wonderful. I'd like to see it."

Since the man had to have felt the same lack of spark Melody did, she decided to assume he meant her studio. *Not* her home. "Of course," she said. "Come by some afternoon and I'll show you around. We can talk about lighting, backgrounds, and lay out a plan that would fit in with your campaign." Keeping her tone professional rather than hopeful, she said, "If you're working with an ad agency, maybe you could bring their rep with you." Wishful thinking, that she could get an in with a local PR company so quickly after setting up shop, but it was worth a try.

"I haven't hired anyone yet," he said. "But I'd like to see your studio anyway. How about now?"

She started in surprise. The man certainly was anxious. But if he was going to give her a week's worth of portrait work, now was absolutely fine. "Of course. Let's go."

It was only after they'd left the restaurant and she was driving home that she had the first hint of concern about bringing Jonathan—a man from her sex list—to her studio. Not that she had anything to fear from him; he'd been nothing but polite since the moment they'd met, despite his reputation as a womanizer. But would *she* find *him* more tempting knowing there was a comfortable bed right upstairs?

Apparently not, she decided a half hour later as the two of them stood in her studio, looking through backdrops and examining different lighting effects. Because there was still no attraction. Zip. Zilch. Not happening, now or ever.

Professionally, though, things looked good. Jonathan seemed very pleased by what he saw. He took particular interest in the small platform Mel had set up for children's shots. The man was happily rubbing his hand across the soft green fabric draped over it. "Much nicer than tacky fur," he murmured.

She nodded, surprised he understood. "Exactly! I want to

offer something a little above the ordinary. No bare-bottom babies on white fluffy rugs." Walking over to a shelf piled with props, toys and accessories, she showed him a stack of folded bolts of fabric. "I have lots of different colors and textures."

He followed her over, staring at the drape cloths, a smile on his face. Then he reached out and ran his fingers over the material. For the first time, she noticed how slender and elegant-looking his hands were for a man.

His eyes drifted closed as he stroked one square of fabric—a brilliant blue satin. "This is lovely, isn't it?" he said. "I imagine it would feel just delightful against the skin."

He finally opened his eyes and met her stare. Melody paused, wondering if he was making a move. A man who stroked mere fabric with such delicate precision would probably stroke a woman in much the same way, wouldn't he?

Too bad Mel didn't want to be stroked. She wanted to be *handled*. By someone with big, strong hands. A *particular* someone with big, strong hands.

Suddenly uncomfortable, Melody walked over to the door leading to what had once been a second bedroom in the apartment-turned-studio. "I'll do most of the shots digitally, and my printer is top of the line. But if you want any traditional black-and-whites, I do have a darkroom."

"Fine." He sounded distracted. Then he shook his head once, as if thrusting something out of his mind. "I'm sorry, I just remembered I have an important call to make." He reached for his cell phone, then frowned. "Oh, no, my battery's dead."

"Not a problem. You're welcome to use mine," she said, gesturing toward the front desk where she did her paperwork.

He shook his head. "No, I hate to be so much trouble. And I definitely don't want to tie up your business phone."

As if to underscore his concern, the phone rang. With an apologetic look, Melody answered, not about to risk missing any potential work. Unfortunately, it was a wrong number.

"Listen, it's not a big deal. If you can tell me where the closest pay phone is," Jonathan said after she'd hung up, "I'll get out of your hair."

"I really don't mind...."

"No, absolutely not. I'm not going to keep you from getting any important calls." He tilted his head to the side. "Unless, do you by any chance have a phone upstairs I could use? In your apartment? That way I won't tie up your business phone."

A hint of uneasiness crawled up her spine. She'd just met this man...going up to her apartment with him seemed a bit risky. Despite how professional, charming and friendly he'd seemed— and the fact that she'd once thought about having spontaneous sex with him if she ever had a chance—he was still a stranger. Ted Bundy had seemed charming and friendly, too. "Uh..."

"Of course not," he said, waving his hand as if he'd asked a stupid question. "You need to be down here working and you certainly don't want to waste fifteen minutes upstairs babysitting someone who needs to use your phone." He frowned, though the hopeful look hadn't left his eyes. He was being polite, but he obviously still hoped she'd help him out.

The thought of the company portfolio he wanted her to do, and the realization that she didn't have to be up there with him—since he'd given her a plausible excuse—helped her decide. "You know what? I do have work to do. But you're welcome to go upstairs and make your call." Brushing past him, she walked into the reception room and opened a small wooden door. "These are the back stairs. They go right into my kitchen. The phone's on the wall by the fridge. You can take as long as you need."

"You're an absolute lifesaver," he said, his green eyes nearly glowing with appreciation.

Remember that when it comes time to pay for your portraits.

"It's no problem at all. Just come on back down when you're finished with whatever you have to do."

NICK HAD PROMISED himself Friday morning that he was going to focus on all the other stuff going on in his life, instead of spending any more time thinking of the woman who'd whirled into it so recently. Melody had occupied nearly every thought in his head for the past several days, when he should have been thinking about a lot of other things. Like work.

"You still going to follow up with the drugstore clerk to see if he's come up with anything else on the tourist murder?" Dex asked as Nick paced back and forth in front of his desk.

"Yeah."

"Going to talk to the store owner again?"

He kept pacing. "Sure."

"Going to be able to concentrate on *anything* other than Melody for the rest of the day?"

That made him pause. Slowly turning on his heel, he eyed his partner, who was leaning back in his chair, his arms crossed over his chest. Dex's small smile and the knowing look on his face said as much as his words had. Obviously Nick hadn't done a very good job focusing on the here and now of his job instead of on the where and when of his love life.

"I know how you're feeling," Dex said as he uncrossed his arms and sat up in his chair. "Rosemary had me tied up in knots from the minute we met."

"Seems to me she still does," Nick mused, practically daring his friend to deny it.

Dex didn't even try. "Yeah." Then he cracked a tiny smile. "But being tied up isn't always a bad thing."

Not even wanting to know if his partner was speaking literally—because he absolutely didn't want to know the details of anybody else's sex life—he could only stare.

Dex chuckled. "Kidding." Rising from his desk, he picked up his sport coat and slid it on. "I'm taking a couple of hours off this afternoon. Rosemary's not happy about something and I'm going to try to find out what it is."

Nick didn't want to think about some of the things Rosemary could be unhappy about…like maybe she'd realized she was involved with a guy who would never in a million years let a rich woman take care of him. That he was never going to be the tuxedoed gentleman who could escort her to all the historical society balls and charity events.

Dex was a plainspoken, down-to-earth cop, and he always would be. He hoped Rosemary found a way to deal with that reality. Or else that she ended it now, before either of them got any more hurt.

"Anyway, why don't you take some time off today, too? Go scratch your itch so we can get some work done around here?"

Nick stiffened, not liking the tone in Dex's voice. Melody was no itch. She wasn't just a piece of ass he could have and forget about, any more than *he* wanted to be that for *her*. If that were the case, the two of them could have done something about her sex list and spent the past several days in bed together.

No, he couldn't say he was ready for anything long-term or serious at this point in his life, but a short-term or one-night fling wasn't going to cut it with that particular woman.

Judging by the speculative gleam in Dex's eyes, his friend knew it, too. Before Nick even had a chance to lay into him, he lifted his hand and held it, palm out. "Forget it, I just wanted to see how you'd react. Obviously Rosemary was right and there's a lot more going on between you and Melody than some list."

"Don't remind me of that damn list," Nick muttered.

"Hey, look who you're talking to. At least *your* girlfriend only has three names left on hers."

"She's not my girlfriend."

"Whatever. Anyway, with two of Melody's guys having croaked, you're a lot better off than I am. Rosemary's still got five, which she loves to throw in my face whenever we fight."

Nick knew Dex's girlfriend only had four names remaining on her list, since she'd already checked one off. But he wasn't about to tell his friend that. Then his partner's words sank in. "What do you mean two of them croaked?"

"Didn't I tell you?" Dex said as he walked around his desk, straightening it up. Dex had the neatest desk in the squad. "Rosemary told me that's what the clandestine breakfast meeting was about last week. The men on Melody Tanner's sex list are dropping dead." He shrugged. "Guess it worked—Rosemary's B.S. murder story got you over there, and got Melody there, too."

Then, saying goodbye to everyone on the floor, Dex left, leaving Nick standing alone, thinking over his friend's words.

Melody never had come clean about how Rosemary had tricked her into meeting him. Now he understood why. Her sex list had turned into a death list? He almost laughed at how ridiculous it was, figuring Rosemary must be even better at manipulating people than he'd thought, if she got her best friend to buy that one.

Then he remembered something: the names of the other men who'd supposedly been killed. "Son of a bitch," he muttered. He'd been in the top five with an old four-hundred-pound chef who'd choked on a meatball?

Either the woman had had some very diverse tastes, or she'd wanted the guy for his famous chocolate cake. Hoping it was the latter, Nick decided to find out. After all, there had been a couple of deaths. And there was a connection…Melody Tanner. So it was his duty as a cop to check into it, right?

He kept telling himself that as he cruised the few blocks from the station to her address, practically on autopilot since he'd been coming here every night this week. She hadn't even realized he'd been stopping by to be sure her bastard ex didn't decide to show up in person to harass her. He usually didn't stay long, only long enough to be sure everything looked secure. He'd also had a friend on night patrol swing by on occasion. As far as he knew, she hadn't even noticed, which was exactly how he wanted it.

As he parked outside her building, Nick's attention was caught by movement at an upstairs window, on the second floor. He had a hard time looking at that window without picturing Melody standing in it, wearing her nightgown.

Entering the main door, he prepared to go up the wooden steps to the second floor when he heard her talking. *Downstairs.* Turning toward the sound, he pushed through a door with a small sign for her studio and found her at a reception desk, using the phone. "Yes, I do have an opening for that time, Mrs. Vanderbrenton. I'd *love* to meet the triplets."

Triplets? Three crying kids to photograph? Yow.

He must have made a noise or something, because suddenly she looked up and saw him standing there. She went silent midsentence, and a pretty pink flush filled her cheeks.

He winked. She blinked. Then whoever she was talking to must've started gabbing, because with a hard shake of her head, Melody returned her attention to her caller.

Nick took the opportunity to mosey around, checking things out. Strolling through an open interior doorway, he found himself in another room, where she apparently took the photos. It was huge, with lots of lighting from the windows lining the front wall. Big black drapes were coiled beside them so she could apparently darken the place up whenever she needed to.

Nick had no knowledge of cameras or photography stuff. As far as he could recollect, the only times he'd sat for a picture in the past ten years had been for his military ID, and his police one. But even he realized there was a good chunk of money invested in the equipment taking up every bit of spare space in the room. Cameras, lights, lenses and tripods dominated the left side. And on the right, she had an office area, with an elaborate computer setup and a printer that looked bigger than the copying machine at the precinct. So she was apparently very serious about this photography thing.

Well, if anyone had experience with camerawork, he supposed it'd be a former model.

Glancing through the doorway toward the front desk, he heard her saying something to her caller about the toddlers. *Toddler* triplets? He shuddered.

Involved in her conversation, she appeared to have forgotten he was there, so he took the opportunity to watch her. The woman was incredibly graceful. Even with a pencil stuck behind her ear and her hair flopping over her face as she bent over an open appointment book, she held herself with style. Again, probably that modeling background.

He wanted to talk to her about that—wondering what it must have been like growing up on camera. He'd considered checking her out on the Internet over the weekend, just to see if he recognized any of her commercials or photos—besides the peacock feather one. He didn't think he was a strong-enough man to seek out that particular shot. But scoping her out had seemed too intrusive. Stalkerish. So he figured he'd wait and let her satisfy his curiosity whenever she got rid of the idea that it was too risky to see him anymore.

Which, it appeared, was going to be right about now. Because she'd finished her call and was hanging up the phone.

He held up her coffee mug, which he'd washed after going home Tuesday morning.

"You came here to return my cup?" she asked with a skeptical look.

"Well, yeah. But this isn't entirely a social visit."

She walked around from behind the counter and joined him in the studio, carefully balancing a camera lens he'd been looking at a minute ago. "Oh? Do you need your portrait done?"

His jaw dropped. "Me? No picture taking for me, thanks."

Frowning, she grabbed his chin and turned his face from side to side. "Why not? You've got great bone structure."

Yeah, he had great structures elsewhere on his body, too, which he'd be much more interested in having her handle, but he wasn't going to go there. Yet.

"I think you'd be a really good subject."

"I didn't come here to talk about photography, either," he said, suddenly uncomfortable at the way she was sizing him up. Hell, a lot of women looked at him, but Melody wasn't giving him a sexual once-over. She was almost evaluating him…like a horse she was thinking about riding.

He'd rather she looked at him as a *man* she was thinking about riding.

He needed a shower. A cold one.

"Why did you come here, then?" she asked, still sounding cool and relaxed. But when she turned away and walked over to fiddle around with some screens hanging from the ceiling—apparently backdrops—he noticed her hand shake.

So she wasn't entirely calm and relaxed. *Whew.*

Nick was about to ask her about the two dead men on her list when she pulled at the front screen, a plain brown one, and allowed it to roll up to the ceiling. When he saw what was behind it, he muttered a curse.

"What?" she asked, glancing over in curiosity.

"Who in God's name would want their picture done with *that?*" he asked, staring at the backdrop. The Bird Girl statue.

"Believe it or not, several people have asked if I had this, including the woman I was just talking to."

Shaking his head in disgust, he muttered, "The mama of triplets wants to pose her babies in front of a picture that was on the cover of a murder book?"

Melody shrugged. "I think *Midnight in the Garden of Good and Evil* was as much a Savannah book as it was a murder one."

"Maybe," he admitted. "But it's overdone."

She nodded. "Agreed. However, if somebody wants to pay me to take a picture in front of it, I'd be happy to take them out to Bonaventure Cemetery and do it in front of the real thing."

"They moved it," he said. "Too many whackos. It's at the Telfair Museum now."

Sounding curious, she asked, "Did you work on that case?"

"Before my time. But some of the guys in the precinct did."

Tugging on the offending screen, she let it roll up as well, revealing a plain white screen behind it. Then, without looking over her shoulder, she said, "So if we're done with the small talk, why don't you tell me why you're here."

Hiding a smile, he admitted, "It's about your list."

Melody whirled around and pointed her index finger at

him. "Don't mention that again unless you want to get thrown out."

With a helpless shrug, he said, "Official business, ma'am. I think I need to hear a little more about your obsession with Charles Pulowski of Chez Jacques."

Her eyes closed briefly and she moaned. "Rosemary..."

"Dex."

"Yes, but who told Dex?"

"Rosemary."

"Exactly." Swiping a frustrated hand through her hair, Melody said, "It was his chocolate volcano cake."

"I figured as much."

"I told you I'd never even met the man."

"I remember," Nick admitted, strolling over to her desk. Leaning against it, he added, "But I've been worried, anyway."

"Why?"

"Well, the company I'm keeping on that list doesn't exactly inspire a whole lot of confidence in your taste in men."

She smirked. "You're *off* the list, remember?"

"You just keep telling yourself that." He crossed his arms over his chest. "I mean, first that cheating TV anchor, then the sleazy ex-congressman. And now a seventy-year-old chef who wouldn't even have fit through your door?"

"Cheating?" she asked, ignoring the rest of his comment.

"That Manning guy," he said. "There was a domestic call to his house a year ago."

Her eyes widened. "Was he abusing his wife?"

Shaking his head and grimacing, he explained, "Uh-uh. She'd apparently caught him with his pants unzipped one too many times and put something mighty unpleasant in a trophy cup he'd gotten for winning some boat race. She then tried to brain him with it, without even, uh, cleaning it out first."

She grimaced.

"He keeled over. I wasn't kidding about the heart attack," Nick added. "I'd bet for a couple of days there, when he was in the hospital, his wife was hoping he would widow her and save her the trouble of divorcing him."

Frowning, she muttered, "But this is Savannah, so when she did divorce him, I bet she *still* got the house."

Before he could ask her what she meant, he heard a noise from the reception area. Melody obviously heard it, too, because her eyes widened and her mouth dropped open.

"Somebody else here?"

She nodded, her face getting pale for some reason. When he looked through the open doorway, he understood why.

"I'm done, and I can't thank you enough, Melody." Jonathan Rhodes walked through the reception area but stopped in the doorway to the studio. Continuing in his staccato-fast lawyer voice, he added, "You've been a godsend, but I really have to go now, so I'll be in touch soon, okay? Very soon." The man's face was red, as if he'd just exerted himself, and his hands were jammed in the pockets of his suit coat. He looked disheveled for this time of day on a weekday.

Nick swallowed. Hard.

"Uh, okay," Melody finally mumbled. Before she could say anything else, the man was gone.

As for Nick, well, he couldn't speak at all. Because the air seemed to have gotten very thick since he'd last inhaled.

"He, uh, was upstairs," she said.

Nick stiffened, even his jaw got tight.

"He needed to use the phone."

He cast a quick glance toward her reception counter, where a phone stood all functional and everything.

Melody followed the look. "He was using the phone in my apartment because he didn't want to tie up my business line."

"Right. What *did* the pervert want to tie up?"

Her gasp was audible. "Look, I know what you're thinking."

He doubted it. Because all he'd been thinking since the minute Jonathan Rhodes had appeared in the doorway was that Nick should have taken Melody to bed Saturday night and not let her up again. Then she wouldn't have had time to even consider hooking up with any other man on her list. Nor would she want to.

"But it was just business," she was saying. "He wants me to do some portraits for him and his associates in his law firm."

"Associates?" he asked, not even trying to keep the skepticism from his voice. "The slimeball operates all alone doing his dirty work getting scumbags off on technicalities. And he apparently spends every dime he has on women. I hear he's got money troubles."

That seemed to really surprise her, because Mel's forehead furrowed in confusion. "You're sure?"

"I'm sure. I interact with enough local attorneys to know. Now, why was he really here? And why didn't you admit it?" Shaking his head, he added, "Tell me you're not even *thinking* about acting on that insane list and jumping into bed with him."

She didn't answer. Instead, she simply stared. And kept right on staring. Which made him feel about two inches tall for even suggesting it.

"I apologize," he said roughly, not accustomed to saying the words to anyone. "I already know you better than that."

She nodded once to accept the apology. "He said he wanted portraits, so we met for lunch. When we got back here he asked to use my phone but didn't want to tie up this one. He went right up those stairs, probably stepped two feet into my kitchen and stood there talking on the phone until he came back down again."

Nick glanced at the slightly open doorway, which concealed a back set of stairs. Confused, he murmured, "The room in the front of the house, directly above us—isn't that your bedroom?"

"Yes, why?"

"Because I saw someone in that window when I pulled up."

Melody tilted her head, staring at him as if to see whether he was serious. "I'm sure you were mistaken."

He didn't think so. But he'd made enough accusations today. He didn't want her thinking he was making any more. "Maybe," he admitted. "So, back to these dead guys…"

"Rosemary was playing on my susceptibility to conspiracy theories," Melody explained. "She knows I loved *The X-Files.*"

He wouldn't have guessed that about her. Rubbing his jaw, he replied, "Hmm…pretty scary stuff for a chicken."

She chuckled, as he'd intended her to. He just couldn't resist that laugh, the sparkle in her eyes and the way one side of her mouth went up a little higher than the other when she smiled. He had to taste that smile, be part of that laughter.

Not giving her a chance to duck away from him, he stepped close and dropped one hand onto her shoulder. With the other, he cupped her cheek, tipping her face up to his. Her eyes flared as she realized he was about to kiss her. Only the memory of the confusion in her voice Saturday night at the party made him pause, to give her a chance to back away.

No backing away. Instead, she moved closer.

So with a helpless moan, he covered her mouth with his and kissed her until he forgot his own name.

MELODY WALKED like a zombie through the rest of her day after Nick left. She wasn't sure how she'd remained standing during the hot, deep, carnal kiss he'd laid on her in the studio. She *hadn't* been able to remain upright when he'd ended that kiss, given her one intense look, then walked out.

The man made her weak in the knees. It sounded clichéd, but it was still true. She'd collapsed into a chair after he'd gone.

He'd said a lot in the kiss…that he wanted her and he was getting impatient. That he knew she wanted him, too.

He hadn't truly believed she'd been interested in Jonathan Rhodes, or anyone else. How could she be when she wanted to make love with Nick more than she'd wanted anything else in her life? Including everything she'd left behind when she'd divorced Bill.

God, maybe she was being a fool and she should just go for it. Maybe once she had him, the frenzy would diminish, not increase. Hell, maybe the man sucked in bed.

"Ooh, sucked," she murmured that evening as she went into her bedroom to change her clothes.

Yeah, she could definitely think of some places on her body that she'd like him to suck. Starting with her tongue, which he'd so delicately tasted during their kiss today.

It was no use…he would be amazing in bed, she knew it. Any man who kissed like he did, who touched like he did, who said incredibly erotic things like he'd said to her on the street the morning after they'd met, would have to be incredible.

Any man who'd sit outside her building watching over her all night would be just as thoughtful, just as tender. Just as amazing when making love.

So do it, have it, take it.

Do him. Have him. Take him.

And then forget about him?

She'd have better luck trying to forget to breathe.

Rosemary would do it. For that matter, probably even Tanya would. They'd say to hell with what happens the morning after, get tonight while the getting's good.

Pulling her shirt over her head, she tossed it onto her bed, then kicked off her shoes and shimmied out of her slacks. While doing so, her gaze fell on her bedside table, where she'd dumped a lot of junk when she'd moved in last month.

The drawer was open a little. That was funny because, as far as she knew, she hadn't opened the thing since she'd emptied a whole shoe box full of stuff into it several weeks ago.

Opening the drawer, she poked around inside, finding nothing but the same six-months-old magazines, some lip balm, a bottle of hand lotion and a dusty condom packet that had probably expired before the turn of the century. Nothing terribly exciting. Certainly nothing a hotshot attorney would be interested in. So probably she was imagining things.

But the thought that Nick really had seen Jonathan Rhodes here in her bedroom earlier today wouldn't leave her mind. So out of simple curiosity, she looked around, searching for anything out of the ordinary. It didn't take long to find something: the closet door was open, and she didn't remember leaving it that way earlier. She always kept it tightly closed so the devilish duo didn't go in there and brush up against all her clothes, leaving streaks of kitty fur in their wake.

Walking inside, she looked at the racks of clothes but saw nothing amiss. At least, not until she noticed the pile of scrapbooks on the shelf, which contained remnants and memories from her modeling days. The books had been neatly stacked, all facing the same way, but now the one on top was turned around. Someone had obviously been looking through it. There was only one person it could have been.

Eww. Jonathan Rhodes *had* been nosing through her stuff.
It absolutely gave her the creeps. What could he have been up
to?

The suspicious part of her mind instantly went to the
worst-case scenario. She suddenly wished she hadn't been
marching around in her bedroom in just her underwear, in
case the man had planted some kind of spy device. A little
weirded out at the idea, she reached into her hamper and
yanked out the ratty, torn T-shirt she'd worn when cleaning
her bathroom the day before, and some dingy, torn jeans to
go along with it.

Once clothed—knowing she was protected from any potential perv cams—she reached for the scrapbook. Almost
afraid to look, she pulled it down, opened it and stared at the
first page.

It was totally empty.

"You bastard," she muttered, hardly able to believe it.
Racking her brain to remember what had been on the page,
she glanced at the date on the inside front cover. Somehow,
she could hardly muster any surprise when she realized which
book this was, and what *should* have been on the front page.

"I'm beginning to hate peacock feathers," she muttered.

Because *that* original photo had been on this page. She'd
held on to it for a number of reasons, beyond keeping track
of her career. Someday, when she was old and broke, she
might need to accept one of the offers she'd gotten for the stupid lingerie from fanatic perverts all over the world. The offers had ranged from $20,000 to the chance to "ride the stick"
from a porn star who was reputed to be *very* well endowed.

Having the original photo as proof of the authenticity of
the lingerie would be important should she ever decide to sell
it. Frowning in disgust and still staring at the empty page, she
was suddenly struck by an awful thought. Nick had said

something about Jonathan Rhodes being broke and slimy. Certainly the man had been less than honest with her today, and if he'd been creepy enough to go through her things and steal a photo from her scrapbook, might he not also… "Oh, God."

Dropping the book to the floor, she jerked her attention to the back of the closet, where several plastic bags covered her better clothes. Some of them were air-sealed, like the ones used to protect wedding gowns. Only, one of those air-sealed bags wasn't flush with the others. It was sticking out just a little.

And it was empty.

She couldn't even breathe. If Nick hadn't said something about Jonathan Rhodes being in her bedroom—if she hadn't noticed the open drawer, the open closet, the turned-around scrapbook—well, she might not have noticed the missing lingerie for weeks. Which was probably what the slimeball had counted on.

Mel didn't think, didn't plan, didn't hesitate. Instead, when she stared into the empty bag and realized the son of a bitch really had stolen her valuable lingerie, she marched into her bedroom. Sticking her feet back into her shoes, she grabbed the phone book. "You'd better be listed, you prick," she snarled under her breath.

He wasn't. But she didn't give up. A trip downstairs to her office and one Internet search later and she had the man's address. Which was exactly where she headed.

Ten minutes later, when she found the address—a high-rise on the edge of the historic district—she was still fuming. Still enraged. Still ready to rip that slimy man's head off. To *think* she'd ever even considered having sex with him!

Paying no attention to the cars whizzing by or to the people milling around outside, she illegally parked and marched into the building. As she got on the elevator, she did glance side to side and noticed a couple of dour-looking men frowning at her. They were probably wondering about the looney woman dressed in rags that smelled distinctly of bleach, muttering threats under her breath. She ignored them.

Unfortunately, the men got off on the same floor and turned in the same direction down the corridor. They passed the first three doors, too, which made her a bit nervous. She half wondered if they were following her, though it seemed ridiculous.

The nervous feeling increased exponentially when they stopped exactly where she did, at unit number 4E. Jonathan Rhodes's apartment…where the door stood wide-open.

"Ma'am, do you have business here?" one of the men asked, still looking at her with suspicion in his eyes.

Oh, great. One of Jonathan's Mafia clients? *Maybe this wasn't such a great idea, Mel.* "Um…"

"I'll take it from here guys."

She knew that voice. Oh, she definitely knew that voice! She just wasn't sure how she felt about it. Should she be grateful he'd saved her from being fitted for cement shoes? Or humiliated as hell to run into Nick Walker when she was wearing a ratty, torn shirt and dirty jeans and muttering about wanting to kill a man. "Nick, I, uh…"

"What are you doing here, Melody?" he asked, his tone firm and his expression serious as he stepped to the side to allow the other two men into the apartment.

Too disconcerted to turn the question around and ask him the same thing, she blurted, "I need to see Jonathan. He…I think that man *stole* something from me today."

Nick said nothing. Instead, he stepped out into the hallway, closing the apartment door behind him. "I'm sorry, you can't see him." He crossed his arms and watched her intently, remaining several inches away from her, despite the electric current snapping between them—as it always did.

Finally, clearing his throat, he admitted, "Jonathan Rhodes is dead, Mel. Someone murdered him."

She sucked in a shocked breath, not believing what she was hearing. "I…I can't believe this…."

"It gets worse."

"How could it possibly get any worse?"

"Well," Nick admitted after releasing a long, slow breath, "I think he was wearing your underwear."

CHAPTER NINE

FINDING OUT a man you'd just had lunch with was dead was bad. Learning he'd been murdered was worse. But hearing that he'd been wearing your practically brand-new pink Victoria's Secret bra-and-panty set with the pretty little rosettes and white lace trim that had cost almost sixty bucks took things right into nightmare territory. As Melody absorbed the shock of Jonathan Rhodes's murder, she couldn't help wondering why the bastard couldn't have been wearing the yellow undies that had looked so cute in the catalog but had made her skin look sallow once she'd tried them on.

Well, there was one thing to be thankful for. He hadn't been wearing her valuable peacock set. Which left her with a question: what had he done with it?

"So, you're absolutely *certain* the lingerie wasn't blue?" she asked Nick as the two of them sat in the front lobby of the apartment building. They'd come downstairs shortly after she'd shown up, both to get out of the way of the other investigators and because Melody had almost had a panic attack over having stumbled onto a murder scene. Nick had been all business at first. But when he'd seen her start to shiver, he'd slid an arm around her waist, giving her all his strength, just as he had the day they'd met, when he'd moved her furniture. And at Rosemary's party, when Paige had made her awful announcement. And again early Tuesday morning when he'd parked outside her building.

Whether he'd admit it or not, the man was a born caretaker. She'd never in her life felt as safe as she did during those few minutes when he'd held her against his side, gently leading her to the elevator, then into the lobby. When they'd sat down, he'd stayed close, with one hand on her shoulder for reassurance.

"I'm not color-blind, sweetheart," he murmured. "You did say you had pink underwear like the ones I described. And somebody had written the initials MT on the label."

She nodded absently. "Yes, it probably is mine, though I didn't notice it missing. I'm not in the habit of putting my name in my panties."

"There were initials on the tags of all the lingerie we found in Mr. Rhodes's 'special' closet. I think he liked to keep track of where he collected each of his trophies." Nick sounded furious and she could see the tension in his jaw. His anger could have had something to do with the murder of a prominent citizen in his district. But she knew it didn't.

He was outraged on her behalf. The thought warmed her, even as she grimaced, not wanting to think about Jonathan's "closet." Good Lord, the handsome, suave former congressman had had a thing for stealing women's underwear...and *wearing* them.

"That is so gross. Please burn them when you're done with them. Lord, that man is lucky I didn't come over here and catch him in them...I would've killed him." She realized how bad that sounded the second the words left her mouth. Talk about self-incrimination.

Nick sighed heavily and shook his head. "Do me a favor, okay? Don't say anything like that around any of the other investigators. They don't know how bloodthirsty you are."

"Oh, boy, I'm sorry," she mumbled, feeling her face grow hot. "I didn't have *anything* to do with this, Nick, I swear to you."

"I'm sure you didn't." Then, in a low voice, added, "But I do need to know where you've been for the past several hours."

An alibi? She needed an alibi? This was turning into a nightmare. A bad movie at the very least. "I was at the studio all afternoon. I made a couple of marketing calls after you left."

When he pulled a small pad of paper out of his pocket and started writing notes, she realized just how serious this situation was. It hadn't quite sunk in before—the first thirty minutes after she'd arrived, she'd been too grossed out about what Jonathan Rhodes had been wearing to actually contemplate that the man was dead. That someone had *killed* him.

She didn't know how he'd been killed. She didn't *want* to know. Particularly since she really didn't want to picture her pretty pink-and-white Victoria's Secret bra-and-panty set covered with brains or guts or anything.

Taking a deep breath and visualizing her entire afternoon, she continued, "At around three, I called Rosemary…Dex was there when she answered, and he left a few minutes later. I was on the phone with her for over forty-five minutes." Not trying to hide her sarcasm, she added, "I was telling her how *very* much I appreciated her letting Dex know about the dead guys being on my list, so he could tell you, so you could come talk to me about it."

He chuckled, but Melody didn't feel like laughing. Because she suddenly thought about the list. The dead guys. God, Jonathan Rhodes made *three*. How utterly, totally creepy. Men she'd once wanted to have sex with really *were* dropping like flies all over Georgia.

A fleeting curiosity about whether Bill had been taking his cholesterol medication crossed her mind, but she quickly squelched it. She wanted her ex humiliated and broke. Not dead.

"What happened after the phone call?" Nick asked.

"Believe it or not, I had a walk-in at around four. A couple who wanted an engagement photo and information for their wedding. I was with them until about five-thirty. After they left, I locked up, went upstairs to change, saw that something was missing and came right over here." She glanced at her watch. It was now seven o'clock. "Wouldn't leave much time for any, uh, murderous side trips."

Some of the concern eased from his expression and, beside her, she felt his body relax a little bit. "You should be fine. I don't know the time of death, but by the looks of it, I'd say it was sometime during your session with the engaged couple." He snapped the book closed. "You will give me their names and phone numbers once you go back to your studio, right?"

"Absolutely. The bride was named Jade Maguire…I knew her years ago in high school. I have her number and Ryan's— the groom's—contact information written down on my desk."

After he tucked the notebook back into his pocket, he almost visibly left his cop role behind and again became Nick, the man. She nearly sighed in relief.

"One more thing I have to ask," he said, his voice deceptively quiet. "You said you hadn't noticed the pink set was gone, so that's not what you came over here looking for." He leaned back on the sofa, crossing one ankle over his knee. "What was it that you were missing?"

Melody wondered briefly how to explain the peacock lingerie. It would probably sound ridiculous that she'd come marching over here chasing after a bra and panties that she truly hated. But they *were* worth a small fortune. "He took a picture from a scrapbook," she admitted slowly.

His brow shot up. "That's all?"

"Well, no…he also took the blue bra-and-panty set I was wearing in that picture."

A tiny smile appeared on those sexy lips. "Uh…was it peacock blue?"

"Oh, crap."

He knew. Nick knew she was the Peacock Feather Girl. He'd probably seen the picture that had made it look like she was hardly wearing anything at all. How utterly embarrassing.

"It's okay, I doubt anyone upstairs recognized you," he murmured. "I certainly didn't. Dex mentioned it."

"Good old Rosemary," she mumbled, shaking her head.

Then Nick straightened and leaned forward, dropping his elbows on his knees. "Melody, I think it is possible Jonathan Rhodes took your very famous lingerie, as well as the pink set he was wearing. He had a—hell, I don't know how to describe it—I guess you'd call it a shrine or something, in his secret closet where we found the body. There was a padded hanger, with candles all around it, and a poster-size blowup of *that* picture on the wall behind it."

"Oh, my God," she groaned. No wonder he'd mentioned the cops not recognizing her: he'd been trying to make her feel better about the fact that every officer in Rhodes's apartment had probably seen that poster. Hopefully he was right and they *hadn't* recognized her from the photo that had made her leave the modeling world behind out of sheer embarrassment. Not to mention the need to have a normal life.

A normal life with the prick with the drill. That hadn't worked out so well. As for the embarrassment thing? Yeesh. Not so well, either.

"I guess, if you think about it, the peacock set really would be the Holy Grail of women's undies to a true collector," he said. Then, looking curious, he asked, "How did you end up with it, anyway? Do models usually get to keep the stuff they've modeled?"

"Not usually. But Luscious Lingerie was a pretty small company and they were having serious financial problems at the time. They offered me the lingerie I'd modeled since they couldn't come up with my full salary."

Just as well. If she'd had the money, Bill would simply have ended up with that, too.

"Gotcha," Nick said. Then he continued, "Anyway, the peacock lingerie is not in his 'shrine.' The hanger was empty and I would have recognized it if it were among his…collection." His tone revealed his distaste for whatever else had been in Jonathan Rhodes's closet. Aside from Jonathan Rhodes.

"Okay," she mumbled, staring at him in confusion and disbelief. "So you think *two* different people stole my underwear today? Jonathan and whoever killed him?"

He stared at her. "That seems far-fetched, doesn't it?"

"Well, yeah!"

"Which is why," he said, his tone even and his expression grave again, "it's fortunate that couple walked into your studio this afternoon."

IF NICK HAD THOUGHT the murder of a tourist in an antique shop had been bad, it was nothing next to someone offing a former congressman dressed in a bra and panties. The whole city was talking, speculating, whispering. If somebody wrote a book about this case, he just prayed they had the good sense not to put a graveyard statue on the cover.

So far, he'd kept Melody out of the spotlight. He wanted

to keep it that way. The woman was lucky that engaged couple had come into her studio completely by chance on Friday afternoon. Because even after they'd confirmed her story—and the timing—his lieutenant had kept a suspicious eye on the owner of the stolen underwear.

According to the medical examiner, the victim had been shot approximately two to three hours before his body was discovered by a friend of Rhodes's, who had a key to the apartment. Between Nick's own visit to the studio, Melody's phone call with Rosemary, and her walk-in clients, Melody Tanner was in the clear. He didn't even have to evaluate why he was so relieved by that…his interest in Melody was already much too intense to be convoluted with any suspicions of murder.

He'd never really believed her capable of it, anyway. Other than the fact that she threatened murder every ten minutes, Nick didn't think Melody had a violent bone in her body. And frankly, with her friends, he didn't blame her for the threats.

"How's Melody holding up?" Dex asked, interrupting Nick's train of thought. The two of them were back at the precinct, going over the crime-scene report. It had been four days since the murder and everything else had slid to the back burner for those in the precinct.

"I don't know. I haven't seen her since Friday night."

His partner's brow shot up. Hell, Nick couldn't figure it out himself, so he sure couldn't explain it to Dex. But for some reason, Mel was avoiding him, back to not taking his calls unless she absolutely had to. There had been two necessary phone conversations: one to give him the information on the engaged couple, and the other to confirm that her pink lingerie had been taken. She'd cut both calls short.

"You sure that's wise?"

"She's not a suspect," Nick said, immediately stiffening. "Her alibi's good."

"I know that," Dex's said in the calm, reasonable voice that had been known to make criminals blab anything, thinking he was their best friend. Unlike Nick's piercing, silent stare that intimidated them into doing the same thing. "I'm saying, we still haven't found her rather infamous underwear. What if it wasn't a random robbery by whoever killed Rhodes? What if the person who shot him had that motive all along…to steal the things Rhodes had already stolen from Miss Tanner?"

Nick raised a scoffing brow. "Murdered for a pair of panties and a bra? That's pretty out there, even for Savannah."

"I'm just saying…there wasn't much else missing from the apartment. It's possible the perp grabbed a few things on the spur of the moment to cover up his real objective. And since there was no sign of forced entry, we have to assume it was someone Jonathan let into the apartment. Maybe someone who had an interest in the same types of things."

"Like wearing famous women's underwear?" Nick's tone revealed his skepticism.

"Yeah."

Ridiculous. Outrageous.

Possible?

"Shit," Nick muttered. "I'd hoped she was out of this altogether."

"I don't think she is," Dex said. "Aside from her lingerie, there's still the list connection."

"You don't *really* believe somebody's knocking off men she once talked about having sex with, do you?"

Holding his stare evenly, Dex murmured, "I wasn't the one who had the Atlanta PD fax over the report on the death of that golfer, Kenny Traynor."

Nick shifted his gaze, wondering how his partner had found that out. He didn't wonder for long—Dex was a quiet observer. He eventually found out *everything.* "Just covering bases."

Dex didn't let up. "Which means *you've* considered it, too."

Yeah. As much as he hated to admit it, he *had* considered the possibility that the deaths were connected. But he hadn't wanted anybody *else* to know he had considered it…not even Dex. He wanted Melody well and truly out of this thing, completely untouched by the three strange cases that were, in a small way, actually connected to her. Through the damn list.

"The Atlanta police ruled it an accident," he explained. "A bizarre one. Traynor died in the locker room of a big country club when he decided to stick something *other* than his finger through a small hole in the wall."

Dex wasn't successful at hiding a flash of amusement. "A *really* small hole?"

"Uh-huh."

"Poor guy." Schooling his features back into his normal, reserved expression, Dex continued, "So did somebody on the other side of the wall get a little offended and take a butcher knife to…it?"

"No," Nick said, marveling yet again over the stupidity of his fellow man. "He, uh…*bumped* into some frayed wiring. Since he was still wet from his shower, the poor dumb bastard went and electrocuted himself."

Dex closed his eyes and shuddered. Even Nick shifted in his pants, as he had when he'd first read the report…the whole thing—not the skimpy details released to the public.

"And the chef?"

Rubbing a weary hand over his eyes, Nick leaned against the side of his desk. "You saw him. It looked pretty basic to me. The guy was throwing meatballs into the air and catching them in his mouth like some people do with grapes or peanuts."

"But meatballs don't go down as easy," Dex said.

"Exactly. It was late, he was alone and drunk. Accidental choking."

There was that stupidity quotient again. It must have been what kept the gene pool thinned out since the black death had pretty much been wiped out and there were no more mastodons running around to take care of natural selection.

Dex frowned and crossed his arms, looking as confused as Nick about this convoluted set of circumstances. Could there possibly be a connection between the men on Melody's list, or with Melody's *underwear,* and three weird deaths, for God's sake? Or was it all some huge, bizarre coincidence?

If this were a book or a movie, Nick would roll his eyes and say there was no such thing as that much coincidence. But in his life as a marine and as a cop, he knew coincidence was alive and kicking and more bizarre than any fictional scenario an author could dream up.

"What did Rosemary say about this whole mess?" Nick asked, curious to know how Melody's friends were handling the situation.

"She's worried. She's been going over to Melody's apartment, trying to talk her into coming to stay at her place."

"She sure has the room," Nick said, his voice deceptively quiet. He had never talked to Dex about Rosemary's wealth... but the size of her house made it pretty obvious. "Speaking of Rosemary...everything okay? You find out what's bothering her?"

Dex's mouth tightened a bit. If Nick didn't know him so well, he might have missed that small sign of tension.

"She really wants me to get to know her father. She's having a family dinner tomorrow night."

He said the words *family dinner* like someone else might say cannibalistic feast.

"Well, have fun," Nick murmured, wishing his friend luck.

"About Melody…I guess she's as stubborn as Rosie. She's staying put in her apartment."

Stubborn. Yeah, the woman *was* that.

"Does Rosemary really think there's any kind of connection here?" Nick asked. Though Rosemary was a pain, she was sharp, and she knew Melody better than just about anybody. Though, not as well as Nick wanted to know her.

"She thinks it's *probably* a strange coincidence, but if it turns out not to be, we should look at Melody's ex-husband."

"Her ex?" Nick had been curious, but he hadn't gone down that road yet. Melody's ex-husband seemed more like a cowardly heavy-breather than a killer.

"Yeah. I guess their split was pretty…unpleasant, and Melody initiated it. Rosie thinks this Dr. Todd guy might be angry and desperate enough to plot some pretty wild revenge."

"Like murder?" Sounded crazy. But he'd heard of stranger scenarios. "Is the guy unbalanced enough to kill guys his ex-wife once fantasized about?"

"If so, you'd better start wearing your vest, since there's only two of you left on that list," Dex said. His tone was serious, but his lips quirked. "Speaking of which, three down and only one to go before you win by default."

"Bite me."

The comment didn't even phase his partner. "You going to follow up on the ex?"

Nick nodded slowly, thinking over the ramifications. Of the ways in which Melody Tanner really could be caught up in this situation. "What if this person wasn't doing it out of jealousy, but rather out of some kind of revenge? Wanting to set Melody up for it? If she hadn't had those walk-in clients Friday, she probably wouldn't have had an alibi."

"Which makes her ex even more interesting."

Nick nodded, agreeing completely. Melody probably wouldn't like it, but he had no choice. He was going to have to pry into her past, her private life. And see what he could dig up about her divorce from Dr. Bill Todd of Atlanta.

"I don't want to do this to her," he murmured, realizing it was entirely true.

"I know."

"God knows I wouldn't want someone poking around in the charred remains of my marriage."

Dex remained silent.

Nick sighed heavily, dropping his head back and looking up at the ceiling. He really had no choice. He was going to have to investigate what had probably been a very painful and ugly time in her life.

"But not now," he whispered.

"Hmm?"

He straightened, giving his partner a look that dared him to argue. "I said not now. Tomorrow's soon enough."

And it was. Whatever ugly circumstances surrounded Melody's divorce, they'd still be out there tomorrow.

For tonight, however, he just wanted to *be* with her. Without any of the other garbage that had been surrounding them practically from the moment they'd met.

Just…be with her.

IT HAD BEEN a few days, but as time went by, instead of starting to recover from what had happened to Jonathan Rhodes, Melody still couldn't get it off her mind. She'd never known anyone who'd been murdered. Never known anyone who'd *known* anyone who'd been murdered!

Sure, like everyone in America, she'd seen cop shows and movies where bodies flew, blood spattered and victims fell prey to ax-wielding psychos wearing hockey masks. But she'd almost become immune to the concept—even to the word. *Murder.* Somewhere along the way, she'd stopped grasping the enormity of it.

She grasped it now, though. Between the time Rhodes had left her studio Friday afternoon—with her underwear tucked into his pockets or down his pants, *eww*—until that night when she'd gone to confront him, someone had gone into his apartment and shot the man dead.

Oh, yeah, she definitely grasped it.

The media was all over the story, particularly Channel 9's Angie Jacobs and Drake Manning, who were the last reporters to socialize with the dead man. That had been at Rosemary's party, where they'd been chatting so normally with Rhodes and with Melody. At first, the duo had played up the connection, accentuating their own personal grief. They'd each taken on the role of distraught former friend.

Until the underwear stuff had started coming out.

That'd definitely changed things. Both reporters had backed off on the personal angle, going in for the kill and digging up anything they could on the former congressman's "perversions." Jonathan Rhodes had gone from prominent attorney and friend to twisted sicko and pariah between two eleven-o'clock newscasts. *Rabid dogs.*

Melody had stopped watching the coverage. And now, finally, on Tuesday evening, she was almost starting to feel herself again. At least she wasn't jumping at every noise in the old building in which she lived. She was the only tenant—since the unit right upstairs from hers was vacant—and every creak or moan in the foundation of the old townhouse had startled her all weekend.

Now, though, she realized as she made herself a light dinner, she was doing okay. At least she was finally putting the image of her blood-streaked underwear from her mind and not stewing so much over where her peacock panties had ended up.

Oh, she was still mad about it. But it was out of her hands. She had to think that whenever the police caught up with Jonathan's killer, they'd find out what had happened to Melody's underwear, too. Hopefully *not* after it had been worn by another sicko guy with a penchant for silk and feathers.

Pouring herself a glass of wine, she took a sip and began to fill a pot of water. She'd decided on penne pasta for one. When she heard a knock on her front door, she smiled and added more water to the pot, figuring it would instead be pasta for two. It appeared she was once again going to have a dinner guest. That was no surprise. Ever since Friday night, Tanya, Rosemary and Paige had taken to popping over for any number of reasons, none of which were the *real* reason.

In truth, they were supporting her however they could. Not to mention trying to get back on her good side after their loose lips about the whole list thing.

Expecting to see Paige's wide smile and a homemade cake, or Tanya's jet-black hair and a bottle of Jack Daniel's...or Rosemary holding the latest editions of every fashion magazine, Melody walked to the front door and pulled it open.

No wide smile. No cake. No liquor and no magazines.

Just pure, living, breathing temptation.

"Nick," she breathed.

"You should have asked who was here, since you don't have a peephole."

Yes, she should have. At least then she might have been able to mentally prepare to see Nick Walker again in the flesh. Oh, such big, yummy flesh.

Feeling heat flood her cheeks, she instinctively reacted to his words…and her own hungry response to his nearness.

She shut the door right in his face.

Leaning her forehead against the doorjamb, she sucked in a few deep breaths, ordering her pulse to stop racing and her heart to stop doing that crazy, out-of-rhythm jerking in her chest.

He knocked again.

"Who is it?" she whispered, more in a stall for time than to make him laugh.

But laugh he did. "That's better. Now let me in."

Lifting her wineglass to her mouth and gulping down a big sip of merlot, she slowly did as he asked.

"Hi," he said.

Unable to help herself, Melody raked a thorough look over him, from bottom to top. Nick was dressed the same way he'd been on the day they'd met at the diner—in tight, soft, perfectly broken in jeans that rode low on his lean hips. A hunter-green T-shirt emphasized his thick arms and wide shoulders. His cheeks were a little stubbly since it was well after five o'clock, and his hair was rumpled, as if he'd run his hand through it in frustration at least ten times today. But what really did her in was that devastating half smile on his delicious lips as he stared at her from the hallway.

Oh, Lord. Oh, mercy. *Oh, yum.*

Being away from the man hadn't lessened the driving, overwhelming hunger she'd felt for him from the moment they'd met. It had only made it more intense. She'd been an utter fool to think not answering his calls or trying to avoid him would make him easier to forget. After all, hadn't she already acknowledged—at least to herself—that he was unforgettable?

"This is a surprise," she finally said, shocked to realize she sounded perfectly normal. Not all crazy-hungry-horny-desperate like she felt.

"I didn't call first since I figured you wouldn't answer, anyway. Are you going to invite me in?"

How about I just do away with the words and rip off my clothes here and now? Is that a good enough invitation?

Managing to keep her clothes on and her libido constrained beneath what was left of her dignity, she stepped back and ushered him in. He immediately looked around the living room of her apartment, his gaze assessing. "Nice." He stepped closer to one wall, where a number of her framed photos were displayed. The ones she was most proud of. "Yours?"

"Yes."

He peered closely at a shot she'd done of an old Jamaican woman in a brightly colored sarong, complete with beads and rooster claws around her neck. "I think I've seen her in Colonial Park Cemetery."

"Probably. She holds services there. She didn't even charge me for the first shot. After that I had to pay her."

Nick chuckled, understanding immediately. That was Savannah. "You're good."

"I hope other people agree with you," she said as she locked the front door. "So far, there aren't crowds lining up to let me prove it."

He continued walking around her apartment, checking it out. "It's a lot brighter than most places around here. I like the woodwork."

She followed his stare, seeing the short divider wall separating the living and dining rooms, so tons of light from the big front windows could spill throughout the apartment. Opening up the space by removing most of the wall between the two rooms had been her suggestion.

To the left, where there'd once been a closet, a pantry and a laundry room, there was now one big work space, eliminating the need for one wall and two doorways. Meaning more light, more air, more room to appreciate the beautiful aged oak floors that had been resurfaced and brought back to their warm luster.

"Brian and Rosemary's father let me have a say in the renovations up here as well as downstairs," she said as she put her wineglass on the coffee table. "There were Spanish-speaking workmen tromping through here for the first few weeks I was in town and I had to camp out in the empty apartment upstairs for a while." She smiled. "With Paige's furniture, as I'm sure you recall."

"Oh, yes, I certainly do," he said, his tone wry. "Rosemary's folks must like you a lot."

"They were like my family when I was growing up. I spent more time at Rosemary's house than I did at my own, sometimes spending days at a time there. I pretended she and Deidre were my sisters and Brian my pesky, spying brother."

Most people would chalk that up to typical childhood stuff, when kids would practically take up residence in each other's houses during long, endless summers. Somehow, though, Nick saw past that to the truth she hadn't been revealing. "A real home, huh? A way to get away from the commercials and the photo shoots and the parties? An escape from the life everyone must have thought was perfect…everyone but you?"

Her jaw dropped. How the man had gotten that much information out of what she'd thought was a relatively normal comment, she had absolutely no idea. But he was one-hundred-percent dead-on.

Yes, Rosemary's family had been a little better off than the average middle schooler's. Still, their lives had been *way* more normal than Melody's. At least there was a mom and a dad, a sister and a brother in Rosemary's house.

Melody had only ever had directors and photographers. Designers and PR experts. And of course, through it all, her mother. Jessica Tanner hadn't been what anybody could describe as a Betty Crocker type. More like a Joan Crawford.

"How did you know that?" she finally asked, wondering if she was really so easy to read. Had the resentment she'd felt toward her mother for all those years *not* gone away, as she thought it had? Did something in her eyes betray the fact that she'd wanted to jump for joy when Jessica had moved to Europe with her new husband, and had barely even called for the past several months…so she had no idea about the divorce? Or had she just had a "poor little rich kid" tone in her voice?

"Me and my brother spent most of our summers at my cousin Virgil's house when we were kids. Maybe not for the same reasons you stayed at Rosemary's. But maybe not so far off, either." A shadow darkened his eyes. "It was sort of a normal life at his place. Definitely better than being home alone with our dad when our mama was at work."

His tight tone and the stiffness of his shoulders told her there was a wealth of meaning below his comment, and she wondered if he'd meant to reveal so much. Probably not. Nick was a contradictory man—at times flirtatious, at times dead serious—but so far, he hadn't been the type to reveal his feelings. Other than desire, of course.

So, no, she doubted he was trying to start some kind of "whose childhood sucked more" conversation with her. Which was almost too bad. Because as much as she loathed the thought of telling anyone about her crazy upbringing, she'd like to know more about Nick's. Every time she met him, she grew more and more curious about what made him tick.

Remembering something he'd said once—about his hometown being hell—she couldn't help wondering what Nick's life had really been like. What had prompted his shotgun wedding at the age of eighteen, and his quickie divorce? Had that thrust him into his military career, where he'd obviously charged full steam ahead into the danger zones from which others were fleeing?

She wanted to know. Wanted to understand him because then, maybe, she'd be able to make sense of the almost brain-zapping attraction she'd felt for Nick Walker since the first time she'd laid eyes on him. Even more…maybe she'd be able to figure out what to do with that attraction. Shove it into oblivion, in the furthest recesses of her mind?

Or grab it in both hands and *have* the man right on her living-room floor.

After being away from him for four long, lonely, hungry days, the living-room floor was looking better and better.

Stalling so she wouldn't have to decide what to do, she headed toward the kitchen. "I was about to put a pot of water on the stove," she explained. "I'm making some pasta for dinner."

"Good. I haven't eaten yet."

She paused in the doorway to the kitchen, giving him an arched look over her shoulder. "You inviting yourself to dinner?"

Offering her a lazy smile and a slow nod, he followed her. "Uh-huh. That okay?"

There was that cockiness again. So why did she suddenly find it cute instead of annoying? "As long as you remember that I am not using my wiles to finagle you into a dinner date."

"Given the way you said you cook, I definitely don't consider myself finagled."

"That's not much of a way to get invited," she retorted.

"I already was invited. By me. Remember?"

Laughing helplessly, she nodded. "Okay. But remember, certain topics remain out of bounds."

"Like the *L* word?"

She nodded, glad he instantly knew what she meant. "Right. You say the word *list* or mention dead lawyers wearing my underwear and I'm kicking you to the curb."

He stuck out his hand. "Deal."

Before thinking better of it, she reached for his hand, to shake it and seal their bargain.

Bad move. Oh, Lord, bad move. Because his touch was so warm, so strong. Firm. Electric.

Their palms slid against one another, their fingers almost entwining. Nick's hands were firm, a little rough, not a soft dentist's hands like the only ones that had touched her intimately for most of her adult life. His were a man's hands. A lover's hands.

They touched absolutely nowhere else. But suddenly Melody felt more intimately caressed than she had in her entire marriage. "Nick…"

"It's okay," he murmured, immediately understanding. As if to emphasize that, he pulled his hand away, looking at it with a somewhat dazed expression for one second before fisting it and shoving it into his pocket. "A friendly dinner, Melody. That's all I'm asking for. No lists, no panties. No stolen kisses." A wicked half smile tugged at his lips and his eyes twinkled. "No talk of sensual late nights with sweet-smelling air and pools of moonlight on the bed."

She gulped, her body immediately growing warm and aware, remembering the sultry words he'd said to her on the street the day after they'd met at the diner. "Yeah. Right. None of that."

"We're only two people getting to know each other," he

added softly, stepping a few inches closer, until the tips of his shoes almost touched her bare toes.

She swayed a bit, drawn by his warmth, wanting to breathe a little deeper, to fall a little farther, to fill her head with the spicy scent that was unique to this man's skin. "Yes." She slid her foot forward, her eyelids growing heavy as a slow, languorous sort of want oozed through her veins. "Are you sure this doesn't break your no-dating rules?"

"This isn't a date," he whispered.

"Just a friendly dinner."

"Right."

So why was she already so tense, on edge, ready to jump right out of her skin?

"Melody," he said, his voice low and intense, "there's one catch. One thing I need to say…that I want you to know."

Oh, no. He was involved. He was in love. He was impotent.

"I know I'm not supposed to bring up the *L* word, but I have to tell you this before we…go any further."

She scrunched her eyes closed, preparing for the worst.

"I'm glad you didn't do it. *Really* glad."

Opening one eye, she peered at him. "You what?"

As if he could read her mind, he grinned. Pulling his hands from his pockets and crossing them in front of his chest, he admitted, "What, did you think I was going to say you were right that first day and I like guys?"

"I am pretty sure we've established that you don't."

"I still haven't quite forgiven you for ever thinking it."

"Sorry," she mumbled, "I wasn't thinking entirely clearly that morning."

"I remember." His smile faded. "But you were clear enough to know you weren't going to hop into bed with somebody just because you'd given yourself permission to six years ago."

Melody's jaw dropped.

Nick reached up and ran the back of his finger along her cheek, across her chin, finally scraping it over her lips, which she instantly snapped shut.

"What are you saying?" Her voice was thready and weak.

He met her stare, something warm and intense making his dark brown eyes glow. "I guess I'm saying I harassed you so much, gave you such grief about it, because I didn't *want* to be a name on a list to you. I wanted you to shoot me down."

There was a strange note of vulnerability in his voice, which got to her more deeply than his words. For all his tough-guy persona and his no-nonsense-cop attitude, Nick Walker had the same deep-down worries and concerns that she did.

He didn't want to be used. Didn't want to be taken advantage of. Didn't want it to mean nothing.

Which was exactly the way Melody had been feeling. She simply hadn't admitted it to that extent, hiding behind the pretext that a man like Nick would be too hard to walk away from and that she didn't have the nerve to risk another heartbreak.

She'd been telling him that she was a coward. Weak. And this man, this big, strong, thoughtful man, had just basically admitted the same thing.

Amazing what his words did. Because as she stood there in the doorway to the kitchen, absorbing the fact that Nick, too, was afraid of being used, she began to feel a surge of strength. Her blood pounded in her veins and her head cleared, as if someone had blasted her with a heady dose of fresh air.

She suddenly felt sure of herself. Sure of what she wanted… at least for right now. She was suddenly brave. *Ready.*

"I understand," she said. "And you're right…I wouldn't have jumped into bed with someone for the sake of getting back in the singles game." Willing him to understand, she admitted, "I know I need to move on—my friends are right about that. But my list definitely wasn't the way to do it."

He nodded. "I know." Then, his lips curling in a tiny smile, he added, "So maybe dinner is a good start."

"Dinner?" He still wanted to eat, while she was beginning to realize that maybe she had grown some guts back? That maybe she was ready to reach out and take the man she knew, the man she *wanted*…not merely the one she'd dreamed about six years ago?

"Yeah," he continued, still delicately caressing her jaw. "If you don't mind, I'd really like to stay for dinner. No lists, no ugly divorces, no murder investigations. Just you and me, starting over." He moved his hand, now cupping her entire cheek, and she couldn't resist curling into his palm. "Starting *something*," he concluded.

Starting something. Oh, those words were so simple but so surprisingly heady. Melody had always liked being at the start of something new, with glorious possibilities lying in wait ahead of her on the path.

The glorious possibilities with Nick Walker might be beyond anything she'd ever imagined. It simply remained to take that first step and see what happened. "Starting something. I think I like that idea." She rubbed her cheek against his warm skin, until her lips brushed the fleshy part of his palm.

Nick's breaths grew more deep. "Me, too," he said softly. "Let's not think about what's next. Let's just…start."

Yes. That's exactly what she wanted to do. Somehow, all those doubts, those crazy wonderings about Bill and his other women and her own shortcomings didn't seem to matter right now. Despite a few hiccups with murdered lawyers and stolen underwear, things in Savannah were going well. When she evaluated it, she thought she might even have to describe herself as happy. For the first time in a very long time.

There were no whispering voices of doubt telling her to back off, to play it safe. Maybe they would have if Nick had kissed her passionately and said, "Let's go to bed." But he hadn't. He simply wanted to have dinner. To start.

And after waiting a long, difficult six years, Melody realized she was ready to do just that. Oh, yes, she was definitely ready.

Only, she didn't merely want dinner. She wanted something much more dangerous. She wanted to be in the arms of a man who'd admitted he was almost as afraid of being used as she was.

Really, when she thought about it, there was only one way for them to move forward. To *start*. And that's exactly what she wanted to do.

"Nick?" she said, continuing to rub her lips, then the tip of her tongue, over his palm.

His eyes were closed, his breaths even deeper. Which somehow gave Melody the courage to say, "Can we *start* by making love?"

CHAPTER TEN

NICK HAD BEEN PREPARED for a lot of things when he'd shown up at Melody's door. A lousy dinner and some good company. Some laughter. Some concern about the murder and worries about lists.

Not this. Not a sinfully sexy invitation from a woman he'd wanted since the minute he'd laid eyes on her. "Melody…"

"Shh," she whispered, delicately kissing the inside of his hand, then nibbling a path to his wrist.

Her touch sizzled, fried him completely. Made every nerve ending in his body come right to attention in anticipation of where that sexy mouth would land next.

He could definitely make some suggestions.

But he couldn't go forward, not without being sure *she* was sure. And not without knowing why she'd changed her mind. "I didn't come here to pressure you," he said, the words hard to push out of his tight throat.

"I know." She stepped closer, until the front of her body—clad in a loose sundress that scooped low over her mouthwatering curves—brushed against the front of his shirt. "Now *I'm* pressuring *you*."

He hesitated for a second, wanting it, wanting *her*, but wondering if he'd be a world-class shit for taking her when a few days ago she'd practically begged him for more time.

The woman had been through a hell of a lot in the past couple of weeks. A stalking ex-husband, pushy friends who kept embarrassing her. A twisted pervert murdered after stealing her lingerie.

And him. The guy who'd spent practically every minute he'd known her either harassing her or trying to get into her pants.

Nick dug down and found some deep reservoir of nobility. "You don't have to do this."

She was silent for a second. During that second, he decided nobility was overrated.

"I know. I *want* to do this."

He restrained from shouting hallelujah, but just barely.

Straightening, she looked him in the face, her blue eyes clear and unhesitating. "This isn't about any list or any past desires or any long-term plans for the future. It's about now. Being true to what I really want for the first time in as long as I can remember." She reached up and pushed at the strap of her sundress, until it fell from her shoulder. Then she pushed at the other one. "And what I really want is you."

Her softly spoken words repeated in his ears and he stared searchingly into her lovely face.

"So, Nick," she whispered, reaching up to run the tip of her finger over the top hem of her dress, "Can I have you? Please?"

Could she have him? A bigger question might have been, did he have anything to give? What he could possibly have to offer this funny, sexy, beautiful woman, he really had no idea.

He was a cop making lousy money. An ex-marine who'd seen too much ugliness. A good old boy who'd never set foot inside a college classroom. A bad-tempered divorcé who didn't believe in love and had been estranged from his family for ten years.

God in heaven, why would she *want* him?

And more importantly, why should he get to have *her?*

"Stop thinking about it, Nick," she said. "I see you analyzing it, but just stop." She didn't wait for his reply. Instead, she gave one tiny push. The dress gapped down, then fell to the floor.

"Oh, God," he whispered, closing his eyes. It was his only defense. Because Melody looked like sin in silk.

Finally looking at her again, he let his gaze linger on the lacy, skimpy, strapless bra that pushed up from the bottom but did little to cover the top curves of her full breasts. Below that, a skimpier pair of panties barely covered the sexy triangle between her legs.

He wondered where the upset, nervous woman had disappeared to. Because standing in front of him was Eve incarnate.

"I'm not going to regret it," she whispered, as if reading his mind. Her hand rose, shaking a little as she placed it on his chest. "If I'm going to start my life over, I want it to be now, with you, being as intimate as two people can get. I need you, Nick. I need this even if whatever we start doesn't last any longer than until tomorrow."

That was all it took. That certainty. And her nearly naked body swaying toward his, silently begging as much as promising.

He was lost.

Wrapping one arm around her waist, Nick tugged her tightly against him and covered her mouth with his. She tasted warm and earthy, like the rich red wine she'd been sipping, and like sweet, tempting woman.

He licked at her full, soft lips, groaning when she parted them and met his tongue with her own. The kiss deepened, giving and taking, lethargic desire making every stroke a sensual delight, until he felt sure he knew every intimate detail of her mouth. He could hardly wait to know every intimate detail of her body.

Kissing this woman needed to go on a list of his own—the list of the top-ten pleasures of his life. He'd say it was number one…but he had a feeling that spot was going to be taken pretty quickly by what was going to happen next.

Needing to taste even more of her, to breathe deeply and inhale her soft, flowery fragrance, he ran his mouth along her jaw, then to the most delectable skin below her ear. Sucking lightly on her neck, he nibbled her earlobe before growling, "Where, Mel?"

She moaned and arched her head back, silently inviting him to taste his way down her throat, until he pressed a wet, openmouthed kiss to the vulnerable hollow. "Here. Touch me here," she replied, moaning deeply as she took his hand and laced her fingers through his, before pulling it to her breast.

He groaned again as her soft mound filled his palm, unable to resist pushing the bra down so he could slide his fingers over its taut tip. She hissed when he caught the sweet, pebbled nipple between two fingers and stroked it, rolled it, lightly squeezing it until she was almost shuddering.

"I've been thinking about this for days," he whispered.

"So have I," she admitted. "Years."

He stiffened, unable to help it. "I don't want to hear about the years, Melody. Not the years I was just a nameless stranger to you, a picture in a magazine."

"That's not what I meant." She cupped his face, running her fingers through his hair and holding him still so she could meet his eyes. Hers were clear, honest, genuine. "I meant, I've been dreaming of making absolutely incredible love—for the first time in my *life*—for years. I've fantasized about wanting someone as much as I want you *right this very minute* for as long as I can remember. Because I've never had that, Nick. Never."

Even as he nearly groaned at the thought that this amazing woman had never had a decent sex life, a part of him—a big part—was damn glad he was going to be the first man to show her just how incredible it could be.

He'd show her that if it killed him.

Running his free hand up her back, he reached for the clasp of her bra and unfastened it. When it fell to the floor, he looked down at her beautiful breasts, heaving and tight, smooth and round and positively delicious.

Melody closed her eyes, arching her back in an unmistakable invitation. She wanted more…more of his hands, more of his mouth. More of everything.

Bending low, he held her around the waist with one arm while exploring one breast, then the other. Sampling here and nibbling there, he teased her, tasted her, licked her, blew on her…not taking one of those sensitive tips into his mouth until she was literally shaking in his arms and panting.

Only when she was frenzied, begging almost incoherently for more, did he cover her with his mouth and suck hard. She cried out, muttering, "Yes, yes, yes," as he thoroughly suckled her. Twining her fingers in his hair, she held him tight to one breast, while with one hand he toyed with her other nipple, until she was whimpering and muttering needful things. Hungry things. Erotic things.

She tasted so sweet, her body a heady mix of a gentle fragrance and musky woman. And she felt so good, with her soft skin against his rough cheek.

"Where, Melody?" he growled against her breast, needing to know whether she wanted him here, now, or up against the wall in her living room? Or on the bed. Or the kitchen counter. Hell, he'd have her on the hard wood floor, as long as he got to *have* her.

She misunderstood again. This time, when she grabbed his hand, she was almost rough as she pushed it down her body…down over her soft belly. Then lower, until he was skimming the thin elastic waistband of her panties with the tip of his pinky.

"Here," she cried as she arched her hips forward to take that intimate touch. "Please, Nick, touch me here."

He didn't need to be asked twice. Closing his eyes, he dipped lower, tangling his fingers in her soft curls until he found her swollen clit and scraped a slow caress across it.

"Oh, Nick," she cried, her weight growing heavier against his arm as her legs began to shake. "Please don't stop," she cried.

He pushed her panties down, letting them fall to the floor. Continuing to stroke her with his thumb—to tease and tempt and arouse her—he watched as her excitement grew. With her hair wildly tangled around her face, her lips apart and a flush of color splashed over her cheeks, she looked every inch a woman being pleasured.

He'd never seen her looking more beautiful. *Never.*

"Where?" he growled, not sure himself now what he was asking. Because he was having a grand old time letting her dictate where she wanted his touch next.

She didn't answer with words. Instead, she tilted toward him, pushing her pelvis into his palm, inviting him to explore deeper. When he did—when he sank his finger into her tight, wet channel and felt her clench around him—they both began to pant and heave at the intimacy of it.

"Oh, yes, *there.*"

Not really caring anymore if she wanted it on a soft bed or up against a hard wall, he grabbed her by the hips and lifted her so she could wrap those amazing legs of hers around his waist. She rubbed against his cock, taking her pleasure as she had that night in Rosemary's office. But this time only *his* clothes separated him from the hot, steamy place where he planned to lose himself for ages.

Carrying her to the couch, he continued kissing her, pausing only to let her push his shirt up and toss it to the floor. Her cool hands memorized his body while she bit and licked and sucked as much of his neck and shoulder as she could reach with her hungry mouth. As if she couldn't get enough of him.

It was almost painful to let her go, let her drop to the couch so he could take off the rest of his clothes. But he didn't plan to be separated from her for long.

Remembering the condom he'd tucked into his pocket—just in case—he grabbed it and tossed it onto the coffee table. Then he reached for his belt buckle.

"Uh-uh," she muttered, her eyes devouring him. "Not so fast. It's *my* turn."

MELODY REALIZED how crazy with need she was when she saw the way her own hand shook as she lifted it toward Nick's slim hips. It was intense, overwhelming, this desire. She wanted Nick Walker so much she could hardly think, could barely breathe. Any questions that had been in her mind before tonight were completely gone, replaced entirely by hunger.

Because she was about to get what she'd wanted for *years*.

She hadn't been kidding when she'd told Nick that for the first time in her life, she was going to have some really fabulous sex.

The sex she'd had before her marriage had been uninspiring The sex she'd had during her marriage had been boring.

This sex…well, she already knew it was going to be mind-blowing. Worth waiting a lifetime for.

Any lingering doubts about whether the sexual problems she'd had with Bill had been her fault—because she really was pretty but passionless, as he'd accused her of being—had completely evaporated. With Nick she felt not merely passionate but positively on fire. She needed him to do everything to her, with her. Once and then over and over again until the rest of the world ceased to exist.

She was shaking, flying, quivering, her entire body feeling like one giant nerve ending that sparked in reaction whenever he brushed the tips of his fingers over her. Or kissed her. Or licked her. "Oh, yes…."

Almost dying from the excitement, she reached for Nick's belt. Unfastening it, she slid the black leather out of each loop of his jeans with agonizing slowness, to heighten the delicious anticipation. Hers *and* his. Funny how desperate hunger was suddenly making her want to slow things down, to draw everything out so she could savor it. After she'd unfastened the metal button of his jeans, she even stopped completely.

Scooting to sit on the edge of the couch, she parted her legs and tugged Nick closer, until he stood between them. The rough denim scraped against her inner thighs and she quivered in response. "I've wanted you between my legs since the first time I laid eyes on you. You know that, don't you?"

"I know." Then, as she brushed her bare breasts against his jean-covered hips, he groaned. "Melody…"

"Where?" she said, mimicking his sensual strategy. She leaned close, knowing her slow, steady breaths were touching his skin, increasing his tension. "*Where*, Nick?"

He closed his eyes and dropped his head back. "Anywhere. Everywhere."

A half inch more and she was brushing her lips over the ropy muscles striping his flat stomach. His hiss of pleasure urged her on. Smiling, she licked ever so lightly, right beneath the top of his waistband. His hiss turned into a groan.

"Honey," he said, his tone almost desperate. "You've got to let me…"

"I'm doing just fine." And *finally* she began to unzip.

As she did so, she almost held her breath, a wealth of questions scurrying through her mind, the way they did the first time she did anything.

Did he wear boxers or briefs?

Boxer briefs. Black ones. Tight ones. *Lovely.*

Did he like the way she let the backs of her fingers slide oh so lightly against his erection as she continued to lower the zipper?

"You're killing me here," he muttered hoarsely.

Oh, yeah. He liked it. She'd venture to say he loved it.

Would he try to take over, try to push his clothes out of the way from pure impatience?

Uh-uh. He remained still, letting her set the pace. His driving need was evidenced only by the flexing muscles rippling through his body as he clenched in preparation for the expected pleasure of her next touch.

A patient man. A controlled man. A big man, judging by the tightness of his zipper against his erection.

Her blood pounded, even as every bit of spare moisture in her body descended right between her legs. She shifted a little on the couch, incredibly swollen, sensitive and ready.

"This is killing me, too, but it feels so good," she whispered. The slow buildup…she'd always loved it. "Did you know I did a ketchup commercial on anticipation?"

He groaned. "Do *you* know I'm going to die if you don't hurry up?" His eyes remained closed, his head back as he muttered, "I could have unzipped every prom dress at my high school in less time than this."

Grumpy, grouchy. Adorable. Sexy. She giggled, loving the way he let her tease and torment them both, before finally lowering the zipper as far as it would go.

"Thank you God," he muttered, his voice half laughing, half choking.

Putting her palms on his sides, she savored the quiver of his hard muscles beneath her touch. In one easy stroke, she lowered her hands, pushing his jeans down over his lean hips and his hard legs. Finally they hit the floor.

She could have let him step out of them, take off his shoes and kick the jeans away. But she liked having him trapped here. Between her legs. At her mercy. So she wouldn't allow him to move an inch.

"Mel…"

"Almost," she whispered, still delicately licking the skin low on his belly, below his tan line. Now her cheek was brushing against that thick ridge of rock-hard heat, which strained against the black cotton, as her fingers had before. The man was nearly incoherent, muttering under his breath.

Anticipation. Build it. Ache for it.

Breathing against the fabric of his shorts, she ran the tips of her fingers over his flat stomach, brushing against a few scars. They made her wonder—but she'd ask later. Much later. When her body wasn't so hungry and her mind wasn't filled with pure sexual desire.

She couldn't wait any longer. Hooking her fingers in the elastic waistband, she tugged the briefs away and pushed them down as one last, fleeting question shot through her mind.

Big or small?

The briefs fell. And she couldn't prevent a moan from escaping her lips. Oh, gracious, *big*.

She didn't think she could get any wetter, or any more excited. But the sight of him ratcheted everything up until she was almost unable to remain upright.

Nick looked ready to explode, to dive into her, but Melody found one last measure of strength…enough to do something she'd long fantasized about doing.

Her breasts were *so* sensitive. And he was *so* close to them.

Giving him no warning, she looked up to meet his eyes, then shifted closer, until his throbbing hard-on was brushing across one of her tight nipples. A few inches more and he was nestled between her soft curves. Hard. Hot. Heavy.

She moaned with pleasure, loving the sensation of skin on skin. *That* skin on *this* skin.

Leaning closer and squeezing her breasts together to make a tighter channel, she heard his groan of pleasure as she slowly slid up and down. That helpless sound gave her the confidence she needed to take things just a bit further. Hungry to taste him, she lowered her head, brushing her lips and the tip of her tongue against that smooth, warm male skin, licking off a drop of moisture there.

His groan turned guttural and his control seemed to snap. Putting his hands on her shoulders, he pushed her back until she reclined beneath him. His shoes and clothes were off within two seconds, and one more past that, he was yanking a condom over himself and following her down onto the couch.

"You ask me *where* and I won't be responsible for my actions," she managed to whisper between chopping breaths.

"I know exactly where I'm going."

And he did. Oh, he most definitely did. With one strong, powerful thrust he went right where she wanted him to. Deep inside her, stretching her, filling her, bursting into her, exactly as an explosion of delight burst throughout the rest of her body.

Crying out, she threw her head back, jerking a little as the sensations rocked her for several long, delicious seconds.

Nick remained completely still, buried within her but not moving. When she could think again, she found him watching her, a look of pure satisfaction—and hunger—on his face. His dark brown eyes glittered and a half smile lingered on that incredible mouth of his.

"Okay?"

"Oh, very okay," she whispered hoarsely. Then, to make sure he knew she was in for the long haul, she added, "By the way, I am *definitely* not done for the night."

His smile broadening, he began to move, drawing out, then driving deep, each thrust feeling better than the last. "Good thing, honey, because I do believe you're two up on me."

Pressing against him, she realized what he meant. He had brought her to a shattering climax in Rosemary's office, and again just now.

She groaned, loving the way he touched her, inside *and* out. His kisses on her neck, the brush of his fingers on her breast and his stubbled cheek against her jaw had her nearly going out of her mind with pleasure. As did those delicious strokes deep within her. He rocked and she rolled and time stood still.

"Well," she finally whispered, while she was still capable of thought, "I'm a fair-minded person. I am definitely willing to let you catch up." The tension was already building again, the sensations rolling through her, her body signaling her as she went higher and higher toward another climax. "But I have to warn you…I'm…I'm getting one heck of a head start."

Then she was over the peak. Shaking, shattering, sighing as Nick drove into her with a few rapid, mind-blowing thrusts.

The last thing she heard was his deep groan of pleasure and a few whispered words as he let the pleasure wash over him, too.

"Okay. That's three to one."

IF JONATHAN RHODES WEREN'T already dead, Drake Manning would have killed him. Gladly.

It was one thing to keep a slightly open secret about your proclivities among your closest friends. It was another entirely to get caught not with your pants *down*, but with your panties *up*. And dead, to boot.

Few people knew of their close friendship, which was the way they'd both preferred it. Rhodes had given Drake some free legal advice on occasion, particularly during his divorce last year. In exchange, Drake had used his standing at the TV station to ensure stories about some of Jonathan's clients received a slightly better-than-fair treatment.

It had been a good arrangement. And since the two of them shared a delight in poker, in boating and in women, their friendship had grown rapidly. They'd even found common financial interests. Including, recently, a mutual desire to aid a riverboat-gambling proposal being lobbied for by a few local, er…businessmen. Some of Jonathan's shady clients had liked having an in with the local media…a chance to get less-than-flattering stories removed from the inspection of the press and to get some good PR whenever possible.

Drake had liked the money. Some might call it accepting bribes at the expense of his journalistic integrity. He preferred to think of it as his future alimony fund.

Jonathan's thing for ladies' panties had been a surprise, but Drake had laughed it off as drunken rambling when his friend had first mentioned it a year ago. Later, when Jonathan had said the same thing while sober…well, Drake had quickly gotten over it. He was no saint in his bedroom. If he enjoyed leather and handcuffs, why couldn't his friend get the same satisfaction from silk and lace?

But what was fine in private was far from fine when it was in the public eye, particularly for people like Drake who were already so very *much* in the public eye. Guilty by association, that's how most viewers—and TV execs—would look at it. That was why he'd had to back off and play down his friendship with the murdered attorney soon after his death. He'd done so the minute more risqué details had leaked out about the murder—like the fact that Rhodes had been shot while wearing ladies' underwear, in a closet full of lingerie. Hopefully, Drake had disassociated himself soon enough.

"You still seething over Jonathan? There's no way you could have known how he'd be found. God, it makes me sick to even think about it."

Drake didn't so much as glance over at Angie Jacobs, who reclined on some pillows on the other side of his bed, smoking a cigarette. He hated her smoking in his apartment, especially since smoking was one of the first things he'd had to give up last year after his heart attack. But considering she'd just blown him with more skill than any professional, he didn't think he ought to complain.

"I should have known about that damned closet," he said instead. "Or you should have. I mean, you slept with him the weekend before he died, didn't you?"

"Jealous?" she asked, sounding amused and pleased at the thought.

"Hardly."

Frankly, beyond giving an admittedly superior blow job and having a finely tuned nose for any scandalous story in Savannah, Angie meant nothing to him. Which was exactly what he'd told her the night of Rosemary Chilton's party when she'd tried to make him jealous by flirting with Jonathan Rhodes. She'd been furious—typical Angie—and had gone home with the other man.

Drake hadn't cared. He hadn't wanted to hang around, anyway, since Angie wasn't the only one of his exes present at Rosemary's party. For a decent-size city, Savannah could still be so small-town. Things had gotten a bit uncomfortable when he'd looked across the crowd and spied a familiar pair of dark, angry eyes.

Besides, Angie turning to Jonathan had provided an easy out from what was already becoming a stale relationship. Drake would have left it at that since he was pretty tired of Angie anyway, but somehow the two of them had found their way back together after Rhodes's murder. Frankly, it was good to have an ally in a storm of controversy and they were *both* in the eye of the station executives. Besides, in a weird way, he kind of got off on doing a woman who'd been fucked by a murder victim less than a week before his demise.

"Believe me, if you were a bit jealous, you'd have no reason to be."

He wasn't.

"Because when Jonathan asked me if he could try on my panties before I left his place last Saturday night, I thought I was going to throw up. The sick bastard." Her voice shook with anger.

Drake didn't want to imagine how she'd responded, but he'd bet it wasn't pretty. If Rhodes had bought it the weekend of Rosemary's party, he'd have suspected Angie of the crime. God knows, considering how rough she occasionally liked to get in bed, she didn't have any problem with violence.

Sometimes he wondered if his heart was up to the kind of sex he had with Angie. But, frankly, his dick had always called the shots over his heart…which hadn't boded well for his marriage.

Angie stirred, rolling to the side of the bed to get up. She never stayed long, having learned in the two months of their sexual relationship that he didn't like clinginess. So she was obviously playing this cool, not pushing things, treating their surprising reunion carefully.

Good. Because the *last* thing he wanted was for her to think tonight meant anything. He'd already been down the married path, and the long-term-mistress one. He had no interest in doing either one again. The marriage had cost him a heart valve, a ton of money and months' worth of embarrassment. Not to mention the college yacht race trophy he'd been so proud of.

The mistress, who'd expected to become the next wife, had been even more vengeful.

So short-term flings with women who weren't in the position to make demands were just the ticket. From the flight attendant he'd been banging in June, to Angie here, he much preferred meaningless sex to commitment.

"Do you think it's true that the underwear he was wearing when he died belonged to that woman we were talking to at the party?" Angie asked as she pulled her clothes on. "That photographer friend of Rosemary's?"

"You mean the one that dark-haired cop couldn't take his eyes off of?" he asked, amused. "The cop you, if I recall correctly, looked ready to leap on?"

"Shut up," she snapped. "He's a low-class nobody."

She couldn't fool him. Angie had worn her lust for the man the way some women wore cheap perfume—until it practically oozed from every pore of her body.

"Jonathan did seem rather taken with her, didn't he?" Drake said, remembering her original question. "My source on the PD confirms she was one of the last people to see him alive Friday, and the police have questioned her."

"I know." Angie dragged deeply on her cigarette, then flicked it into a nearly empty glass of water on the table by the bed.

Drake frowned, wanting her to leave.

"I'm wondering," she continued, "what her relationship is with Detective Walker."

"The nobody?" He didn't bother to hide his sarcasm.

Her eyes narrowed, as did her lips. "For your information, my main concern is what, exactly, Jonathan might have said to that woman. Since she is obviously acquainted with Detective Walker, and he's investigating the murder, it might be worth finding out what she knows about your...*arrangement* with Jonathan."

Drake didn't blink, didn't move a muscle. He just stared at Angie, who continued to fidget around with the zipper on her tight skirt. She finally noticed his lack of response and looked over. "What?"

"I'm not sure I know what you're talking about."

She gave him a sly, catlike smile. "Jonathan did like his pillow talk. I know now why you killed that story on his money-laundering client. And why you did the exposé on the council member who was fighting so hard against the gambling legislation."

Son of a bitch. Jonathan had talked to Angie about their arrangement.

"Don't worry, I don't plan on telling anyone. If that perverted bastard hadn't gotten himself killed, believe me, I would have wanted in on the action."

Yes, he suspected she would have.

"So you see, don't you, why I'd like to find out what this Melody Tanner knows. Strictly for *your* sake, of course."

Oh, right. His sake. If it would get her an anchor slot or

bring her to the attention of CNN, Angie would serve his weak heart up on a platter without a second's hesitation. "Well, maybe you should cozy up to the cop and see what he knows," he suggested, knowing his taunt would piss her off.

It did. "Fine. Forget it. You can laugh all you want and I'll sit back and watch when that woman leads the cops right to your door. Maybe they'll want to know how 'close' you and Rhodes really were…in a business sense of course."

They stared at each other across the expanse of the bed and, for a second, Drake considered lunging across it and smacking her. But he somehow managed to offer her a smile of truce instead. "Thanks for the suggestion. Maybe it *is* worth checking out this photographer…just to make sure she doesn't know anything."

Though he hated to admit it, he realized, as he said the words, that Angie might be right. In order to get close to the Tanner woman's underwear drawer, there was no telling what Jonathan Rhodes might have let slip.

"Now, why don't you let yourself out?" he asked, not trying to hide his boredom. She walked to the door, pausing only when he said, "And, Angie? Leave the key."

Her eyes flashed and she fisted her hands at her sides, knowing what he meant. But at least she left without a scene.

Which was good. Because Drake had some damage control to do. And the place he needed to start was with the woman: Melody Tanner.

CHAPTER ELEVEN

NICK HADN'T BEEN SURE how Melody would react after they'd made love on her couch Tuesday night. But the woman had surprised him, as usual. There'd been no embarrassment. She hadn't expressed any regrets, didn't blame herself or him.

No. Instead, after they'd both recovered enough from their passionate encounter to at least breathe normally again, she'd simply pulled her dress on over her naked body and invited him to stay for dinner, which he had.

Her pasta sucked. But the sex more than made up for it.

Funny, he would have expected their intimacy to make things more strained between them. But they'd laughed through dinner, talking, sharing sips of wine and opening up a little more about silly things. Movies. Pets. Her lousy cooking and his bad temper.

They'd talked about everything from the heat wave to the play-offs to Rosemary and Dex. She'd asked about Joyful and he'd given her the *Reader's Digest* version of his childhood there…leaving out a few details. Like what it had meant growing up the younger son of the town's meanest drunken bully.

He'd asked her whether she'd really been the Oscar Mayer kid and she'd confirmed it by introducing him to Oscar…one of her cats. Her cats liked him, though he still hadn't figured out who C.C. was named for.

She'd told him what it had been like to "come and play" on *Sesame Street* as a five-year-old. And he'd told her about Johnny and Emma, their upcoming wedding, and even, just a bit, about the scandal that had brought the two of them together.

Somehow, it seemed that making love had let them completely remove the stress and expectation of her list, of the way they'd met. Of the murder. Everything else had been left at the door...everything except Nick and Melody and their overwhelming chemistry.

By the end of the evening, he'd been absolutely sure of one thing: Melody Tanner was a funny, vivacious woman who had a wicked sense of humor and a laugh that deserved to be bottled and sold as a drug. Because he felt high whenever he heard it.

When he'd left at around ten, he felt they'd completely eliminated the wall of embarrassment and mistrust she'd erected between them shortly after they'd met. That she'd let down her barriers and allowed herself to be the real Melody...charming, funny, happy and confident. And sexy enough to stop his heart.

It had been about the finest evening he'd ever spent with a woman. Which made *this* so much harder to take.

"Good God, Mel," he mumbled as he looked over the newspaper photos he'd tracked down on the Internet Wednesday afternoon. "No wonder you needed a list...even then you must have suspected you were marrying a bastard."

He hadn't wanted to do it, but the thought that Melody's infamous list might actually have something to do with Jonathan Rhodes's murder made it necessary to look into Melody's past. And what an awful past it had been.

The media coverage of the spurned-wife scandal had been brutal. The Atlanta papers seemed to have delighted in taking potshots at the former model who'd come up with such flamboyant revenge against her cheating husband last year. The pictures had been grainy and black-and-white, but in spite of that, the images of a paint-smeared Melody being rescued by a fireman on an extension ladder were quite shocking.

He had to hand it to her, the billboard thing had been inspired. It was just too damn bad she'd gotten caught.

"I hate this," he mumbled as he shut down his computer.

He hated what he had to do. Absolutely hated that he had to go back over to Melody's place and question her about her ex-husband, letting on that he knew all about her ugly divorce. What she'd done. What it had cost her. Everything.

He needed to know one thing from her, the one thing the papers hadn't been able to report: how had Dr. Bill Todd reacted? With perhaps *murderous* anger?

Figuring he'd at least try to recapture the good vibes from the previous night before he hit her with what he knew, he decided to wait until dinnertime to talk to her. So, without calling to give her any warning, he knocked on her door at six o'clock Wednesday night with a large pizza in one hand and a bottle of wine tucked under his arm.

This time, she asked who it was. "Good girl," he replied. Then, louder, he added, "It's the pizza guy."

"I don't open the door for strange delivery men unless they work for Cartier."

He laughed. "No diamonds. Will anchovies do?"

Opening the door, she raised a brow as she saw the pizza and the wine. "Anchovies? I thought you had a thing about fish."

"I was kidding. Pepperoni and green pepper. It was the least I could do since you supplied dinner last night."

"Did we see each other last night? I can barely remember. Must not have been that memorable."

Striding through the door, he set the pizza and wine on a table by the door and caught her around the waist. Planting a deep kiss on her laughing mouth, he mumbled, "Ringing any bells?"

"Hmm. Might need more reminding."

He kissed her again. Deeper, hotter, the little whimper in her throat telling him just how much she liked it.

That whimper also reminded him he had to stop. Going further with Melody—going to bed with her again—wasn't an option until he admitted that he'd spent much of the day digging into her past, prying into her most painful, private moments.

Letting her go with a regretful shrug, he stepped back and picked up the pizza. "So, what do you say?"

"How do you know I haven't already made something?"

"It's pizza. *Is* there anything else?"

"Ah, yes, the perfect comfort food for every pathetic single woman who doesn't want to eat canned tuna fish with her cat every night," she said as she followed him.

He put the pizza on the counter, and set the bottle beside it before turning around to give her an incredulous look. "Pathetic doesn't come close to describing you, darlin'. I don't think you'd have to spend one evening alone for the rest of your life if you didn't really want to."

"Maybe I do want to."

With a half smile he asked, "You want me to go?"

She hesitated for maybe the length of one slowly inhaled breath, then shook her head. "No."

Good thing. Because he wasn't going anywhere. Not only because he wanted her with the desperation of a man who'd had only one incredible night with her. But also because he had to figure out a way to question this woman about what must have been the most humiliating time of her entire life.

Other than the thing with the dead guy in her underwear, of course.

This still wasn't exactly dating, he reminded himself. Coming to her house with pizza and wine, or pulling up a plate for some extra pasta, or having crazy hot sex on her living-room couch was not dating. So he wasn't feeling the least bit tense or uptight, the way he normally did whenever he considered actually jumping back on the stupid relationship bandwagon.

What he and Melody had, other than a hot-enough-to-melt-the-arctic-shelf attraction, was a sort of friendship. At least, as much of a friendship as you could have with someone you wanted to smother in chocolate and then lick clean.

"This is the kind you like, right?" he asked, gesturing toward the bottle of red wine.

"Yeah. Though pizza goes better with beer, doesn't it?"

He certainly thought so. But Melody didn't seem like a beer-drinking kind of woman.

She put that supposition to rest by reaching for an open bottle that had been sitting on her small kitchen table. "There's more in the fridge."

He didn't need to be told twice. Grabbing a bottle of beer, he untwisted the cap and drank gratefully from it. The wine he'd save for later—Melody might need it when they got around to talking business. *His* business.

But not now. For now, he simply wanted to enjoy talking to her the way he had last night after they'd…well, just *after.*

"So, you never did answer my question last night about your mother," he said as he leaned against the counter and watched her open the pizza box, bending over to sniff appreciatively.

"Did you ask me a question about my mother?"

"Having a hard time remembering our conversation?" he asked, knowing what *he* most remembered about the previous evening.

She stretched a little, a lethargic smile on her face. "I remember a lot of questions...mostly involving the word *where.*"

Heat washed through him. "You know, I was asking where in your *apartment* you wanted to go."

Nibbling her lip and looking sheepish, she replied, "Sorry. I didn't realize that."

A bit of color spotted her cheeks and Nick marveled at how utterly adorable this woman could be. A paradox, really...one minute strong and confident. Then intensely sexual. Then uncertain and nervous. And now, so cute and embarrassed.

Clearing her throat and getting out some plates and silverware, Melody said, "What was it you asked about my mother?"

Knowing she was intentionally changing the subject, steering clear of anything more intimate—for *now*—he answered, "I asked if she was happy with this rich new guy you said she married."

Swiping a thick lock of auburn hair away from her forehead, Melody shrugged. "Well, that's not a question. That's a given. My mother, money and men. Three *M*'s that just seem to go together."

"What about Melody?" he asked. "That's another *M* word."

She put a slice of pizza onto a plate and carried it over to him. "We get along fine...now that she's on another continent."

"Does she know you're back in Savannah?" he asked as he sat down at her small kitchen table, pushing the chair to make room for his legs beneath it.

"Nope. As far as she knows, I'm still happily burying my

head in the sand about my marriage and living among the rich and bored in Buckhead, right outside Atlanta."

She'd said something similar last night, when talking about her mother/manager. "Hasn't your ex said anything like, uh, 'Your daughter found out I'm a cheating, gutless slug and divorced me' when she's called?"

She snickered, then replied, "She hasn't." Sitting down opposite him, she continued, "Hasn't called, I mean. I phone every other week or so, and remind her that if she needs me to call my cell. So far there's been no need."

Glancing down at his plate so she wouldn't see the sudden flash of sympathy in his eyes, he asked, "What if *you* need her?"

She lifted her beer. "I haven't needed her for a long time. Not since I was sixteen and had myself legally emancipated."

"Ouch."

"Oh, yeah. Ouch is right. She wasn't happy at first, but, believe it or not, our relationship improved once the issue of money wasn't standing between us. I paid her a salary, and only rarely let her make decisions for me regarding my career." She sighed heavily. "Though, honestly, I did let her talk me into one doozy of a mistake there at the end."

He somehow knew what she meant. "The peacock set?"

She nodded.

"Was it such a mistake? It sure made you famous."

"Infamous. Imagine my delight in being recognized for that."

He didn't have to think very hard. Because, yeah, he knew firsthand how much attention she'd gotten. He'd been one of the lechers making raunchy jokes about the Peacock Feather Girl, like so many of the guys in his unit.

A bitter taste of shame rose in his mouth, as well as indignation for the crap Melody had endured. At the instigation of her own mother, who should have been protecting her teenage daughter. Not exploiting her.

"Anyway, that was the beginning of the end for me. I decided to quit and eventually my mother realized she wasn't going to be able to talk me out of it."

"Yet you gave up all the emancipation and freedom to get married a couple of years later." Nick wasn't purposely trying to turn the topic of conversation to Melody's ex. They'd get to that soon enough. Right now, he really was just interested in hearing why she'd made some of the choices she had.

She rolled her eyes as she bit into her pizza. A few moments later, she mumbled, "I think I was trying to live a commercial."

He didn't follow. "Okay..."

"You've got to understand, I grew up in front of the camera. On TV, I was always one of the happy, smiling members of some happy, smiling family." Wiping her mouth with her napkin, she explained, "Whether I was sneaking a dog into the house and giving it a bath, or squeezing the toilet paper or naming my bologna, I had this glimpse of what other people's family lives might be like. And they were very different than mine."

Made sense, he supposed. In the same way he used to imagine everybody else's family life back in Joyful had to be much better than his own. Of course, in his case, he'd probably been right.

"So I guess when I met Bill, I somehow thought I was going to end up like one of the families in the commercials I'd made as a kid." She sipped her beer, then shook her head. "I guess if I'd ever appeared in an ad for a horror movie, or a safe-sex campaign, I might have been more prepared."

Nick lifted his own beer, focusing on the bottle, which his

hand tightened around. Melody was opening the door he'd needed to get through. Discussing the end of her marriage. A topic his job required him to delve into…but damned if he wanted to do it.

It was such an invasion. He'd already invaded her so much by digging up her most ugly secrets. Having to admit it—and to dig even deeper, in person—made it that much worse.

Damn, sometimes he really hated his job. And right now there were no bullies or cowards he could bust to make it all worthwhile. He wished that he could.

One thing was sure—if he ever found Melody Tanner's ex-husband lurking around here, stalking and harassing her, he was going to make the man wish he'd never set foot in Savannah.

"So marriage wasn't what you thought it'd be, huh?" He sure could understand that, since his had been a nightmare, too.

"Oh, no."

"He cheated?" he managed to ask.

A snort preceded her answer. "Only with anything that walked. Or blinked."

Remembering Melody was caught up in this case in some way, and figuring the sooner they found Jonathan Rhodes's killer the better, he swallowed hard. Keeping his voice even and his tone relaxed, he said, "Hence the barnyard animals remark."

Her quick, shocked gasp told him she'd instantly grasped his meaning. Which was what he'd wanted—to be honest with her. But it still felt like a huge betrayal.

She froze, staring at him with confusion in those blue eyes before lowering her slice of pizza to her plate. "You've been investigating me?"

"I'm sorry, Mel."

"How *could* you?"

"I had to."

She rose from the chair. "I can't believe you did this."

"I didn't have a choice." Hoping she'd hear the regret in his voice, he added, "I wish I hadn't had to do it. But I did. Your…situation could be important to the Rhodes case."

She threw her arms into the air and glared at the ceiling. "My humiliating, horrible divorce could be related to a murder?" Stalking across the kitchen, she smacked her hand on the countertop, keeping her back to him. "So that's what this was all about? This 'something' that you wanted to start…it was all part of your investigation, wasn't it?"

Low blow. Very low. Nick followed, walking over to stand right behind her. Close, but not touching.

It didn't matter. Even without touching her, he was suddenly flooded with the sensual memory of what had happened last night. Just twenty-four hours ago they'd been wild and crazy. Sweet, hungry, intense passion had erupted between them when he'd said he wanted to start something.

So how she could think he'd only said it to get her to let her guard down so he could investigate her cut him deeply. "You don't mean that. You know it's not true."

He lifted his hand, wanting to touch her, to reassure her that he wasn't the lying, using prick she was imagining him to be. His palm hovered above her shoulder, one inch above her warm, bare skin. But he didn't lower it, knowing he couldn't cloud the issue with their physical attraction right now. Not until she cleared her head and accepted what they had to do: talk about her ugly past in Atlanta.

Oh, there were so many things he'd rather do. Like put his hands on her shoulders, bend down and kiss the side of her neck. Slide his fingers over her shirt and delicately stroke the sweet curves of her breasts. Make her wet and hot and hungry and take her—fast and wild—bent over the kitchen counter just like this.

Somehow, Nick managed to thrust the image away.

"Last night was exactly what we both intended it to be," he said in a thick whisper. "An end to the wondering and a start to something else. Whatever that is, I don't know and I don't think you do, either. And I don't think either of us really *needs* to know anything more than it wasn't about a damn list or famous underwear or anything else."

She didn't turn around, didn't acknowledge his words in any way. But her pulse wasn't beating so wildly in the side of her neck, so he continued, "One thing *is* for sure, Melody. I didn't make love to you so I could get you to trust me with your secrets. I didn't begin to look into your past until today. And then…" Knowing it wouldn't be easier to hear, he concluded, "Well, it wasn't too difficult to get the details. I didn't need to seduce them out of you."

She turned around, but he didn't back off to give her more room. They were standing only an inch apart, practically nose to nose. He silently urged her to trust him, to know that he hadn't intentionally set out to hurt or humiliate her.

When she spoke again, he knew he hadn't succeeded.

"I want you to leave."

THOUGH SHE'D HOPED her welcome-home party for Melody would break the ice between her father and Dex, Rosemary now knew it hadn't worked. With a house full of people, there had been no real reason for the two of them to talk. Definitely no opportunity for any of that silly male bonding that men seemed to think was so important.

She *wanted* them to bond. Dex was an amazing man and for some absolutely unfathomable reason, he loved her. Really, truly, honest-to-God loved her. He'd said so, just a cou-

ple of weeks ago. And as crazy as she thought he was for loving her, someone who was almost as shallow as she was selfish—which was exactly what she'd told him—she'd also
realized he meant it.

She hadn't said it back. Rosemary Chilton might have ice
in her veins when negotiating a high-end real-estate deal. But
she had chicken's feathers on her backside when it came to
admitting her feelings.

That didn't mean she didn't feel them, however. She great-
ly feared she'd gone and done it but good…she'd fallen in
love with a strait-laced, serious, hard-nosed cop. Which
meant she wanted everyone else she loved to love him, too.

Especially now. When things looked like they were about
to get very…complicated.

"I'm so glad you all could make it tonight," she said to everyone seated around her dining-room table Wednesday evening, not wanting to think about the phone call she'd gotten
from her doctor yesterday.

"Thanks so much for having us all over," Patty, her stepmoth-
er, said with a bright smile. She knew Rosemary was trying to
work on Daddy, and was doing everything she could to help.

Of course she would. Patty had been a lot like Dex once
upon a time. A Northerner, an outsider, a working middle-class
person. Also a widow with a young son, who'd instantly
treated Deidre and Rosemary like her own daughters.

She'd been wonderful for Daddy, who'd been crushed by
his divorce from Rosemary and Deidre's mother. Rosemary
didn't even like to think of how her father had retreated into
himself after Mother had run off with her tennis instructor.
But he'd recovered, thanks to Patty. So why her father
couldn't see that Dex was just as wonderful for his younger
daughter, she had absolutely no idea.

He'd better start seeing it quick, though. Because Dex was

going to be around for a long, long time. Especially once he found out what Rosemary had been too nervous to tell him.

"This was a sweet surprise honey. I'm sorry Carl is out of town," her sister said, obviously also feeling the tension in the quiet room.

Rosemary wasn't particularly sorry. Deidre's husband, Carl, was a boring, strait-laced, smooth-talking businessman who happened to be their father's golden boy. If he'd been here, the differences between him and streetwise, plain-speaking Dex would have been all the more obvious. Not to mention that Brian would retreat into his silent shell, or stutter helplessly, as he always did when their brother-in-law was around.

Thankfully, Carl was a snob as well as a financial guru, so he had no designs on Brian's job as their father's "rent collector." He had once joked that if he'd wanted to be a landlord, he wouldn't have bothered going to college.

The prick.

"Don't you want wine with your dinner, Rosemary?" her father asked, glancing at the sweet tea she was sipping.

"No, this is fine," she said softly, wishing she'd never come up with this family dinner idea. She'd been feeling queasy enough without adding an excruciating get-together to the mix.

"So, Dex, are you working on that awful murder case involving that former congressman?" Deidre asked. "I can't believe we all saw that man just a week and a half ago. Bet Melody is really mad at you for inviting him, Rosemary."

If her sister had been close enough to kick under the table, Rosemary would have done it. She settled for a glare, instead.

"Melody Tanner?" her father asked. "What does she have to do with Jonathan Rhodes?" Then he frowned. "I can't imagine she was friends with him. I was surprised enough that you invited him to your home, Rosemary. He wasn't a very nice man."

"W-wasn't much of a *man* at all," Brian mumbled, as usual fading into the background when the family was all together.

Rosemary almost grinned, knowing her brother was referring to the women's panties thing. But it wasn't exactly a good topic of conversation for the dinner table.

"I am on that case," Dex said evenly as he sipped from his water glass. "But I can't talk about open investigations."

Her father didn't react one way or the other.

"Melody's almost like one of our own girls," Patty said with a smile. "She and Rosemary were an incorrigible duo." Giving Brian a fond look, she added, "Brian didn't know what to do with himself when Rosemary's friends were around."

Her brother flushed. The last thing Rosemary wanted was for poor Brian to start stammering that he hadn't followed Rosemary and her friends around whenever they all came over because of his infatuation with Paige, so she quickly changed the subject.

"Dex is from a long line of police officers, did I tell you that?" Rosemary said to fill the silence.

Her father nodded, cutting his roast beef. *Stubborn man.*

"His father is the police commissioner in their hometown in Pennsylvania, and one of his uncles is chief of detectives."

"So why did you move here?" her father asked, finally looking directly at Dex instead of at the wall, the floor or his plate. "Why didn't you stay *there* to go into law enforcement?"

Not good. There was a belligerent note in the question, as

if he were saying he wished Dex had never come to Savannah at all.

Please be patient, sugar.

"I wanted to do things my way," Dex replied. "Completely on my own, without any family influence paving the way."

Oh, Lord have mercy, *that* was the wrong answer.

Her father lowered his fork. "You're saying you don't have respect for your family, for your father?"

Dex met his stare evenly. "I'm not saying that at all. I simply didn't want anything handed to me by virtue of my last name. I don't want anything I didn't earn on my own."

Since Daddy could trace his money back three generations to his great-grandfather, who'd started his fortune with a lumber mill up the river, that wasn't a great answer, either.

"Rosemary, these potatoes are just delicious. I must have the recipe," Patty said brightly, obviously seeing the train wreck about to happen, too.

"And do your father and uncle appreciate your rejection of their way of life?" her father asked.

Rosemary covered her eyes, suddenly wishing the roast beef had been a little more well-done, because she really felt sick to her stomach.

"They respect me," Dex said, his tone as stiff as his set-in-granite jaw. "If my father doesn't like the choices I made, he still knows they were *my* choices to make."

"And the green beans!" Patty chirped.

"The rolls are wonderful, too," Deidre said, obviously realizing things were heating up.

Daddy's silverware was on his plate, his hands flat on the table, and a hint of steel sparked in his gray eyes. Rosemary knew the look.

Hell.

"It's hard enough being a parent without having your child

throw everything you value into your face." Now he was looking at *her*. "Rosemary, for instance, chose to go into real estate of all things and insisted on buying this house when I wanted to *give* it to her."

She'd be paying for it for the next four decades, too, but she didn't regret that decision.

"I would've taken it," Deidre mumbled into her wineglass.

God, Rosemary wished she could have a glass, too.

"*You* have a *husband* who provided you with a nice house," their father said, never taking his eyes off Dex.

Oh, that was a dig. Now the vinegary taste of salad dressing was churning around with the too-rare roast beef. Rosemary sipped some tea, praying for an earthquake or something to end this miserable gathering. Never again…she was never going to try to force people together ever again. She'd learned her lesson.

"That's one of the things I admire most about your daughter," Dex said. "In spite of being somewhat…meddlesome, she has a keen business sense and is very independent."

Rosemary felt a little better because of the warmth and hint of admiration in Dex's voice. But she was going to get him for the meddlesome comment…once she stopped feeling as if she was on board a boat being tossed about by twenty-foot waves.

"Young people nowadays don't comprehend the importance of family tradition," her father continued, his face now red.

"When tradition comes at the expense of free thinking and independence, I'd say that's a good thing."

Rosemary moaned, her body aching as much as her head. Her tummy was rolling around and she dropped a hand to her lap, wondering how rude it would be if the hostess upchucked all over the platter of mini fruit tarts about to be served for dessert.

"I feel sorry for your father," Daddy snapped.

And Dex pushed his chair back from the table, not red faced but pretty tense nonetheless. "I think I've had enough to eat. It was wonderful, Rosie."

"Rosie?" her father snapped. "You call my daughter *Rosie?*"

Rosemary couldn't stand one more second of it. Throwing her hand over her mouth, she jumped up. "Enough," she said with a moan. Glancing to her right, she added, "Dex, you need to be a little understanding, because someday you could be in his shoes, wondering why your son wants to be a ballet dancer instead of a cop." Then she stared at her father, sitting to her left. "And Daddy, you need to back off, because the man you're snarling at happens to be the father of your first grandchild."

Silence descended. Her stomach heaved one more time.

And Rosemary promptly ruined the fruit tarts.

MELODY DIDN'T KNOW whether or not she'd really wanted Nick to leave when she'd ordered him out Wednesday night. Not until he'd actually done it.

Then she'd realized she hadn't.

"He did what you asked him to, dummy," she reminded herself later that night, when she was sitting in her living room, sipping a cup of hot tea and going through a box of tissues.

Yeah. He'd done what she'd asked. He hadn't been happy about it, and he'd told her he'd be back soon, when she'd had a chance to realize he'd looked into her past for a very good reason. And then he'd walked out the door, leaving his pizza—and her tangled emotions—behind him.

So why was she feeling so upset about it?

"It wasn't like him," she told C.C., who was curled up on

her lap. Oscar, on the other hand, was watching from the top of the entertainment center, where he liked to perch, pretending to be king of his domain. That cat always managed to get himself into the highest spots available...then couldn't get down.

"It wasn't like Nick to just go," she said. With no arguments, no teasing. He'd simply looked at her as if she'd wounded him, made his parting comment, then walked out.

Over the next couple of hours, after she'd allowed herself to rage and fume and be embarrassed, she'd realized he had a point. She'd accused the man who'd made unbelievably fabulous love to her just twenty-four hours ago, on this sofa, of sleeping with her to get information on a case.

"Bull," she muttered. He wouldn't have done that. He *hadn't* done that.

So now it wasn't anger at being used that kept her from picking up the phone and calling the man. It was pure embarrassment. Because he'd seen those pictures. He'd read those articles. He'd peeked into her psyche at a time when she'd been so out of her mind with anger and hurt that she hadn't been herself.

And maybe that's why he'd left without an argument. Perhaps seeing that side of her, the vindictive, vengeful woman who'd been humiliated in the media then thoroughly berated in court, had left him feeling less attracted to her.

"How could it not?" she whispered.

C.C. just kept purring.

The cat was nice company, but she wasn't very talkative, and Mel *needed* someone to talk to. It was too late to call Paige, because her husband was a little tense about how much time she spent with the "girls."

Another man who called women girls. Ugh.

Rosemary was having a family dinner and, while Melody

was dying to find out how it was going, she didn't want to interrupt. She'd find out tomorrow whether or not her friend had been successful in creating some sort of friendship between her father and Dex.

"Tanya," she whispered, wondering what route her friend was on this week. It was doubtful she'd be home, but she might still be reachable. Dialing Tanya's cell number, she crossed her fingers that the other woman wasn't in flight somewhere over Nebraska. Thankfully, Tanya answered on the third ring.

"Hey," Melody said. "You at the gate?"

"On the ground in Milwaukee," Tanya said, sounding weary. "Fog delay. So your timing is absolutely perfect."

The two of them talked for a little while, small talk, really, so Melody could work up a way to tell Tanya about the whole having-sex-with-Nick thing, before moving on to the whole ordering-him-out-for-investigating-her thing. But before she could do either one, she realized Tanya wasn't her usual cheerful—if sarcastic—self. "Hey, you don't sound good."

"Some drunk coacher stuck his hand up my skirt when I was handing him his pretzels."

"Did you slug him?"

"*Accidentally* spilled a can of tomato juice all over his lap. That chilled his sorry ass out."

Chuckling, Melody still realized Tanya was upset about more than an unruly passenger, which, to be honest, she dealt with on a regular basis. Though, how anyone would have the courage to put his hands on the woman, who was almost six feet of gorgeous, walking attitude, was beyond her. "That's not all, is it?"

"It's been a shitty month. *Couple* of months."

Her friend hesitated. Feeling incredibly selfish that she

hadn't been there for anyone else's troubles but her own, Mel said, "Go on, spill. What is it? Can I do anything?"

Tanya's voice was dry. "Got a gun?"

She choked out a laugh. "What?"

"Sorry. Bad joke given your week," Tanya said. "I...hell, I guess I just realized sometime over this past summer that I'm twenty-seven years old and I have once again let myself be used by someone who didn't give a damn about me beyond being a great lay and being able to get good air fares."

Whoa. An unconfident, sad-sounding Tanya? This was so off-the-wall. Tanya had balls. Bigger balls than most men. Not to mention more self-confidence than anyone Melody had ever known. And some guy had broken her heart? "I'll get a gun."

Tanya laughed, finally sounding truly amused. "You got enough problems, girlfriend."

"What's one more murder investigation among friends?" she asked, suddenly feeling better herself, too. "By the way, who, exactly, told you you're merely a *great* lay? Because I distinctly remember back in high school when Reggie Denton told the entire basketball team that you were a *fabulous* lay."

Her friend chortled. "Yeah. Right before I broke his fuckin' arm."

"There's my girl."

Melody could hear an airport loudspeaker in the background announcing that the weather conditions were clearing. So Tanya probably needed to get back on the job.

"Maybe that's been my problem," Tanya said, sounding distracted. Confused. "I used to break a guy's arm, now I go off and cry."

Tanya had met a guy who'd left her in tears? Some things were beyond comprehension. "That's a problem, all right. If anyone knows, it's me. But eventually those tears do dry up."

Tanya sighed, her relief audible. "I hope so. Thanks for calling, Mel. I needed to talk, I guess. Maybe more than I thought. I'll be home around this time tomorrow night and I'll buzz you. Let's plan on getting together soon, okay?"

"Anytime, sister."

A call for boarding sounded in the background. Tanya said, "Don't kill anyone before then, okay?"

Grinning, Melody replied, "Don't throw any groping passengers out the emergency exit."

"Deal."

Hanging up, Mel realized she felt a whole lot better than she had a half hour ago. Amazing how her friends could always lift her spirits. She was glad she'd been able to repay the favor for Tanya tonight, who'd sounded more upset about this guy she'd been involved with than Melody would ever have expected.

Glancing at the clock and realizing it was after ten, she decided she was relaxed enough to go to bed. Things were looking okay. And they'd look better in the daytime.

But before she could get up and turn out the lights, the phone rang. The cordless phone was still in her lap, so she picked it up, a tiny spark of hope that it was Nick warring with a hint of concern about her prank caller. Just to be sure, she checked the caller ID before answering.

The number wasn't blocked, and it was local. Unfortunately, she didn't think it was Nick's. She answered cautiously. "Hello?"

"Ms. Tanner?"

Okay, not Nick, but not a heavy-breathing sicko, either. "Yes."

"Ms. Tanner, you might not remember me, but we met recently at Rosemary Chilton's house. My name is Drake Manning."

She almost dropped the phone. Good God, was this "let Melody's past come back to haunt her" month? Why on earth would yet another man she'd put on that stupid, awful list be calling her, especially at this time of night?

"Please excuse the hour," he said smoothly, as if he'd read her mind. "I'm doing the late-night program this week because a colleague is on vacation. We're working on our coverage of Jonathan Rhodes, and, since I hear you were one of the last people to speak with him, I wondered if you would consider talking with me about it."

Talk about the guy who'd stolen her underwear, then gotten himself shot while wearing them? Uh-uh, no way, never. She'd rather eat Oscar and C.C.'s cat food for a month than go on TV and humiliate herself again. Once in a lifetime was enough for anybody. "I don't think so, Mr. Manning."

"Please, Ms. Tanner, it's not for public consumption." He paused. "Jonathan was a friend of mine. I'd like to understand, if I could. I'd consider it a real favor if you'd meet with me. Just for coffee or something?"

She didn't want to. She almost wanted to warn the guy to stay a thousand yards away from her, given that three of the five men he'd been grouped with on her Men Most Wanted list had dropped dead in the past eight weeks. One with a little help.

But something in his voice, the note of genuine regret maybe, made her take pity on him. He'd had to cover his ass on the air, but in the early hours after the murder, Drake Manning had clearly been mourning a friend.

"All right, Mr. Manning," she said. "Coffee it is."

CHAPTER TWELVE

SOMETHING WAS seriously wrong with Dex. Nick had figured that out the minute the two of them had met at the station Thursday morning for a meeting with the police commissioner on the Jonathan Rhodes case. The other detective was always quiet and circumspect, but today he'd been damn near brooding. When Draco, another detective on their floor, had asked Dex to confirm the name of a witness, Dex had almost snapped his head off. Totally out of character for Mr. Laid-Back.

Even figuring he already knew what the problem was, Nick had asked his partner if anything was wrong. Dex had mumbled something that could have been "nothing" or could have been "everything" and hadn't said another word.

On any other day, Nick would have tried to find out more. To at least see if there was anything he could do to help his friend. It was doubtful, since the dark expression on Dex's face was instantly recognizable to any other man who'd gotten himself all torn up in the guts about a woman, as Dex obviously had. And the only woman in his life was Rosemary.

If she'd broken up with him because of the difference in their social stature, Nick was going to tell her where she could go, regardless of whether she was Melody's best friend.

Melody. She was the reason he hadn't hassled Dex too much about his dark mood. Because he'd been unable to get her off his mind since he'd left her apartment the evening before, still wondering where exactly he'd made such a wrong turn. Was it in making love to her when he'd known he was going to have to pry into her past? Was it telling her what he'd learned? Should he have asked her first, giving her a chance to explain things her own way?

Whatever he *should* have done, he couldn't change what he *had* done. Or how she'd reacted to it.

He'd investigated and she'd erupted.

"You've got to talk to me sometime," he muttered as he looked up at her apartment window Thursday night. It was nearly ten, and though he wondered if her neighbors were looking outside, recognizing his car and figuring there was a stalker or a criminal staking out their street, he couldn't make himself drive away.

He hadn't sat outside her building like this for a few nights. But for some reason, today, an unidentified worry was gnawing at him. He didn't believe in superstition or ESP or any of that crap, unlike a lot of people in this town. But he did believe in intuition. Cop's instinct, whatever. And something had been telling him all day that Melody needed him. So after putting in an extra long day at the station and grabbing a late dinner with some of the guys, he'd cruised down her street before heading home.

Her apartment was nearly dark. She could already be in bed, asleep. And he was probably just being paranoid. Still, something made him sit here, in the quiet stillness of the night, for a minute more, hoping the feeling of uneasiness would dissipate.

It wasn't until he saw her emerge from the front door of her building that he realized he'd been totally busted. Cringing, he gave her a sheepish wave as she stalked over to the car looking like an avenging angel. Which was incredibly sexy.

"Unless you're staking out another drug dealer on this street, you've got some explaining to do," she said as she opened the passenger door and leaned inside.

"I was on my way home and I wanted to—"

"Wanted to what, spy on me?"

His hands tightened on the steering wheel. This had been a very bad idea. "Look, I'm sorry. I had this feeling."

She rolled her eyes.

"Stupid, I know. But I felt like maybe you needed me."

She said nothing for a second, staring at him across the darkness of his car, hopefully assessing his words. Or trying to figure out what to say. Then, with a determined look she said, "I don't plan on *needing* anyone ever again, Nick."

His gut knotted up.

"I'm tired of people thinking they have the right to take care of me, or know what's best for my life."

"I wasn't—"

She cut him off. "But, I *am* ready to speak to you again."

Locking his car, he followed her inside and up the stairs to her apartment. Once inside, he stepped out of the way, watching her lock the doorknob and throw the bolt. With the light from a small lamp and the television playing mutely on the other side of the room, he got a better glimpse of her face. Beautiful, of course, but she also looked tired. Tense. "You okay?"

She nodded. "It's been a long day." Heading toward the kitchen, she asked, "I'm going to make some tea. Want a cup?"

Tea. Gag. "Got any coffee?" He regretted the request one second after the words left his lips because he suddenly remembered what her coffee tasted like.

"Just decaf."

Decaffeinated brown flavored water couldn't taste much worse than regular brown flavored water he supposed. "It'll do."

Once inside, he sat down in the living room, picking up

one of her cats—the one named after the bologna—and scratched him behind his ears. Melody returned from the kitchen and sat down on the other side of the couch.

"So, are you speaking to me again?" he asked softly, still eyeing the cat.

Even in the soft lighting of the room, her tension was visible, but she admitted, "I know why you felt you needed to look into my divorce. I understand that much."

"Good."

Anger made her voice tight. "But I don't understand why you had to be so damned secretive about it."

She had a valid point. He'd been feeling like a first-class heel about that all day. "I'm sorry. I should have trusted you enough to ask you. You could have told me what I needed to know."

"Like I was going to tell you all the ugly details?" she said, looking skeptical. "I doubt that would have happened."

"Well, maybe subconsciously that's why I didn't ask."

She fell silent, watching him pet the cat, a pensive expression on her face. Finally, in a low voice, she asked, "So, how much do you know?"

He continued running his fingers through Oscar's soft hair, knowing better than to look at Melody, to show any sign of sympathy. She'd hate that. "I know you were married to a big slimeball who tried to get your underwear during your divorce."

Her expression softened.

"And I know that just because I found out you have a temper doesn't mean you and I can't keep…going forward."

"Going forward? Is that what you call it?" Confusion rang clearly in her voice. "We're playing around with this tension, pretending we can have some kind of sexual relationship, when on the side you're investigating me and I'm wondering how I ever had the nerve to get naked and crazy with you."

"Naked and crazy?" That sounded good to him. If only she hadn't sounded so dismayed when she'd said it. "Was that such a bad thing?"

She rose to her feet, striding to the kitchen. "You said you didn't want to be a name I scratched off your list. Well, dammit, I sure don't want to be nothing but an investigation to you."

Nick lifted the cat off his lap and immediately followed her. He had to clear up that notion immediately. "Lady, you are a lot of things to me, but *just* an investigation definitely isn't one of them." Taking her by the upper arm, he held her still, determined to make her believe him. He wondered if she could hear the crazy, wild beating of his heart, and if she knew what it meant. He also wondered if he was brave enough to tell her.

His pulse was beating as out of control as his thoughts for one reason: he was afraid. Because right now, Melody could order him out of her life for good…and he feared that more than anything he'd ever experienced on the streets of Savannah.

He might not know *what* they'd started, but they'd started something. And damned if he was ready to let it end. Not when, for the first time in as long as he could remember, his life was feeling so incredibly right.

"Melody, don't shut me out. I'm sorry I had to pry into your past. I'm a shit and a bastard and you have every right to tell me to go to hell." She opened her mouth as if to do just that, so he quickly continued, "But I swear to you, I didn't *want* to invade your privacy. I never would have done it if I didn't think there was at least a slight possibility that your ex-husband could be tied up in this somehow. I would have let you tell me on your own time, in your own way."

"By painting it on a billboard?" she snapped.

He tried to keep a grin from tickling his lips but couldn't quite manage it. "Damn, girl, you give good revenge. But somebody needs to teach you about covert operations."

"Don't you dare laugh at me!"

"Not laughing at you, honey." No, he wasn't laughing at her. He was about to go on…to tell her how much he admired her strength, particularly because of the way she'd moved here and gone on with her life, despite a divorce settlement that had, even to a novice like him, seemed incredibly unfair. But before he could do it, the phone rang.

"It's late," he said, immediately on alert.

She looked at him, then at the phone, which continued to ring. Then she let out a slow, steady breath. "It's probably my friend Tanya. She's supposed to be getting home around this time tonight."

Still unsure, he nevertheless stepped out of her way, letting her pass. Reaching for the cordless receiver hanging in a cradle on the wall, she pulled it to her ear. "Hello? Hello?"

His whole body grew tense as he saw Melody's slim jaw tighten. Even from a few feet away, he could see the way her chest began to heave.

"Hang up," he snapped.

She ignored him. "Look, you twisted creep," she snarled into the phone, "you'd better stop calling me. You got the last bit of blood from this stone. I have nothing more for you to take, Bill, so go to hell and leave me alone."

Once she'd slammed the phone down, she glared at Nick, heat and anger snapping almost physically between them. "You want to investigate my son-of-a-bitch ex-husband? How about figuring out how he keeps getting my personal phone number even though I've had it changed twice since I moved here."

Nick clenched his back teeth, not wanting her to see his sudden fury. "Have you gotten a lot of these lately?"

"A couple. I don't like to answer when the caller ID is blocked, but I never know if it could be a potential client who got my home number from a friend." Melody's sudden burst of angry bravado appeared to abandon her, because she crossed her arms in front of her chest, running her hands up and down as if to warm herself. "He doesn't say anything, just breathes deeply. Or sometimes he makes little moaning sounds, as if he wants me to imagine him *doing* something to himself…while I'm on the other end of the line." She sounded revolted.

"The sick bastard," Nick said tightly, striding over and putting his hands on her shoulders. Unable to help himself, he pulled her into his arms, holding her against his chest. He twined one hand in her thick hair while the other pressed against the small of her back.

Making small, gentle circles with the tips of his fingers, he murmured soft, comforting things, until he felt the tension slowly ease out of her body. "I'll take care of him, Melody," he whispered. "I'll make sure he leaves you alone."

And he meant it. No matter what else happened, he was going to see to it that Melody never shed another tear, never had another moment's pain, because of the SOB she'd married.

"I don't need you to take care of me," she said, pulling away and running a weary hand over her eyes. "But if you want to help me figure out how to get him to leave me alone, I guess I'd better tell you a little more about who we're dealing with."

DRAKE MANNING WASN'T feeling well. It was quarter to eleven, he was about to go on the air for the late news, and all he could think about was getting it done and going home.

He *hated* this schedule. A man of routine, he liked his regular noon and six-in-the-evening slots. The next time the eleven-o'clock anchor wanted to go on vacation, they could just get one of the beat reporters to take over the desk. Like Angie. Heck, maybe if he put her up for the job, she'd stop glaring daggers at him for dumping her again.

"Are you okay, Mr. Manning? You're looking pale, even with the foundation."

Forcing his annoyance away, he met the stare of Marla, the station's cute young makeup girl, in the lighted mirror of the greenroom. "No, actually, I'm not quite up to par," he admitted, giving her the kind of self-deprecating smile that made his TV viewers want to welcome him into their homes every single day of the week. And made him look much younger than his forty-four years. "I stopped and grabbed a late dinner on my way in tonight. Mexican food doesn't seem to agree with me these days."

She gave him a worried frown, bending to put a motherly hand on his forehead. Which gave him a nice shot of her cleavage down the loose neckline of her blouse. "You feel warm."

He was definitely feeling warm. Particularly because Marla—who he'd always flirted with but never seriously pursued since she seemed happily married—was now brushing those nice round tits of hers against his shoulder.

Hmm…maybe she *wasn't* so happily married.

"You're so kind," he murmured, lifting a hand and patting her fingers, which rested on his shoulder. "Such a good person."

"Oh, *thank* you, Mr. Manning."

Her expression was almost adoring. Why had he never noticed that before?

"A little more spray, sweetheart, all right?" he said softly, not wanting a single hair out of place when he was on the air. And wanting a nice shot of her ass as she bent over to grab the hairspray off the counter.

"Of course," she said, reaching around him, giving him the view he'd wanted.

Now things were *definitely* heating up. Drake was surprised to realize he was getting a hard-on, right here in the greenroom where people wandered in and out all the time.

Actually, he'd been feeling sexed-up a good bit of the day, ever since he'd had coffee with that photographer, Melody Tanner, this morning. The woman had the kind of mouth that could make a man beg. It'd been damn hard to keep focused on Jonathan Rhodes—and what he might have spilled to Miss Tanner…nothing, apparently—when all he could think about was exactly where he wanted her to put her juicy lips.

"Is that all right?" Marla asked, tucking in the few last errant strands of his hair before she sprayed it into place.

He nodded, not even able to speak, wondering why he was getting a world-class woody merely from sneaking a peek down a woman's shirt, which, frankly, he'd been doing since the age of ten.

He was usually much more controlled. Having had a lot of sexual experience—a *whole* lot—he'd become adept at keeping cool at inappropriate times. Usually it was no problem. But now…well, though he tried a few mental tricks, Drake Junior simply wasn't obeying orders. His faithful friend just kept swelling up until big Drake had to shift in his seat.

Even the thought of the ugly scene he'd had in the parking-lot forty minutes ago couldn't calm things down. He'd been ambushed by a woman he'd been banging before Angie, who'd chosen now—two months after he'd ditched her—to confront him about it. The thought of the anger in her face should have been enough to shift his cock into standby mode, but even that didn't help.

"Watch your eyes," Marla said as she coated his black hair with another layer of strong spray. When she was done, she put the bottle down and looked at him quizzically. "Are you going to be all right?"

"Mmm-hmm," he mumbled, feeling hot all over. Particularly in the groin. Too bad he had to go on the air in ten minutes, because with the size and strength of his hard-on, he could undoubtedly turn Marla into a fan for life.

"Now you're getting flushed. Want me to get you your soda?"

Nodding, he watched her in the mirror. She jiggled as she walked to the other side of the greenroom to pick up the large foam cup he'd put there when he'd arrived.

He could definitely use his drink, because the cup didn't contain soda. With a hefty tip, the bartender at the place where Drake had stopped for dinner had been accommodating enough to put a Sea Breeze in a to-go cup, any hint of alcohol nicely disguised by the strong smell of grapefruit juice.

"Is there anything else I can do for you?" Marla asked after she'd brought it back over and handed it to him.

Oh, he could definitely think of one or two things. He smiled, wondering how she'd react if he took his hand off his lap and let her figure out exactly what he wanted her to do for him.

But no. Angie had taught him a serious lesson about messing around with anybody at work. "Thanks, Marla, but I'm fine."

She gave him another smile—so pretty, so young and sweet—and then sauntered out, her little butt wagging. When he was alone in the greenroom, he rose from his stool, suddenly feeling a bit light-headed. He actually almost stumbled, although that was probably no wonder, considering his dick was throbbing so much he was ready to fuck the first thing that moved.

"Down, good buddy," he murmured under his breath before lifting his drink and sucking from the straw. Hopefully the alcohol would help him get through the next half hour.

Putting the nearly empty cup on the counter, he tapped his chest and took a deep breath. "Got to leave some juice for the old ticker." It probably wasn't so great for his heart to have nearly every ounce of blood in his body centered in his wanker.

Still, as he walked out of the greenroom toward the soundstage, he had to admit it felt good to know he was strong and virile enough to be able to get it rock hard, without even touching a woman, only a year after open heart surgery. Damn good.

And as soon as the eleven-o'clock news was over, he was going to say to hell with it, find Marla the makeup girl, and screw her until she couldn't walk anymore.

MELODY TOLD Nick everything.

It wasn't easy. It wasn't pretty. And she couldn't do it without switching from tea to wine.

As if knowing she needed her space, Nick didn't sit with her on the couch, where she'd curled up with one arm wrapped around her upraised legs. Instead he'd taken a seat on the floor, his long legs crossed in front of him, one forearm resting on the seat of a chair.

Just looking at him down there, his thick hair tousled, his lean jaw lightly stubbled and his brown eyes so attentive made her shiver in reaction. Trying to disguise that, she sipped from her glass. The warmth of the rich red wine oozed through her body, helping her forget she was revealing some of her most painful memories to someone who'd made incredible love to her forty-eight hours ago. Who'd given her multiple orgasms and left her hungry for more. Many more.

"First man-induced orgasms I've had in a long time," she murmured, not even realizing she was speaking out loud until she saw Nick's brow shoot up.

"I beg your pardon?" he said.

Hell, once she'd gotten over her anger at him for investigating her, she'd spilled her guts to the man. After what she'd revealed, Melody had absolutely no blushes left. So she certainly didn't feel any heat rising to her cheeks as she explained, "Before Tuesday night, it'd been…a long time since I'd been intimate with anyone. In fact, that night at Rosemary's was the first time I'd had a man's hands on me in over two years."

A flash of something hot and sexual appeared in his eyes, but just as quickly disappeared. "So you stopped sleeping with the prick with the drill long before the end of your marriage?"

She laughed softly, amused at how Nick had zoned in on Bill's nickname—the one she used with her friends, and in her own brain. "Yes. Like I said, it wasn't only the rumors of Bill's infidelity…which I strongly suspected but couldn't entirely prove. But it was how wild those rumors were. I became…*cold*. I guess that's the word. He left me cold."

On the chair, his fingers curled into a fist. His voice low, he said, "You are not cold, Melody Tanner."

She met his eyes, took strength from the attraction and warmth she saw there, then explained, "But I grew cold with *him*. As he did with me. There was no intimacy. How could I have trust and intimacy with a man who used to take out my modeling scrapbooks and show them to anybody who came to our house?" Sipping again and shaking her head, she fell silent.

"Like you were a trophy in a case," he murmured, understanding without further explanation.

"Exactly. Can you imagine what it was like sitting at a dinner table with three other couples, knowing…just *know-ing*…the men were remembering the first time they saw that peacock feather picture?" She shuddered. "Not to mention their wives who had to hate my guts."

"Nobody could hate you. If anything, I'm sure it made them see Bill for what he was."

"Yes. A collector. I was a prize, one he wanted other people to envy him over. The Peacock Feather Girl, the swimsuit model. The fantasy…not the real woman. *She* didn't interest him. Especially once the initial excitement of his possession wore off." Lowering her voice, she added, "Thank God."

Nick's entire body appeared tense, and his jaw was almost granite as he gruffly said, "You should know, since it's been an issue for you in the past, I don't…I've *never* had anything I could pass on to you. It makes me *sick* that a husband would put his wife at risk like that."

She immediately knew what he meant, and though they'd used a condom the other night, she appreciated him saying it. "Thank you," she whispered. Even after all these years, and even though she'd had absolutely no regrets about making love with Nick, something inside her warmed and unfurled at his openness. Maybe because she'd never had it before. "And for the record, the worst never happened. I'm—"

"You don't need to say another word," he replied, still looking almost ferocious. On her behalf, she knew.

She imagined this man would be something to see if he ever truly got enraged at someone.

"He's never quite gotten over you walking out on him— denying him his prize. Has he." It wasn't a question.

"No, I don't think he has, judging by the phone calls and the way he spoke to me when he was here."

That did spark an even stronger reaction from Nick. He shot straight up, rising to his feet, his fists clenched and his eyes blazing. "He was here? In Savannah?"

"In this building," she admitted. Still hating to remember the ugly scene, she explained, "The day we met. Do you remember when I was trying to move the mattress? That was why I was so stressed out that day. Bill had said he was in town on business and thought he'd stop in to say hello. What he really wanted was to gloat and show off the new Rolex he bought with *my* money."

"Did you ask him what the hell kind of business he was doing? I thought he got all your money because he claimed he could never be in business again?"

"Good point," she admitted with a soft laugh. "He said he was involved in something 'big' with some businessmen here in town, again taunting me about what he had that I didn't. I asked him to leave me alone. To be content with what he'd taken from me, to go on with his life and let me go on with mine. That's all I'd ever wanted."

"To go on with your life, just have him leave you alone?"

She nodded. "It seemed reasonable, and frankly, I thought the financial trade-off was worth it. Otherwise, I might have fought the judge's decision. Or at least dragged my feet, making him work harder for his victory."

Nick paced across the floor, his boots pounding against the hardwood, revealing his anger. "And what happened? Did he do as you asked? Did he leave you alone?"

"Well, he hasn't stopped calling, that's for sure," she said with a disgusted frown.

He finally stopped pacing, leaning against the arm of the couch and looking down at her. "Melody, do you think he could have had anything to do with what happened to Jonathan Rhodes?"

She immediately shook her head, the response instinctive. "No. He's a bully and an ass, but I don't think he's a murderer."

Nick didn't appear convinced. "It's amazing what people will resort to when their pride is at stake."

That certainly was an understatement. "Right. Like climbing up onto a billboard and vandalizing it."

Some of the tension seemed to leave him and he managed a slight smile. "Yeah. Like that. But he's lucky you reacted with a paintbrush. Believe me, in the four years I've been on the force, I've seen wives resort to guns, knives and frying pans a lot more often."

"Maybe if he'd come home that night, I would have reacted violently…directly at him. Instead I lashed out at his billboard, knowing I'd hit him where it would hurt the most—his pocketbook."

He grunted. "Which is why it totally blows that he got all your money because of it."

"Yeah, it totally blows," she said with a deep laugh.

Her own laughter amazed her, and she froze, realizing what she'd just done. She'd never thought she'd be able to laugh about that awful night. But somehow, talking about it to Nick had seemed to open up something inside her. To allow her to let go of some of the humiliation and rage and view it from his perspective. God…to *laugh* about it.

Nick reached over to the coffee table and picked up his half-empty bottle of beer. After he sipped from it, he murmured, "There's one thing I don't get."

"What?"

He hesitated for a brief second, staring into her eyes as if gauging whether or not to continue.

"What?"

"Tell me why you're so sure you're not ready to move on with your life. I mean, despite what happened between us Tuesday night, I don't think you've fully recognized yourself as the woman I see. The woman most of the world sees."

His words took her completely by surprise. She'd been expecting something else on the murder investigation. Not something so personal. "I don't quite follow."

"I mean," he continued, "if you were totally messed up in the head about why he didn't want you—why he cheated—maybe I could understand you having some kind of confidence issues. Relationship issues." He slowly moved down to sit beside her on the couch. His khaki-clad hips were just a few inches from hers, but they didn't touch. But it *felt* like they were touching.

Suddenly the air felt warmer, and she began to tingle. Not from the wine, but from something much more intoxicating. This sweet-talking, incredibly sexy man.

Who seemed determined to psychoanalyze her.

"But it sounds to me like you know exactly the way your ex's mind worked. You know it wasn't you—it had *nothing* to do with you. So why is your confidence still shaky?"

Melody didn't know what to say and not only because his physical proximity seemed to be sapping all her energy and her brain power. Nick's question was nothing she hadn't asked herself. Bill's betrayals, his attitudes, his obsessiveness had all been obvious from early on. Nick was entirely right: she'd still let the failure of their marriage—and even her husband's cheating—weigh on her as if they'd been her fault. Yes, she'd worked up the nerve to have an incredible, sinfully delightful sexual encounter with Nick, but in her mind, she'd never stopped wondering when the other shoe was going to drop. When Nick was going to see whatever it was that Bill had seen in her. What he'd found lacking.

    Knowing he was waiting for an answer, she admitted, "I was
the stupid one who mistook the need for a normal life for love.
I married him for all the wrong reasons, when I should have
been letting myself grow up and be a normal twenty-one-year-
old."

    "So you wanted love. It's not a crime. What he did…now
that's a crime." His voice grew more quiet, and even more
intense. "You've been carrying the weight of your failed marriage on your shoulders, Mel, when you should have heaped
it on that bastard's head. Along with about a ton of bricks."

    She couldn't say anything. His words bounced around in
her mind, making so much sense yet seeming so simple. Her
logical mind suspected her ex-husband was simply incapable of fidelity. That no woman would have been able to hold
his attention. Her emotional side, however? Well…it hadn't
quite caught up.

    Still, maybe Nick was right. Maybe it was time she
stopped letting her marriage color every other experience in
her life.

    Yes, she'd been stupid to fall in love with an ass—or at
least the life she thought that ass was offering her. But the
rest of it…well, the rest of the blame was Bill's. From his first
affair to his last brag session about his famous wife, he'd used
her, exploited her and taken her for granted. Until she'd had
enough and had gotten out. All on her own.

    Well, maybe with a little help from a can of paint and a
news helicopter. And some firemen.

    But she'd really done it. She'd had the strength to walk
away from something she knew was wrong. So how could she
now claim to not have the strength to walk *toward* something
she knew could be very, very right?

    Especially when she already knew it was very, very *good*.

    "You going to stare into that glass like it holds all the secrets of the universe? Or are you going to admit I'm right?" he asked softly.

She tore her gaze from the sparkling burgundy depths of her glass and looked over at the man sitting beside her. So big. So strong. So intuitive.

So utterly desirable.

Oh, Lord, she wanted him again. Wanted him desperately. Whether she was good enough to hold him—to keep him—suddenly didn't seem to matter anymore. Later…she'd think about what he'd said about her marriage later. For now, she just wanted him.

She was about to tell him so—and ask him to stay the night—when she realized he was no longer looking at her. Instead, he was staring toward the muted television, his head tilted to the side and a puzzled expression on his face.

Melody followed his stare. "Oh, great, *him*," she muttered.

Drake Manning was doing his smarmy thing in front of the camera. Funny how completely unattractive she now found him, the man who she'd thought was so handsome six years ago. Not just because every hormone in her body seemed to have Nick's name stamped on it, but also because Drake was one slimy character.

She figured now probably wasn't the best time to tell Nick she'd met the reporter for coffee this morning. She had a feeling that could kill the suddenly intimate mood.

Besides, coffee had been a wasted exercise, since Manning had been more interested in staring at Melody's chest than he had been in his late friend, Jonathan Rhodes. The Channel 9 anchor had been decidedly gross. And Paige was right, his hair simply didn't move. It would have stayed perfectly coiffed if he'd been sucked up in a wind tunnel.

"Let's turn it off," she said, turning away from the television.

Nick wasn't even looking at her. "There's something wrong with him. Where's your remote?"

Curious now, Melody retrieved the remote control from between the cushions of the couch and hit the volume button. She quickly saw what had gotten Nick's attention— Drake Manning *didn't* look well. His face was pale and sweaty under the lights of the television studio. He was reading the news, but his breaths were audible, choppy, magnified by his microphone.

"Looks like he's coming down with something," Melody said, wondering when they were going to take pity on the guy and fade to commercial.

Nick said nothing, still staring intently at the screen.

Listening to the television anchorman go on about an upcoming historical festival, even Melody grew more curious. Because his voice was growing weak, then loud, shaky, then firm. "Where the heck is an obnoxious used-car commercial when you need one? Why is this guy still on?"

"I have no idea," Nick said. He leaned forward, dropping his elbows onto his knees, still focused entirely on the television.

"And now, we're going to…going to…" Drake Manning's eyes widened and his head dropped forward. Something in his lap or at his feet had obviously caught his attention.

Looking up into the camera again, he stammered something. Then, to her surprise—and probably the surprise of the entire TV viewing audience—the anchorman stood up from behind his desk.

When he stood, he became a lot more visible. A *whole* lot. Way, way, *way* more visible.

"Oh, my God," she whispered, seeing where Manning's hands were situated. *Exactly* where they were situated. She scrunched her face up in distaste. "Is *that* what they do behind the news desk these days?"

"If that's the case," Nick said, his voice dry, "it's no wonder they can smile through tragic stories."

Before she could even accept the fact that a well-respected Savannah celebrity was grabbing his groin on live television, Melody's mouth dropped open and her words dried up in her mouth. Because *now* Drake Manning was stumbling out from behind his desk, one hand clutching at his chest.

People on the set of the television news show scrambled into the picture, the weather guy leaping out from the front of his blue screen and yelling for someone to call 911.

Only the cameraman seemed to maintain his journalistic sleaziness…er, standard…and remained focused on the star of the Channel 9 news team. The camera shot held steady, fully capturing the view of Drake Manning falling to the floor, landing flat on his back.

Melody gasped. Nick grunted. They both stared, as did most of Savannah probably. Who could possibly have turned away from the sight of the famous local newscaster lying sprawled on the floor of his studio? His arms were wide, his eyes open. And, most shockingly, his trousers were, uh… tented.

Noticeably tented. *Astoundingly* tented.

"Nick, is that…"

"Yeah, it is," Nick said, already reaching into his pocket for his cell phone. "I've got to say," he added while he dialed a number and waited for his call to connect, "I think now I understand why Drake Manning was so popular with the ladies."

Yeah. Judging by the enormous bulge in the crotch of Drake Manning's pants, so did Melody.

CHAPTER THIRTEEN

IF IT HADN'T BEEN for the recent deaths of three men on Melody's infamous list, Nick might have at first thought Drake Manning had simply dropped dead of a massive coronary on the job. He wouldn't be the first hard-living fortysomething man to do so. The visible erection notwithstanding, the guy *did* have a heart condition.

But somehow, from the moment he'd arrived at the hospital where they'd taken Manning Thursday night and learned the famous newscaster hadn't survived, he'd had a feeling the death had been anything but natural. So after calling Dex to meet him, Nick had gone back to the potential crime scene to see what he could find out.

"Do you really think the M.E.'s going to find something that will turn this from a normal heart attack into a murder?" asked Jerry Gates, a detective from the First squad. The guy was looking into Manning's death, since the Channel 9 studios were in his precinct. Fortunately, though, he'd been receptive to Nick and Dex's presence because of the possible connection to the Rhodes case.

"Yeah, I do," Nick said, rubbing wearily at the corners of his eyes. They'd been here at the studio all night, and it was nearly seven. He'd been up for twenty-four hours and since he'd slept like crap the night before that, he was dragging. He needed coffee, pronto.

They'd spent much of the night talking to Drake Manning's co-workers. The more they did so, the more convinced Nick became that the man had been a victim of more than merely a weak heart. One of the crew members had allegedly seen Manning arguing loudly with a woman in the parking lot shortly before the broadcast. The news director had also admitted Manning had problems with some of his co-workers, who disliked his ambition. And his womanizing.

"Manning and Rhodes were in bed together on some business deal, huh?" Then, snickering, Gates added, "Considering the way he looked right before he keeled over, he wanted to be in bed with *somebody*."

Cop humor. Gruesome, but necessary for surviving the darker side of the job.

"Yeah, we've stumbled across a few mentions of Manning in some of Jonathan Rhodes's files," Nick said, not wanting to get into any specifics on any *other* connection between the two men.

Like Melody's list.

Melody. He glanced at his watch, realizing it was probably still too early to call her. He'd promised to stay in touch as he'd bolted from her apartment the night before but he hadn't had a minute to do so.

"The lab found something in Manning's drink."

Nick looked up as Dex entered the office, where he and Gates had been interviewing every employee who'd been in the building during the eleven-o'clock program. "Let me guess," Nick said. "A male sexual performance drug?"

Dex nodded. "Yeah. Judging by the amount in the few ounces of liquid left in the cup, someone put a supersize dose of the stuff in there."

"Talk about embarrassing…OD'ing on the little blue pill." Gates looked back and forth between them. "Is it possible the guy had a hot date last night and was just overzealous with his medication?"

Nick immediately shook his head. "The man had a heart attack last year. No doctor would have prescribed something like that. And even if he got it illegally, Manning wouldn't have been stupid enough to take that big a dose."

Dex nodded, looking somber. "Somebody slipped it to him."

Gates didn't argue the point—it was the only thing that made sense. No matter how much he wanted to get laid, no man would be foolish enough to take massive doses of a drug that affected his most valued body part.

Dex crossed his arms and frowned. "From what the make-up girl said, Manning's cup was sitting on a counter in a public room when she arrived. There were probably twenty people in the building at that time."

"It could have been anybody," Gates said. "Maybe even from wherever he got the drink to begin with."

Right. Meaning they had a long day of work ahead of them.

Gates left the office, heading for the men's room, leaving Nick and Dex alone. His partner was wearing the same dark expression he'd had yesterday, so apparently whatever had put him in such a rotten mood hadn't gotten any better. Nick wasn't going to ask his partner what was wrong. Dex knew him well enough to know he could talk to him about anything if he needed to.

"I need to tell you something," Dex said, his tone serious.

Okay, apparently he needed to.

"I obviously didn't realize we were going to catch this one today. I've got a flight booked to Pennsylvania late this afternoon and I'll be flying back tomorrow morning. I already put in for the time off."

Nick's eyebrows shot up. Apparently something serious was going on at home. "I'm sorry, is there anything I can do? Is it your family?"

A half smile tilted the other man's mouth. "I guess you could say that." The smile faded. "Rosemary's pregnant."

Nick froze, not sure he'd heard his friend right. "Oh, man, for real?"

"Yeah."

Nick thought about it for a long minute. Once upon a time he'd been exactly where Dex was. Only his situation hadn't turned out so well. "You're sure the baby's…"

"It's mine," Dex replied, unhesitating.

Nick nodded. "You dealing okay?"

Dex shoved his hands into his pockets, looking more unsure than he ever had about anything in the two years Nick had known the man. "I don't know. I love her."

"I know you do."

Shaking his head, Dex began to pace across the office. "I just hadn't expected this."

"But now it's happened. So the question is, how do you feel about it?" Nick asked quietly.

"Happy. Scared. Pissed off. Overwhelmed. Excited."

That about summed it up, Nick supposed. "How about Rosemary? What's she thinking?"

For the first time, Dex averted his gaze, staring at the floor. "I haven't talked to her since she told me Wednesday night."

Eyes narrowing, Nick asked, "Why the hell not?"

Dex shook his head. "It wasn't an ideal situation. Her family was there when she blurted it out to all of us then threw up all over the dining-room table."

Nick bit his bottom lip to prevent a chuckle.

Dex didn't seem to notice. "I think her father would be

very happy if I got kidnapped and thrown aboard a Russian trawler, never to be heard from again."

"Tough shit."

Dex finally looked up.

"I mean it, man, what her family thinks doesn't matter. It's what you and Rosemary want that's important." Shaking his head, he continued, "You do what is best for you two and your kid. What her father wants or doesn't want is his problem, not yours."

Remembering the shotgun wedding he'd endured—and the way it had thrust him in a completely different direction than he'd ever envisioned for his life—Nick had a strong feeling of empathy for his friend. "Whatever you do, Dex, do it for the right reasons, not because it's what somebody else wants you to do."

Dex nodded once. "I will. And actually, I already know what I'm going to do. That's why I have to go to Pennsylvania."

Before Nick could ask anything more—like why, exactly, his friend was leaving the state when his girlfriend had just told him she was going to have his baby—Gates returned from the men's room. Dex immediately shut down. Not unexpected—his partner wasn't the type to discuss his personal life in front of a near-stranger. So Nick was left to wonder why Dex had to go home this weekend.

If he found out Melody was pregnant, the last place he'd want to go would be Joyful.

Whoa, man, that had been a random thought. He'd only known the woman a few weeks, and he was already thinking about stuff like families and babies? Insane. Utterly out of character. But completely true.

What that meant, he had no idea. Funny though, that Joyful had crossed his mind now, considering he was supposed to be heading there tomorrow for Johnny and Emma's engagement party. He wondered if Melody would want to take a ride with him across the state. And wondered if it was too early in their relationship to ask.

"To hell with it," he muttered. "I'm asking anyway."

Looking at his watch again and seeing it was after seven, he decided to try to get in touch with her before things got crazy with people arriving for work at the TV station. "I'm going to go make a call," he murmured, giving Dex one more nod of support.

His partner acknowledged the gesture with a nod of his own.

Figuring Mel probably hadn't gotten much sleep and could very well have sat up all night waiting for a word, Nick left the room to phone her. When she answered on the first ring, he figured he'd made the right choice.

"Nick?"

"Yeah. I didn't wake you, did I?"

"I don't think I slept at all. I saw on another channel this morning that Drake Manning didn't make it. They said it was a heart attack…is that true?"

Leaning one shoulder against the corridor wall, he wondered how much to reveal to Melody. He wished he could reassure her—could tell her that Manning had indeed died of natural causes. But he couldn't lie. "It was a heart attack…but we're not sure what caused it. It looks like he was drugged. We're not sure if that caused the heart attack or not."

Her sigh was audible. "Drugged by something that made him, uh…"

"Yeah."

Another sigh. "That's gross."

"Pathetic," he agreed.

"Sounds like a woman thing."

"How so?"

"I mean, it sounds like something a woman would do. Killing a guy like that…well, I think I'd be looking at any woman he's recently used and abused. Or maybe his ex-wife."

She was right, and Nick had been thinking along the same lines. Funny how quickly she'd leaped to the same conclusion. "It looks like I'm going to be here a while longer. We're talking to everyone who spoke to him yesterday."

"Oh."

That tiny sound made him pause. Because something—his intuition—told him she *hadn't* simply been making it out of disappointment that he wouldn't be back over anytime soon.

"What's wrong?"

"I was going to tell you last night when we saw him on the news, but you left so fast."

He rubbed his weary eyes, almost knowing what she was going to say next. "Tell me what?"

Clearing her throat, Melody explained, "I met Drake Manning for coffee yesterday morning."

Wonderful. Absolutely perfect. Just what he needed to hear.

She hurried on. "He called me and asked me to meet him because he wanted to talk about Jonathan Rhodes. They were good friends."

Yeah, good friends. Slime one and slime two. "What time was it?"

"About ten. It was really nothing. We met at a coffee shop around the corner, sat outside for a half hour, then I left to go take team photos for a local high school football squad."

Sounded innocent enough. Not that his lieutenant was going to believe that when he found out. "You sat outside the whole time? With lots of people around?"

"Absolutely."

"Was he by any chance drinking juice out of a foam cup?"

"Uh-uh. Coffee out of a ceramic mug."

Okay. That was better. But he was still going to have to tread very carefully. He was now officially sleeping with a woman who might somehow be involved with two murders.

No, he didn't for a moment suspect Melody had anything to do with the deaths of Drake Manning or Jonathan Rhodes. Any more than he thought she'd shoved a meatball down Charles Pulowski's throat or held that golfer in Atlanta at gunpoint and made him stick his dick in a wall.

But four deaths in two months…two in one week. That was one hell of a coincidence.

"I'm going to have to come by later to take your statement," he said wearily.

Her voice subdued, she replied, "That's fine."

God, he hated to leave things on that note. So cool and impersonal. If he'd turned the damn television off last night, he might right now be waking up in Melody's arms after an incredible night of sensual pleasures.

He had to close his eyes at the very thought of it. Nick wanted her so much it hurt. He wanted to slowly remove her clothes, to kiss every inch of her beautiful, soft body. To stroke away every unpleasant thought and love her until the rest of the world didn't exist.

As if she read his mind, she asked, "After you take my statement, are you going off duty? I mean, am I only going to be seeing Detective Walker today?" Clearing her throat, she added softly, "Or am I going to be seeing the man I wanted so much to make love with last night?"

The cop in him said to back off. To cool their relationship to a purely professional one. Not just for the sake of the case, but possibly for Melody's own good.

If somebody was out there knocking off guys to get at her—either to frame her, or to claim her—the last thing he needed was to let his emotions get any more entangled with the woman. She needed him to be clearheaded and professional. Not emotional and berserk with the need to protect her.

But it wasn't the cop who answered. It was the man. "As soon as I'm off duty, I plan to take you to bed and not let you up until we're both on the verge of starvation."

"Oh, thank God," she said, sounding relieved. With a soft laugh, she added, "I think I'll go now and stock a cooler full of food to put in my bedroom."

Finally feeling the tension ease out of him, Nick laughed as well, wondering how he'd ever thought his life was pretty good before Melody had been in it. Because every time he spoke with her, every time he looked up and saw her smiling face, he realized she was doing the impossible. The woman was working her way into his heart. Making him wonder if there really were second chances for people who'd been as unlucky in love as both he and Melody Tanner had been.

He didn't know yet. But one thing was sure—as long as he had breath in his body, he was going to make sure she was okay.

ROSEMARY WAS dying to tell her friends about her amazing news—that she was going to have Dex Delaney's baby. She'd been ready to explode for days, ever since she'd gotten the call from her doctor confirming what she'd suspected for a couple of weeks. And she'd fully intended to call Paige, Tanya and Melody and have them meet her so she could tell them in person.

But another darn murder had interfered.

"What rotten luck," she muttered as she trudged around the house Friday morning dressed in a bathrobe and fuzzy slippers. There was no point in getting dressed. Considering how difficult it was to get through a morning without losing her breakfast, she had the feeling she'd be back in bed before noon. Not only because of the morning sickness that had plagued her for the past couple of weeks, but also because she was so heartsick over what had happened Wednesday at dinner.

God, she needed to talk to Melody. Her friend was just the person to share her happiness—and her sheer terror—about her pregnancy. And she would also be able to help Rosemary figure out what to do about Dex. Unfortunately, she didn't suppose Melody would be in a cheerful frame of mind, considering yet another of the guys on her Men Most Wanted list had keeled over dead.

Definitely rotten luck.

She wished Dex was around so she could ask him for the details. But he wasn't around...and hadn't been since Wednesday evening. "Dammit, Dex, get your ass over here," she whispered, looking at the phone, which had remained ominously silent all day yesterday and again this morning.

He wasn't very happy with her. Oh, sure, he'd done a good job disguising his shock when she'd so foolishly dropped that little bombshell on his head in front of her entire family. He'd been incredibly sweet, taking care of her, helping her up to her room to lie down. Kissing her on the forehead, he'd told her to stay in bed and take it easy.

One tender, fleeting touch of his hand on her stomach had said even more. But they'd both known they couldn't have *that* conversation with her family in the house. So Dex had gone back into the lion's den to face her father.

Lion's den...how appropriate an expression. Her father had roared all right. She'd heard him from her room. Splashing some cold water on her face, Rosemary had come back downstairs to try to smooth things over, only to find that Dex had left.

Without saying goodbye. Without telling her how he felt about the baby. Without *anything*.

She hadn't heard from him since.

"I'm not calling you," she snapped at the phone, even as hot tears rose in her eyes. She dashed them away angrily, attributing them to pregnancy hormones. Because Rosemary Chilton didn't cry over *any* man. "You can just forget it, sugar, because I am not chasing after you."

She only hoped Dex would come back chasing after *her*. Given the way her father had acted, that might be questionable.

Simon Chilton, for all his insistence that he was a modern, reasonable man, was still remarkably old-fashioned and a bit hotheaded. He certainly wasn't happy that she was pregnant by a cop to whom she wasn't even married. He'd made that pretty clear to Dex. Which was obviously why the man she loved had left minutes after learning he was going to be a father.

The rest of the family had been wonderful. Patty hadn't even tried to hide her excitement. And Deidre had asked a million questions. Since Deidre had been talking about having a baby for a while—but had been thwarted by her asshole husband—she seemed to want to experience pregnancy vicariously through Rosemary.

Brian had stammered his congratulations, telling her he expected that he and Melody would be the baby's godparents.

The baby. Her baby.

She dropped her hand to her stomach, wondering when she'd start feeling pregnant instead of merely nauseous. Hopefully soon enough to deal with whatever was going to happen with Dex.

Whether he came back or not, stood up and behaved as the man she knew, or turned into a rat bastard she'd never want to know, she was going to have to be strong. Both for herself and for this baby, whom she already loved so very much.

"You hang tight in there, little guy," she whispered. "Your daddy's going to come around sooner or later. And after I kick his ass, we're all going to be real happy. Mama guarantees it."

MELODY WATCHED for any snippets of news on the Drake Manning case throughout the day Friday, hoping for a glimpse of the detectives investigating the case. She needed to see Nick's face.

The way they'd left things last night had made her tense and unsure. Yes, she knew he still wanted her…as much as she wanted him. But had anything else changed? Was he eyeing her with suspicion now? Because, really, this was getting beyond ridiculous. Melody had heard of people being bad luck, but she'd never imagined she might one day be cursed. They might as well start calling her Madame Melody, the deadly divorcée of Savannah.

"Come on, come home," she muttered as she looked at the clock and saw it was now after five.

She realized she'd said the word *home* a moment after it left her mouth. How utterly strange. This wasn't Nick's home. She hadn't even quite grown accustomed to it being *her* home yet. So why would she think such a thing?

It was too early to think that way. Much too soon to think she could have a future with the man. Could grow to love him.

"No," she whispered. She *wasn't* going to do that, wasn't about to open herself up to the kind of pain love could bring.

Sex was one thing. A torrid, passionate, deliciously wicked affair, that was all she'd mentally signed on for the other night when she'd asked him to make love to her.

Not the deep feelings that had left her pacing her apartment all day, wondering where he was, if he was okay. If he was thinking the worst about her.

If he'd already decided she just wasn't worth the trouble.

C.C. and Oscar stared at her as she paced around, until Melody felt almost judged by the felines. "Okay, so maybe I *do* still have some unresolved baggage," she admitted out loud.

Maybe the things Nick had tried to convince her of the night before—like the idea that no woman would have been able to keep a man like Bill Todd faithful—were going to be harder for her to accept than she'd hoped.

"But I'm trying, dammit," she said.

It was just awfully hard to try when every hour that went by made her suspect more and more that she was setting herself up for another major heartache. She hadn't even been able to reassure herself with a brief visit—a professional one—because Nick had ended up sending someone else over to take her statement, telling her he was too close to her to do it.

Her friends would have been a great distraction, and she would have liked to hear their reactions to Mānning's death, but none of them were available. Tanya wasn't answering her phone. Paige was working at her secretarial job. And Rosemary was apparently coming down with something. Sounding stuffy and tired, she'd admitted she was lying down and Melody had cut their call short.

So there'd been no easy way to get her mind off the man who'd occupied her every waking thought—and her every deep, erotic dream—for many days now.

At least she'd gotten some work done. She'd gone downstairs for a couple of hours, touched up some pictures she'd done for a local businessman needing a publicity shot. She'd manipulated the man's under-eye bags right out of existence.

She'd also worked on her new company Web site, which had gone live last week. The site featured a number of shots Melody had taken of Savannah and her people and was, if she did say so herself, quite nice. Plus she'd begun working on a proposal for the engaged couple who'd provided her with an alibi last week. Thankfully, they still wanted to work with her, despite a visit from the police.

Sitting back to look at it, she realized her schedule was showing signs of life. As was Melody.

Unlike most of the men on her list.

When she finally heard a knock on the door at seven o'clock, she almost raced to answer it. Yanking it open and seeing Nick standing there, dressed in the same clothes he'd been wearing last night and looking as if he wanted to collapse into the nearest chair, she grabbed his hand and pulled him inside.

"You look awful."

"I should have gone home to shower," he said, running a hand over his eyes. "But I knew if I did, I'd pass out and I didn't want to wait until tomorrow to see you." Grinning, he admitted, "I owe my neighbor big-time for taking care of my shoe-chewing mutt last night and today."

Smiling, she led him to the living room and pushed him onto the couch. "I'm glad you didn't. Now, what's first? Food, shower or sleep?"

"Kiss," he replied, tugging her down, too. She fell onto his lap and met his mouth with hers for a deep, slow kiss that made everything else fade into insignificance. Tilting her head and curling closer into him, she twined her fingers in his hair and met every lazy thrust of his tongue with an equally seductive one of her own. Without a single word they said a lot of things. Mainly that it felt so incredibly good to be together.

When they finally drew apart and she saw the way his eyes were closed, his long lashes resting on his cheeks, she frowned. "You still awake over there?"

Without even opening his eyes, he nodded. "Oh, yeah."

But he didn't look as if he'd be that way for long. "Why don't you go in my room and lie down?" she asked with a light laugh, tracing her fingers down the side of his face.

The man had an amazing face. Someday she was going to talk him into posing for her. *Naked.*

He caught her hand in his and kissed her fingertip. His eyes were wide-open now and his intimate smile told her he was feeling more hungry than tired.

"Did you miss me today?" he asked, his voice throaty.

"Oh, I guess you crossed my mind once or twice," she said with a saucy shrug.

"Ditto."

She wondered if he'd been thinking the same things she had. If he'd reached the same conclusions…as in, none. No conclusions about the future, at least not for Melody. She didn't know what was going to happen tomorrow, she just knew she had to continue to take what she could get today.

Now.

"If you don't want a nap, why don't you at least go take a nice hot shower while I get you something to eat?" she said.

One of his brows rose. "Uh, are you *making* it?"

"Ha-ha," she said, regretfully rising from his lap. "It's not too hard to cut into a nice round of brie, warm up some crusty bread and open a bottle of wine."

"Can I have a steak on the side?" he asked, half laughing, half groaning. "And some fries? And a cheeseburger?"

Chuckling, she pulled him to his feet. Nick was enjoying this, she could see by the twinkle in his eye. He liked the idea of her pampering him.

Well, frankly, she kind of liked it, too. He'd adopted the role of caretaker so many times since she'd met him. Now she was in a position to repay the favor.

Putting her hands on his back, she pushed him toward the bathroom. "Don't fall asleep in the shower and crack your head open on the edge of my beautiful big bathtub. Blood might stain the hardwood floors and Brian would never forgive me."

"That landlord of yours ever fix your pipes?" He gave her a decidedly lascivious look over his shoulder. "Because while I'm here, I'd be happy to check things over."

"All fixed," she said with a smirk. "Now go."

"Maybe you should come with me to make sure I don't pass out from sheer exhaustion," he said, turning around to face her.

"I thought you wanted food."

"I'd rather devour you."

Suddenly the playfulness was gone from his face, replaced by serious, deliberate want.

She swallowed hard. Which was all the hesitation he needed.

Without warning, he scooped her up in his arms and strode into the bathroom. "What about your exhaustion?" she asked, laugher on her lips.

"I'm suddenly feeling much more energetic." When they reached the bathroom, he lowered her to stand on her own. "And I need someone to help me wash my back."

Reaching for the old-fashioned spigot, he turned on the water—hot, then cold—and plugged the drain. By the time he looked at her again, Melody was already holding out the jar of bubbles. Vanilla scented. He uncapped it, sniffed appreciatively, then dumped half the bottle into the tub.

She laughed softly. "There's not going to be enough room for you in there with all those bubbles."

He didn't say anything, he merely began to untuck his shirt, his every move slow, deliberate and sultry, hinting of his mood.

Slow. Deliberate. Sultry.

Oh, heavens, it was going to be an amazing night.

Nick tugged the shirt off, revealing his strong chest and rippled stomach. Then came his boots, his pants. Until finally he was completely naked.

Melody grabbed the door handle, trying to remain steady. Because Nick was the living example of male perfection. Broadshouldered, slimwaisted. Hard, masculine and ready.

And he wanted her. *Her.*

"Now you," he murmured, reaching for the loose cottony fabric of her dress. He pulled it up and tossed it away, hissing when he realized she hadn't been wearing a bra. His eyes grew even darker as he stared at her bare breasts.

Melody kicked off her shoes, then pushed her panties to the floor until she stood in front of him just as naked. "I guess you want to make sure I don't get my clothes wet when I scrub your back?" she asked, her voice more seductive than teasing.

He didn't say a word. He simply reached out to slide one big hand over her hip, his rough palm fitting perfectly in the indentation of her waist. "Come here."

He drew her up against him, their skin meeting to create a new type of friction. Dropping his mouth to hers, he kissed her until they were sharing breaths, their hearts beating in unison.

"Oh, I've missed you," she murmured as the excitement of his touch washed over her. Desire slid throughout her body. Particularly in the hollow core of her, where she'd been dying to be filled by him again.

Saying nothing, he turned off the water, then picked her

up again and stepped over the side of the old tub. Melody almost purred when Nick lowered himself into the steamy, bubbly water, settling her on his lap. Her back was to his front, and his arm draped with deliberate possession around her waist. He tugged her back so she could recline on his chest.

It was heaven. Perfection. Hot and steamy and slippery. Beneath her bottom, she felt the delicious strength of his arousal and knew how this bath was going to end.

But Nick didn't seem inclined to make it end anytime soon.

"The water hot enough for you?" he murmured as he lazily stroked her belly, her midriff and the bottom curves of her breasts. Every movement was lethargic, uncalculated, made only for the pleasure it brought to them both.

She nodded, leaning her head back to rest on his shoulder, with her cheek rubbing against his neck. "It's wonderful."

They remained as they were for several long minutes. The silence was broken only by the sound of their own breaths, and the occasional muted drop of water falling from the faucet into the bubbles beneath it. And Melody's nearly inaudible sighs.

She couldn't do much *other* than sigh and quiver in delight as Nick continued a slow exploration of her body, lightly tracing patterns and swirls all over her with bubbles. On her rib cage. Around her belly button. Between her breasts, at the base of her throat. Everywhere but the one or two spots—the three or four spots, actually—that would likely send her flying out of her mind.

"Mmm," she murmured when his touches grew a bit more deliberate. More heated. More intimate.

His fingers, slick and soapy, moved lower, dipping into the curls between her legs, teasing, promising, then pulling away.

Dipping again, lower now, but tormenting her by brushing past to instead stroke her hip.

"Nick," she said with a groan.

He laughed throatily, delighting in his own wickedness, and continued to torment her. Kissing the side of her throat, he increased the intensity. With one hand, he continued to caress her hip and her thigh, drawing closer and closer to the empty place between her legs, where she *so* wanted to be touched. Nick slid the other hand up her body to cup her breast, flicking his thumb over her nipple until she gasped, "More, please."

"Where?" he asked teasingly.

She wasn't going to allow any miscommunication this time. Covering both his hands with each of hers, she pressed one of them even harder against her breast, while showing him exactly where she wanted the other one.

"Oh, yes," she groaned when he finally stopped torturing her and slid a finger into her wet folds.

He whispered sweet things against her neck as he continued to kiss her, to suck her earlobe and nibble on the skin beneath it. Mimicking the way he was going to be making love to her soon, he moved his finger in and out of her, slowly, deliberately. His thumb rubbed her a bit higher, where she needed to be touched most. And as everything spiraled together, with one of his hands on her breast, the other pleasuring her between her legs, and his sweet whispers in her ear—she came in a shaking rush of delight.

She arched back, kissing his jaw as she rode out the orgasm. When she could breathe again, she turned in his arms and covered his mouth with hers, needing to taste him. Needing everything he could give her.

Keeping her mouth against his, she maneuvered her legs

around his waist. A tight fit in the tub, but so utterly worth it. "I want you so much," she whispered, almost shivering as she rubbed against his body, now all hard and hot and wet.

"Wait, I need to get…"

"No," she replied, knowing immediately what he meant. "I took care of it." She wanted absolutely nothing between them this time…wanted to feel only skin against skin.

He cupped her face in his hands. "You're sure? I'll understand, and I want you to feel safe, Mel."

"I feel safer with you than I've ever felt with anyone in my entire life." Which was completely true.

He smiled, visibly pleased by her confession. Smiling, too, Melody began lowering herself onto him, taking him into her body a little bit at a time. Every inch was a revelation and a joy…obviously not just for her. Nick's eyes closed and his mouth fell open as she wrapped herself around him completely, taking everything he had to give in one deep, deliberate stroke.

"I love the way you feel inside me, Nick," she whispered in his ear as she remained still, savoring his penetration, the way he filled her, almost like her other half.

"I love it too, honey," he admitted.

She began to move, the water and the bubbles and his skin combining to overwhelm her senses. Feeling so close to him—so incredibly close—she gently ran her fingers over a small scar on his chest. Then on another one lower, under his ribs, silently telling him how much she ached for any pain he'd ever endured. She kissed the military-looking tattoo on his upper arm, thankful his heroism hadn't cost her the chance to know him. To have him.

Soon the intensity grew, carrying them higher until neither of them could speak. He began to give and she began to take and they both splashed and thrust and kissed and loved and came. Until the water grew cool and neither of them could move.

Finally she collapsed in his arms, kissing his neck, overwhelmed by two realizations. First, that with this man, every time they made love was more amazing than the one before.

And second…that for the first time in as long as she could remember, Melody was truly happy.

CHAPTER FOURTEEN

NICK WOKE UP just before dawn, blinking and looking around in the darkness to get his bearings. The bed was smaller than the one in his apartment, but his feet weren't asleep from the weight of a heavy, pain-in-the-ass dog sprawled across them for half the night.

It took only a few seconds to remember where he was, particularly because Melody was curled up beside his naked body. She sighed in her sleep and burrowed closer, as if sensing he was pulling away from her, even if only in her dreams.

Nick dropped an arm across her waist and watched her sleep. He hadn't slept all night with a woman in years. Not since he was married, as far as he could recall.

It was nice. Damn nice.

The realization stunned him. Because it implied that he'd been lonely, or missing out on something.

He'd been alone for a long time—ten years—and he'd gotten used to that. He had friends and he had his job. In the service, he'd always had a mission. Now he even had a nutty dog who drove him crazy but still made him laugh and was a true companion.

But, he had to admit, he hadn't had anyone he loved for a very long time. If ever.

Sure, he loved his mother…and his brother. But as far as romantic love? Well, frankly, he didn't know that he'd *ever* experienced it. He'd thought he was in love as a teenager, but it had been just that—a teenage thing. He sure as hell hadn't loved his ex-wife, Daneen. And he'd never loved any of the women with whom he'd had occasional sexual flings. So he'd almost gotten used to thinking of himself as incapable of it.

Why then, when he looked at Melody Tanner's sleeping face, did he feel so completely overwhelmed with some nearly unidentifiable emotion?

Apparently realizing he was awake, one of Melody's cats began to meow. Glancing down at the foot of the bed, he saw C.C. looking up him, her green eyes glittering in the murky, predawn light of the room. When she knew she had his attention, she turned her head to look at something above her. When he followed the cat's stare, he realized what she'd been focused on.

"How'd you get up there, tough guy?" he asked, seeing the other cat, Oscar, way up on a plant ledge on the far wall.

Looking at the furniture in the room, Nick realized the adventurous cat must have jumped from the seat of Melody's rocking chair to the back of it, then up onto her dresser. A hop to the top of her armoire would put the cat within claw-scratching distance of the ledge.

Which was exactly where he was perched.

"You're stuck, aren't you?" Nick asked softly, laughing at the animal who looked much too proud and disdainful to meow for help. Good thing he had C.C. looking out for him.

Carefully shifting his arm from under Melody's shoulders, he got out of bed and padded across the room. Cats…almost as much trouble as dogs. Who knew? But at least his feet hadn't fallen asleep under C.C.'s weight.

"Hold on, little guy," he murmured to Oscar as he pushed the rocking chair close to the ledge. Getting up on it, he balanced carefully, holding a hand out for the cat. "Come on, bologna cat. Let's go."

Oscar sniffed his hand, then carefully put his paw out. And just as quickly pulled it away.

Bracing himself with one hand on the wall, Nick leaned higher, trying to coax the cat forward. "Come on, Oscar, my ass is hanging out in the wind here."

Eventually the cat lurched forward, bounced off Nick's hand to the armoire, then down to the floor, where he took off like a shot down the hall.

The cat had good reason to take off running. Because as he jumped, he managed to knock a small plant off the ledge, sending it careening toward Nick's head. Only a quick leap from the chair and out of the way saved him from a thump on the skull. Nothing, however, could save him from the dirt shower he got as the thing tumbled end over end on its way down.

"Dammit," he muttered, looking down at the specks of dirt covering him from shoulder to foot.

Behind him, he heard a snicker. Cringing, he slowly checked over his shoulder and saw Melody sitting up in the bed, watching every move he made. She was grinning widely, looking bloody adorable with her hair wildly tangled around her face and the sheet tucked up around her breasts.

"You think this is funny?" he said in a low growl. "Maybe I'll rub this dirt off all over you."

Her eyes widened and she scooted back in the bed. Holding the sheet with one hand, she stuck her index finger at him. "Back off, big man. Step away from the bed and proceed directly to the shower."

He threw his head back and groaned. "God Almighty, another shower? Am I never going to get to eat?"

Melody's wicked laugh told him exactly where her X-rated mind had gone at that one. The way his cock perked right up told him his had followed suit. His mouth went wet with another kind of hunger...the hunger to lick the inside of her thighs and taste her warm, womanly folds the way he had a few hours ago.

"Scratch that. Food's overrated."

Brushing the loose bits of soil from his shoulders, he stepped toward the bed, giving her the kind of lascivious look that made nuns clutch their habits. But before he could get too far, something crunched under his foot. Something hard and jagged.

"Shit," he muttered, figuring he'd stepped on a piece of the planter. But looking down, he saw the small terra-cotta pot a foot away, still remarkably intact, lying on a few crumpled palm fronds and a pile of dirt. "What the hell..." he murmured when he saw just what it was he'd stepped on.

At first, he almost scratched his head, his not-quite-awake brain not processing the small box, the wires spilling out of it, and the tiny glass circle that looked like an eye.

Then he realized what he was looking at. And froze.

"Melody," he murmured, very slowly bending down to look more closely at the broken square of plastic, "are you into kinky stuff like making sex movies?"

She laughed, then throatily said, "No, can't say I am. Why, do you have some naughty ideas going on in your devious mind?"

He didn't answer. Instead, he carefully picked up the twisted, broken box by the tip of a torn internal wire and rose to his feet. Absorbing what it meant, he immediately looked around the room. At the phone, the pictures on the wall, the grate for the heater. Any number of hiding places.

His whole body growing tight as raw anger washed over him, he somehow managed to keep his voice steady and calm. "Honey? I want you to get up and get dressed, okay?" His jaw so tight it hurt to get the words out, he added, "But keep the sheet around you."

She immediately opened her mouth to question him but quickly fell silent as she saw what he was holding in his hand. He lifted it higher, letting the first rays of the dawn slanting in through the gaps in the curtain illuminate it.

"Is that what I think it is?" she asked, looking stunned then horrified.

"Yeah." Feeling violated on his own behalf, but way more on hers, he said, "It's a hidden camera." His whole body shook with fury as he said what they were both thinking.

"Somebody's been watching you."

BY THE TIME Dex showed up at her house at eleven o'clock Saturday morning, Rosemary had worked herself into an absolute state. Watching from her upstairs bedroom window while he parked on the street and walked to the front porch, she seriously contemplated pitching a vase out the window onto his head.

"Thinks he can ignore us, huh?" she muttered, her hand resting on her flat stomach. "He's got another think coming, sweet angel. That man is not a coward, so we sure aren't going to let him act like one."

When the doorbell rang, she took her good sweet time going downstairs to answer it. Dex was obviously in an impatient mood today, because he jabbed at the thing three times before she swung the door open. "Well, Detective Delaney, isn't this a nice surprise." Steeling herself not to notice the fatigued look on his unshaven face, or the way his hair was sticking up and his usually immaculate clothes were rumpled, she added, "Stopping by to invite me to join the neighborhood watch program?"

"May I come in?"

"Oh, by all means," she replied with exaggerated Southern hospitality. Stepping back, she gestured widely with one arm. "My home is yours."

His whole body stiffened, which, she instantly realized, was one of the problems. As if she hadn't known already. He didn't like *her home.* Which basically equated to her life.

"How are you?" he asked quietly as she closed the front door.

"Oh, I'm peachy. Unless, of course, I think of peaches. Or any fruit that might go in a tart. Then I just want to throw up."

His green eyes shifted down and he looked at her stomach. Rosemary put a protective hand there.

"How far along are you?" he asked, still so quiet, so focused, so tired.

"Three months," she said, crossing her arms and leaning against the foyer wall.

"That far…?" he asked, sounding slightly dazed.

Loosening up a bit since she'd heard genuine emotion in his voice, she grudgingly added, "My cycle's been off, but I've never been exactly regular, so it didn't sink in at first."

He nodded slowly. Unable to stand the small lines of weariness beside his eyes, or the tired slump of his shoulders, Rosemary sighed. "Come on in and sit down." She tried to brush past him to go into the living room, but Dex caught her arm and stopped her. It was the first time he'd touched her in three days. And she suddenly wanted to cry. To throw her arms around him and ask him where he'd been. To hit him. To make love with him. To beg him to want the baby as much as she already did.

"Rosemary…"

She also wanted him to call her Rosie.

"I'm sorry," he said softly, running his hand lightly up and down her arm.

Sorry that she was pregnant? Sorry for dropping off the face of the earth? "Sorry for what?" she asked, hearing the almost desperate note in her own voice.

"Sorry I disappeared. I had something to do."

She pulled her arm away. "Oh, right, I'm sure there were *tons* of things that were more important than this."

She tried to walk away, but Dex stopped her, this time putting both hands on her upper arms. "Not more important. But something I *had* to do."

Without another word, the man she loved reached into his pocket, retrieving something. "Rosemary Chilton, I love you."

Oh, God, such relief…

"I want you. I want the baby. I want us to be a family."

She closed her eyes, sighing loudly and deeply.

"I want to take care of you. To provide for you," Dex said. "I want you to come with me, to raise our child…to be my wife."

She opened her eyes with a little gasp. She and Dex had never talked marriage. And even though she knew he was a very moralistic man, she wasn't sure he'd want to take that step yet.

When she saw what Dex held in his hand, she began to understand where he'd been and why he'd had to go away.

It was a ring. A stunning old-fashioned ring, with a square-cut diamond surrounded by tiny sapphires. Probably an antique, most likely an heirloom. Almost certainly something important to Dex.

"I went to Pennsylvania to get this from my grandfather. He's been keeping it for me since my grandmother died," he said, lifting the jewelry for her to see. "It's for you."

Okay, so he wasn't on his knees, and he hadn't exactly *asked* her to marry him so much as he'd told her he wanted to. But this was as close to a marriage proposal as she'd ever gotten. And she was pregnant. So she started crying anyway. "Oh, Dex, why didn't you tell me you were leaving? I've been out of my mind with worry."

"I'm sorry. I needed to pull my head together. It hasn't been easy to figure out because of…" He looked around her house, his mouth tightening as his gaze fell on the elegant furniture, the antiques, the artwork. "Because of all *this*."

The money. She'd always known he had a thing about her money.

"But I have decided we can make it work, Rosemary," he continued, stiffening his shoulders.

A man shouldn't have stiff shoulders when he proposed. That should go in wedding planners' handbooks. It just looked…ominous.

"All you have to do is walk out of here and come with me. I don't make a great salary, but if we move back to Pennsylvania, I could make a good bit more to support us."

She laughed a little. "Sugar, you don't need to go to work for your father. I know that's never been what you wanted."

Something flashed in his eyes, maybe a hint of relief that she truly did understand him. But it quickly disappeared. "I'll do whatever it takes."

"I don't care how much money you make, I've got plenty of that."

Whoops. Wrong thing to say because Dex's jaw tightened. "I'm not touching your money. I'm not living in your house."

Rosemary's head started to pound. This stern, harsh-sounding man was so unlike the Dex she knew. The Dex she loved.

"If this is going to work, you have to leave all this, Rosemary. Live within my means and raise our child the same middle-class way I was raised."

She didn't think she'd heard right at first. This hard-sounding person standing in front of her *couldn't* be the same man who'd playfully smeared an entire jar of raspberry jelly all over her—and then licked it off—a few short weeks ago. Dex wouldn't possibly ask her to move far away from her family, to give up everything she had—her home, her life, her career—because his *pride* wouldn't allow her to keep any of it.

His pride. *His* money. *His* job. *His* life.

What about her life? Hers and the baby's?

"Well," he said, still standing there so rigid and strong, as if he'd rehearsed this whole thing in his mind a dozen times and was afraid to deviate from the script, "what do you think?"

He lifted the ring again. No dropping to one knee. No embracing her, pressing kisses all over her stomach to welcome their child into their lives. No assurances that he didn't care where they lived or what they lived on, as long as they were together.

Not her lover. Not her love. Not the man she wanted to be her baby's father.

No. Just a harsh, inflexible cop.

"What I say…" she murmured as she walked back to the door, her heart breaking with every step "…is no."

He looked stunned for a second—the first completely genuine reaction she'd seen since the minute he'd arrived. But it quickly disappeared. "You're just emotional."

Nodding, she admitted, "Yes, I'm very emotional. But I'm also sure of what I want. And it isn't to start a life with someone who coldly plans out our future without a single thought about what I want. Not with someone whose pride is so great he can't see a wife as his partner, in all ways, accepting what both of us can bring to the table. Figuratively *and* literally."

Opening the door, she stepped out of the way and gestured

him toward the exit. "So I'm sorry, my answer is no. I'm not accepting your terms."

He remained silent, shocked.

"And now I think it's time for you to leave," she said, wondering where she'd gotten the strength to say that with such conviction, when deep inside she knew it was the last thing she wanted.

Somehow, she found one more deep reserve of strength. Enough for two more words.

"Goodbye, Dex."

MELODY HADN'T ever imagined meeting Nick's family this early in their, uh…whatever they had. Knowing the Walkers didn't live nearby, and that she and Nick hadn't even yet figured out what kind of a relationship they were caught up in, she'd assumed any family introductions were a long way off. But here she was, sitting in his car, not far from a Georgia town called Joyful, about to meet the Walker clan.

Nick had assured her he'd planned to ask her to come with him anyway, but the camera incident made it that much more important to him that she did. He didn't want to leave her alone after what had happened.

She wondered if Nick's family would take one look at her face and see the rage there.

Because, oh, rage was what she felt. What she'd been feeling for hours since they'd left her apartment, dropped her cats off with Paige and gone by Nick's place to pick up Fredo, who was sprawled in the back seat. And the anger had built throughout every hour of their drive across the state.

She'd done a pretty good job disguising her feelings when Nick had first revealed the Internet camera someone—oh, wouldn't she love to know who—had hidden in her bedroom. Keeping the sheet around her, as he'd suggested, she'd calmly gotten up, gone into the bathroom, puked, then put on some clothes. By the time she'd come back out, Nick had already put the camera into a plastic bag and was on the phone with someone. From the sound of it, another cop.

He'd tried to get her to stay in her kitchen while he and the other detective who showed up scoured the rest of her apartment—and her studio downstairs—for any additional disgusting spy devices. She hadn't. Instead she'd followed them into every room, watching as they pried off grates, searched behind switch plates and carefully examined her telephones.

The fact that they'd found nothing else beyond that one camera on the plant ledge in her bedroom, which had apparently been positioned just perfectly for spying on her when she was undressing or sleeping—oh, God, how utterly revolting—didn't make her feel better.

So the pervert hadn't wired her whole building. That didn't mean he hadn't gotten an eyeful, watching her in the privacy of her bedroom. Changing, crying, thinking, sleeping.

Making love with Nick last night.

She felt nauseated again. But she didn't figure Nick would appreciate her getting sick in his new-looking car.

"How much longer?" she asked, seeing by the road signs that they'd skirted past Atlanta by about sixty miles. That was as close to that city as she ever wanted to be again for the rest of her life.

"Another half hour at most," Nick said.

They were the first words they'd exchanged in a while, both of them quietly absorbing what had happened this morning. But now that they were near their destination—near his family, where they'd have to put on a happy face for his brother's engagement party—she needed to talk. Needed to understand and to unload. To vent and to speculate.

"Okay, so tell me," she said, her voice surprisingly calm. "Who could have done it?"

Nick's jaw tightened. "I have my suspicions."

"Beyond that," she said, immediately knowing he was thinking of Bill, who was first on her list, too. "I want to know, in technical terms, who may have had the capability and the opportunity to do it."

He told her. "The camera was a small, wireless one that had to have been networked to a router somewhere close to your place…but maybe as far as several buildings away. From that router, whatever was being filmed could have projected to an Internet site."

She gasped at that implication. "The Internet…"

"Don't think that way," he muttered, knowing exactly where her thoughts had gone. "I'm sure whoever it was set up his own private little Melody address for his viewing pleasure." His hands were white on the steering wheel, as if he was gripping someone's throat, reminding Melody of the man's temper. "We searched online, and nothing came up."

Small comfort. But she chose to grab on to it like a lifeline. "And the camera didn't need a computer of its own? Every one I've seen is connected to its own system."

"A computer's not necessary with this wireless type. These things sell for a couple hundred bucks. All you need is a power source—which was up there for a plant light, most likely. And a wireless system to network it to."

Spying had gotten so simple. Made her rethink her long-held belief that the Internet was the greatest thing since control-top panty hose. "Pretty easy to do, then, huh?"

"Yeah. But we'll find him, Mel. Your part of town has a lot of businesses, so there could be a lot of wireless networks, served by a lot of ISPs. But we're already looking. Sooner or later, we'll track down the right one and find out who set this up."

She trusted him. How could she not, given the confidence in his voice? "It shocks me how easy it must have been for someone."

"Yeah. It could have been installed there and hidden in the leaves of that plant within a matter of minutes."

Minutes for someone to invade her privacy and put her up for public consumption. As if she hadn't had enough of *that* in her lifetime.

"Meaning," Nick added, "that it could have been your ex, the day he came to harass you. Was he ever alone?"

She sighed heavily. "I don't know how long he was in the building before he found me up on the third floor that morning."

"Bastard." Shaking his head, Nick continued, "It also could have been Jonathan Rhodes, when he was stealing your underwear."

They were the most likely suspects, she knew. But they weren't the only ones. "There were workers in and out of the apartment for days while I was living upstairs."

"Did any of them stand out as suspicious?"

"Not really. Other than the foreman, most of them spoke Spanish, so I couldn't understand them."

He didn't look the least bit relieved. Without another word, he reached across the console and took hold of her hand. Lifting it, he brought her fingers to his lips and kissed the back of them.

Her heart flipped a little.

"You didn't have to whisk me out of town, you know," she said softly. "Once you made sure the apartment was secure, I would have been okay there."

Ignoring the road in front of them, Nick looked over, his expression incredulous. "Are you crazy? You think I would have done that?"

His vehemence was nice, but she'd meant what she said. She was tired—damned tired—of reacting instead of acting. Of basing her choices on the actions of other people.

Maybe she was finally recovering. Finally regaining her nerve and her strength. Because the last thing seeing that camera had made her want to do was run. No. It had made her want to fight.

Only one thing had caused her to agree to come with Nick to his hometown. She wanted to be with him.

"You're sure your brother and his fiancée won't mind me crashing their party?" she asked, still feeling funny about it.

"Positive."

Considering Nick had flat-out said he wasn't going unless she came with him, she suspected he was right. "And you can afford to be away from work?"

"One day's all right," he admitted, though she sensed his concern. Nick wasn't the kind of man to bail on his responsibilities. Which said a lot for how much he cared about his older brother, who she was going to be meeting in a very short time.

When they pulled into Joyful, Melody was struck by two things. First, the town was incredibly pretty—the picture postcard she'd imagined the first time she'd heard its name. And second, the streets were darn near empty. It was nearly dinnertime on Saturday, yet only a few cars chugged up the main road through town, and no one walked along the sidewalk outside the cute shops dotting the street.

"Where is everyone?" she asked, looking around in confusion.

Nick sighed audibly. "At the party, I guess."

"The party? The party we're going to?"

He nodded. "I expect so."

She couldn't quite wrap her mind around it, having lived in big cities for most of her life. But when Nick pulled up in front of a small café shaded by some huge, beautiful pecan trees, she realized he might be right. Because the parking lot was overflowing. Cars, trucks, motorcycles. They were jammed into every corner.

Unless Emeril had made a pit stop here to do some cooking, she suspected that Nick's brother and his fiancée were a very popular couple.

"Maybe this wasn't such a great idea," she whispered. "I expected to meet your family. Not your whole town."

Nick shook his head. "I do believe most folks here in Joyful would say they're one and the same thing."

And a few minutes later, inside the café, Melody realized the man was right. The pretty restaurant, with fixtures and furniture that looked brand-new, was filled with laughing, talking people, whose voices all seemed to unite to call out, "Nick!" when they walked in.

He was immediately surrounded, and Melody stayed back, watching every person, trying to figure out which one was his mother, and which was Johnny.

She immediately ruled out the pudgy guy with dark hair, who bore a slight resemblance to Nick but was much shorter. Hearing him called Virgil, she realized this was a cousin—the one Nick and his brother had gone to spend time with during their summers.

When they were scared to be home with their father.

That was a conversation she was going to have with Nick Walker one of these days. And soon. Having revealed everything to him about her own life, she realized she knew darn little about his. At least, the life he'd lived before his time in the military.

She was still thinking about it when a very pretty woman with short, platinum-blond hair appeared at Nick's side and threw her arms around his neck. Nick hugged her back.

Melody's whole body grew stiff, taut with tension. Her breathing slowed as a pounding began in her temples. She didn't know who the woman was, but she was beautiful and she was in Nick's strong arms.

So much for thinking she was fine, that she'd recovered from the emotional garbage left over from her marriage. Because obviously, judging from the sharp stab of pain in her stomach, she'd been fooling herself. Not if seeing Nick hug another woman, probably in complete and total innocence, could make her so instantly tense. Panicky, almost.

She nearly took off. Her feet edged backward, toward the door, but she barely got a few inches before she bumped into something big. Something hard. Something human.

A pair of hands dropped onto her shoulders to steady her. "Whoa there."

Spinning around, she looked up into a pair of twinkling green eyes and a face that looked very familiar. It was Nick's face, but a little different. Not only in the color of the eyes, but the laugh lines beside them. His smile was broad, his whole body relaxed and laid-back. Unlike his brother.

For that's who this had to be. She was looking at Johnny Walker. The groom. Who'd just caught her trying to bolt out of his engagement party. "You're Johnny," she managed to say.

"Uh-huh. Don't think we've had the pleasure," he replied, never losing that open, welcoming expression.

"She's with me."

Melody closed her eyes for a second, not knowing whether to be relieved that Nick had walked up behind her or not. She wasn't ready to turn around and face him, that was for sure. Not when she was still all jumpy and jittery because he'd been hugged by another woman.

Johnny Walker's smile broadened, emphasizing the lean lines of his face, which was almost as nice as his brother's. Stepping around Melody, he threw his arms around Nick's shoulders and hugged him. "'Bout time you showed up, I was getting worried. Have you seen Emma Jean?"

"He has, but he neglected to tell me he brought a friend," a woman's voice said. "Nick, you big dope, she looks exhausted from that long drive. Did you even offer to get her a drink?"

Melody couldn't muster up any surprise that Emma Jean, Johnny's bride, was the blonde Nick had been hugging. The realization didn't make her feel better about how badly she'd responded when she'd first seen her. It merely reinforced what she'd already suspected.

She hadn't reacted out of jealousy but rather out of *habit*.

A habit she needed to break if she wanted her relationship with Nick to have any chance whatsoever of working.

"Em, this is Melody Tanner. I kidnapped her and brought her along for the ride," Nick said.

Emma Jean's smile was wide and genuine. "I'm *so* glad to meet you." She sounded as if she meant it. The other woman's voice wasn't a soft, Southern drawl like her groom's, but instead held almost a European accent. "Is this your first visit to Joyful?"

Melody liked the other woman's face, which looked like it'd reveal every feeling Emma Jean ever experienced. When the woman stepped closer to Johnny and slid an arm around his waist, there was no denying the expression of absolute joy.

"Yes, it is. And I'm glad to meet you, too," Melody murmured. "Sorry to crash in unannounced."

"It's not a problem, not at all. In case you haven't noticed, we expected a crowd," Emma Jean said, laughing as she looked around the full-to-exploding restaurant.

Melody was about to reply when she felt a hand squeeze her butt. Sucking in a shocked breath and hoping no one had seen Nick's inappropriate gesture, she turned around to glare at him. And found herself nose to nose with a cackling old man.

"Who…did you just…"

"Mr. Terry," Johnny said with a forbidding frown. "You'd better keep your hands to yourself."

"Is she one of *your* friends?" the old man asked Emma Jean. He wagged his eyebrows, which were in desperate need of a pair of hedge trimmers. "From your movie days?"

Movie days? Melody didn't quite understand the reference, since from what Nick had said, Emma Jean worked as a financial advisor. And a partner in this restaurant.

Emma Jean rolled her eyes and sighed. "Mr. Terry, you know that story wasn't true. By the way, that's *Nick Walker's* lady friend you groped."

The old man's eyes widened and he looked over to see Nick, watching him like a hawk, all simmering energy and dangerous heat. Lord, Melody hungered for the man.

Nick would never in a million years lay a hand on an old fellow who looked like a stiff wind would blow him over. But Mr. Terry obviously didn't know that. "I thought she was a bridesmaid," he said, sounding plaintive.

"Are you pinching my bridesmaids?" Emma Jean said, her fists on her hips.

"Just a bit," the old man said with a deep sigh. "Used to be I could pinch a lady's behind and she'd slap my face. Now they only laugh." He looked almost mournful.

"Do you want me to slap your face?" Melody asked dryly, hearing Emma Jean snort.

Mr. Terry nodded, looking so hopeful Melody was tempted to do as he asked. But with her luck, the old guy would keel over and die. And she'd had her fill of dead guys this week.

Johnny shook his head. "You'd better be careful, Mr. Terry. Claire Deveaux will do more than slap your face, she'll knock your teeth out."

The old man responded with a phlegmy chuckle. Clamping his lips shut, he made some slobbery sound in his mouth. After a second, he pushed a full set of dentures out from between his lips, shook them at the crowd, then sucked them back in. "Too late for that," he said once his teeth were back in place. He sounded terribly pleased with himself. "Now, where is Ms. Deveaux? We'll see how good her aim is." And he went off to look for Claire, whoever that was.

Melody couldn't help laughing, despite the fact that some toothless, dirty old man had just felt her up. Somehow, the unexpected moment had eased her tension, letting everything else slide away for the first time all day. All the questions and uncertainty she'd had on her shoulders for so long had somehow lightened in this place where there were no ex-husbands, no shaky businesses, no corpses, no hidden cameras.

She felt good. Better than good. She felt *joyful*.

"I'm glad I came here," she said, really meaning it.

"I'm glad you came, too," Nick said softly, dropping his arm possessively across her shoulders.

Emma Jean and Johnny both watched, speculative but also appearing to approve. Which made Melody feel even better.

So with a genuinely relaxed and playful wink at Emma, she said, "Okay, Nick, you big dope, where's my drink?"

CHAPTER FIFTEEN

NICK'S FAMILY HAD LOVED Melody. He'd known they would, of course—what wasn't to love? But considering the way her life had been going lately, he'd half wondered if she'd tense up and be reserved around strangers.

Uh-uh. Maybe for the first five minutes in the crowd of Joyful lunatics she'd held back. But she'd quickly loosened up…to the point where she'd let Mona Harding—former porn star turned restaurateur—drag her up to the front of the room with a bunch of other bridesmaids to join in on a chorus of "I Will Always Love You." It was Johnny and Emma's song…apparently a remnant from that infamous prom night. Nick's wedding night.

My, how life did turn.

By the time they neared home Sunday afternoon, he was feeling both glad and regretful that he'd taken Melody to meet his folks. Glad because she'd had a wonderful time and because his mother had downright adored her—pulling him aside to tell Nick that if he let her get away, he'd regret it for the rest of his life. And glad because Melody seemed so happy. The tension had been erased from her body and she'd laughed more in that twelve-hour period than she had in days.

Regretful because she'd harassed him mercilessly for his life story all the way home.

Damn, Georgia was a big state. There was no way to evade

her questions when the two of them were trapped in a car with just a slobbery dog for company for several hours.

"So you definitely weren't the Steve Urkel of your high school," she said, referring to the conversation they'd had at Rosemary's party. "From what Emma Jean says, you got straight A's only in fighting and breaking the heart of every teenage girl in town. Especially once your big brother left for college."

He rolled his eyes. "Em's got a big mouth."

"Do you still have your yearbook? I want to see a picture of Daneen."

He almost drove off the road. "Why in hell would you want to do that?"

"So I can at least scratch her eyes out on paper, if not in person," Melody said matter-of-factly.

Oh, he loved her like this. The woman was in a feisty mood. Feisty and adorable, sexy and irresistible.

Not that he'd resisted her much the night before. They'd spent many long, glorious hours sharing a room in Joyful's one and only bed-and-breakfast, making that creaky antique bed moan even louder than Melody had. He'd explored every inch of her body, tasting and touching, kissing and licking her until she came in his mouth, purring like C.C. did when she was petted.

She'd scratched like C.C., too, judging by the marks on his shoulders. But they were worth it.

It was a good thing they'd left early this morning. Because by noon, he was sure the whole town had been gossiping that Nick's new lady friend was a screamer. So went the Joyful rumor mill, which had once condemned Emma Jean as an ex-porn star.

"She's just lucky I'm never going to set foot in Atlanta again as long as I live," Melody muttered.

Still talking about Daneen. That Melody had been so indignant on his behalf when he'd told her the whole story of his marriage was the only good thing that had come of talking about it. "She's ancient history. From what I hear, she's hooked up with some music teacher and is finally trying to be a better person."

She snorted. "Leopards, spots...ever heard of them?"

"I hope it's true. For Jack's sake," he murmured.

Melody obviously heard something in his voice that made her realize how uncertain Nick's feelings still were about that situation. She reached out and took his hand. "He's a nice boy. I'm glad his mother let him come up to visit your mom this weekend so he could be at the engagement party."

Nick nodded. "He's a good kid." He fell silent, as always feeling a little confused whenever he thought about Jack. Wondering how things might have been different.

"Sometimes you have to trust that life turns out the way it's supposed to, you know?" she said softly. "If you'd stayed with Daneen, you might have been there to raise Jack, but you wouldn't have been there for those children in Kosovo. Would you?"

Her words left him stunned. Reeling. Because during the many times he'd thought about his life and the way things had turned out, he'd never once made that association. Never. Though it was a very obvious one.

He'd lashed out and joined the marines to escape the disappointment of his life. He'd been an angry kid. But the military had made a man of him, the kind of man who actually excelled under pressure, who was at his best when he was taking care of people.

"As much as I know you wish you'd had the chance to be a really good father—to prove you're not *your* father—it just wasn't the right time for it to happen."

Not his father. Someone had obviously talked to Melody about his family. Probably somebody named Emma Jean Frasier.

Not quite sure what to say, he simply nodded, keeping his eyes forward and both of his hands on the steering wheel. Her words bounced around in his head, and he knew they'd keep bouncing until he'd had a chance to sit down and really think about them. To rethink *everything*.

Suddenly, another father came to mind. Dex. Given the way Melody had spoken all weekend, she didn't know her friend, Rosemary, was pregnant. Nick wasn't about to tell her. That was the kind of thing that needed to be told by the people involved.

Besides, he didn't want to bring up anything that might raise barriers between them. Because the odds on Rosemary and Dex's chances weren't exactly great.

Not that they didn't love each other. A fool could see they did. But he didn't know if love would be enough. When two people were on such different levels—at such different places in their lives—emotionally, physically, financially—it would be damn hard to make it work for long. It would take a lot of determination and courage. Patience.

He supposed that was what it took to make any relationship work over the long term. Not that he'd ever been in one long enough to find out. Not that he'd ever even wanted to.

But glancing over at the woman next to him, turned sideways in her seat so she could reach over and scratch Fredo behind his fluffy ears, he began to wonder if, in him, he had what it took to try.

And what it would take to find out.

NICK HAD TRIED to talk Melody into going back to his place with him—to stay there until he found out who had planted a spy device in her apartment. She'd refused. No pervert was going to keep her out of her own home. Not now that she finally had a home that was entirely her own.

"I'm sorry, I'm not leaving," she said as they stood in her living room arguing about it shortly after they'd walked in the front door. "You checked everything again. It's clear."

"You're not staying here by yourself, Melody. I mean it."

She didn't like the rigid tone in his voice, but reminded herself he was simply going into protective cop mode. He'd left the playful, flirtatious lover at the city limits, and had been tense and on edge ever since they'd gotten back to Savannah.

"Well then," she said, trying to tease him out of his unrelenting stiffness. "If you're so worried, maybe you should stay here with me tonight." Stepping closer, she slid her arms around his neck, tangling her fingers in his thick hair. Tugging him close, she brushed her lips across his, coaxing him into responding.

He resisted for a half a second. Then, with a helpless groan, he wrapped his arms around her and drew her so tightly against him her feet left the floor. His mouth opened on hers, consuming her in a fiery kiss that was deep, hungry and almost desperate. He communicated a lot with that one kiss. Mostly that he still wanted her. Craved her.

And oh, God, did she want him. Now that she knew her apartment was clear of bugs or spy-cams, she wanted to rip her clothes off and have him right here in her living room. "Take me, Nick," she demanded, not caring about anything right now except *having* him. "Take me."

He did as she asked without hesitating, yanking her jean skirt up, his mouth never leaving hers. Tugging her panties out of the way, he plunged a finger into her already drenched body. He set a frantic pace, matching the strokes of his hand to the rhythmic plunges of his tongue in her mouth.

She was just as desperate, just as frenzied. She needed to reclaim this place. Needed to make it hers again. This was her home, and if she wanted to have wild, hungry, up-against-the-wall sex, she damn well should be able to do it without fears that somebody might be watching.

Grabbing at his jeans, she fumbled around, unbuttoning, then unzipping. She tugged his briefs away, slipping her hand inside to clutch at his thick erection and stroke up and down, knowing that with their hunger, it wouldn't take much to send both of them spiraling over the edge.

"I need to be inside you *now*," he muttered thickly, backing her up until her thighs hit the short divider between the living and dining rooms. It was the perfect height, she realized, as Nick, still kissing her as if he needed her mouth to survive, lifted her and set her on the edge of it.

He didn't even take his pants off, or her skirt. Shoving his jeans and briefs out of the way and stepping between her parted legs, he plunged into her with ravenous, crazy passion.

Melody dropped her head back and cried out. Bracing herself on the ledge with her hands, she let Nick drive into her, over and over, until they were both panting and shaking. And, very shortly, climaxing almost in unison.

When they were spent, still heaving in deep, shuddering breaths, Nick wrapped his arms around her and picked her up. Melody held him tightly around his neck as he carried her to her bedroom and lay down with her on the bed.

"This is your place," he said between deeply inhaled breaths. "You can do whatever you want here, Mel. Nobody's ever going to violate your privacy again. I swear."

He understood. Without her having to say a word, he completely got what had driven her to such desperate want, to nearly rough passion. He'd known what she needed. And he'd given it to her. Which, she realized as they lay on their

sides, face-to-face on her bed, his arms still around her and
her legs still around him, was what the man always seemed
to do.

She was about to open her mouth to thank him, and maybe to ask him how he already knew her so well, when something began to hum against her inner thigh. "Uh, that a
vibrator in your pocket, or are you just happy to see me?" she
asked with a laugh.

"My phone's on vibrate. You'd have better luck reaching it
with your foot than I would with my hand," he said with a laugh.

Melody quickly released him, sliding away on the bed as
he sat up and tugged his phone from his pocket. "It's Dex,"
he said when he looked at the caller ID "I'm sorry...."

"Go ahead. I need to go clean up, anyway."

While Nick talked to his partner on the phone, Melody
went into the bathroom and got herself back together. Or, as
back together as she could after such wild, spontaneous sex.

Maybe she was turning into a nympho. Because thinking
about all that wild, spontaneous sex was getting her aroused
again. Good Lord, she'd had the man half-a-dozen times in
the past three days and she was already hungry for more.

"Bill," she told her own reflection, picturing her ex-husband's face, "I wasn't cold. You were just a *lousy* lover."

Logically she knew her husband couldn't hear her, but it
felt good—damn good—to say it out loud. She was still smiling about it when she left the bathroom, finding Nick standing in her living room, fully dressed and tucking his phone
back into his pocket.

"Sorry to come and go, but I need to get to the station."

She snorted at his bad pun. "Come again, anytime."

He grabbed her and pressed a quick, possessive kiss on her
lips, then strode toward the door. "I'll try to come back tonight. You'll be okay with Fredo?"

She looked at the dog, who'd commandeered himself a sunny spot in front of the window, and nodded. "We'll get along fine…since C.C. and Oscar aren't here."

Nick's hand was on the knob, but he paused before turning it. "You know, I've been wondering. Oscar's named for bologna. What's C.C. stand for?"

"Cap'n Crunch. I thought she was a boy when I got her," she explained with a shrug.

"Ahh," he said with an understanding nod.

"It's better than Tampax, right?" she asked.

"You did *those* commercials, too?"

She nodded ruefully. "Someday, we'll have to go through my whole portfolio."

"I'm going to have to start watching TV Land for old commercials."

"Don't I wish," she said with a grin. "If I'm on TV Land, that means residuals. I don't think Bill got the right to those in the divorce." Wow, she was even laughing about her ex stealing all her money. She was definitely getting better.

Nick opened the door, stepping into the hallway. But before he left, Melody asked, "So what did Dex say? Do you have some kind of lead on the murders?"

"Yeah. He's questioning a suspect in the Manning case."

She grew curious, wondering who had killed the man just a few short hours after she'd had coffee with him. "Who is it?"

"The connection was bad. I only caught part of the name."

"Was I right about it being a woman?"

He nodded. "Yep. The person Dex is questioning is female."

"I figured."

"Dex found out who Manning had the argument with in the parking lot Thursday night. Apparently it was some stewardess he'd been dating a couple of months ago. One he'd dumped."

"And you think she came to take revenge?" she asked, stepping out into the upstairs hallway with him.

"That's the thinking."

"What was her name?" she asked, still curious about Manning's strange, very public death.

"Oh," he said, apparently remembering he hadn't answered that question earlier. "She's an African-American woman named Williams." He turned toward the stairs. "Tina…something like that, I think. Tina Williams." Blowing her a quick kiss, he hurried to the stairs, going down them two at a time.

Melody remained still, unable to turn around and go back into her apartment.

Tina Williams? Oh, God. Please, not *Tanya* Williams. Not her friend, the flight attendant who'd been so unhappy Wednesday night on the phone. Who'd been crying over a creep who'd used her and dumped her. Not her friend who was getting back into town late Thursday night…the friend who had sounded ready to fight back instead of crying anymore over some guy.

Not the one who'd sounded so disgusted whenever Drake Manning's name was mentioned. "Oh, Tanya, no," she whispered.

Feeling panicky, Melody hurried back inside her apartment and dialed Tanya's number. There was no answer at home, and none on her cell. Nearly desperate, she found the phone book and came up with the name of one of Tanya's friends, who worked with her at the airline. The other woman told her she hadn't seen or heard from Tanya since Thursday…when they'd landed at around nine in the evening.

Every call hammered another spike of worry into Melody's skull. Until, finally, she realized there was no other choice but to find out the truth for herself. Sticking her feet into her sandals, she grabbed her purse and headed for the door.

She didn't want to worry her friends, but she decided to call them, anyway. Rosemary did have some great connections in this town. And if Tanya needed a lawyer…

"Don't think like that," she reminded herself.

She dialed Rosemary's number as she locked her apartment door. By the time she was sitting behind the wheel of her car a few minutes later, she'd also spoken to Paige, who would have been livid if they'd left her out of this. The two women had been equally horrified, and equally determined to do something.

Of course, they'd all come to the same conclusion.

If Tanya was indeed at the police station, then that's exactly where her three best friends needed to go.

NICK RECOGNIZED Melody's friend Tanya as soon as he arrived at the station and spied her through the two-way mirror, sitting in the interrogation room. Dex, too, obviously knew the woman's identity. He was waiting for Nick outside the room, pacing up and down the hall, looking like utter hell.

Dex's usually precisely neat clothes were rumpled. His hair was sticking up and his face looked as if he'd been sleeping on a bed of nails…or not at all. His partner didn't get this torn up over the job. Which left Nick with the distinct impression that things hadn't gone well with Rosemary.

"Is that who I think it is?" Nick asked, ignoring Dex's personal problems. They had a job to do…and if that was Melody and Rosemary's friend sitting in the other room looking both angry and terrified, he and Dex were going to be in a world of hurt.

"Yeah." Dex ran a frustrated hand through his hair, which

explained the sticking-out-all-over look. "I didn't know it was her until I showed up at her place to talk to her."

"How'd you get her name?"

"One of Manning's friends. Manning apparently had a fling with her a couple of months ago and dropped her, the same way he seemed to drop every woman he was ever involved with."

"Shit." This had just gotten *very* sticky. "Does Rosemary know?"

The fatigue disappeared from Dex's face as his entire body stiffened. "I haven't spoken to Rosemary since yesterday."

Unable to let his friend think he didn't give a damn about what was going on, Nick said, "You talked to her about... things?"

Dex nodded.

"And she didn't like what you had to say?"

Dex's harsh laugh sounded unfamiliar to Nick. "She told me in no uncertain terms that she wouldn't marry me, and to get out of her fancy house and out of her life."

Whoa. Nick had suspected Rosemary could be a flaming bitch, but that sounded way over the top, even for her. From what he'd seen, the woman loved Dex. Even if she didn't want to marry him, he still couldn't see her being so cruel about it. "She actually *said* those things?"

"She turned down my proposal," Dex said flatly. "I told her I wanted to marry her, and tried to give her my grandmother's ring, which I'd flown up to Pennsylvania to get." Dex shook his head, sounding more dejected than angry all of a sudden. "She told me she wasn't giving up her house, her town, her life."

That made Nick curious. "Why would she have to?"

Finally Dex stopped eating up the cracked linoleum floor

with his long strides. Looking at Nick as if he were thick in the head, he said, "I can't support her like that."

Nick didn't understand his friend's attitude. "Seems to me Rosemary makes a good living…so why would you have to support her at all? The two of you could live just fine on what you both make." Then, not quite believing it himself, he speculated, "Unless, of course, you're some kind of male chauvinist who doesn't want to let your wife work outside the home." He immediately shot down his own theory. "Of course, Rosemary works out of her house, so that's kind of a moot point anyway, isn't it?"

"I'm not a chauvinist," Dex said, sounding shocked at the accusation. "If Rosemary was an accountant or a salesclerk, or a pilot or a doctor, I wouldn't care."

Crossing his arms and leaning laconically against the wall, Nick said, "Yeah, sure, I can see why that's *so* different. Realtors being so much more rich and successful than doctors and pilots and all."

Dex must have realized how stupid his words had sounded, because he shook his head. "It's not what she does for a living."

"You just said it was," Nick said softly, playing devil's advocate for some reason. Maybe because he hated to see his partner so ripped up. And maybe because he knew Melody would hate to have her best friend's heart broken. Which, he was beginning to suspect, was exactly what was going on.

Dex's pride had spoken. And Rosemary's pride had answered.

"It's not her job. It's her lifestyle. Her big house, her rich family, her parties. I'm not cut out for any of that."

Pursing his lips, and nodding, Nick said, "Okay, I can see that. Of course, I don't suppose Rosemary's going to be having many parties with a baby running around. And I sure don't see that woman letting her rich family have any say in how you two raise your kid. She's a strong-minded one." Straightening and stepping closer to his friend, he continued, "Strong-minded enough not to want to be dictated to by anyone. Not her family." Lowering his voice, he added, "Not even you."

Dex froze, only the tightening of his mouth showing the direct hit Nick's words had been.

"Did you ask her what she wanted?" Nick asked, suspecting the answer already. "Or did you tell her how it was going to be?"

Dex didn't answer, which was answer enough.

"Hell, man, did you at least romance her before you told her she had to give up her life to keep such a great prize as yourself?"

"Fuck."

That was answer enough, too.

Dex looked completely stunned. "I blew it. I didn't even *ask* her to marry me, I told her I wanted her to. No getting down on one knee, no flowers." His friend's green eyes grew suspiciously misty. "I wanted to say all that, to tell her how happy I am about the baby. But I walked in and saw that house and those antiques and just found myself throwing down the gauntlet."

"Sounds to me like she picked it up and socked you in the jaw with it." Dex was lucky the woman hadn't done it literally, as well. If Rosemary weren't pregnant, she might have.

"I should go talk to her."

"I think you're forgetting something," Nick said, nodding toward the interrogation room, where the best friend of *both* the women in their lives was still cooling her heels.

"Damn. Why this? Why her?"

"I don't know," he replied. "But I think it's time to find out."

Leaving Dex to figure out how to fix the relationship he'd screwed up, Nick entered the interrogation room.

"It's you," Tanya Williams said, sounding stunned and angry. "You were at Rosemary's party."

"Yeah. I'm Nick Walker. Dex's partner."

The woman met his stare without flinching. "I didn't have anything to do with what happened to Drake. I swear to you."

He pulled out a chair and sat across from her, remaining silent, assessing her posture, the sound of her voice, the steadiness of her hand and the gleam in her eyes. He didn't know this woman at all beyond knowing she was Melody's friend. One of the infamous "list" ladies. Yet somehow, when he looked at Tanya's brave-yet-terrified face, he realized he believed her.

"Okay," he said. "I need you to tell me everything you know about Drake Manning. Starting with anyone else who might hate his guts as much as you obviously do."

WHEN ROSEMARY SAW Dex at the police station, her first instinct was to kick him. Her second was to throw her arms around him and hold on like they were the last two people on earth.

Her third was to kick him again.

"Where is she?" she asked, storming right up to him as he stood in the hallway outside the precinct's coffee room. Rosemary had visited him here before, so she had a good idea of the layout. She turned toward the interrogation area. "In there?"

Dex took her arm. "She's fine. Nick's with her."

"She needs a lawyer."

"No, she doesn't."

Rosemary smacked his hand away. "I watch *Law And Order*. You can't hold her without a lawyer."

"We're not holding her at all," he said quietly, trying not to touch her again. "We're talking to her. She gave Nick some information that could help. I got word from the crime lab five minutes ago that they matched a fingerprint they found on Drake Manning's cup to the same person Tanya mentioned. I think your friend's in the clear, Rosie."

Rosie. Oh, drat the man, why did he have to call her Rosie now when she was so angry and had all her defenses in place? God, it had been hard driving over here today after she'd gotten Melody's frantic call. The last person she wanted to see was the man standing in front of her, looking so tired and so unhappy yet still so utterly desirable. Even now, when he ran a weary hand over his eyes, Rosemary's heart flip-flopped in her chest.

"Nick went back in to tell her he'll take her home." Dex laughed, though it sounded forced. "It looks like all this fuss over your friend's list was a big series of coincidences."

That distracted her. "What do you mean?"

"The person we're focusing on didn't have anything to do with Melody's list. A fax came in yesterday from the detective in Atlanta who investigated the death of that golfer. He says the surveillance cameras outside the ladies' room show the man was alone when he had his…accident. No foul play."

She breathed a sigh of relief. "So there's no way the cases are connected. Not even to the chef with the meatball?"

"An accidental choking, just like we always thought."

Oh, this *was* good news. Melody was going to be real relieved to find out she wasn't some Typhoid Mary. Remembering one more thing, though, Rosemary frowned. "What about Jonathan Rhodes?"

Dex shook his head. "We're not sure yet. That investigation is still open. But the more we look into the man, the more I'm convinced he was offed by one of his own clients. Or some ruthless business type he was trying to crawl into bed with."

"Wearing women's panties?" she replied, unable to resist.

Dex laughed, his tense face finally easing into those familiar laugh lines. Those much-loved laugh lines.

Rosemary stiffened her spine and forced herself to think of the unlovable cretin who'd showed up at her door yesterday morning. "I'd better call Melody. She was going by to pick up Paige and bring her down here."

He groaned. "Oh, please call off the cavalry. I don't know if the precinct can handle all four of you."

Glaring, she said, "You can't handle *one* of us." Then her hand dropped to her stomach. "Make that two."

She'd expected Dex to react angrily, to turn back into that stiff-lipped man who'd handed her his ultimatum yesterday.

Instead, he did something much more shocking. Without sparing a single look around the station—which, though not as full as it would be on a weekday, was still populated by people—her big, strong cop dropped to his knees.

"Dex, what are you…"

"I love you," he said, his voice unwavering. Putting his hands on her hips, he pulled her close, until his face was near her stomach. "I love your mommy. And I can't wait to meet *you.*"

The world spun a little off-kilter, a crazy sense of dizziness sweeping through Rosemary's body. Down the hallway, she spotted a few familiar faces but didn't even think of taking her attention off the man kneeling in front of her, saying such amazing, tender, wonderful things.

"I want us to be a family, to be together," he said. "But I realized I never even asked what you want. So I'm asking now, Rosie. Do you want me?" He reached into his pocket and dug out the ring he'd offered her yesterday. "Will you have me?"

She sucked her bottom lip in her mouth. "Do you really want *me,* Dex? The real me, warts, temper, bossiness, money and all?"

He slowly rose to his feet, stepping close to her so his face was only an inch from hers. His dear, tired face, now looking so hopeful, so full of love. "I want you any way I can get you, Rosemary Chilton. Please say you'll be my wife."

Over Dex's shoulder, Rosemary saw Melody, Paige, Tanya and Nick watching with smiles on their faces.

It couldn't possibly match the one on hers. Almost laughing with the sheer joy of it, she threw her arms around Dex's neck.

"I'll marry you, you big, slow Northerner!"

He cupped her face in her hands and tenderly touched his lips to hers, sealing their promise with a sweet, loving kiss. When they finally pulled apart, he didn't let her out of his arms, as if he were afraid she wouldn't come back. "Soon?"

She nodded. "While I can still fit into a gorgeous dress." Then, wanting to make sure there were no misunderstandings, she added, "By the way, Dex, I've got one hell of a mortgage on that house. If we do this, it's as partners. Fifty-fifty."

He quirked an eyebrow. "On a Georgia detective's salary?"

Rosemary grinned. "Sixty-forty. But you pay the phone bill."

Dex rubbed his chin, pretending to think about it, looking so darned cute. "Oh, you drive a hard bargain, ma'am."

"You're looking at the best broker in Savannah," she said, almost purring. "You don't want to haggle with me, sugar."

He stepped back and stuck out his hand, taking hers to shake it. "Okay, Miss Chilton, you have yourself a deal."

CHAPTER SIXTEEN

THERE WAS NOTHING like a chicken burrito and a margarita—
or in Rosemary's case, an ice water—to celebrate an engagement. And a pregnancy. And a get-out-of-jail-free card.
Which was why Melody, Paige, Rosemary and Tanya met at
their favorite restaurant that night.

They sat at *their* table. Served by *their* waiter. Toasting
with *their* margaritas—and water. And feeling very much a
foursome. Just like old times…except for a *few* updates.

"I still can't believe you're having a baby," Melody murmured, looking across the table at Rosemary, trying to picture her friend heavy and round…a mother. A wife.

"Me neither," Paige said. "You're not exactly glowing.
When is she supposed to start glowing?"

"I don't know," Tanya said, sipping her drink. "But she's
right, Rosemary, there's no glowing that I can see. You look
like crap."

"Spoken like a woman recently released from jail," Rosemary replied with a smirk.

"Bite me, Rosie, baby," Tanya said with a sweet smile.

Ahh, heaven. This was what Melody had needed. What
she'd longed for. Her friends…no, her family…together
again. So *why* did she feel something was missing?

Or maybe *someone* was missing.

"Okay, Tanya, give us the condensed version," Rosemary

said, tackling the subject they'd all been dancing around since they'd sat down thirty minutes ago. "What happened between you and Drake Manning?"

Melody's heart tightened for her friend, who suddenly looked so lost, so bereft. So unlike the strong, amazing woman they all knew and loved.

Tanya didn't try to bluster or joke her way out of it. Instead, she simply said, "He hurt me."

Three little words. But they held a wealth of emotion and heartbreak. Melody reached over and grabbed Tanya's hand. Paige dropped an arm across her shoulders and hugged her, and Rosemary gave her a nod of understanding.

"After talking to Mel Wednesday," Tanya explained, squeezing Mel's hand back, "I decided to be the person I used to be, and go tell him off for what he did, instead of crying about it. So I went to the studio and we had it out in the parking lot Thursday night. Then I left and went to a hotel on the beach for a couple of days to be alone."

That explained why nobody'd seen her.

"Are you…does it hurt?" Paige asked. "That he's gone?"

Tanya thought about it, then slowly shook her head. "I'm not grieving, if that's what you're asking. I really had gotten over him in the two months since we split up. I'm not happy the man's dead, but I can't say I'm real broken up over it, either."

Tanya sighed deeply, nodding and murmuring something to herself. Then, looking as if she were shaking off her sadness, she lifted her glass and drained it in one long sip. By the time she returned the empty glass to the table, she had a smile on her face. "Okay, enough about the *dead* dick with the *big* dick. Melody, I want to hear about your hot *Time* magazine hero."

Paige nodded so hard her curls bounced. "Me, too."

Tanya continued, "I have to say, if that man had used a few persuasive techniques on *me,* I'd have been confessing to giving stock tips to Martha Stewart."

Reaching for some sour cream to put on her burrito, Melody chuckled. "He's, uh…amazing. Wonderful."

Paige sighed. Rosemary smiled. And Tanya rolled her eyes. "Yeah, yeah, but I want to know what he's like in the sack."

The restaurant owner, whose face had lit up like the Rockefeller Center Christmas tree when they'd come in, happened to be passing by at exactly the right—or wrong—time. He frowned, looking shocked by Tanya's words.

Oy. Ricky the restaurateur really *did* have a thing for her. A serious one, apparently, because with one more disappointed look in her direction, the man walked out of his own restaurant.

"Come on, girl," Tanya prodded, not even noticing. "Was it worth waiting six years for? Worth everything you've been through?"

Was it worth it? Oh, there was absolutely no question about that. Nick was amazing. The sex was phenomenal. Every hour they spent together was more magical than the last. He made her laugh and he made her crazy. He teased her and listened to her, bossed her and understood her.

Was Nick worth it? Yes. Most definitely.

Acknowledging that much wasn't hard. But it did force her to confront something else. Something she hadn't wanted to face, hadn't wanted to consider. Something absolutely terrifying. "Oh, God," she whispered, "I'm in love with him."

Her three friends didn't laugh or razz her. They all got quiet, probably hearing the dismay in her voice.

"You weren't looking for that," Rosemary said softly.

She shook her head. "I didn't think I'd ever fall in love

again for the rest of my life." Still almost dazed, she looked around at her best friends, seeing their concern. "This wasn't supposed to happen. It was supposed to be easy, blameless. Not something that could hurt me."

Paige leaned over and touched her hand. "He hasn't hurt you, Mel, and maybe he won't."

"He wouldn't want to," she admitted, not doubting that for a second.

Tanya cleared her throat. "But?"

"But…if it doesn't work out, I'm going to end up a wreck again." She looked at Rosemary, who'd held out for what she wanted—what she believed was best—for herself and her child. "*You* were strong enough to know you'd be okay on your own. I don't know if I've reached that point yet. And getting involved with Nick so soon after coming here, I haven't had a chance to find out."

It was true. During her life, she'd gone from being her mother's cash cow, to Bill's trophy. Moving to Savannah was supposed to be about not needing anyone. Not being used by anyone, ever again.

Yes, she'd begun to blossom into her new life, to reclaim her friends and her career and her own home. But she'd also gone and fallen in love with someone who could shatter her all over again. Someone who could already make her heart stop if he even innocently hugged another woman. Someone who demanded the right to protect her, when what she most wanted was to stand up for herself. "I don't know that I'm ready for this."

"You think it's too soon after your divorce?" Paige asked. "Since it's only been a few months?"

"Bullshit," Tanya said. "We all know your marriage has been over for years, Melody Tanner. So don't use that as an excuse not to go after something good."

Something good. Something great. But something she didn't know if she could handle.

"So this is the infamous place where brides and brides-maids gather to write lists."

Instantly recognizing Nick's voice, Melody jerked her gaze upward, sucking in a breath and ordering her heart to stop hopping like a Mexican jumping bean in her chest. "Hi."

"Hi," he said, just as softly, giving her an intimate smile. He bent down and brushed his lips across hers, giving Mel hope that he hadn't overheard any of their conversation.

"I hope you don't mind that we stopped in, but we thought you might want to know how things worked out," he added.

Beside Nick stood Dex, who was bending down to kiss Rosemary's cheek. He whispered something in her ear and she smiled sweetly.

Now she was glowing. Even Tanya would have to admit that.

"I know this is for women only," Nick continued, "but can we join you for a couple of minutes?" He looked at Tanya. "I think I owe you a drink."

"Anyone who wants to buy me a drink can pull up a chair at my table, anytime, cutie," she said, immediately scooting over to make room.

Dex and Nick grabbed two chairs from a nearby empty table and pulled them up. Nick was close to Melody, so close his jean-clad leg brushed against her bare one. Which instantly made her remember the way his jeans had brushed against her inner thighs earlier that day, when they'd been so hot for each other they hadn't even paused to take off all their clothes.

He looked at her, his eyes darkening. She had no doubt he was remembering exactly the same thing.

"So, was it *her?*" Tanya asked, breaking the seductive memory.

Paige squealed. "Ooh, we're going to find out who did it? It was a woman? I figured it was because only a woman would hit a man where it would hurt the most." She looked around at the others. "Men are much too protective of penises to do that to another man."

Nick and Dex each gawked while the women at the table chuckled, well used to Paige's jabbering. And her volume.

"So, was it Angie?" Tanya asked, looking as certain as if she already knew the answer.

Melody immediately placed the name. Angie was the reporter who'd been with Rhodes and Manning at Rosemary's party.

"Yeah," Dex said. "She confessed."

An enormous weight disappeared from Melody's shoulders with those three words. She'd been hoping Drake Manning's murder had nothing to do with her, and Dex had just confirmed it. Because Melody had never had anything to do with the prime suspect before that night.

"I knew it." Tanya looked at the women at the table and elaborated, "Drake mentioned her Thursday night when we were arguing, saying something about yet another angry, spurned woman." Her jaw clenched. "He said we should comfort each other."

"The creep," Melody muttered.

"She says she didn't mean to kill him," Nick said. "She was furious because he'd dumped her twice in one week. It was more than someone with her ego—and her temperament—could take. She can be one vindictive woman. Believe me, I know."

Reaching out to grab a handful of chips, Nick also casually picked up Melody's glass and sipped some of her margarita. His actions were so natural, so comfortable, as if they were a long-established couple.

She looked away, wondering why that thought hurt instead of helped. Why her mood was getting darker the longer they sat here, so close, yet already separated by the doubts that had filled her mind before he'd arrived. She desperately wanted to recapture the good feeling she'd had a little while ago—before she'd been stupid enough to start analyzing her feelings for the dark-haired man sitting beside her.

Impossible. She couldn't be near him—so very close to him—without feeling way too much. Nick's arm was draped casually across the back of her chair. He was sitting so close she could smell the spicy cologne he wore, which instantly reminded her of burying her face in his neck, breathing in every bit of him that she could get when they made love.

No way could she force herself not to respond. Not to *feel*.

"What'd she mean to do, if not kill him?" Paige asked, wide-eyed. "Get him so horny he'd take her back by default?"

"She wanted to humiliate him," Dex said. "Completely and totally embarrass the man by making it too uncomfortable for him to sit in front of a camera and report the news."

Melody thought about it. Though it was possible, she wasn't entirely convinced. "She had to have known he had a heart condition, and that giving him so much of that kind of medication could be dangerous."

"Especially since she slipped it into his grapefruit juice," Nick said. "Apparently they don't interact well together. Another strike against Manning before he took the first sip."

"You think she's lying to make herself look better?" Melody asked.

He shrugged. "It's possible. We may never know. From

what the coroner says, the level of the drug in his blood-stream wasn't as high as we'd first thought. But even a couple of one-hundred-milligram pills, combined with his bad heart, were enough to do him in. Whether she meant to kill him or not, that was the result. She's been charged with murder."

So it was done. They'd caught the person who'd killed Drake Manning. And from what Rosemary had told her as they'd left the police station earlier, the police had come up with several other theories about Jonathan Rhodes's death. Theories that, thankfully, didn't include her. Or her list. Or her underwear.

"I sure wish I knew where they were," she muttered.

"Where what were?" Nick asked, obviously overhearing.

"My peacock underwear," she said with a sigh. "I don't suppose they've shown up on eBay?"

He shook his head. "Afraid not, darlin'. We may never know…at least, not until we catch whoever killed Rhodes. It could be something as simple as the killer liked the look of them and decided to steal them for his wife or girlfriend."

Well, she supposed another woman wearing her underwear was slightly less gross than a man wearing them.

"Mel, do you want to come by and get C.C. and Oscar after we leave?" Paige asked, completely changing the subject.

It was a welcome shift. They'd talked enough about death.

"Do you mind if I do it in the morning?" Melody asked, suddenly feeling weary. As much as she'd loved being here with her friends, she now wanted to go. Maybe being alone would help her figure out what to do about her confusing situation—a situation other women might think wasn't confusing at all.

It was for Mel, though. Confusing as hell, yet really a

very simple problem, when it came right down to it. She was in love with an amazing, sexy man who took her breath away.

But she didn't know if she had the strength to try to keep him.

IT HAD BEEN A LONG DAY, but now, knowing at least one of the homicides he'd been working had been cleared, Nick was feeling pretty good. When he looked at Melody, he felt better than good. Great might describe it. Blissful—as sappy as it sounded—might not be too far off, either.

Because he'd fallen in love with the woman. He hadn't quite believed it was possible, and he still didn't know if he'd be any good with this new emotion, but he didn't doubt that was what he felt. For the first time in his life, he really *got* it.

He loved her. He wanted her. And now, after this miserable, ugly day, he was damn glad to be with her.

There was only one problem. Melody was pulling away. Rather than being outwardly glad that a killer had been caught, that her one friend was blissfully happy and her other friend no longer under suspicion for murder, she looked anxious. Withdrawn.

It could just be fatigue—it'd been a long couple of days, especially with the camera nightmare in her apartment. They'd gone on a cross-state trip where she'd met his entire family, not to mention the population of Joyful. And their own relationship had been like a crazy amusement-park ride, going up and down, spinning out of control when neither one of them had really expected it. They'd scaled some high peaks and plunged to some dark depths. All in such a short time.

But he didn't regret one minute of it. He was willing to

bet Melody didn't, either, no matter what was weighing on her mind right now.

Maybe it was everything else still left to deal with. Solving the Manning case hadn't shed any light on Melody's Peeping Tom. So he wasn't feeling any less tense about that situation. But he was pretty convinced that either Jonathan Rhodes or Melody's ex had planted the camera.

Rhodes certainly wasn't in any position to do it again.

As for Dr. Bill Todd…well, from what Nick had learned about the man today from the Atlanta PD, he had new troubles of his own. So maybe he wouldn't be so anxious to harass his wife anymore. If he *had* been the one spying on her, he definitely wouldn't once Nick got through with him.

"I'm sorry, everyone, but I'm really tired. I think I'm going to call it a day," Melody said, confirming his suspicion that something was wrong.

He immediately rose from his chair.

She waved a hand. "Don't worry, I can get home just fine. I have my car. Why don't you stay here and eat? I know you've got to be starving."

Staring at her, shocked she'd even suggest it, he sensed the others around the table growing quiet and watchful. Melody's friends looked a bit nervous, as if they knew what was going on in her mind. Judging by Tanya's deep frown and the way Rosemary was nibbling her lip, they weren't too happy about it, either.

"I'm fine," he said slowly. "I wasn't planning on staying, anyway, especially if you're not going to." As if he would. As if she really *wanted* him to. "Besides," he added, meaning only to tease her, "I'm not letting you out of my sight after everything that's happened."

Okay, maybe that wasn't the right tactic. She looked away,

her expression even darker, her shoulders slightly slumped. "I don't need you protecting me," she muttered. "I am capable of looking out for myself."

Definitely not the right tactic. "I know you are," he replied. "But that doesn't mean I can't worry about you. Since I have to come to your place to get Fredo, anyway, I might as well just follow you now."

She frowned, as if she'd forgotten about the dog. But she stopped arguing.

Saying goodbye to everyone else, Nick escorted her outside. Funny how Savannah had been so bloody hot lately, because the expression Melody was wearing was downright chilly. She didn't say a word as he held her car door open for her.

As he followed her back to her place, Nick began to figure out what was wrong. He mentally kicked himself, recalling the way she'd insisted earlier today that she didn't need to be protected. That had been right before they'd had some of the most incredible, mind-blowing sex he'd ever experienced, so maybe he should get a break for not remembering it right away.

She'd repeated the words at the restaurant. Looking out for herself was obviously important to her. But Nick couldn't change who he was. He took care of people he loved.

Loved. There was that word again, all bright and shiny, just waiting to be said out loud.

He wondered when he'd have the courage to say it. If she'd someday have the courage to say it back. He certainly didn't expect miracles; Melody could very well have a "once burned, twice shy" attitude like Nick had for the past decade. That he could get past his mental obstacles a bit sooner was understandable. She might need a while before she reached the same conclusion he had: that they were perfect together.

Realizing Melody had gotten ahead of him at a stoplight,

he pressed the gas harder. By the time he got to her street, he saw her car was already parked. She wasn't in it. Pulling up behind her hatchback, Nick got out and walked to the door of her building. Before he could even try the knob, the door opened from the inside.

"Hi. Here's Fredo," she said, sounding out of breath. As if she'd raced up the stairs to grab the dog, then flown back down here so he wouldn't have to come up.

She handed him the leash and Fredo jumped up to give Nick an enthusiastic greeting. Scratching the happy mutt behind the ears, he murmured, "What's going on?"

"What do you mean?"

"I mean," he said, a wary kind of tension building in his head, "I know something's wrong. Are you all right?"

She nodded, stepping outside to join him on the front stoop. "I'm fine. Maybe a little tired."

He couldn't contain a wolfish smile. It was instinctive when this woman was around. "So let's go to bed."

Wrapping her arms tightly around herself, Melody shook her head. "I need to be by myself for a while."

The tension in his temple turned into a pounding. "How long's a while?"

Melody finally looked up at him, meeting his even stare. There was no disguising the confusion in her eyes, or the tight pull of her mouth.

The woman was unhappy. Unsure. Not the Melody he'd been falling in love with over the past several weeks. He was looking at the one he'd met that very first day, out on the sidewalk where she'd taken a nosedive onto her mattress.

"What happened?" he asked, his body growing taut with anxiety, like it did when he sensed something bad was going down on the street. Right now he sensed something very bad was going down on his life.

"Nothing happened," she said. Her voice shook a tiny bit. "I just realized I need to take some time, Nick. Things are going too fast. I'm afraid I've let myself get off track lately. I'm not achieving what I set out to achieve when I came here."

That made zero sense. "A new life? A new start? Some happiness? Tell me you haven't achieved all of that…and more."

She shook her head. "I can't deny that. But I don't know that I can handle this right now. I don't know that I can handle *you*. I'm afraid I've been fooling myself, fooling both of us about how I feel, what I'm capable of feeling."

He stiffened even more. Because he'd heard that refrain before. He'd certainly been played the fool before, starting way back ten years ago when he'd been a duped eighteen-year-old husband. "*Fooling* me?"

"I don't want to be hurt again," she said, running a hand through her auburn hair and rubbing at her temple. "I don't want to need you. I don't want you taking care of me."

She fell silent. But the next logical sentence rang in his ears, anyway. *I don't want you.* He heard it. She had to have heard it, too. It was almost tangible, hanging there in the few inches of night air separating them.

"You want me to leave you alone?" he asked, his body rigid.

There were tears in her big blue eyes. And there was agony on that beautiful face.

But she said it anyway.

"Yes, Nick. I do want you to leave me alone."

MELODY'S HEART BROKE when Nick turned without a word, walked down the front steps, got into his car and drove away.

He hadn't said anything. Not one thing. He'd simply held himself in that stiff military way and left.

This wasn't like the night she'd asked him to leave but hadn't really wanted him to. Because, in her mind, she knew asking him to leave was the right thing to do. At least until she sorted things out for herself.

Somehow, though, she'd expected a few words, a brief conversation. At least an assurance that he understood she simply needed more time. Maybe even that he'd wait.

She didn't expect him to wait for long. She wasn't that selfish a person. Still, she'd expected he'd understand at least a little bit.

But no. Nothing. Not a word. Just that rigid, inflexible posture and a march to his car. And out of her life.

"Oh, my God, please not forever," she whispered as she shut the door and went upstairs to her apartment. As she walked into her living room, she acknowledged she might have lost the best thing she'd ever had. Being strong, confident and independent was one thing. But being in love…being loved in return…well, she didn't know if there was anything better than that in life.

"It can't be too late," she murmured, already wondering what to do. Wondering if the anguish she felt now, figuring she'd lost him, was indication enough that she should never have let him get away. Especially not without telling him how she felt.

She thought about calling him and asking him to come back so she could better verbalize her concerns. Or, hell, maybe just jump on the man and take him to bed, since that had been one place she and Nick never had any problems communicating.

Melody nearly reached for the phone, but before she could, it rang. She jerked in surprise at the shrill sound. Sending up a quick prayer that it was Nick calling from his cell phone a couple of blocks away, she answered. "Hello?"

She held her breath, hoping Nick was trying to find the right words. But there was only silence.

Not wanting to think her sick, heavy-breathing stalker might have caught her at a moment when she was already so frigging depressed, she snapped, "Hello? Who is this?" When she got no response, her jaw tightened with anger. "Go to hell."

"Melody? It's me. Bill."

"Ahh, it speaks," she said, not trying to hide her sarcasm. "What's the matter, you afraid you're going to hyperventilate with all that heavy breathing so you decided to talk this time?"

"I'm in trouble."

"You're going to be if you don't leave me alone. Call me one more time and I'm shoving your phone right down your heavy-breathing throat." Wow, that felt good.

"I don't know what you mean," he said, his voice holding a hint of a whine. "I haven't called you in months."

She didn't want to hear that, didn't want to think her ex hadn't been the person harassing her. Because that would leave her wondering who had. Suddenly feeling weary, she rubbed her eyes and shook her head. "What do you want, Bill?"

Her ex-husband said nothing for a second. In the background, Melody heard yelling, and the clang of metal. "I'm in trouble."

Like she was supposed to care? "What, did you pick up another case of the clap?"

"You're so sarcastic," he said, sounding hurt.

Ha. It took emotions to feel hurt. Bill didn't experience them. "And you're wasting my time. Goodbye, Bill."

"Wait, please." His voice rose in desperation. "I'm in jail."

That got her attention like nothing else could. Stunned, she slowly sat down at her kitchen table. "You're kidding."

"No, I'm not. And I need you to do something for me."

Her bastard of an ex-husband was in jail and was calling her for a favor. There had to be some kind of divine retribution in this moment, she just knew it. But her curiosity wouldn't let her dwell on it yet. "Why are you in jail?"

"That doesn't matter. Look, I need some money."

Melody started to laugh. Real belly laughs. When she could finally speak again, she said, "You must be joking. I don't have any money, you moron. You stole it all."

Someone yelled in the background again and Bill's voice grew lower, more desperate. "It's not funny, Mel, they have me in this dirty place…with these…these *men!*"

Oh, divine retribution indeed. "Sorry, big guy, they don't let male prisoners room with female ones. Not even sexual miscreants like you. Now, I have to go."

"Melody, please, I'm desperate. I don't have any cash right now—I invested it in a couple of business deals that don't look like they're going to pay off anytime soon. And the court hasn't taken care of the house yet, so you're still on the deed. I need you to co-sign so I can use it as collateral for the bail bondsman."

She absorbed his words, realizing he was totally serious. The man who'd ripped her life apart and left her with nothing was calling on her to bail him out. Figuratively and literally.

It was unbelievable. Shocking. Almost operatic.

Part of her knew she should be a better person, rise above the past and feel some sort of pity for the man. But deep down, Melody could only think that sometimes karma was a really good thing. "What did you do?"

"We don't need to get into that."

"If you want me to even *consider* helping you—" not that she seriously was "—you'll tell me what you did."

Bill hesitated. And Mel started to hang up. "Bye."

"Wait! I, uh…I met someone on the Internet. And I went to meet her and her friend at a hotel."

Oh, gag.

"I didn't know they were underage." He whimpered. "Mel, they're using words like *Internet stalking* and *statutory rape.*"

That was all she needed to hear. The man didn't deserve a single ounce of pity—not that she probably could have mustered one up, anyway. "I think you'd better call your friend the judge and ask him to hurry up on that title work," she said slowly, not taking satisfaction in it, but instead feeling a strong sense of calm. Relief, almost. Because in this brief, five-minute phone call, Bill had confirmed every suspicion she'd had about her marriage. And her husband.

He hadn't just been a cheater. He'd been a sexual deviant. Nick was right…no woman could have satisfied him. What he'd done to her had absolutely nothing to do with Melody and everything to do with his own weaknesses.

"What are you saying?" he asked, sounding panicked. "Mel, you *have* to help me."

Suddenly feeling at peace, Mel smiled. "No, I don't have to do anything for you. I was serious about the judge—you're going to need the court to change the deed really fast, because I'm not signing a thing." He began to sputter and she added, "Have a great time in jail…sure hope none of the other inmates find out you were seducing little girls."

"Melody!"

She hung up. Hung up on her ex, on her shitty marriage. Hung up on the unhappiness and the uncertainty. Hung up on the past.

Funny, because she was suddenly feeling anything but hung up. In fact, she felt free for the first time in ages.

Humming under her breath, she put the phone back in its cradle and walked out of the kitchen. She kicked her sandals off, padding barefoot toward her bedroom. It was too bad she didn't have anyone here to share the great moment—not even her cats—but honestly, deep down, she knew it didn't make any difference. She might want other people to be part of her life. But she knew she really could do okay alone. Having someone in her life was a choice, not a necessity. A choice she was ready to make.

"Now, to make Nick understand that." She just hoped he was a firm believer in a woman having the right to change her mind. Because one thing was for sure—she wanted him back. Pronto. And that was why she was going into her room to change out of the stale clothes she'd been wearing all day, since they'd left Joyful. Once she'd gotten herself looking a little better than a limp dishrag, she was going over to Nick Walker's apartment to tell him she was ready for the bikini, even though half an hour ago, she'd been convinced she only wanted a leather coat.

He'd understand. "Please let him understand."

Still smiling, Melody walked into her bedroom and opened her closet door. Flipping on the closet light, she began looking through her clothes, trying to figure out what to wear for a groveling session and some serious makeup sex. Her eyes immediately shifted toward the back of the closet and the sealed clothing bags, half-wishing the stupid peacock set was still here. Because it sure would make a statement if she showed up wearing that, a raincoat and nothing else.

She'd decided on a cute sundress when her brain processed what her eyes had just seen. Melody froze, still staring straight ahead. It took her a few seconds and a few deep gulps of air, to work up the nerve to look again toward the plastic bags.

"Oh, my God," she whispered.

Because it was there. Her famous Luscious Lingerie set

was hanging there, right where it had been before Jonathan Rhodes had stolen it. The bag was sticking out a little past the others, and the peacock-blue was unmistakable.

Still, she had to be certain. Taking two slow steps, she felt her heart begin to race and her blood roar in her veins. Reaching for the bag, she pulled it away from the others, unzipped it and confirmed her suspicion.

There was no mistaking it. She was looking at the bra-and-panties set that had once made her so infamous. Moaning, she closed her eyes as the implications flooded her mind.

Someone had broken into her apartment and put the lingerie back in its place.

"You weren't supposed to find it so soon."

Melody's eyes flew open as a quiet voice spoke from behind her, in the bedroom. If she'd thought her heart was racing before, it was nearly bursting when she spun around, instinctively reaching for something she could use as a weapon.

"Who are you?" she asked, wishing Fredo was still here. Wishing *Nick* was here. Wishing she'd bought a gun as Tanya had jokingly suggested. "What do you want?"

"Don't be afraid," the male voice said in that deep whisper, made more eerie because she was staring from her brightly lit closet out into her darkened bedroom. "I'd never hurt you."

Yeah, like she was going to buy that one. Melody felt along the wall under her clothes until her fingers brushed against her old set of golf clubs. As gingerly as she could, she began to slide one up, slowly, keeping her hand—and the club—hidden.

"I thought you were going out, I didn't realize you were going to come right back up after you got the dog." The whisper got a bit louder. "That dog barked when I tried to come in. I had to wait upstairs all day. But when you took him, I came down real quick to p-put your panties back and hide the new camera."

God, that voice was creeping her out…making her shake, but also sparking her fury. Because the sick man had just confirmed he was the one who'd been spying on her.

"Who are you?" she asked, her voice steady and strong.

"Please, d-don't be afraid, Melody."

And suddenly she understood. Even before he stepped out of the shadows into the light so she could see his face, Melody realized who'd been making her life a living hell for weeks.

"Brian."

CHAPTER SEVENTEEN

FOR THE FIRST ten minutes after he drove away from Melody's place, only one word rang in Nick's head. *Fooling.*

She'd been fooling him, fooling them both. She'd said the word herself, and somehow, it had been all he'd heard of their entire surreal conversation.

Nick had had quite enough of playing the fool over a woman. He'd sworn never to be used that way again after his divorce. So what the hell had he done?

Exactly what he'd sworn not to do.

Fredo seemed to sense his dark mood because he remained solemn in the back seat, not making a sound. The dog didn't even do his usual trick of standing up and trying to peer through the front windshield at the oncoming headlights, while invariably leaving a line of drool on Nick's shoulder. But Fredo was lethargic. Depressed. Well, they said dogs sensed human emotions. And his were pretty damn dark right now.

"Love isn't worth it, Fredo," he said, shaking his head as he steered onto the highway. "It's too big a risk."

Within another mile or so, however, he had to admit one thing: the past few weeks, well, he'd almost say they had been worth it. That being with Melody, watching her blossom and come alive, become the woman she was capable of being, had been worth tonight's disappointment.

"She's one hell of a woman, whether she felt anything real or not," he said aloud, using his dog as a sounding board.

Fredo barked softly, a growly little sound of agreement.

That was the part that got to him. He couldn't wrap his mind around the idea that Melody *hadn't* been feeling it, hadn't been experiencing the same emotions Nick had. He couldn't have been all alone in their relationship—it had been two-sided.

They'd been in sync with each other, both in bed and out of it. She'd somehow known exactly what to say to make him finally let go of the guilt he'd been carrying about Jack. Just like he'd known the root of her insecurity had been because she'd blamed herself instead of her ex for their divorce.

"She felt it," he said, confirming it out loud. "So why would she claim she didn't?"

The curiosity nagged at him, so much that he had to start replaying their conversation, her exact words. "Fooling both of us," he murmured, remembering the anguish on her face when she'd said it. Funny how he'd heard the word *fooling* more than he'd seen the anguish. He saw it now, though. He had a feeling when he went to sleep, he'd be seeing it behind his closed eyelids.

"She's afraid," he murmured, beginning to put it together. "She's not sure of what might happen and she's afraid."

But she wasn't a coward. He'd seen a lot of evidence of that. Physically, Melody Tanner wasn't going to take shit from anybody. Emotionally...well, that might be another story.

What would it take to lay a skewered heart on the line so soon after it'd been charbroiled in a rotten marriage?

"Trust. Confidence," he whispered.

Fredo barked again.

"Security. Certainty that you aren't going to be made a fool of…" His voice trailed off as Mel's words began to make sense.

Fredo finally moved, his face appearing beside Nick's shoulder, as if he'd finally recognized the change in his owner's mood. Because his mood had definitely changed.

"I'm an idiot." Fredo didn't disagree.

Melody wasn't going to put her heart out there to be chewed up and spit out again, not unless she had confidence—and trust—that she wasn't alone in her feelings. Nick hadn't given her much reason to have that confidence. He'd never told the woman how he felt about her.

Maybe if he'd simply said the words, let her know that he loved her and that she could trust him, she wouldn't have felt the need to back away. Or at least they could have talked about slowing down. Instead he let his pride force him to leave without a word.

"I'm as dense as Dex," he told the dog.

At least he hadn't gone to another state. In fact, he'd barely gotten out of the city. Even that was too far, but he quickly remedied it by turning around at the next exit ramp.

She might not be ready to do anything about it, but no matter what, Melody deserved to know he loved her.

IT TOOK MELODY a couple of long moments to wrap her mind around what she was seeing. Brian, Rosemary's stepbrother, whom she'd known since childhood, was standing in her bedroom. In his hand was another of those wireless cameras.

Looking at her as if she should apologize for coming home and interrupting him, he said, "I wasn't expecting you, Mel."

"What is this all about, Brian?" she asked, not stepping out of the closet. She also didn't release her grip on the golf club.

"I wanted you to be happy. To get your underpants back for you," he said, misunderstanding her question.

She stared at the camera. "I mean *that.*"

"W-well, that was part of making you happy. So I could watch you and do anything you needed." He stepped closer, into the doorway of the closet, blocking her exit. "That's how I knew that m-man had taken your panties. I saw him. I couldn't watch all the time…but I was that day. He was per-perverted."

Melody closed her eyes, hoping Brian wasn't saying what she thought he was saying.

"It's okay, though. I got them back and he never put his dirty hands on them. He said so. He wrapped them in p-plastic and treated them like gold. Just like I did once I got them back."

Her vision blurred and her head felt as if she were spinning on a theme-park ride. It was almost too much to take in.

Rosemary's stepbrother had killed Jonathan Rhodes, she knew it. And he'd done it out of some kind of twisted devotion to *her.* The man who'd always seemed a bit slow but still normal was obviously *far* from it.

"Brian, *how* did you get them back?" she asked, needing to be certain.

He scrunched up his forehead, looking angry. "He sh-shouldn't have been wearing your pink ones. I only went there to take them b-back. I used my p-passkey since Simon owns the building."

Of course. And Brian took care of all his stepfather's properties. Meaning he had a key to *this* apartment, too.

"But he h-had them on, M-Mel, and I got s-so mad."

Killing mad. Her stomach heaved. Especially because Brian was looking very angry now, his face growing red as he stumbled over more of his words. Since childhood, Brian's slight stutter was always aggravated when he was most stressed or upset.

"I have to know, Brian. Are you responsible for everything that's been happening to me? The camera, the calls?"

His anger evaporated so quickly she wondered if she'd imagined it. He looked at her as if it were the most simple explanation in the world. "Only because I love you. I always have. Rosemary thought it was Paige I loved. But it was you."

He loved her. So he'd killed a man and stalked her.

This was going to be a movie of the week on Lifetime someday, she just knew it.

Melody remained quiet, thinking fast, trying to determine whether or not this man, who'd confessed to murder, was a serious threat to her. One thing was sure, no way was she going to set him off by telling him his feelings were not reciprocated.

"You weren't ready. I knew that," he said, sounding so reasonable. "And now that I'm the l-last one on your list, I can wait, Mel. Until you *are* ready."

Her list? Her fucking list? "I don't know what you…"

"I heard you and that man in Rosemary's office the night of your party. You took h-him off the list and put me on it. I'm number one."

Her jaw dropping open, Melody finally edged closer, needing to understand how any of this could have happened. "Brian, that list was a joke. Nothing but a joke."

He shook his head, as solemn as a child who knew only black or white, unable to distinguish the gray. "N-no, it wasn't. You went out with that policeman before you scratched him off. And you went to lunch with Mr. Rhodes, too."

Which meant nothing, though she didn't think she could make him understand that. "Brian, I never would have done it."

"I kn-know that!" he said. "You're good. You were waiting for the right one. Nu-number one. Me. Your landlord."

Racking her brain to try to remember exactly what she'd said that night when she and Nick had argued, she vaguely recalled saying something about putting anyone—including her landlord—on her list instead of Nick. Brian had been listening, probably through the French doors leading out to the veranda. And he'd obviously taken her literally. As her *landlord*.

She wondered if he'd seen the intense passion that had erupted between her and Nick, but figured he couldn't have. If she remembered correctly, she'd shut the door and made sure it was draped.

Nick. Oh, God, did she ever wish she hadn't sent him away tonight, for a whole bunch of reasons. Not the least of which was that she had no idea how to handle an unbalanced murderer who'd been watching her and had killed out of love for her.

"So when do you think you w-will be ready, Mel? Soon? Because I've waited such a long time for you. Watching you has made it even harder."

Watching her.

"I n-never watched you in the bathroom or anything," he said, sounding self-righteous. "I didn't want to invade your privacy. And it wasn't all the time. Some nights I'd want to be closer to you, so I'd sneak upstairs into the empty apartment with my l-laptop and w-watch you sleep, knowing you were r-right below me."

Her stomach heaved. The only thing that kept her together was the realization that Brian hadn't been watching Friday night when she and Nick had been making love in her bed. She had the feeling he wouldn't be so calm now if he had seen that.

She shook her head, "Brian, I'm sorry, you misunderstood. The list was a joke, I didn't mean it."

He stepped into the closet, suddenly frowning. "Don't say that. You d-did mean it, Melody." That red tinge appeared in his cheeks again and his normally placid face twisted into a frown. "You c-can't be an Indian giver, not w-when you said I'm n-number one." His breathing was growing deeper now and he seemed to be having a hard time holding it together. "The list says I w-win."

He reached for her, still looking angry, not at all the man she'd grown up knowing.

Still, Mel didn't really believe he'd hurt her. Not until he grabbed the front of her blouse and ripped it down the middle.

NICK KNOCKED on Melody's door, waiting outside her apartment for her to answer. When she didn't, he knocked again. "I know she's there," he muttered to Fredo, who stood next to him in the hallway. "Her car's still parked right outside."

Still no answer.

She might be in the shower. Or asleep. Maybe she just couldn't stand seeing him right now. But something wouldn't let him turn around and leave.

It was that feeling, the same feeling he'd had a couple of other times. The feeling that had driven him to sit outside her apartment on those nights, watching for some unknown danger that he'd sensed but couldn't identify.

Fredo growled. Looking down, Nick saw the normally placid dog's ears lying back on his head and his fur standing upright. The dog was staring at Melody's door.

At that moment, Nick knew his intuition had been correct. Something was wrong. No way was he leaving, not until he made sure Melody was all right.

Nick hadn't been a cop for four years without learning a thing or two about locks, and Mel's was a piece of cake.

Thankfully, she hadn't thrown the top bolt, just the knob, so he was inside her apartment within about twenty seconds.

The kitchen light was on, and it cast a pool of illumination across the living area, which was empty. He took one step toward the lit room, but Fredo had other ideas. With a yip, the dog leaped away, taking the leash right out of Nick's hand. He ran toward the back of the apartment—toward Melody's bedroom. Nick, reaching for his gun, was right behind him.

He simply wasn't prepared for what he found.

Melody, with her blouse hanging open—obviously ripped—stood over a man, clutching a golf club like a broadsword.

"Mel…"

"Oh, God, Nick," she said, dropping the club and throwing herself into his arms. "I'm so glad you came, I didn't want to have to hit him again. I'm afraid I might have given him a concussion as it is."

She was afraid she might have injured the creep lying on her floor? Nick was going to do a lot more than that to the man. When he looked at Melody's blouse, now just rags barely covering her beautiful body, he knew he could easily kill the man.

He reached for him. "That bastard's going to wish he'd never left Atlanta."

"No," Melody said, grabbing his arm. "It's not Bill."

Surprised, Nick squatted down beside Fredo, who was growling over the unconscious figure, obviously standing guard. He rolled him over and was shocked to see Rosemary's brother. "Brian?"

She nodded. "I don't know how I'm going to tell Rosemary or her family. This is awful, Nick. I think he's really sick."

Checking the man's pulse to ascertain that the lump on his skull hadn't been fatal, he slowly rose to his feet. Melody was shaking now, reacting to what had happened. Nick holstered his gun behind his back and pulled her into his arms, trusting Fredo to watch Brian.

"It's okay, honey," he whispered, rubbing his hand up and down her back. "It's over."

And over the next couple of hours, he realized it truly was over.

He'd called for uniformed backup while Melody had changed her clothes. While they waited, she filled him in on everything. Brian's obsession, *and* his confession.

The man had regained consciousness by the time the EMTs had arrived, but they'd taken him to the hospital anyway, with an armed escort who'd arrest him as soon as he was declared fit. Brian had tried to speak to Melody before they'd taken him, but she'd walked away.

Knowing she dreaded having to tell Brian's family, Nick made a call to Dex. Between the two of them, they decided the best way to proceed was through Simon Chilton. Dex had gone to see Brian's stepfather immediately. He'd called back a half hour ago, confirming that while Simon had been devastated, he'd remained calm and had told his wife and daughters. Dex was still with the family, helping them sort through their options.

Nick suspected one of those options might be a mental hospital. From what Melody had told him about the way Brian had acted and the things he'd said, that sounded like the best place for the man.

Finally, after Nick and Melody had both given statements to Draco and Jones, two of the other detectives from his precinct, they were once again alone in her apartment. After walking the detectives out, Nick had returned to find Melody in her room. She'd changed into an oversize cotton nightshirt, and was sitting cross-legged in the middle of her bed.

She hadn't turned the bedroom light on. But the puddles of light spilling in from an outside streetlamp, and the glint from the hallway were enough for him to see her. To remind himself that she was absolutely fine.

He walked across the room, watching out the front window while Draco and Jones pulled away.

"Rosemary called while you were outside," she said.

Nick immediately tensed, not knowing how the other woman had reacted to the accusations against her brother. Brian was family, after all. If she hadn't believed Melody, or had blamed her in any way, Mel would be crushed.

"She asked me to forgive her, to forgive all of them, for not seeing Brian had a problem." Mel continued looking down at her hands. "For not stopping him from hurting me."

Relief eased the tension from his shoulders. Maybe Rosemary was wiser than he'd given her credit for. She'd certainly been right about standing up to Dex during his craziness. "I'm glad. They'll make sure he gets the help he needs."

"I hope so. I still can't believe it happened, you know?" She shook her head, sending her soft auburn hair gliding over her shoulders, picking up a glint of gold from the streetlamp. "I keep feeling I'm watching a movie of the week."

"It would probably be on that chick station."

She smiled a little for some reason. The first smile he'd seen on her face in hours. God, he was glad to have it back.

"You know," he said, thinking of why this had happened, of what had sparked Brian's rampage, "I'd happily burn that list of yours…if it hadn't led to us meeting."

She glanced up. Maybe she'd heard the note of intensity he couldn't keep out of his voice.

"I suppose I feel the same way," she admitted.

And suddenly he knew the subject had changed. They'd finished dealing with murders and cameras and stalkers. Now they were talking about them, Nick and Melody. They both knew it.

"Why did you send me away tonight?" he asked, crossing his arms and leaning against the wall.

She countered with a question of her own. "Why did you come back?"

He frowned. "I forgot Fredo's water bowl…why do you think?"

Swallowing visibly and twisting her hands together in her lap, she said, "I sent you away because I was afraid."

"Afraid I'd hurt you." His voice was low.

She nodded. "And afraid I didn't know my own mind, that I couldn't trust my own feelings."

He was about to tell her she could trust his when she continued, "But I knew I'd made a mistake. I came in here to change so I could go to your place and tell you…something."

Straightening, he approached the bed, moving slowly, not wanting to startle her when she was finally opening up. "Tell me what?"

Melody nibbled her lip, her head down. Eyeing him through a few tendrils of hair that fell over her face, she said something that made no sense at first. "I was going to tell you I'm not going to move to Antarctica, and I'm not going to eat my way through February and April." She breathed deeply, as if to calm her slightly shaky voice. "I wanted to say that I know you're going to fit me as well in June as you do right now."

And he got it. Immediately. She was referring to the crazy conversation they'd had a while back about shopping for a bathing suit when she was looking for a leather coat.

Unable to contain a small smile, he nodded. "Does that make me the pink-spotted bikini?"

Melody giggled, the sound washing over him like a cool,

clean blast of fresh air. Unexpected, cleansing and utterly delightful.

"I love you, Melody," he said before the laughter had left her lips.

She froze. Her lips parting, she simply stared at him from the center of the bed, as if not sure she'd heard correctly.

"I love you," he repeated.

"Is that what you came back to tell me?"

"Yeah. I also wanted you to know I'll wait if you need more time." Lord, he hoped she didn't need too much of it. Because it was already killing him to think of walking out of here tonight and being away from her until morning. Much less being away from her for days. Weeks. Months. He might lose his mind.

He sat on the edge of the bed, shifting to face her, but not going too close, not crowding her in any way. "I also want you to know something. I'm not a cheat. When I give my word, it's unbreakable."

She inched closer. Just an inch, but it was something.

"I will love you as much twenty years from now as I do today, and I swear to you, I will never break your heart. I'll never let you regret it if you allow yourself to love me, too."

Another inch. Another deep breath. Another sigh. And finally, another smile. "Oh, Nick, I don't have to give myself permission to love you. I fell in love with you when I was sure I would never love anyone again."

He dropped his head back, closing his eyes, letting her words and the surety in her voice fill his head. Letting her presence—her whispers, her scent, her sweet, sweet face—fill every corner of his memory.

When he felt able to look at her again, he found her watching him.

"You know," she said, "I started loving you the moment I

looked out my window that night and saw you sitting in your car, watching to make sure I was okay."

That was still a touchy subject. "I know you don't want to be protected," he said, remembering her arguments from earlier that day. "And that you're capable of taking care of yourself." Thinking of Brian and that five-iron, the woman was more than capable. "But I've got to tell you, Mel, it's who I am. I'm a bossy, arrogant cop and I'm going to have a hard time ever letting you put yourself in danger if there's anything I can do to stop it."

"How about if I promise not to put myself in danger?" she asked, that little smile still playing about her lips.

She eliminated the final space between them, rising to her knees and sliding her arms around his neck. "I love you, Nick Walker. I don't need time. I don't need any more reassurances." Laughing softly, she added, "I know you know I can swing a golf club, so I'm not at all worried about some floozy catching your eye."

"Impossible," he said, shaking his head. "You're the only woman I see."

She communicated her happiness—and her emotions—by kissing him sweetly, lightly, delicately.

That lasted about ten seconds before Nick had had enough. Wrapping his arms around her, he hauled her close, parting his lips over hers, making love to her mouth the way he wanted to make love to her body.

She tasted so damn good. Perfect.

They shared everything they were feeling in the silence of the kiss, and soon it was enhanced by want. Hunger. The need they'd had for each other since the minute they'd met.

"I've never made love to someone I loved…and someone who I knew loved me," he muttered against her mouth as he pulled his shirt off and tossed it away.

When he reached for the bottom of her nightshirt, however, she stilled his hand and backed up. "Then we'd better make it something to remember, don't you think?"

Without explanation, she slid off the edge of the bed, standing in front of him in a puddle of moonlight. Her expression confident and inviting, she began to lift up her night-shirt. Slowly. Her teasing was surely going to kill him before the night was over.

It was like the first time all over again. The excitement was just as powerful, the want just as overwhelming. His impatience was driving him wild. "You are one beautiful woman, Melody Tanner," he managed to whisper.

"And you are one beautiful man, Nick Walker."

He was about to reach for her, to rip off the shirt she was taking her own sweet time with, when he spied a flash of blue between her legs. "Holy mother of God…"

She pulled the shirt a little more, revealing the thin, feathery strip riding over each hip. And those dark swirled peacock feather eyes riding low on her body. Right above the place where he wanted to lose himself forever.

"Ah, I see you recognize it," she murmured as she continued to pull the shirt up. Revealing her hips. Her midriff. Then more of that sultry blue—the bottom of the bra.

"Oh, yes, ma'am, I definitely recognize it," he said, wondering how he could get the words past his tight throat. He choked out a rough laugh. "Considering it's more than likely evidence, I don't think I'm going to forget it."

Melody tugged the nightshirt completely off and dropped it to the floor. As she stared at him, her blue eyes glittered as brightly as the skimpy lingerie she wore. She stepped closer, her whole body swaying, so feminine, so soft and desirable. His fantasy girl come to life.

Only, she was no fantasy. And she was no girl. She was his woman, his mate in every possible way. Or she would be, as soon as he put his ring on her finger. Which would happen as soon as she was ready.

"If you think I'm giving this up for somebody to use as evidence in a murder trial, you're sadly mistaken," she said, her voice challenging, her stance provocative. "If anybody wants this off my body, they're going to have to come and get it."

He needed no more invitation than that. Rising slowly from the bed, Nick stepped toward her.

"It's mine," she added, licking her lips but not backing away as he approached. "And from now on, honey, what's mine, I *keep*."

Melody was talking about more than lingerie, now, he knew it. Just as sure as he knew what she was saying. "You can keep me as long as you want me," he said. *Forever would be nice.*

She lifted a hand to his face, rubbing the pad of her thumb over his lips. Nick kissed her fingers, then caught her hand in his own and began tugging her closer.

"I've wanted you all my life," she whispered before gliding into his arms. "Wanted someone to love me for who I am, and to make love to me until I'm sure I'm going to die from the pleasure of it. Someone who's good and honorable and honest. Brave and sweet and sexy."

He rolled his eyes. "Don't overdo it."

"I'm not overdoing a thing," she whispered as she slid her arms around his neck and leaned up until their faces were only a breath apart. "You're my dream man. My fantasy guy. Number one on my list, now and forever."

He laughed softly. "As long as I'm the *only* man on your list."

"I wouldn't have it any other way," she whispered.

Her lips were so close to his they nearly brushed together, separated by only the tiniest sliver of late-night air.

And then, there was nothing between them at all.

EPILOGUE

ROSEMARY AND DEX WERE married in a small civil ceremony six weeks later. Nick served as best man, and Melody as maid of honor. Tanya and Paige were witnesses.

The rest of the Chiltons would see them later at dinner. Because of the stress in Rosemary's family, the couple had decided on this low-key wedding, not wanting to wait, not wanting to delay their joy over the baby they were expecting.

The baby seemed to be a source of joy for all of Rosemary's loved ones, who were still struggling to understand how Brian had gotten so sick without anyone ever realizing.

Brian was in one of the best hospitals in the state, visited often by his sisters and his parents. Nick thought it doubtful that he'd ever be competent to stand trial, considering the psychiatric evaluations. Maybe that was just as well…Simon and Patty might not ever have their son back, but at least they didn't have to fear for him in prison.

It still made Melody sad to think that Rosemary wasn't getting the big church wedding with the long white gown that she'd always dreamed of. Somehow, though, when she saw the way the bride and groom looked at each other after they'd said their vows, she had the feeling they didn't give a damn.

They were crazy in love. And love was enough.

Meeting Nick's eye from the other side of the judge's chambers, she completely understood.

God, life was good. Miraculous.

With Nick by her side—living with her, working with her, loving her every minute of the day—she felt capable of anything. Including, she had begun to suspect, accepting his proposal of marriage. He'd asked her a week ago, telling her she didn't have to answer until she was ready. That she could take as long as she needed. Somehow, looking at the man who'd burst into her life a few short months ago, she began to realize she *was* ready. No more questions, no more doubts. She was absolutely certain she'd found the love of her life.

Maybe Rosemary had been right. Maybe it had been fate.

Or maybe Melody was simply the luckiest woman on the planet.

"So," Paige said as they all prepared to leave the courtroom after Dex and Rosemary had been pronounced husband and wife, "Tanya, you're the last single one. We've got to get you a man."

"Huh. I'd rather have a vibrator," Tanya said with a snort.

The judge coughed. Nick and Dex rolled their eyes. And Melody, Rosemary and Paige all burst into laughter.

Yeah. Life was so good. It'd taken a while, but Melody truly believed she'd finally gotten to the place she was meant to be, with the people she was meant to be with.

Her family. And her love.

"You know?" Melody said as they walked out the courthouse doors into the sunny, cool November day, "It hardly seems fair that Rosemary didn't get to have a bachelorette party."

Nick's arm, which was around her waist, tightened a little. He already knew where she was headed.

Paige's nod sent her curls flying. "Yeah, no fair."

Tanya piped in, "Rosie, after you push that puppy out, we're going to throw you one hell of a party."

The new bride, who'd just started getting a bit of a round tummy, nodded. "I'll be *so* ready for a glass of wine by then."

"Or a margarita," Paige said.

Dex and Nick both groaned. Loudly.

Dex gave Rosemary a stern look. "Only on one condition."

"Yeah," Nick said, not taking his eyes off Melody.

The two of them finished in unison, "No lists."

Rosemary and Melody looked at each other from a few steps away, shared an "aren't we blessed" moment, then separated to get in their cars.

Once inside with Nick, Melody put her hand on his leg. "You won't have to worry about me wanting to make a list at *my* bachelorette party. Once in a lifetime is enough for me."

He opened his mouth to say something, probably "damn right." Then her words sank in and a slow grin curled his gorgeous lips up, until he was flashing those two incredible dimples. "You trying to tell me something?"

"Maybe I am."

But before she could say what, Nick threw the car back into Park, hopped out of the driver's seat and came around to the other side. Melody watched, incredulous, as he tugged her door open and pulled her out to stand with him. Then he reached into the front pocket of his suit coat and lifted a small velvet box.

Lowering himself to one knee in the middle of a bustling Savannah square, he said, "Melody Tanner, will you be my wife?"

She saw her friends all pausing on their way to their cars, and began to smile. Then to laugh. And when she nodded, she also began to cry.

Because yeah, it was good. It was all good.

As far as Melody Tanner—soon to be Walker—was concerned, life just didn't get any better.

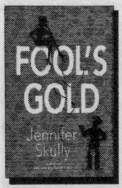

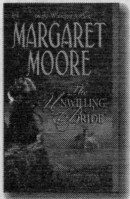

Enjoy a classic tale of romance that will
warm hearts this holiday season,
by #1 *New York Times* bestselling author

NORA ROBERTS

GABRIEL'S *Angel*

Pregnant, alone and on the run to protect her unborn child, Laura Malone
finds herself stranded on a snowy Colorado road and at the mercy of
Gabriel Bradley. Fortunately he wants only to provide her shelter. As they
weather the storm together, a bond is formed and a promise made—one that
will keep Laura safe and one that will give Gabe a new reason for being....